Avery Press
New York • London

The Dark Action

The Dark Action First Edition, 2021.

Cover design by Sarah Cook Design.
Author photograph (at back): Troy Aossey.

Avery Press, USA.
Manufactured in the United States of America.
All rights reserved.

ISBN: 978-1-7348774-0-3

The Dark Action

THE SECOND BOOK IN THE DEVLIN SERIES

LANDON J. NAPOLEON

Praise for the *Devlin Series*

The Dark Action (Book 2)

"Landon J. Napoleon's novel aptly showcases a lawyer's hectic workload... what truly propels the tale are the meticulous steps the lawyer Connor Devlin takes to reach resolutions. The author weaves distinctive characters into myriad legal wranglings. All of these cases generate an unwavering pace... A riveting legal tale that's more true-to-life than melodramatic."

—*Kirkus Reviews*

"Meticulous... The core of the story is procedure, and on that front Landon J. Napoleon excels. The depth of knowledge regarding legal matters... lend this procedural a refreshing, real-world feel that seasoned mystery readers will appreciate."

—*Publishers Weekly*

"I loved this book, which is unique in the way it accurately portrays the process of being a trial lawyer outside the courtroom. I read a lot of novels in this genre, and this was right up there with the best. Can't wait for volume 3."

—Jeffrey Leon, past president American College of Trial Lawyers

"Landon J. Napoleon has nailed it with rapid-fire and intriguing plot development wrapped in crisp dialogue. The book sharply illuminates the truth all actual trial lawyers know universally: justice is won or lost long before the judge ever swears in the jury... won or lost in the dramas and drudgery of indefatigable investigation and preparation with the inevitable setbacks awaiting. A riveting work."

—A. Clifford Edwards, president (2019-2021) International Academy of Trial Lawyers

The Rules of Action (Book 1)

"Briskly told and well-drawn, this legal thriller does what many courtroom-based novels and television shows do not: It stays true to the actual practice of trial law... A fast-paced tale of justice in action and a remarkably accurate portrait of a trial lawyer's daily grind... Prospective law students are frequently encouraged to read law-student memoirs or legal hornbooks, but for a realistic view of litigation and a great deal more action, they'd do well to add this legal thriller to their reading list."

—*Kirkus Reviews*

Praise for Landon J. Napoleon's debut novel *ZigZag*

"*ZigZag* is one of the boldest and most original first novels to appear in a long time. It's also very funny, in a way that only the raw street-song of truth can be funny. Landon J. Napoleon has written a gem."

—Carl Hiaasen

"A remarkable debut portraying the inner life of a disturbed ghetto teenager as he attempts to grow up in the frightening world he's inherited... An unaffected, moving, astonishing insight into the heart of a troubled, silent genius."

—*Kirkus Reviews*
(starred review)

"...this mixture of comic adventure and paean to the values of volunteerism is a vivid read and impressive debut novel."

—*Library Journal*
(starred review)

"...affecting first novel that explores the survival of the human spirit in an atmosphere of deprivation and cruelty."

—*Publisher's Weekly*

"...Landon J. Napoleon's first novel is an affecting work."

—*The Dallas Morning News*

"Landon J. Napoleon conveys the strength of the human spirit through his wonderful creation, and in the process tells an engaging and enriching story."

—Barnes & Noble *Discover Great New Writers*

Books by Landon J. Napoleon

Devlin Series novels

The Rules of Action (Book 1)

The Dark Action (Book 2)

Other novels

ZigZag

Deep Wicked Freaky

The Flatirons

Nonfiction

Angels Three: The Karen Perry Story

Burning Shield: The Jason Schechterle Story

Author's Note

THE *DEVLIN SERIES* **OF NOVELS** are works of fiction inspired by, and based on, the actual career arc of a prominent trial attorney, starting in 1970. In all instances, I changed the names and altered certain facts and legal situations to protect real identities. The end result is fictitious works based on real events and cases.

However, references to pop culture, music, events, politics and various court cases and rulings are all historically accurate, including in most instances the actual names of the lawyers, politicians and principals involved in those events.

For Deb Stelzleni,
my guiding light.

"Often the best way to relax is to just go back to work."

–Steve McQueen

Prologue

Midtown Phoenix, Arizona
Christmas Eve 1983, 11:42 p.m.

DELANEY DUNNE HAD ALWAYS WANTED TO BE A LAWYER, not a midnight fixer dispatched on this twisted deed. Double-D, as his crew now called him, also hated December, when winter finally descended upon the desert with its pain-in-the-ass rain and cold that fogged the windshield on his orange 1980 Pontiac Firebird Trans Am. He wheeled into a darkened and deserted parking lot, backed into a space facing Central Avenue and killed the headlights. He left the V-8 engine rumbling and gnawed at his fingernails.

Why was he here at this odd hour on a holiday? He knew the question contained the answer, which further rankled his sour mood. He wiped the inside of the windshield with his jacket sleeve so he could see the building across the street, one of the midtown high-rises, disappearing around the tenth floor into an uncharacteristic, heavy fog. He bumped up the heat, rolled down his window and stuck his head into the night. He closed his eyes and let the tiny droplets pinprick his face while he pulled in some deep breaths of cold air to settle his nerves. Then he looked into the

1

mottled cityscape and repeated the mantra in his mind: inches and seconds. Back inside the car, he rolled up the window and listened to the Queen tune. Even at low volume the bass thump of "Another One Bites the Dust" was impossible to resist, his head bobbing.

Inches and seconds.

Point was, victories in the game of life often came down to the narrowest of margins. Winning a Super Bowl. Getting a fox in the sack. Committing crimes without getting caught. Dunne watched the building entrance: there was not another human being anywhere in his field of vision up and down the street on this eerie night in the city. This one should be as easy as the first.

Inches and seconds, Dunne. Don't get cocky.

A nagging feeling of failure clung to the after-dark fixer, despite being the first in his family to graduate college—a bachelor's degree in history down in Tucson. After a sub-par LSAT score almost killed the career track entirely, he was accepted to exactly one law school: Nova University in Florida. He'd never heard of it, either, because it had just opened in 1974, the same year he applied. Nonetheless, he was in and on the path to what he believed would be a noble pursuit.

Then, over beers less than an hour before he was set to depart for Florida to begin law school, Dunne found himself at an unlikely crossroads—with a tantalizing job offer from a stranger, an opportunity that had materialized out of the blue. The hook that snared Dunne was that he had grown up poor: the allure of a get-rich-quick yellow brick road was too intoxicating for him. Just like that, Delaney Dunne had ditched the law-school idea and made a turn that, nine years later, had him sitting here in the darkness on a rainy Christmas Eve.

Inches and seconds.

Delaney Dunne, Esq., never came to be. If he had become a lawyer, he might have been advocating for a client in a court of law earlier this very day. Instead, he was here huddled in the dark mist on Christmas Eve, his heart racing as he finally saw the target. Dunne switched off the radio. He did not want to do this anymore—not any of it, not the small jobs and especially not the big ones like this late-night dispatch. And yet there was some invisible hand pushing him along the road he had chosen all those years ago. Just as he'd read in that Joseph Conrad novel: "It was written I should be loyal to the nightmare of my choice."

The man had just emerged from the building, the gold-framed rotating doors spinning slowly behind him. He stopped and looked up in disbelief, like all

2

Phoenix residents flummoxed by the sheer audacity and annoying inconvenience of precipitation. He wore a black polyester suit, with black leather wingtips, a wrinkled white dress shirt and a black tie loosened at the neck. He turned to his right and started walking north on Central Avenue beneath a phalanx of towering, silhouetted Canary Island date palms, a tropical outcrop in a sea of urban hardscape.

Dunne waited until he could barely see the lone figure through the watery curtain. Then he released the clutch and eased the Trans Am into the street, turning left across the wide boulevard to head in the same northbound direction as his target. The rain intensified into a thundering downpour. Dunne fumbled to find the windshield wiper control and almost lost sight of his target. Distracted by the rain and still trying to steady himself, he forgot to turn on the headlights as the sky unleashed.

Inches and seconds.

The man in the suit could now see the glowing white sign for the parking garage, which was just ahead, across the street and to his left. He stepped off the curb to cross the street.

Fifty yards out, Dunne shifted rapidly, grabbing second gear and then third, and floored the accelerator. The man was hoofing it, with a quickened pace to beat the rain, so Dunne had to cross two lanes and ride down the center turn-lane of the wide street. This had to be done right. Now midway across the street, the man could not hear the surging engine through the din of the pounding rain. Soon he was almost to the safety of the opposite curb, forcing Dunne all the way across the southbound lanes to intersect his target. But then the man suddenly stopped walking, trying to remember if had left an important document on his desk and wondering whether he should go back to check. Dunne had not anticipated the target stopping; he quickly veered the car right at more than forty miles an hour, trying to miss the target as instructed.

Instead, the man turned his head, saw the blacked-out vehicle at the last second and succumbed to the brutal impact.

Part I

The Detective

Chapter One

TRIAL LAWYER CONNOR J. DEVLIN was ready. Nine years of litigation had brought him here, to the legal equivalent of the Last Chance Saloon: the verdict in the final appeal. Win or lose, Devlin was ready, because there would finally—mercifully—be no more doorknobs to rattle. No more motions or maneuvers. No more calculated plays, gamesmanship or bluffs. No more formal channels of recourse. Win or lose, there would simply be closure for both sides after a protracted legal war.

Devlin also hoped the end of the case would concurrently end a new torment, which had turned 1984 into a macabre nightly ritual: interruption insomnia. Stripped down to his white boxers, covers long ago thrashed to the floor, now Devlin did what he did each time he came to this place that neatly halved the black night. First he exhaled in audible frustration. Then he turned and stared at the lit white numbers until the next digit flipped down.

2:32 a.m.

He never had difficulty falling asleep. But then, at the appointed hour, his mind racing through a hundred different details in dozens of cases, he was wide awake again, which triggered the standard Buffalo maxim.

CHAPTER ONE

What the fuck.

Devlin's maddening affliction had only intensified in the last few days as he awaited the news on the landmark nursing-home case *Kay Pearson v. Flynn Enterprises.* But he also feared that even resolution in that legal matter would ultimately not end his nightly torment—which meant Devlin might not ever get a good night's sleep.

2:33 a.m.

Devlin knew every solo operator—entrepreneur, oil wildcatter, country music crooner, abstract painter, trial lawyer—needed the same thing: a breakout hit. Devlin had had a few near-misses on that front. Big City Auto Sales was one, and whether he won or lost on appeal, the Pearson case had at least put him on the map in the legal sphere. Clearly Devlin's career would not end if he lost. But after nine years trying to close out one case, the unease of a major appeal loss was prominent. The first decade-plus of his career was Devlin's legal infancy and childhood, sketching the outlines of who he would become in his profession. The tilt of the final outcome in this case had the power to solidify, or besmirch, that legacy.

This is what Devlin did in these wee hours: ponder the greater meaning while pretending he might fall back asleep. Early in his career, with the indefatigable Trevor Walsh as master skirmisher and co-conspirator, Devlin had first cut a swath through the criminal courts and then perched squarely as a practitioner in the civil arena. Devlin pondered how it was possible that the steady march of time could slow to this geologic pace in the wee hours. This level of plodding was the domain of tectonic plates and lateral moraines, not the long nights of a trial lawyer. Devlin exhaled. He was merely a spectator to parallel ridges of mental debris, frost-shattered and deposited along the sides of this godforsaken endless struggle, another glacier block of ice frozen in time.

Devlin grunted aloud, exasperated, and was out of bed and flipping on the bathroom light. The insomnia always demanded action: just give up for the night and stop the flip-flop. Better to be up and moving than enduring endless thrashing. The dark dance whirled; Devlin uncapped the toothpaste, started the rhythmic *swish-swash* across his teeth and replayed the verdict from the Court of Appeals in case number PB1977-002736, *Kay Pearson, plaintiff, v. Flynn Enterprises, defendant.* The case had been the crowning moment that capped the seventies and first decade of a greenhorn's career. Four years of toil squared against a defense team led by the vertex of the bluebloods, the ever-annoying namesake partner from Bell & Bauer: Richard Bell. That Devlin had thrown the final ace, and put one over on the man he derisively

LANDON J. NAPOLEON

thought of as "Sniff," was national news in the legal world in this precedent-setting case. Devlin won $200,000 in compensatory damages, which covered the roughly fifty grand he'd sunk into the case for his investigation and high-priced expert witnesses. Then there was the big bombshell: the ice-cold $12 million in punitive damages the jury had said was due to Devlin's client. But of course, Dickie Bell's savvy was limitless, and he'd pulled a few cards of his own straight from the bottom of the deck during the appeal process.

Since Devlin had nothing but time—2:34 a.m.—he always went back to the U-turn. The fact that he could mentally replay, verbatim, the judge's decision on appeal was not a good sign: *The award of punitive damages in this case was the result of passion and inflammation caused by improper conduct by counsel. These damages bore no reasonable relationship to the compensatory damages. This court finds prejudice generated by conduct of counsel and hereby vacates any award of punitive damages.*

2:35 a.m. *Swish-swash.*

Of course, Devlin had immediately filed an appeal to that decision—his last option—by requesting that the Arizona Supreme Court take up the case, which it eventually did. Then, opening briefs and oral arguments by both sides. Devlin had been consummately prepared when he presented his argument. All told, the appeals process burned another four years on a case that began in 1975. At least his client, the daughter of the deceased, had already been paid the compensatory damages after the original verdict in 1979. At the time, Devlin only took what he needed to cover his expenses, giving her the remaining $150,000 even though he was due one-third of that amount. She had suffered enough, and the growing revenue stream from Devlin's other cases afforded him this flexible selflessness.

And there it was again, the glacial grind of the legal system and process, the steady march eroding his seminal victory. The same forces that had created the Grand Canyon—time and pressure—had stalled a career in the geologic equivalent of one Planck length.

2:36 a.m.

Devlin rinsed and spit, and stared into the mirror as if he might foretell the future if he just achieved sufficient concentration. Now the entire matter was with the Arizona Supreme Court. That they'd taken Devlin's appeal was a small victory in itself. But there was probably zero chance the five white men would reverse the lower Appeals Court ruling. Devlin was staring at fourth down from his own one-yard line, with one second left on the clock, in the middle of a history-making

Buffalo blizzard whiteout. He needed the Hail Mary of all desperation trick plays to pull off this miracle. He tried to find solace: the court could take away the money, but Devlin's precedent-setting victory at trial court would always stand.

Except he couldn't take moral victories to the bank. He'd been waiting years for the punitive payout himself, which would really put him in a flush position. Meanwhile, he still had a legal practice to run with all the attendant costs and overhead, not to mention expenses he was fronting on all his other cases. He'd sold his collector cars, too, not because he couldn't afford to keep them, but because as Devlin's caseload intensified he realized he was unlikely to ever have time to drive and otherwise enjoy the vehicles.

He still lived here in the three-bedroom, two-bath townhouse in Scottsdale with the resort golf course as his backyard and the redolent orange blossoms in spring bloom. Devlin & Associates was operational, too, in the red-brick building on Third Avenue in Phoenix, with his one full-time associate: go-to assistant Nadia Flores, who had become something of a surrogate mother to the East Coast transplant and was a steady and reliable force in Devlin's career ascension.

Devlin might have mused about some other topic, such as making a mental note to go see Al Pacino do a manic turn as Tony Montana in *Scarface*, which was getting big buzz. But instead, the aging case still consumed him. When the state Supreme Court justices issued their ruling, win or lose, the legal well would be tapped: no more appeal channels, no more depositions, settlement conferences or slick strategies to play. Devlin had already acquiesced to the reality that when the music stopped this time, he would be the lawyer left standing without a chair. If a legal career was supposed to get easier after fourteen years, for Devlin the forces of physics seemed to be precariously perched to thwart him. Devlin glanced at the clock again and shook his head.

2:39 a.m.

What the fuck.

Chapter Two

"YOU WIRED?"

Instead of answering the question, Sloane Monae was thinking about the gun, the one armpit-holstered on her client's bodyguard. She and the two men sat in the back of a black limousine in Gallup, New Mexico, on a miserable frozen day. The early-March sky was a depressing blotch of black and purple, and the loud wind pounded an icy wall of rain against the car. A cacography of spray paint littered the plywood that had replaced the glass in every storefront of the corner strip mall, foreclosed at some point during Jimmy Carter's presidency. The only other vehicle in the potholed parking lot was Monae's low-slung blue 1978 Datsun 280Z.

During the five-hour drive up from her apartment in downtown Phoenix, the radio jock had said something about record cold throughout the region. But right now Monae was not thinking about occluded fronts. She was thinking that she'd never been asked that question before, even when she was breaking bread with snitches, victims and defendants in Texas—the tattered and tattooed cavalcade of rogue humanity she had encountered as an investigator in the Dallas County District Attorney's Office. Or after she'd made the move west to Phoenix, to hang her own shingle as a private detective.

CHAPTER TWO

An armpit holster? So obvious. For her part, Monae never went anywhere without her Paloma Picasso black leather shoulder bag, with its gold chain hardware, embossed logo and stylized gold "X" at the clasp. And inside that petite bag at her feet was her service weapon from her years on street patrol: a double-action revolver—a short-barreled, Colt .38-caliber Detective Special. Monae preferred the rugged simplicity of her revolver over the newer semi-automatics: no magazines to fumble with, and no safety to manipulate. Just draw, aim and pull the trigger. It went "bang" every time. And if it didn't, just pull the trigger again.

The man who had asked the question, Mickey Conrad, was the mayor of Silverton, Colorado, a tiny tourist hamlet fabled for its mountain scenery and still-operational steam locomotive. He had chosen this dreary high-desert plateau as a midway meeting point between Silverton and Phoenix. Conrad was a decorated Vietnam helicopter pilot, and he visibly suffered the lingering emotional after-effects of shuttling the bloodied and the dead during combat. Back stateside he had launched a lucrative, also illegal, part-time operation using his pilot skills to transport marijuana from Mexico. On one of those flights, he crashed his plane—stuffed with fat bales of electric lettuce—in Northern Arizona. His face still bore the cuts and the contused coloration of healing from that crash; he had definitely eaten some serious leather.

Conrad had the frantic mien of a man on the run, and kept fidgeting and scratching at his neck. Then he'd gaze out the window as though he was expecting someone at this forlorn stop on the way to nowhere. But the sleet blurred any possibility of seeing anything other than random blobs of watery color, so he'd shift in the seat and start working at his neck again. The weeping scratches never got a chance to scab over.

"You better not be wired. You better not be a cop, or I swear to Christ…"

The enormous bodyguard seated across from them looked like he could don a Wookiee suit and stand in for Chewbacca. Instead he was wearing a black leather jacket; he shifted again in the seat just enough so she could once again see the holstered silver revolver.

Mickey Conrad's stiff-arm approach to a woman who was actually on his side was not unusual: Monae had acquired a similar and inherent distrust of all involved, whether cops, detectives, defendants, victims, witnesses, defense lawyers or prosecutors. Especially the latter two, because no one lied more skillfully. Sitting here in a hole-and-corner meeting, with the gun-toting Wookiee and this skittish potential client, Monae neither trusted nor feared Mickey Conrad. For now, Conrad was just another guy with a story and a problem. She had heard hundreds of similar tales, so the story itself almost didn't matter; she was here to fix the problem.

"Check this out," she said, pulling back her tweed coat sleeve to expose a white-and yellow-gold watch with delicate lines and an elegant shape.

"Yeah, so?" Mickey Conrad scratched his forehead.

"You know what this is?"

"Beyond the obvious?" A surge of wind shook the limousine. Conrad grabbed at the seat as though the car might roll over.

"It's a 1928 ladies Rolex Tonneau," she said. "It was my grandmother's. Then my mom wore it for years, and she gave it to me when I graduated college. Criminal justice at UT, in Austin."

"A college degree *and* you learned how to tell time. Congratulations. All while I was saving you and your hippie sellout friends from Communism."

Not exactly the intended effect. "That's not the point. What I'm saying is, do you think a cop would wear a watch like this?"

Mickey Conrad just shrugged. Then he pulled her wrist closer and put an oily thumbprint on the vintage crystal. He grimaced and pushed her arm away as though it smelled like cheese left in the trunk of a car for a week. "I don't know, maybe. Anyway, could be a knockoff."

"Yeah, it could be, but it's not. And I'm not a cop. But let me be completely transparent: I *was* a cop, for three years. And then an investigator for the Dallas County DA's office. I'm not here to get the drop on you, but to *help* you. So, right now what you need to do is lose the tough-guy bullshit and tell me what happened. Then, if you're lucky, I can help you clean up the mess you made."

"*I* made?"

Monae shook her head like a disapproving teacher. The only thing defendants said more than "I didn't do it" was "It wasn't my fault."

"You know, Mr. Conrad, if you walk around all day and notice it's always dark and gloomy, it might mean you have your head up your ass."

"You talk to all your clients like that?"

"Just the ones who need a reality check. Yes or no: do you want to go to prison?"

"You think you can get me off?"

"Yes or no."

"I can't go to prison. I'll go nuts in there. I just can't." Conrad scratched at his neck, both hands, as though he had fleas. Monae carefully rubbed the face of her watch on her blouse and nodded toward the mayor.

"Look, it's unlikely you're going to prison on a first offense. With the right lawyer, we should be able to get you probation."

"What do you mean, right lawyer? I thought you were my lawyer."

"I can fix this. But I'm not a lawyer. We need an Arizona attorney to represent you in court."

"And why probation?"

"Look, if you got popped blowing a red light with a couple joints in your pocket, well, that's one thing. But you got nailed with three hundred pounds of stinkweed inside your plane. That's a very different thing. Best case, you're still going to be on paper. So whatever probation wants, probation gets. If probation says, 'Hmmm, looks like rain,' then, with all due respect, Mr. Mayor, you'd better be opening an umbrella with a smile your face."

There was something about this hard-boiled world—the flat-faced Wookiee bodyguard and the mayor's own criminal hubris—that was irresistible to Monae. She was quick on the uptake, and could be making truckloads of legal tender in many other career endeavors. And the tall, reedy brunette, with her demure girl-next-door charm paired with stunning stockinged legs, could easily play those cards as a foray into the corporate hierarchy dominated by male grunts in precise suits. But this tough daughter of blue-collar working parents had always wanted to be in these cobwebbed crawl spaces instead, going toe-to-toe with the felons and miscreants who at least embraced their lies and cheating with an honesty that made them more honorable than their white-collar-criminal counterparts. Out here, blunt force respected blunt force. Conrad threw a brick; Monae heaved a cinder block. This was the work world she loved, a black limousine in Gallup, New Mexico, being slapped with rain, where she got to set out the pecking order.

"You can do all that?"

"No. I can be one-half of the team that represents you to do all that, help file paperwork and stand by you in court while your brilliant defense lawyer says all the right things with such lyrical and delicate diplomacy that the judge will be lulled along as though he's hearing the alluring strains of Homer's sirens."

Mickey Conrad was street-smart, but he didn't want to admit he wasn't too good with American history. Instead he nodded knowingly. Providence had deemed that this impressive young woman would be both smart, with her fancy college degree, and tough enough to meet here on her own and push back even when it was two against one. Conrad liked that. She wore a long black skirt with a side zipper, an untucked white blouse and black leather loafers. Topping it all off was Monae's favorite coat, which she had rarely been able to break out in the cloying Texas and Arizona heat: a semi-fitted, mid-length jacket crafted from British milled tweed with a funnel neck. Conrad decided that if he ever had a daughter, he would want her to be just like Sloane Monae.

On the other side, Monae had intentionally dropped the Greek literature reference to establish her intellectual superiority. It was a subtle play, one she always knew had worked when the other person didn't say anything. Conrad had no clue— so now they'd sorted out, diplomatically and without embarrassing anyone, that she was Buck, *The Call of the Wild* intellectual lead dog. She liked that it built credibility with a client, but on an unspoken, subconscious level, because men didn't like to be told they were idiots (which in so many cases they were, in her humble estimation).

"Remember, you're the one who's going to have to right this ship," she said. "That starts now. Everything will hinge on you keeping your nose clean until we get to court. Then a spotless probation period: you don't even jaywalk, feed a parking meter or think about running a yellow light. For at least a year, and likely more. One misstep at any point along the way, and your charge goes to a felony. So it will be you, not me or the skilled defense lawyer we find, who makes this thing right."

The mayor nodded. His sallow, bruised and stubbled face looked like he hadn't slept in days. But underneath the tough-guy words and bodyguard show of power was a scared man who needed help. A man who had answered the call to serve his country and then got spat on when he came home. A man who had become a criminal and was terrified of jail, but was also despondent that he'd destroyed his credibility as the mayor of an American municipality.

Monae studied him, a nonviolent offender caught doing something stupid. If he didn't step on her plan, she would likely be able to work through the system to keep this guy from getting a prison number. No, Monae wasn't a party girl herself, and had never dipped a toe into the hippy-dippy dope scene. That just wasn't her bag. In fact, she was a college scholarship athlete who had never done drugs and barely drank alcohol, which had helped her stay sharp and drill seventy-mile-an-hour spikes at opponents on the volleyball court. For her, Conrad clearly deserved a second chance, forgiveness and a little grace. Her hard currency of reality was not without empathy. This was exactly the type of person she had always envisioned helping by staking out a career in the criminal justice system, on the side of the fence where the bottom-feeders lived out their dramas.

"We should talk about my fee," she said.

"OK."

"You're a Colorado resident, but because you crashed in Northern Arizona we're going to be in the Mohave County court jurisdiction. Assuming we find our person in Phoenix, that means six hours of driving round-trip plus travel expenses every time your lawyer has to appear in court. He or she probably won't know the judges up there, either, so we're going to want to do a little research on whomever we get. We're going to aim to avoid a trial, but we'll still need to ask around and find some witnesses to understand the case top to bottom and make sure there aren't any surprises out there. There aren't any surprises out there, right?"

"Surprises? Like what?"

"I always like to start with the freezer."

"What?"

"Yeah. Any dead bodies, large amounts of cash or anything else that doesn't belong next to the Swanson Hungry-Man?"

"No. Nothing like that."

She gave him the hard look and another chance to come clean, because there was always something. If it wasn't in the freezer, then maybe in the toilet tank or inside a mattress. Again, defendants aren't as good as cops and lawyers at lying.

"What?" the mayor said.

Silence. Nothing made people squirm more than saying nothing. Mickey Conrad scratched his head again and then his neck. "OK, this is probably nothing, but I do have a little weed back at my house."

"A little weed."

"Yeah."

"How little?"

"Not much."

"*How* 'not much'?" she asked.

"I'm talking maybe ten pounds."

"Ten pounds is not much? I guess it's all relative, when you were caught with three hundred."

"This last little bit is premium, sticky bud here, not that dried-out road weed your unemployed brother-in-law will try to pass off. They had a warrant, but missed it during the search. I actually hid it inside a wall where the insulation goes. Except up high so it's less obvious where I had to patch. That's nothing, right?"

"I didn't hear what you just said," she said. Freezer. Toilet tank. Mattress. She added "wall cavity" to the list. "But hypothetically, if a client was charged with, say, a major drug trafficking felony, it might make sense, hypothetically, for that client to not have drugs on, or anywhere near, his person, including hidden in the wall cavity of his primary residence. That would be my hypothetical recommendation to someone in that situation. And any client who was not willing to follow such a hypothetical recommendation would need to find help elsewhere."

"So, what, flush the weed?"

She sighed. "Hypothetically."

"Man, that's a nice stash to just flush. What if I gave it to a friend?"

She was already shaking her head. "Look, people talk. People always talk. And you're the mayor of the town. You follow?"

Conrad grudgingly nodded. "OK, not even just a little for personal use? It calms me."

"So would meditation or going for a run." Monae turned her head and stared at the rain.

In his best surly-teenager voice, Conrad said, "Man, you're a real buzzkill."

"Are we clear?"

"Yeah."

"Yeah what?"

"Yeah, I'll get rid of it."

"Good. Now, taking everything into consideration, my retainer for this case will be $25,000. That will cover my fee and the lawyer I'll find. Our expenses are on top of that."

"That's a lot of jack."

"That's what Jill said."

Conrad smiled. "Still sounds high."

"Ah," she said, "the irony, straight from the lips of the marijuana mayor."

"You got a way with words. Guess that comes at a price."

"Look, if I keep you out of prison and you get your life back, it's the deal of the century."

"Yeah, but if we lose? It's like rolling the dice."

"Perhaps. But I can help you beat the house."

The mayor nodded again. "You got an answer for everything." Conrad exhaled audibly, a mixed sigh of anxiety and relief. "All right. Let's do it. Chacho."

The Wookiee bodyguard produced a weathered, black leather bag with a shoulder strap. The mayor took the bag, unzipped it and dug around. Then he looked up and smiled.

"Cash all right?"

Chapter Three

"IT'S LEANDER FARLEY ON THE PHONE from the state prison in Florence."

Devlin, sitting in his office in the red-brick building on Third Avenue, asked Nadia Flores to repeat what she'd just said through the squawk box. And yes, he had heard correctly.

"How did he get my number?" Devlin asked, his eyes burning after another middle-of-the-night session thinking about his cases.

"I have no earthly idea, Connor," she said. "Put him through, or tell him you're out?"

Leander Farley. Devlin had to search for the name through the warped-glass memory of fourteen years of legal practice. Back to his unconventional compatriot Lucky, the one-armed oracle with an impressive criminal and law enforcement network. One Friday night over beers Lucky had mentioned a state cooler inmate, a former Tucson plumber and drug kingpin, who was on death row for successfully conspiring to murder a competitor. More specifically, Farley ordered a hit by having the guy thrown down a mine shaft.

Farley would never again breathe in freedom, but he fancied himself a gentleman barrister. He spent his days reading case books, diligently studying the law and quickly rising to prominence as the resident jailhouse lawyer. Lucky had asked Devlin if he'd send Farley an outdated set of Arizona Revised Statutes books. Devlin had Nadia Flores send the books to Farley with a short note from Devlin. A month later, Farley had called Devlin to thank him for the gift. Somehow, Farley was apparently a death-row inmate with easy telephone privileges. Despite Farley's horrific crime, Devlin still had a soft spot for people engaged in their own redemption even when facing such a bleak specter.

"Connor?!"

"Yeah, sorry. Put him through."

"I've got a case for you," Farley said without salutation.

"OK, well, my docket's pretty full, Leander." That was no lie; at last count Devlin was juggling some forty different cases. He had plaintiff cases, both large and small, along with more than a dozen insurance defense cases that put Devlin on the other side of the plaintiff v. defense equation. This was a unique angle: a plaintiff lawyer doing defense work, which always put Devlin three jumps ahead of the plaintiff's lawyer in such cases. Due to that unique skill set, people hired Devlin to take on especially difficult defense cases. In each, Devlin's first priority was to resolve the case without beating down the plaintiff. These cases provided a steady revenue stream and a reliable way to cover overhead. One of those cases had Devlin defending a stripper who had been driving blind-drunk in the middle of the day and crashed into another car driven by a pregnant woman who, thankfully, only sustained minor injuries. Devlin did not have much patience for such idiocy from his own clients, and he was personally appalled by the drunk woman's behavior. To take the case, do his job, get paid and still look at himself in the mirror, Devlin would focus on doing what he could to help the plaintiff. He would offer the policy limit of $100,000 upfront, which was way more than the plaintiff's lawyer could hope to get in court for what, in the end, was only a soft-tissue injury case. To head off an end-around by the plaintiff, Devlin was going to keep his client out of the courtroom altogether.

"Just hear me out," Farley said, snapping Devlin back.

There was a loud, static buzz on the jailhouse phone that necessitated Devlin holding the receiver about six inches from his ear and simultaneously straining to hear Farley. As Farley started, Devlin was again wondering how he had such easy access to a phone.

"So, his name is Bobby Swift. He's in on a thirty-year stint. The night he was arrested, Swift was out of his mind on heroin and LSD. After robbing an all-night gas station in Tucson, for some reason he retraced his steps and pumped six .38 slugs into the store clerk. The store clerk survived, or Swift would have been facing straight murder one. Instead he got attempted murder."

"Sounds like a real pillar of the community. What do you want from me?"

"He's not a murderer."

"Only by chance. He's no Rhodes Scholar, for sure."

"Just come down and meet him. You'll see what I mean. Bobby's not a scumbag."

"Another glowing character endorsement."

"No, what I mean is he's learned his lesson. Now he needs your help. Kid's only 24. I'll bet you did some stupid things when you were 24."

Devlin smiled. First thing that popped into his mind: going to the Tom Jones concert the night before the bar exam. "Sure, but I never shot anybody. Your boy's playing in a whole different league of stupid."

"There was a recent U.S. Supreme Court case for a post-conviction remedy. Bobby Swift fits the profile."

The mere mention of any high court brought it all back again, *Kay Pearson v. Flynn Enterprises,* and put the bad taste in Devlin's mouth.

"I don't know, Leander. I'm going to have to think about it."

"If we can get his conviction overturned, don't you think he deserves a second chance?"

We? Devlin thought. But with that question Leander Farley had again tapped Devlin's Catholic soft spot: forgiveness. Still, Devlin had been trying to keep his practice steered toward personal injury ever since Trevor Walsh had lured him into the seedy underworld of the morning chain at the courthouse and that turn-and-burn, roller-coaster world. Devlin's aim was to help true victims who had been unjustly wronged, not this wannabe *Death Wish* Charles Bronson. But the second-chance angle was already nibbling at the fringes of remote possibility.

"Just come down, and I'll introduce you. You know I wouldn't blow smoke up a fellow counselor's ass."

OK, first, Devlin did not really know Leander Farley; they had only spoken once before now. And second, fellow counselor? Still, Devlin admired his pluck. "All right. Based on what I've heard, I can't make any promises. But send the case file, and I'll at least take a look."

"That's fair. That's all I ask."

"One more thing: in the unlikely event I do this, I'm assuming it would be pro bono. There's no way this Bobby Swift can pay me, right?"

Farley laughed. "Actually, trust me, counselor. That's one front our boy has covered. Payment will not be a problem."

"OK, well, that's very non-specific and mysterious. But we'll leave it at that. Send that file."

"It will be on your desk inside a week."

Devlin hung up. The phone call had sparked long-forgotten memories for him, about those early days hustling defense cases and breaking it all down with One-Armed Lucky, the uneducated legal sage. They'd lost touch and hadn't seen each other for years. In that moment of reflection Devlin decided there was a piece of news Lucky deserved to hear in person: the final appeal ruling in *Kay Pearson v. Flynn Enterprises,* the case Lucky had referred to the young upstart he'd dubbed "Big Time." Devlin grabbed the phone book, looked up AAA Bail Bonds and dialed, but the woman who answered said Lucky had left more than a year ago. Last she heard he was working as a handler at the dog track. As soon as Devlin hung up, Flores rang again.

"There's a gentleman here to see you."

"What was the name of that dog track Ann Pearson went to with Lucky?" Devlin asked.

Silence. "Am I supposed to know what you're talking about?"

"Pearson. Wrongful death. Maybe five years ago? I think it was on Washington."

As Devlin waited for her to answer, she came in and partially closed the door, resolute as always and dressed in her slacks and long-sleeved blouse, a combination she wore daily regardless of the season. "There's someone here to see you who said his name is CandyMan."

"CandyMan?"

"That's what he said," she whispered. "Says he knows a motorcycle cop you represented, and the cop thought you were really good."

Devlin knew hundreds of cops, because he had spent years among mouth-breathers like Bobby Swift. In turn, Devlin was around the cops who hauled in those perpetrators and showed up in court to testify. The criminal defense world was a meet-and-greet into the mind and psyche of every Sue Grafton bad guy and sleuth. Especially with the cops: after doing case interviews or following up leads, the inevitable shop-talk always ensued. Cops loved to bullshit about everything and nothing in particular, but they loved to talk about cop stuff the most. They went on and on about weapon calibers and their best target groupings at the range. They talked about who'd seen the deepest plunge of cleavage on a traffic stop, and the jack-hole civilians who got tickets just for being jack-holes. They detailed foot chases, takedowns and collars. They bragged about who'd encountered the dumbest perps doing the most unbelievably stupid things. Cops loved to whisper gossip, too, about the chief and who he was promoting next, who was banging whom up and down the chain of command, who might be dirty, and every other manner of cop minutiae. Cops loved to openly complain about lawyers, judges and the crooked legal system, too. They especially griped about open-and-shut cases that fell apart in the courts—like sand through their fingers—because witnesses and even victims refused to cooperate. In fact, most cops couldn't talk about anything else except being a cop. They were glacially slow to warm up to civilians, but once they figured out Devlin was a straight shooter, they opened up to the point the lawyer would eventually have to crowbar himself away from the conversations with some invented excuse. A quick glance at the wrist and "I'm late for court" usually worked best.

Out of those friendships and constant encounters, Devlin got the idea to start a group legal plan specifically for law enforcement. As a loss leader, for just $2.50 per month any cop who was a paying member could call Devlin any time for legal advice. He'd just signed up his 400th cop. In turn, personal injury work started to trickle in from those same cops on his plan. The general tenor of the cases was: *my wife/brother-in-law/friend got rear-ended/jackknifed/T-boned by some woman driver/hippie/white-trash asshole who ran a red light/didn't yield/was going twenty over the limit,* etc.

Devlin was dreaming about sleep and still racking his brain trying to come up with the name of the dog track. *Regal* something... and he needed to prepare a brief for the judge for a pre-trial settlement conference scheduled for July in a medical malpractice case with a client named Darcie Savoy.

"I don't have time for CandyMan today. Tell CandyMan to make an appointment. Or better yet, tell him we're not taking any new clients right now."

Flores leaned in. "Devlin, I think you should tell him. I don't want to be the one."

"Why?"

She got even closer and whispered, "Because he looks like he might break things if I tell him something he doesn't want to hear."

"Break things? What are you talking about?"

She motioned. "Go look. He brought his girlfriend, Sunshine." She could not contain her amusement, and broke out laughing.

"Sunshine? What in the hell."

Devlin stood, cinched his tie knot, slipped on his suit jacket and peeked into the lobby. CandyMan and Sunshine were, indeed, quite the pair. They might have walked straight off a Hollywood back lot after an open call for "biker and his old lady." CandyMan was about five feet, ten inches but went about 220 pounds, with a professional beer belly. His muddied tattoos, up and down both arms, were starkly visible, uncovered by his white tank top. Shaggy brown hair, a wild beard, faded jeans and black boots completed the ensemble directive sent out by the casting director. His biker mama fit the part, too: short and pudgy with voluminous, jiggly breasts—huddled masses yearning to breathe free in every direction—and a weathered complexion that added ten years to however old she really was.

Devlin gave up on the name of the dog track, flipped the charm switch, smiled, stepped into the lobby and motioned to them both. "Connor Devlin. Please, come into my office."

Once seated in his office, the duo introduced themselves. CandyMan and Sunshine, it turned out, had legally changed their names to match their job title and demeanor, respectively. In other words, he sold pot, and she was always lit up thanks to her old man's wares.

"How can I help you?" Devlin asked absentmindedly, now back to mentally searching for the name of the dog track.

Personable and spirited, CandyMan spoke with surprising articulation and eloquence in describing his motorcycle accident, the resulting nagging hip that needed to be replaced, and his desire to have Devlin as his lawyer based on the cop recommendation. CandyMan's story immediately touched Devlin. How could he *not* help this guy? The biker's unique charm and resolute spirit sealed the deal. Despite being impossibly busy with a Herculean caseload, Devlin had already decided he would do everything in his power to help CandyMan in his quest to regain his mobility. Before they left, Devlin had signed up a new client with his standard letter of agreement, stating that there were no upfront fees and that Devlin's cut was one-third of whatever injury settlement or jury award they might get, plus his expenses.

TRUE to Leander Farley's word, five days later Devlin was reading the file. Robert Earl Swift was at the apex of the Swift family of screw-ups, a bloodline gone bad. Now 24, he'd already done six years in prison for the attempted second-degree murder. In his letter to Devlin, Farley suggested appealing Swift's conviction with a Rule 32 petition, a legal version of a get-out-of-jail card. Under a Rule 32 petition, Devlin could appeal by articulating one of three reasons: ineffective counsel, newly discovered evidence, or substantive change of law. Devlin would use the third option, because when Bobby Swift was originally sentenced, the law stated that he was not eligible for parole until twenty years into his sentence. With the new U.S. Supreme Court precedent, Swift was eligible for parole after a "reasonable time," which was a subjective definition and the core of what Devlin would have to articulate. And certainly, a ruling by the U.S. Supreme Court would fall under "substantive change of law." The evidentiary hearings would take place in Tucson, in Pima County where Swift had committed his lame-brain crime.

If successful, Bobby Swift would be entitled to re-sentencing. Farley's legal theory was spot-on, but Devlin still didn't love the case or the defendant at first glance. Devlin was reluctant to help spring a moron who had inflicted such violent pain on another. The other issue was that while Leander Farley was reasonably intelligent and presented himself well, he, like everyone else pounding sand in a six-by-nine, had a credibility gap as wide and long as the black Lincoln Continental Devlin once drove. His current ride was a 1983 cherry-red Chevy Blazer. Everything in Farley's letter would have to be held out for further analysis, corroborated and fact-checked, all of which would eat up more valuable time. If he took the case, Devlin would have to prepare a brief and file it to get a preliminary hearing.

Right then, after years on the mental back burner, it hit him. Devlin rang Flores, who answered on the first ring.

"Royal Palms Kennel Club," Devlin said proudly.

"What?" she said.

"I told you I'd get it. The name of the dog track."

"Is there a to-do here?"

"Can you please call them and ask... oh shit, what was his real name?"

"Whose real name?"

"One-Armed Lucky."

"Who?"

"The guy. He used to refer cases. You know. Shit, what was his name?"

"I have another call."

"I'll think of it."

"OK, you do that and let me know."

Reluctantly, and mostly because he had a morbid curiosity to meet both Leander Farley and Bobby Swift, the next day Devlin took a trip down to the state lock-up near Tucson, to have a face-to-face. Devlin headed south on Interstate 10, through the sun-blasted and oddly beautiful moonscape of the Sonoran desert, in the gleaming Blazer he'd bought new after convincing the Chevy dealership to sell it to him minus the factory engine and transmission. The general manager had been perplexed at first, then suspicious, and finally hesitant but agreeable to removing the engine and transmission and selling Devlin the remainder of the vehicle without any warranty. Devlin then had a speed shop drop in a 454 big-block crate and a beefed-up automatic four-wheel-drive transfer case that made it feel like 1970 all over again.

At first glance, Bobby Swift was exactly as Devlin had predicted: a scrawny, 24-year-old punk wearing a ratty bandana, walking with a puffed chest and sporting arms littered with rudimentary jailhouse tattoos. Leander Farley came to the meeting, too—the death-row inmate with exceedingly loose prison privileges. Swift had a buzz cut; Farley sported a receding hairline and long brown hair pulled back into a ponytail. After introductions, Devlin got right to the point.

"Tell me why I should take your case," he said.

Bobby Swift grunted as though this entire proceeding was an imposition on his busy day of doing zilch. Then he told a predictable tale. His parents were both uneducated, blue-collar and alcoholic. Bobby himself, along with a sister and half-brother, had grown up without much guidance. Bobby found the wrong path by seventh grade, when he started shoplifting. For Bobby, the poor choices and bad behavior all culminated in the worst night of his life. He had only seen the hard light of incarceration since, but offered to swear to Devlin on a fourteen-foot stack of Bibles that he was a changed man and no longer a violent person.

Devlin was doing what he did best, listening and assessing all the unspoken cues. Although he hadn't ruled out the idea of representing this kid, there were still key questions.

"I'm not saying yet that I'll take your case, but if I do we can't have any bullshit between us. None."

Bobby just stared at the lawyer with a haughty look of disinterest and smug defiance.

"There a problem here?" Devlin asked.

"You tell me."

"Bobby, come on now," Leander said. "I vouched for you."

Bobby shrugged his shoulders. "Ain't no problem here, Leander."

Devlin stared him down for a few seconds before saying, "First thing we need to clear up: I won't represent violent criminals. People who do bodily harm to other human beings. Especially for a few lousy bucks. I still have to look at this pasty Irish mug in the mirror every morning. I'm not passing judgment on you for what you did, but going forward, I won't have anything to do with that kind of bullshit. Are you done with that life?"

Bobby Swift looked down while picking at his tooth with a fingernail.

"Is that a 'yes'?" Devlin asked.

Swift looked up. "We all have bad days."

"Yeah, but we don't all shoot people on those bad days."

Swift smirked and held up his right hand. "Scout's honor. I won't never do nothing like that again."

Devlin sighed and nodded. If this was the best front the kid could put on, he wasn't exactly bankable. But Devlin had also been around enough offenders, con artists and rotters to sense the kid, while trying to play it tough, was really crying out for someone to help him.

"OK, one more thing we need to clear up. Your boy Leander said you can pay me, correct?"

Swift laughed. "Sure. Whatever you need."

Now that was a negotiating stance that triggered suspicion. "This isn't dirty money I'm going to regret taking?"

"Less'un you don't like the idea of liquid dinosaurs gettin' you where you need to get."

"What in the holy fuck?"

"Oil," Swift said.

"He can pay you whatever you need," Farley said.

"Well, that may be, but I want to know *how* he has money to pay me. I want to know whatever it is you need to tell me so I don't ever get surprised. Ever." Devlin thought, this one was courtesy of Trevor Walsh, the wild-eyed former prosecutor and mentor to the young Devlin. The manual never failed: *Rule #2: Never be surprised— surprise is death.*

Leander slid Devlin a small piece of paper. "Here's the contact person. Call them, and they'll set up whatever payments you need." It was a female name, and "Philadelphia Bank and Trust" was written below a phone number.

"I'm not following."

CHAPTER THREE

Bobby Swift nodded at Leander, who then told the story. In the 1920s, Bobby's paternal grandfather had won a large parcel of Texas scrubland in a backroom card game. In turn, the grandfather became an oil wildcatter and eventually tapped black gold on that otherwise worthless tract. Despite a dysfunctional family upbringing, Bobby Swift and his two siblings were now the sole heirs to one of the richest oil-royalty incomes in the United States: averaging north of $50,000 *a month* each to Bobby and his sister; and about $25,000 a month to their half-brother. The life of a lawyer: the wild tales and almost-unbelievable circumstances of clients never got old. Of course, Devlin would need to vet what Bobby Swift was saying and get back to him.

Liquid dinosaurs. At least the kid had some imagination. Then the name popped into Devlin's racing mind: Larry White. That was One-Armed Lucky's real name. Devlin made a mental note to call the dog track once he got back to his office.

AT the row of tables directly behind Devlin in the prison meet-up room, a female defense attorney had just finished meeting with a client and now sat talking with another woman dressed in a navy suit.

"I did a little digging and found out the sitting judge is also ex-military," the woman in the suit told the attorney. "My hunch is the brotherhood bond will play favorably."

"What's the venue again?" the attorney asked as she dug through her attaché case and prepared for her next client.

"Mohave County Superior Court."

"Page?"

"Kingman."

"What is that, like, couple hours each way from Phoenix?"

"More like three. But I built the drive time into the retainer."

"Which is how much?"

"Your end would be ten thousand," Sloane Monae told the attorney.

"And you want to try to keep him out of prison?"

"That's the goal."

"I'm not sure that's possible given the facts of the case."

"Well, that's why he needs someone good. Like you."

"Let's just suppose, by some miracle, we can plead him out to a non-designated, open-ended offense: you think this mayor can keep his nose clean while he's on paper?"

"I do," Monae said, thinking of Mickey Conrad's freezer, and then the wall cavity he'd described, and wondering if he had done as promised. It was this Phoenix-based defense attorney's suggestion that she and Monae meet here at the state lockup, in between clients, because the high-demand counselor's schedule was otherwise booked solid for the next month.

Then Monae noticed a man in a crisp tailored suit standing at the row of tables next to theirs. His back had been to her, but when he stood and turned she discreetly took note. The first thing a woman noticed, at least one who was almost six feet tall in her bare feet, was a man's height. Likewise, playing at the University of Texas on a volleyball scholarship had given Monae and her teammates an uncanny ability to peg people's heights, because they were always assessing the front line of the competition. She put him at six-foot-three, which was in fact his exact height.

That he was tall was a good start. He was not James Bond good-looking—he had a paler complexion and a sort of bookish quality—but was undeniably and unconventionally handsome, with a lean frame, clothes that fit just right, a pair of round wire-rimmed glasses and brown hair that seemed long for a lawyer, which he had to be. Who else came to prison in a tailored suit? His stylish cast made him the kind of guy men and women alike wanted to meet. Monae could make her own guesses. His air was that of a soloist. She'd bet on him being a rogue lawyer, calling his own shots in the name of justice. Monae liked her conjured image of this broad-shouldered lone wolf riding the high plains, from town to town, as a protector.

"Seems almost too good to be true."

"Tell me about it," Monae said, distracted by her Western-movie montage.

"What?"

Monae looked back to her conversation partner and caught herself. She'd just been busted checking him out, but she played it cool.

"I'm sorry. Could you repeat that?" Monae said.

"Your case? Ten grand is a nice fee. Like, what's the catch, right?"

"No catch. Just the chance to do the right thing for a veteran. And I'm not a lawyer, so your services are critical."

The other woman pulled out a pen. "Let me jot down your name. Like the painter, 'E-T' at the end?"

"No, it's M-O-N-*A-E*."

"When do you need an answer?"

Just then the tall man turned, made direct eye contact and smiled. Monae glanced away and stared at the floor.

The woman noticed. "Are you OK?"

"Yes. Sorry. The preliminary hearing is in a couple months, so the sooner the better."

"Why are you staring at the floor?" the woman asked.

"The floor? Me? I'm not." She looked up. The handsome lawyer was across the room now, walking away with two inmates in their orange pajamas. Monae subconsciously noted the details of the perpetrators: the taller inmate had a ponytail, and the younger one had buzzed hair and tattoos. Judging by their respective gaits, the taller one's height matched his rank—a notch or two above the shorter kid, who projected his inferiority complex with typical false bravado.

"I'm slammed right now, but it's intriguing. Let you know in a few days?"

"Yes, of course. That's great."

They both stood and shook hands. The female attorney walked away.

What an idiot, Monae thought to herself. That was all very uncharacteristic for her, to get distracted by some stranger. But not just any stranger, *a slickly dressed lawyer*. She shook her head again and laughed.

"Get a grip," she said aloud as she walked toward the door labeled "Exit." Thankfully, the mystery man was gone. And she knew there was little chance she would ever know his name or see him again. She had only come down here to the state lockup to find Mickey Conrad a good defense lawyer, and on that front she had already likely succeeded. The woman Monae had just met seemed wholly capable, although not particularly warm and fuzzy, which didn't really matter. Monae didn't need her to sing about unicorns and hand out cupcakes, just to pull the right legal levers. Monae stepped to the window and took the pen to sign out on the sheet attached to the clipboard. Then, inexplicably, Monae found herself scanning the list trying to decipher which name was attached to the man in the nice suit. There were a dozen men who had already signed out.

"You good?"

She looked up. The uniformed guard was staring at her and nodding at the woman waiting behind her. Monae smiled and noted the time on the large round clock behind his head, glanced down one last time and landed on the name that fit the time parameters: Connor J. Devlin.

"Yes," she said. "I'm good."

Chapter Four

THE DYING LIGHT FRACTURED THE REMNANTS of the day into creeping shadows cast across the vacant urban lot. The unusually cool May weather reminded Devlin why it had been so easy to idle away hours here between two faded brick buildings, atop a table of sun-hardened dirt punctuated by clumps of brown weeds starved for rainfall. There had always been two overturned white five-gallon buckets as makeshift chairs, with the battered-but-reliable radio at Lucky's feet playing sixties and seventies hits. Tonight, the music came from the modern era through the open window of the Blazer: "Always Something There to Remind Me" by Naked Eyes, a catchy pop tune that was a pure earworm. For the first time in years, Devlin had come to this spot on a nostalgic whim—only after going to the Royal Palms Kennel Club to track down One-Armed Lucky. Now that he stood here, the memories came flooding back. Everything was a retread, it seemed: Devlin specifically remembered the original Sandie Shaw version of this song as part of the soundtrack to his start of law school.

DEVLIN had just graduated from Notre Dame, packed the last of his things into his brand-new gleaming black 1967 Corvette with a white convertible top and candy-red interior, and headed west on the open road toward his own manifest destiny: law school. Two days later, he first heard the song as he rolled through the bleak high desert of New Mexico and marveled at the silent bursts of chain-lightning on the enameled black horizon. The sun-parched moonscape was a blunt contrast to the slate-gray arc of the Midwest skies and green grass he'd left behind in South Bend. There was no longer going to be anything to remind Devlin of his time at Notre Dame, nor his youth in Buffalo. In each place, lingering dirty ice ruled for half the year. For the first twenty-two years of his life and education, Devlin had attended a succession of all-male institutions forever imprisoned under dismal, foreboding skies. So as he ghosted through the iridescent desert light south across scorched Arizona, it was like someone had finally found the switch and turned on the lights. Devlin had escaped the grinding weather machine.

Finally he rolled onto the campus of the University of Southern California to begin law school, a place where the vivid light played off any number of beautiful coeds. As his cryogenically impaired bones thawed, creaked and acclimated back to normal operating temperatures, Devlin spent those first weeks in reverent awe of the towering palm trees, glittering sunshine and, of course, the girls. Liberated from the suffocating cloak of nineteen layers of wool, scarves, hats and gloves, the USC campus displayed more skin in a week than Devlin saw through all four seasons in Buffalo or South Bend.

At orientation, Devlin found a back-row seat in an auditorium and took in the murmuring small talk. In addition to the female bounty, he was now surrounded by apex predators, the top of the academic food chain from all the upper-echelon universities. Devlin realized it was now him against the progeny of the powerful. Just a few minutes into the law school dean's opening remarks, which Devlin was only partially absorbing, he felt a clammy heat flash through his body as he wondered how he was going to survive this three-year gauntlet of classroom rigor. That fish-out-of-water realization intensified throughout his first semester, a four-month period in which Devlin had no idea what was going on in his classes. Of course, the law school's proximity to the female dorms, stocked with the free-love miniskirt generation, wasn't helping matters.

One professor, Juneas Duffman, was the smartest and most intimidating human being Devlin had ever encountered. Duffman had graduated number one in his class at Harvard Law and picked up a master's degree in Greek mythology for good measure. Immediately, Duffman was dismayed at the flawed logic revealed in

Devlin's writing. The first assigned paper Devlin wrote did not fare well, as Duffman scribbled: *The worst piece of drivel ever penned by a law student purportedly fluent in the English language.* Slowly, however, Duffman began to recognize Devlin's rare holistic talents: grit, empathy and presence. He flatly told the aspiring lawyer, whom he had started calling "Mr. D," that Devlin would never sit on a federal court bench, much less the U.S. Supreme Court. "You're simply not judge material," he had continued.

Devlin was actually relieved: the thought of listening to lawyers argue all day was not appealing in any way, nor was it how he wanted to make his mark.

"But there's something about you and your presence," Duffman said. "You should think about being a trial lawyer. That is, if I can help you put together two legible sentences." The professor paused, smiled knowingly and then added, "I bet you cut a wide, phallic swath through this campus."

Devlin nodded and smiled, too, as to affirm that assessment, and then later grabbed his Random House dictionary to look up "phallic" and "swath." Gradually, Duffman's academic assessment became prophetic as Devlin studied eight to ten hours every day. With his fascination for assembling facts and case elements, by the end of his second year Devlin's classmates tagged him "The King of Torts." Throughout that final year, Devlin felt a growing excitement for his chosen field. Of course, he did not yet have a grasp of the maddening loopholes and grinding timelines he'd encounter in an imperfect legal system, but the idea of amending people's pain—giving voice to the voiceless—instilled great hope in his idealistic psyche. Unlike most classmates, Devlin took a workmanlike outlook: the law itself was not some ancient and holy instrument surrounded by a golden aura. For Devlin, the law would be the tool he'd use to expose corporate and institutional arrogance, indifference and greed. In 1970, just by graduating, Devlin had survived a brutal attrition rate: from their original class of 125, only thirty-five received their USC law degrees on that day. Although Devlin was among those who had crossed the finish line, he languished in the lower third of the small class.

HOW had fourteen years passed already? Devlin looked around: there was no white bucket to flip and sit on, and all these years later, his one-time compadre was nowhere to be seen. Not because he had moved on from AAA Bail Bonds but because, as Devlin had just learned, One-Armed Lucky was dead. The woman at the dog track had scant details; perhaps a heart condition, or was it cancer? Either way, definitely something that came on quickly and took everyone by surprise. Devlin was saddened that he had no idea this had happened almost two years ago. The woman said she knew Lucky had been cremated and was not sure if there had been a memorial service. With no gravesite or formal marker to pay his final respects, Devlin instead came here to their once-sacred space where *Kay Pearson v. Flynn Enterprises* had all begun, courtesy of Lucky's case referral. Devlin leaned against the red brick wall and just delivered it straight, aloud, into the ether of time and space:

"Well, you one-armed freak, we lost the Arizona Supreme Court appeal. Kay at least got the compensatory damages we won at trial, and our winning verdict stands. But the $12 million in punitive damages the jury said was ours goes away. *Bupkis.* But don't give me any of your shit, because we still beat those bastards straight-up. No regrets. I'd play it the same way again."

A woman carrying a briefcase had stopped in the gap between the buildings and was staring at Devlin. Unfazed, he whispered, "Watch this, Lucky." Then he redoubled his voice and extended his arms as though striding to center stage in a sold-out theatre: "'As flies to wanton boys are we to the gods; they kill us for their sport!'"

The woman looked puzzled and walked away.

"King Lear. That's what we're up against, pal. Anyway, I just wanted you to hear it from me." Devlin leaned against the cool brick and absorbed the urban hum he remembered well from these unique chinwags. A horn honking. The distant wail of a siren. Everything masked by the white noise of rush-hour traffic funneling south to Interstate 10.

"Well," he said, "I have better things to do than hang around here trying to educate your sorry ass."

Yeah, likewise, Big-Time—save them fancy Shakespeare quotations for the foxes, cuz they ain't be working on me.

Devlin smiled: something like that. The banter of their brotherhood. Devlin wiped a tear, instinctively crossed himself and said, "Peace be with you, brother."

Chapter Five

DEVLIN TURNED, WALKED BACK to the idling Blazer, climbed in and squawked the tires with his old pal on his mind. As Devlin drove, any sentimentality quickly faded as he thought about the remaining hours: head to the gym at the Jewish Community Center for some full-court basketball, and then back to the office to burn the midnight oil. Two weeks after meeting Bobby Swift, everything had checked out with his story, so Devlin needed to get to work on the Rule 32 petition Leander Farley had recommended. Devlin crept along in heavy traffic. He was so engrossed in ruminating about his core arguments for the petition that he didn't notice the blazing orb to his left, shimmering behind a sheer veil of wispy clouds. Just before dipping into the desert horizon completely, a fragmented splash of spectacular orange, garish pink and purplish hues exploded across the sky.

WHEN the wind came back into Devlin's lungs, he realized he was flat on his back on the shiny hardwood, staring at a grotesque yeti, a short squat man with every square inch of his body seemingly covered in black and gray fur.

"Who the fuck are you, coming into my lane?" the yeti asked in a thick Brooklyn accent. "Keep that weak shit outta here."

Then Devlin remembered that he had come here to play basketball, he had driven to the hole and then everything had gone black. He extended a hand: "Connor Devlin." Devlin had been playing basketball five nights a week since the mid-seventies, in various city leagues around Phoenix, and had never taken a hit like that one.

"Yeah, the kid PI lawyer from that case that was in the news," the yeti said, laughing. "At least you picked something you don't have to be smart to do. Lamont the dummy. That's your new name." He turned and walked away without helping Devlin up. Devlin got the Lamont reference, which was from the sitcom *Sanford and Son*. *What an asshole*, Devlin thought, not realizing he had just collided with a living law legend.

Phil Goldberg, aka Goldie—which was the only thing anyone had ever called him since he was two years old—was five feet, eight and weighed 260 pounds. He worked 365 days a year, which only partially explained why he had burned through four marriages. He was the son of Russian immigrants from Brooklyn, and had gone to Michigan State University on a full-ride football scholarship back when teams carried three fullbacks, bowling-ball shaped grinders who could annex three yards, between the tackles, on any carry. During his first year of college his father fell ill, so he dropped out to help care for him. When his father died, Goldie was adrift. That is, until the football coach from Brandeis University called to offer Goldie a similar slot on that team and an academic track. After graduating with his bachelor's in history, Goldie went on to University of Chicago Law School, where he graduated first in his class. He stopped in Phoenix in the late fifties on his way to California, and never left.

Brilliant and physically menacing, Goldie had the outward demeanor of an addled long-haul truck driver so foul-tongued he embarrassed other truck drivers with his language. Intellectually, he wrote like a poet. A brilliant legal theorist, his range in the law was unparalleled. He worked out of a small building downtown, across the street from Phoenix Municipal Hospital—where Devlin's back-alley investigator Max Daniels had once gone on a midnight fishing expedition for a missing nurse—in an office without any windows, which a secretary had dubbed The Bunker. Goldie did all his own research and writing. He smoked cigars and drank coffee all day long, and never left his desk to go out for lunch. Instead he stayed in his cave and gnawed on cold fried chicken while he worked. There were cigar smoke-stains up and down the dingy walls of his office that looked like brown water lines. Anyone who worked for, with or near Goldie for an extended period would likely develop emphysema. Why he hadn't himself was more evidence that he was somehow superhuman.

Goldie had risen to prominence as a dominant trial lawyer in Arizona in a career spanning the fifties, sixties, seventies and now into the eighties, with the notion that the courtroom was living theatre. And to Goldie, each case was a play steeped in hilarious, sardonic and tragic themes that became metaphoric tapestries. Goldie immersed himself in the most difficult intellectual legal proceedings: First Amendment law; convoluted insurance, construction and securities cases; and arcane criminal law. By the time he cold-cocked Devlin coming across the lane, Goldie had authored more than seventy-five winning appellate decisions.

"Hey, Lamont, you big dummy." It took Devlin a few seconds to realize it was Goldie, calling him out again as he toweled off his face, the only part of his sasquatch body not covered in sweat-matted hair. "Yeah, you, Lamont. Did you see the blurb in the paper today? About your boy?"

Devlin was confused: was it possible there had been an article about One-Armed Lucky? And today, of all days? Two years after his death? That did not make any sense.

"Yeah, well, he's out. The one-time boy wonder, now a disgraced felon and disbarred attorney. Maybe you can hire him to work for you. Dummy Number Two. 'Dummy & Dummy: Together we almost add up to an IQ of seventy-five.'"

"What are you talking about?"

"Stay with me, potato brains. Your boy, Trevor Walsh? Just got out of the can. Small blurb in the metro section. Oh, but that's right, Dummy don't read good."

The juvenile schoolyard insults had zero impact, but the news the mini-yeti had just relayed hit Devlin like another Goldie forearm across the throat: Trevor Walsh was out.

Later, at home in shorts and a T-shirt, Devlin played a new game in his mind, which was to tell himself that by working well past midnight he would finally, mercifully, be able to sleep five or six hours straight without interruption. But even as he settled in with his legal pad and several Bic pens, Devlin knew his mental exercise was only a chimera. Sleep was not forthcoming any time soon because, as always, Devlin's mind was brimming with case details.

ONE month after the run-in with Goldie, Devlin had barely noticed that the Soviet Union government announced it would boycott the upcoming Summer Olympics in Los Angeles. Devlin was working eighty hours a week, grabbing some sleep and still juggling forty or so cases including the Bobby Swift Rule 32 petition. He sat at his office desk staring at the yellow legal pad. Fifteen minutes ago, he had written the rudimentary basics across the top of the page and then stalled:

IN THE PIMA COUNTY COURT, STATE OF ARIZONA
ROBERT EARL SWIFT, Petitioner,

vs.

STATE OF ARIZONA, Respondent

PETITION FOR RELIEF FROM SENTENCE OF INCARCERATION UNDER RULE 32 OF THE ARIZONA RULES OF CRIMINAL PROCEDURE

Robert Earl Swift respectfully petitions this Honorable Court for relief from his sentence of incarceration. The Constitutions of the United States and of the State of Arizona require a new sentencing proceeding pursuant to Rule 32 of the Arizona Rules of Criminal Procedure.

Devlin knew the next step was to carefully detail the case chronology, sentencing and various appeal attempts. As Devlin sat pondering the difficult and arcane terrain of appellate law, he looked up from his desk and through the doorway into the reception area—and received a heaven-sent jolt of pure oxygen that obliterated any other concern. Without explanation, a brunette had appeared in his lobby. A mystery woman. Her dark, thick hair fell to her shoulders. She had to be over six feet in her black heels, and wore a closely tailored gray suit. She looked professional, tastefully curvaceous and younger than Devlin. Flores came in, partially closed the door and said, "Sloane Monae, to see you regarding a potential case."

"Who is she?"

"Sloane Monae. I'm sorry: I made the appointment when you were out, and forgot to tell you."

"No, I mean, *who* is she? How did she end up here?"

"My numerous talents do not include omniscience, Connor."

"Give me a minute, and then send her in. Please close the door on your way out."

Flores rolled her eyes, walked out and only partially closed the door. Devlin could hear her asking the woman if she wanted anything to drink. Devlin stood and checked himself in the reflection of a framed Knute Rockne poster, tightened his tie knot and ran his fingers through his hair. Then he pulled on his suit jacket and took his spot behind the desk. Flores tapped and came in with the mystery guest, who extended her hand.

"Sloane Monae," she said.

Devlin stood and shook her hand. "Connor Devlin. Pleasure to meet you." And boy, that was no false flattery. This tall, powerful woman smelled as good as she looked, a floral scent that was pleasant but not too sweet or overbearing. As they both sat, Devlin watched as she tucked her long stockinged legs in front of his desk.

Monae was quickly making her own assessments, immediately thinking this guy sure had a lot of framed pictures of himself on the walls, including one where he was standing with another guy in a suit and a kid in boxing trunks. In another he was shirtless, in Notre Dame boxing trunks and looking, well… wow, very fit. His being some sort of pugilist didn't bother her at all; she had been equally fierce on the volleyball court, had flourished through the fighting rigors of the police academy and had held her own in many street scrapes on dirty corners of Dallas. This lawyer obviously liked cars, too. And there was a framed front page of a newspaper showing a graduation ceremony, with a kid in cap and gown reading a newspaper amid the throng of students.

"That you?"

"Yeah, college graduation. Notre Dame."

"Who was the speaker?"

"Eugene McCarthy. He was a senator at the time. And always a poet."

"So, what, you couldn't be bothered for ten minutes with his message of service and social activism?"

"It was really just a goof. Except a photographer snaps that, photo ends up on the front page of the daily and gets splashed all over South Bend. My mother was mortified. My father said it represented the opposite of everything he had been trying to impart throughout my entire upbringing."

"Meaning what?"

"That my work ethic was below the standard demanded by our heritage."

"Irish?"

"You a detective?"

"In fact, I am." A detective, she thought, who better not be making it obvious that she had looked at the shirtless photo one beat too long. She had been right: what kind of lawyer has a framed photo of himself, minus a shirt, hanging in his law office? That's right, a *rogue* lawyer. He had nice eyes, too, and a stellar white smile. There was no way on God's green earth this guy was not already taken. *Stay on topic, Monae.*

"Sounds like your dad set high expectations."

"You could say that. He could out-Irish the best of them."

"Out-Irish?"

"Work until everyone else around you drops."

"Is that what you do?"

"Yes, that's what *we* do. I'm the third Connor J. Devlin. One day my son will be the fourth."

It was a perfect opening: "You're married, then?"

"No. Not divorced, either."

"So, what, you've already decided what you and your hypothetical wife will name your future offspring?"

"Something like that."

"What if it's a girl?"

"Hadn't gotten that far."

"And maybe your hypothetical wife won't like the name 'Connor' for a boy. Maybe she'll want to name him 'Larry' after her father."

"Your father's name is 'Larry'?"

She felt a touch of color on her cheeks. "And how do you know I'm not married?"

"No ring, at least."

"My father's name is Gabriel." Boy, this Connor Devlin did not waste any time. "He taught me from an early age that I could be anything I wanted."

"Like an investigator. Municipal or private?"

"Private. I was a beat cop in Dallas for three years and, like you, wanted to run my own shop. And, like you, that means I have to out-smart, out-maneuver and out-work the competition. Out-Irish them, right?"

"And out-dress," Devlin said, smiling, "Which you have done spectacularly."

Monae thought, *He's already flirting, inside five minutes. Play it cool. Get back to business.* "That brings us to why I'm here."

"Yes, I'm very interested to know."

"I have a potential case, and I'm interviewing attorneys to find the right fit for my client." She already knew Devlin was the right fit as a lawyer, including his street cred and track record, all of which she'd researched after seeing him at the prison. Still, she was going to make him work to earn this case. Plus, she owed it to the mayor to properly vet his prospective attorney.

"As you can guess, I've done my research," she said. "I have to say you've carved out a decent reputation in Phoenix and the greater Southwest. You had that big nursing home case that made the news. As a solo practitioner myself, I respect that—an independent brand name you wouldn't have if you were buried in a big corporate firm."

"Risk and reward," Devlin said. "I could never picture myself as one of the gray-faced, trudging into a hundred-lawyer firm every day. Instead, you and I? Solo operators. It's in the blood."

"Does that mean you would be interested in representing a criminal defendant?"

If it meant the chance to spend one more minute with Sloane Monae, Devlin thought, he would represent Charles Manson. Devlin wanted to leap, but he could not act like an overeager schoolboy.

"That all depends on the case," he said. "I do have extensive experience in criminal defense work, but I've really been trying to steer my practice out of that arena toward precedent-making plaintiff cases. But perhaps for the right case. Tell me about this one."

Sloane Monae spent the next ten minutes briefing Devlin on the Vietnam veteran pilot Mickey Conrad, his crashed plane stuffed with three hundred pounds of shrink-wrapped green bud, and the careful legal guidance she had already given, right down to the Swanson Hungry-Man discussion. She left out the part about the wall-cavity misstep that Conrad better have rectified already. She finally concluded with, "And we would be in Mohave County, which is Kingman."

"Overnight?" Devlin asked, innocently enough, as he calculated the potential time commitment.

"Well, I mean, yes. Perhaps. Not necessarily," she said. "Well, it could be. Overnight. It all depends on the judge's docket, right?"

Devlin nodded. "OK, let me understand the facts of this case. Your client was flying a private plane without a flight plan, at low elevation to avoid any detection, and crashed with three hundred pounds of dope. When the police arrived he was the only person on board, still strapped into the pilot seat; he confessed to the crime and the police arrested him on scene. And there is no other evidence to point to anyone other than your client as the perpetrator of this crime."

Monae nodded.

"What is our defense, then? We can't argue that he didn't commit this crime."

"We're hoping for probation instead of prison time."

Devlin whistled. "That's going to be a tall order." But his mind was already working the challenge. "If there's no defense, then our best strategy would be to mitigate the damage enough that the prosecutor would allow him to plead to an open-ended offense rather than possession. He's still probably going to have to do some time, but much less if the defense strategy works. After serving his time—maybe we can keep it to a year or less—he'd be eligible for parole. If he completes his term of parole without any missteps, then his original charge would get designated a misdemeanor rather than a felony. I'd say that would be the absolute best outcome. And if I take the case, I would not want to misrepresent this strategy to your client as anything other than a real long shot."

"I… may have told him it's unlikely he'd go to prison on a first offense," she said. "With the right lawyer."

"Well, I may be the right lawyer, but I can't change the facts of his case, which are all against us."

"I understand," she said, liking that he had said *us*. "But the right lawyer also gives us the best shot."

"True. Have you already established a fee arrangement?"

Devlin was conflicted. This case was probably 90/10 against keeping this guy out of the clink. Devlin didn't like cases that started with those odds. On the other side of the ledger, taking the case would mean more time with Sloane Monae, an intriguing woman who had just floated into his world seemingly out of nowhere. However, despite her obvious professional and personal assets, she could not factor into Devlin's decision regarding whether to take the case for a potential client.

"Your retainer would be $7,500," she said, straight-faced. After meeting with the first attorney and offering ten large, Monae reconsidered: this was her case and client, and therefore she deserved a bigger end of the take.

"That sounds a tad low to represent a criminal client and keep him out of prison." Devlin's phone rang. "Excuse me."

It was Flores: "I have Trevor Walsh on the line."

Hearing the name knocked Devlin back a bit. Despite the compelling primacy of all things Sloane Monae, he did not want to miss this chance to speak to Walsh. "Would you please excuse me," he said to the detective. "I need to take this call."

"Of course." Monae stood and glided toward the door. Devlin felt a twinge of guilt for taking in the view as she left.

"Thank you," he said. "I won't be long." Then, into the phone: "OK, put him through." After a few seconds Devlin heard the voice for the first time since the seventies.

"What do you say, kid? Long time."

"No shit!" The sound of his old mentor's voice made Devlin smile. "How are you, Walsh?" An extended silence said it all. Devlin scrambled. "Hey, look, don't worry. You'll get back on your feet."

"Still confident, kid. That's good. So, looks like you're still in the game."

"Oh, hell yeah. They'll have to drag me out of here when I'm 85." Devlin had been trying to remember the last time he'd seen, or at least spoken to, his canny sage. Then it hit him. "Hey, you remember the last time we talked?"

"No way, kid. Years, for sure, right?"

"It was before closing arguments in my big nursing home trial. End of '79, right? Remember that? You called me late that night, drunk off your ass, and just started insulting me up one side and down the other." Devlin was laughing. "Remember?"

More silence.

Trevor Walsh. The untouchable, hot-shot prosecutor. In the beginning, he was like a whetted scythe through every defense strategy. Devlin had been in awe at how surgically Walsh argued his cases. Before turning 30, Walsh had already tried and won twenty-two murder cases without a single loss. But now he sounded completely broken. The frenzied Trevor Walsh energy had been hollowed out and replaced by a dark and vague desperation palpable even over the phone. The guy was a shell of who Devlin remembered. It had been Walsh's own sordid obsessions that killed his brilliant career: history-making booze binges, serial sexual escapades and five-figure gambling swings. Then Walsh got on the wrong side of a criminal client and started ferrying cocaine during jail visits, to take off the edge… for both of them. As it turned out, attorney-client privilege did not extend to shared cocaine use, even when discussing legal matters. Devlin had never forgotten the spirit of what Walsh had said during that last late-night drunk-dial. Immediately after the call Devlin had scribbled it on his yellow legal pad with the list of other gems Devlin had been writing down since early in his career. *Rule #9: The side that makes the fewest mistakes wins.* Sadly, Walsh had been making all the mistakes. Ten years Devlin's senior, it seemed odd the tables had turned on him so completely: the student had become the mentor.

"Yeah, I gotcha," Devlin said. "Fuck the glory days, anyway, right? Who needs 'em. Hey, I'm with someone, so I need to let you go, but could you stay on the line and give Nadia your address?"

"Address?"

"Yeah, there's something I have—"

"Look, kid, I appreciate the sentiment. But like you said, glory days and all."

"Just five minutes. I'll give it to you, and then you can shit-can me."

Silence.

"Walsh?"

"Goddamn," Walsh said. "Same persistent pain in the ass."

"Just like you taught me, old man."

Silence.

"So that's a 'yes'?"

"Yeah, yeah, if it means getting you off my ass, sure."

"Good. I'll see you soon." Devlin routed the call back to the woman who kept Devlin & Associates on track, and asked her to get the address and send Monae back in. Once the detective was seated again, Devlin said, "OK, my apologies. Where were we?"

"Old girlfriend?" Monae asked, smiling. "She wants her stuff from the top drawer at your place?"

"There's no top drawer," he said.

"Ah, the strong, independent type."

Speaking of drawers… Devlin pulled open the top-right desk drawer and reached all the way to the back until he felt it: still there after all these years. He'd completely forgotten about it until the phone call. He closed the drawer.

"Sorry, where were we?" Devlin asked again.

"It's OK if you want to continue this some other time," she said.

"Welcome to my world. Seventeen balls in the air. He was someone I used to work with, a veritable genius. Now he's… down on his luck, for sure."

"Sorry to hear that."

"Yeah, he was one of my first mentors. We started a firm together. That motherfucker was really something. Sorry."

"No apology necessary. I rode patrol for three years. Cops and criminals. Not exactly the Queen's English."

Devlin was lost in how far Walsh had fallen.

"So anyway," she said. "Your fee. You think it's too low. But to that I say: your primary responsibility is the hearing. I'll be the lead on everything else."

"Even so, I probably can't do it for less than $9,000." Perhaps it was the horse trader in Devlin, but he couldn't help digging in just a little.

Perfect, she thought. She'd just made an extra grand for herself. "That should work. If you could draft a simple letter of agreement I can get you a retainer check."

She also made a mental note to call the attorney she'd met at the lock-up, to let her know her services would not be needed.

"Done. What's next?"

"Well, I guess we should plan a trip up there to dig around a little. We don't have a lot of time since the hearing is at the beginning of next month."

"Let's do it," Devlin said.

She smiled. She could not deny that she liked his confidence and strength. And the smile… and all the rest. She stood, smiled and handed him a business card.

"Get me that agreement," she said. "Then we'll make it official with the check. I'm looking forward to working with you."

Devlin stood and smiled. "Likewise. Believe me, the pleasure will be all mine."

She could only nod and smile, thinking that she doubted that very much. Devlin could not resist another long look as she disappeared into the lobby and then out the front doors. He sat back in his chair and glanced at the mostly blank legal pad. Amid the slow progress on the Rule 32 petition, her presence had been a very nice, momentary diversion. Then Devlin thought about Walsh again. Devlin himself tried to be a good Catholic, which meant he was also a believer that the right order of things, good and bad, came in threes. That idea got the gears grinding.

First, there had been the news about One-Armed Lucky.

And now Trevor Walsh.

Devlin could only wonder: who would be the third ghost to visit from the first decade of his career?

Chapter Six

THE NEXT WEEK DEVLIN AND MONAE DROVE NORTH to Kingman to investigate the mayor's case. They left in the darkness at 3:30 a.m. so they would have a full work day when they arrived well before eight o'clock. This schedule worked great for Devlin, since he was already up anyway with his mind spinning in multiple directions on various cases. In the days prior, Monae had lined up afternoon appointments with the police officers who had been first on scene at the crash site. Devlin and Monae would use the morning to see what else they might dig up. Devlin also wanted to meet with the prosecutor to discuss a plea deal, but the man was traveling, so that meeting would have to wait.

Devlin offered to drive and, when he pulled up to Monae's apartment in the cherry-red Blazer, she was not surprised at all. She had pegged Devlin from the moment she saw him at the state lock-up, and everything he had done and said thereafter confirmed her intuition. How many buttoned-up lawyers drove a jacked-up Blazer the color of a fire truck? One, which is exactly why she liked Devlin from the start.

For Devlin's part, he too was pleased. In place of the form-fitting business suit and black heels, Monae wore a simple white cotton T-shirt that accentuated her athletic build and again conjured Shakespeare: "We are such stuff as dreams are made on…" Likewise, her entire simple ensemble—hair pulled back into a tight ponytail, Levi's, white canvas Chuck Taylors and black Ray-Ban Wayfarer sunglasses with silver accents—was casually chic while also being sexy. Devlin was out of the Blazer and walking around to open her door, but she was already climbing in on her own. He walked back around and climbed in behind the wheel.

"Morning," he said.

"Coffee," she said.

Devlin had already stopped at a twenty-four hour convenience store, and he handed her one of the two white foam cups with plastic lids.

"I meant let's go get coffee. You're one step ahead. Thank you."

"There's cream and sugar there if you want."

"No thank you," she said, suppressing a smile. "I take it black… like my men."

Devlin started the Blazer and smiled. *Airplane!*

"Surely you have to love Leslie Nielsen."

"I do, and stop calling me 'Shirley.'"

Devlin drove from downtown and onto US-60, which would eventually become US-93 and take them all the way northwest to Interstate 40. From there they'd head west to Kingman. Devlin, balancing his foam cup on his left knee, was thinking through the mayor's case. Monae was still moving slowly toward full consciousness, and stared into the darkened industrial maze off to her right.

"After this cup I'll be human again."

"Yeah, me too," Devlin said, although he had been awake since before 2 a.m. He'd given up on sleep and worked on the Rule 32 petition for about an hour.

Twenty minutes later, they had left the city behind and were cutting through the inky void of the desert, with scattered saguaro cactus arms curved skyward and low, craggy mountains silhouetted by moonlight.

"How'd you become a lawyer?" Monae asked.

"Barely is how."

"Barely?"

"I have two stories very few people have heard, so if I divulge, you have to promise not to judge me."

"No deal. I'm already judging you."

Devlin laughed. "Fair enough."

AFTER high school graduation, at his father's insistence, the young Devlin grudgingly trudged off to college in South Bend, Indiana. He was decreed to pursue a career with a professional credential— doctor, CPA, lawyer— as a lifelong hedge against an Irish-immigrant heritage. This would be another key element in the ongoing "Out-Irish" initiative: naysayers could still call the paddy a dirty harp or a potato eater, but they'd never be able to take away a professional license. At least that's what the senior Connor J. Devlin told his son.

But it was his mother, Claire Devlin, who ushered her only son through this important rite of passage by driving him to Notre Dame. They left Buffalo on a sunny August day, in Dad's gray 1963 Cadillac DeVille, a massive floating boat that would take them east by Lake Erie, across the top corner of Pennsylvania and into Indiana.

On that drive Devlin thought about her daily driver, a 1963 Pontiac Grand Prix, which they'd left home. During high school Devlin had secretly souped it up with three two-barrels and replaced the factory exhaust system with headers and lake pipes. The result was a boss car you could hear coming from three blocks away. Devlin was preparing to take the car to a local track for Saturday night drag races.

"Why is my car so loud now?" his mother asked one day.

"I don't know, Mom. Must be getting old."

One Saturday night Devlin came home late, with a first-place trophy he hid behind the garage. The next morning the trophy was on the kitchen table.

"No more," she told her son. And that was her way: not to be onerous or punitive, but able to draw clear lines. She was never sympathetic to her son's bad acts, but she wasn't going to crucify him, either. Devlin got the message and was too chagrined to ever bring it up again. He did smile every time he heard Mom fire up the Grand Prix.

After the seven-hour drive, Mom stayed several days to help her son get settled. When it was time for her to go, Devlin hugged his mother and watched her drive away for the long solo trip she had ahead. He watched until he couldn't see the car, and he had to admit he already missed her.

The overall milieu of the University of Notre Dame in the fall of 1964 made winter in Buffalo look like a beach-town bender. The sky palette only contained multiple nuances of a single shade: slate-gray. There were no women on campus. Cars, telephones and television were forbidden. Lights-out was 11:30 p.m. during the week and 12:30 a.m. on weekends. By comparison, Devlin considered now, Leander Farley had freer rein, more autonomy and better privileges on death row.

Further, daily mass was mandatory, and that meant every morning at 7:30—even in winter when there was five feet of snow. Devlin found it incomprehensible that he had found a location on Earth where it was more miserably cold than his hometown. And all that was the good news.

The town of South Bend itself, except on football Saturdays, was DOA. The overall bleakness was so grinding on townies and students alike that a collective seething resentment was palpable even under everyone's four layers of wool. The year before Devlin arrived, in 1963, the Studebaker Corporation had shut down its plant and given the town's lifeless spirit a fierce jackboot to the face. Jobs were nonexistent. Hope was a forgotten possibility.

Welcome to college!

Prompted by the motivation to expedite his departure from South Bend, Devlin buckled down, survived the experience, graduated with a 3.5 GPA and earned a degree in Russian literature. With his eye on the West Coast and the University of Southern California Law School if he could get accepted, everything was poised to change dramatically. However, first he had to make his mark on the LSAT. The night before the 7:30 a.m. Saturday exam, a typically bitter February evening, Devlin acquiesced to his roommate's insistence that they go out for a drink. Devlin had nicknamed his roommate Frankenstein because he was just as big as the fictional creature, with a similarly blocky head—and, like the mad doctor's creation, spoke in one-word grunts: *Food. Hungry. Beer.*

"One beer," Devlin had said.

"Beer. One. Go."

"I'm serious," Devlin said. "I'm taking the LSAT tomorrow. That's my future. One beer."

"Beer. Go."

A little after 7 p.m., they left the dorm. Having a car at Notre Dame was grounds for expulsion, so when Frankenstein and Devlin had surreptitiously bought a pink 1954 Buick for $45, they had to stow it in the faculty parking lot. They only drove it when no one was around to identify them as students, which meant under the cover of darkness. The wide four-door was more rust than paint, and had four white-sidewall tires with tread smooth as a bowling ball. The body parts that weren't rusted were a garish pink. With that exterior color and the deep pillow-top interior, they nicknamed their ride "The Womb."

Seven hours later, by 2 a.m. the one-beer strategy was not even a foggy recollection. Devlin and his roommate were so drunk that one of the two cute townie hairdressers they had met at the bar insisted on being the one to drive everyone to her place for further revelry. She lived just across the state line, in Niles, Michigan, in a cramped studio apartment where they drank for another hour and listened to Drifters and Ronettes 45s. Then, for the next two hours, Devlin intermittently passed out and woke up in the stuffy apartment, which felt like 120 degrees with an old radiator glowing bright red and churning away at full bore. Each time he awoke in a sweat there were two sounds emanating from the darkness: the radiator hissing and popping, and the amorous groping of Frankenstein and his new bride.

Devlin eventually sobered up enough to convince "his" girl to drive him back to Notre Dame. Frankenstein was on his own and would have to retrieve The Womb, which they had left at the bar. On the dark campus, Devlin slid over to say goodbye and gave her a peck on the cheek. Then, at 5 a.m. on that Saturday morning, Devlin staggered back to his dorm cursing himself for his supreme idiocy.

"OH my God," Monae said, laughing. "Did you pass?"

"Like I said: barely. I got no sleep. After the proctor distributed the exam, I was certain I was going to vomit. The only thing that saved me was lifting the window to let the cold air oxygenate my brain. I took the entire exam like that, with my head half out the window like some sick animal. It was multiple choice, so at some point I just started marking 'D' for every answer, figuring I'd get at least 25 percent right."

Monae was laughing so hard she almost spit the last of her coffee. Michael Jackson's "Billie Jean" started on the radio, because federal law apparently required that every U.S. citizen hear the song at least twice a day for life. Devlin was laughing, too, and thinking about the denouement of the story, which he had left out. That was the part about the mischievous grin the hairdresser had given him as her head dropped to his lap to send him into the morning darkness on a high note.

"OK, that's going to be tough to top," Monae said. "What's part two?"

"That was my LSAT. Part two was the bar exam."

"No."

"Yes."

"You didn't."

"I'm afraid I did. Why am I telling you my darkest secrets?"

"There's clearly no hope for you."

"I'll save that one for later."

"No fair."

"State and county," Devlin said.

"What?"

Devlin smiled. "Nothing. Just something my dad used to say."

HOURS later, they roared up to the Good Night Motel in Kingman, a dust-ravaged civic blip that was the closest population center to the crash site. Sloane Monae had booked two rooms. The biggest boast of the two-star accommodation, proudly displayed under blue neon, was *COOL AC!!* delivered via rattling window units into each room, apparently so cold it required two exclamation marks on the sign. They checked in, retreated to their separate rooms briefly, and then met in her room where they set up a mini command post. They studied a city map, charted their route and set out. For the first couple hours, Devlin and Monae prowled the diners, coffee shops and retail stores to find witnesses to the crash. Although anything gleaned would not be directly usable in a plea agreement, Devlin told Monae they needed to know everything about that day Conrad's airplane went down: the weather, the craft and the crash itself. The crash had been big news, so everyone in town had at least heard about it, which meant some had seen it, too. Or knew someone who had.

They had both intentionally dressed down for the day in jeans and sneakers, because city slickers in suits and leather shoes stood no chance. Still, the locals were wary of outsiders to the point of cliché, regardless of wardrobe. It took another couple hours, and lots of deft coaxing by both, to finally find a few witnesses willing to talk. The witnesses, however, weren't able to provide much beyond what Devlin and Monae already knew.

That afternoon, they met with the arresting officers, who were more or less duty bound to talk to the mayor's defense attorney. An underling lawyer from the county prosecutor's office sat in to ostensibly monitor the conversations, but she barely said a word. Devlin grilled the officers separately about the arrest procedure, chronology and processing of the crash site, evidence and defendant. He asked them each about the search of the plane and the chain of custody on the three hundred pounds of marijuana. In each meeting Devlin went over and over the same terrain, including the processing, removal and storage of the plane. The cops had squared their stories, and their procedural documentation was pretty solid, but not textbook. Between meetings Devlin highlighted some potentially usable loopholes to Monae, but she had already caught them all on her own. None of this would be needed, of course, if he successfully pled out the case. But he felt obligated, and Monae agreed that they needed to be prepared for trial regardless.

After they finished interviewing the last cop, who worked swing shift, they drove to the chain-link storage yard where the police had stowed the wreckage. Devlin spent the next hour crawling around the wreckage with a flashlight and taking Polaroid photographs for his own case file. By the time they got back to the Good Night Motel it was after 9 p.m. Both energized by the investigation, they paused at the stairwell that ran up the center of the sagging, two-level property. Devlin's room was on the first floor, and hers on the second. The summer evening sky was a fusion of red dust and fading pink and purple in the gloaming.

"Want to grab some dinner?" he asked.

"Yes. I'm starving."

"Should we shower first?" he asked.

Yes indeed, she thought, as Devlin's shirtless torso flashed in her mind again. "Forget that, counselor. Food. I'll give you five minutes for a whore's bath, and then you need to be back here to feed me."

Devlin chuckled. "You kiss your mother with that mouth?" She just smiled and started up the stairs. Devlin felt victorious when he turned and walked back to his room without stealing any furtive glances.

Twenty minutes later they were seated in the back corner of a Mexican restaurant with cracked red vinyl booths and a nineteen-inch TV mounted from the ceiling playing MTV music videos. He and Monae each had a mammoth margarita in a frosted, salt-rimmed glass. They had skipped lunch, and were mowing through the chips and salsa.

"So how about the other story?"

"How about it?"

"Give up the goods, counselor."

He nodded and smiled. "Like I said: no judgment."

"And like I said: forget that."

DEVLIN took a bar exam review course that was next door to the hippest spot in Phoenix, an English pub-themed place called the Wellington. At the time, he was dating a Playboy bunny named Jessica Jean. The night before the bar exam, Devlin thought back to the last session of the review course as the lecturer had offered some final tips. *Get a good night's sleep. Eat a good breakfast. Bring extra pens. Arrive at least thirty* *minutes before the exam start time.* He remembered the fear, the reality of the three-day test and its judgmental backdrop—pass or start over—pushing down with an unrelenting anxiety and weight. The one tip that had really registered in his mind was about getting sleep. After class he and a few new friends wandered next door to the Wellington. As he pulled on the door, Devlin reaffirmed his intention.

One club soda. That's it. Then you get your Irish ass home and in bed.

The packed Wellington was cooking that night. Devlin held court at a large table where he regaled Hot Rod Hundley, a player with the NBA's Phoenix Suns, with true tales of having dinners with his father and Johnny Unitas back in Buffalo. Although the Wellington was going full-bore, the bar exam was holding steady on Devlin's internal radar. So far he had strictly adhered to the club-soda protocol. But then the LSAT ghosts reappeared in the form of one Jessica Jean, the curvaceous schoolboy dream, who playfully pulled two tickets from the deep plunge of her cleavage.

"They're for the Tom Jones concert tonight. Front row, center. I'm taking you!"

Devlin did not tell Sloane Monae that, even almost fifteen years later, he could vividly recall the smell of Jessica's talcum-powdered body with a curvaceous cleft deep enough to hide concert tickets.

"No way," Devlin had told Jessica, his brain already fogged by her siren call. "I have the bar exam tomorrow. And the day after that, and the next day after that. No way."

In the long build-up to the multi-day exam, Devlin had been studying fifteen hours a day. He had so much legal minutiae crammed into his brain that he considered wrapping his head with duct tape lest some arcane fact slip out. But damn, the look she threw his way; that, combined with the sweet perfume, powder and smile, pierced all layers of logic and defense. In that exact moment, Devlin knew he was going to the Tom Jones concert. True to his Buffalo roots, the only appropriate response was simple resignation.

Flat intonation, with shoulder shrug: What. The fuck.

Devlin abandoned the club soda in favor of beer, and cut loose. When it was time for the concert, he took Jessica Jean's hand and pulled her through the gauntlet of drinking and revelry, a chorus of cheers, hand slaps and a few "Way to go, Devlin!" send-offs. Like a million good men before him, the feral call of the rut had swept reason and lucid thinking aside.

What Devlin did not know was that inside Veterans Memorial Coliseum he would be subjected to ridiculous stacks of speakers five feet from his head, rendering him nearly deaf for the first day of his bar exam. Or that he would be surrounded by screaming, pawing women. Or that he'd slap a sweaty high-five with Tom Jones himself while dodging a non-stop firestorm of panties and negligees being tossed at the singer. By 2 a.m. on the morning of the first day of the examination, Devlin was prone on Jessica Jean's couch while she pressed a cold washcloth on his forehead in a fruitless attempt to stop the vomiting. After he got a few clammy hours of marginal sleep, she drove him to the university for day one of his bar exam. The overall parallels and timeline to the LSAT seemed like a cruel cosmic joke.

He stumbled from her car, a brand-new ice-blue Gremlin, his body engulfed in a cold, sweating haze. His primary thought was that he hated Tom Jones, every last lyric he ever sang. More drunk than sober, Devlin fantasized about some random melee breaking out around him—locusts or maybe nuclear war—to yellow-tape the campus and shut down the exam. He stopped and turned. Jessica Jean was still parked, sitting in the Gremlin. She waved and smiled and gave him two thumbs up.

Just as the lawyers during the review course had warned, the bar exam was grueling. Devlin burned through an entire Bic pen *each* day, and by the end had a nagging blister on his right index finger. Similar to the LSAT, he'd pulled it together, sobered up and survived the three-day ordeal without so much as a loud belch. When it was all done he shuddered, of course, at his cavalier attitude. How, he wondered, had he so easily reduced the state bar exam to the equivalent of running down to the store for a carton of milk? At least there was not a shred of lingering doubt or fear about doing well, because he had studied relentlessly and had been ready to take the test. If nothing else, Devlin had decided, going to the Tom Jones concert with a Playboy bunny was intertwined with his inherent proclivity to take risks. He'd gambled, had that once-in-a-lifetime experience, and pulled off the intended result. This approach—where he put everything on the line—defined his life. And his career as a lawyer, too.

"OR," Monae said, finishing her second chicken enchilada, "it just means you didn't learn your lesson the first time."

"I get no mercy from you," Devlin said, pushing away his empty plate. Hall & Oates were going on about God knows what.

"Yeah, in fact," Monae said, "now I'm really questioning my decision to hire you and your obviously flawed judgment. Is it too late to get a refund?"

"What about you?"

"What about me?"

"I'm sure you've made some professional missteps in your—how old are you?"

"Missteps?" she said laughing, almost unable to get it out. "You almost bombed the LSAT and the bar, and you're a lawyer. Those are more than missteps."

"I know it's not polite to ask a lady. But oh well: how old are you?"

"You first."

"Thirty-nine, earlier this month."

"Happy belated birthday, old man."

"You?"

"Twenty-nine, earlier this month."

"Well, young lady, you should respect your elders. Here's to June birthdays. I shared my wayward path to the law. How'd you become a private investigator?"

"How far do you want me to go back?"

"How about to the beginning?"

"Well," she said, holding up her empty margarita glass, "in that case I'll need another one of these." Devlin waved over the waitress and ordered two more.

"I was born and grew up in Denver. Three older brothers. My dad was a truck driver, and my mom a secretary. Neither of my parents, and none of my brothers, went to college. I probably would have followed the family model except I was a rad volleyball player in high school. Basketball, too, and track, but volleyball was my game and my ticket to a different life. I got a full-ride scholarship to UT in Austin and went for criminal justice. That was probably my blue-collar roots. Figured I'd be a cop. When I graduated college in '77, Dallas PD was hiring. Sort of 'right place-right time' as departments were starting to look for more female officers. The general public was slowly becoming more open to the idea of women in blue. Thank you, Angie Dickinson."

"*Police Woman.*"

"Exactly. And the equal opportunity amendment to Title VII in '72 applied to police departments, too. So I rode that first wave of expanding opportunities for women in law enforcement. But still, talk about a male-dominated grunt club."

"How long were you a cop?"

"Three years too many."

"Too dangerous?"

"Partially, yes, but I could always hold my own on the streets. The real predators were in our own department. Being a female cop was rough. There weren't many of us, and it felt like we were constantly fighting two fronts all the time: the bad guys on the outside, and our male fellow officers on the inside. The men in blue were the most relentless threat we faced."

"You're saying the cops were predators?"

"That's exactly what I'm saying. When I came out of the academy I was 22. When you go out on the street they pair you with a more experienced training officer for three months. That officer has to approve you for duty when your training is up. My TO was in his early thirties, wife and two daughters, weekend barbecue grillmaster. He liked guns, red meat and big trucks. My first night in uniform while we're on patrol he put his hand on my knee and told me there were things I might do for him to ensure good marks on his evaluation. That's how it started."

"He said that? On your first shift?"

"Yeah, he did. But he was just the first of many."

"What did you do about it?"

"I did what we always do. I shifted in the seat, pulled my leg away, stared out the patrol car window and asked him an unrelated question about arrest procedure. Just pretended it never happened."

"Couldn't you have gone to your sergeant and reported him?"

"In my first hour on patrol? They already had interchangeable nicknames for the female officers that made it clear where we were in the hierarchy."

"Like what?"

"Dickless Tracy."

Devlin could only shake his head.

"Tits in Blue."

"C'mon!"

"Hot Fuzz."

Devlin was disgusted. "I get the idea."

"Never to our faces, but loud enough that we heard."

"This is all on them, but don't you have to speak up—"

"Speak up? See, men just don't get it. What it feels like… to be stalked into a corner and boxed in. That same week my patrol lieutenant—keep in mind now, this was my sergeant's superior officer, my boss's boss—tried the same thing. Except worse. He was even more blunt and creepier. He told me if I spent ten minutes on my knees every now and again, he would personally guarantee I would make sergeant within three years. And he could make it happen, he said, because the brass was looking to promote—and I'm quoting here—'gash.'"

"He said that?"

"He did."

"That is unbelievable."

"So, yeah, that sort of soured me on the whole cop thing. Too many assholes walking around with guns to compensate for their tiny-dick inferiority complexes."

Devlin laughed.

"I'm sorry," she said. "That was un-ladylike. That's the tequila talking."

"No apology necessary. You should hear the way I talk to my own fucking clients." They both started laughing.

"Now, when you say 'fucking clients,' do we mean as an adjective; i.e., clients with whom you're having sex?" They were both laughing so hard they could barely breathe. "Or... wait—yes, I minored in English, so take that to the bank—are you using 'fucking clients' as a gerund, a type of verbal noun that retains properties of a verb, such as being modifiable by an adverb and being able to take a direct object? And I think we both know what I mean by 'to take a direct object.'"

Devlin was waving her off, to please stop, so he could breathe. Finally, Devlin asked: "Volleyball, criminal justice, English minor, cop... then what?"

"Then what is I found my niche, as an investigator with the Dallas County District Attorney's office."

"Why was that your niche?"

"Being a cop was mostly brawn and some brain. But as an investigator it was all brain. I helped evaluate and prepare cases for court. I served subpoenas and went out to execute search and arrest warrants. And, one of my favorites: locating witnesses."

"I assume you're good at it?"

"Oh, I'm very good, counselor. They can run, but they can't hide."

"How long with the DA's office?"

"Two years. With that and my three years on patrol, I probably wasn't ready to go out on my own, but I did anyway."

"And why Phoenix?"

"I have a dear college friend who was on the UT volleyball team with me. She's from Phoenix, and she knew I was looking for a fresh start after the Dallas PD thing. She invited me out and gave me a place to land. Then I got my own place. I've only been here six months."

"What do you think of Phoenix?"

"The Valley of the Sun," she said. "I love it. It's sunny and clean like Dallas, minus any Confederate connection. It's a city but feels more like an overgrown small town."

"Going back to your PD experience: I'm sorry that happened to you," Devlin said. "That's the kind of corrupt bullshit I take on in my practice. When you turn on the light, the cockroaches scatter."

"Well, yeah, no argument here. But we're talking about ten thousand years of human evolution. That's a tough nut to crack. No pun intended."

"How about Sally Ride?"

"Of course. First American woman in space."

"That's progress, right?"

"Well, yes, and yet women are still being coerced and harassed at work as we speak. And right on cue, look at this crap." She pointed at the TV, which was playing the video of the members of KISS—unmasked!—singing "Lick It Up." The females had no speaking parts and only one purpose, which apparently was to crawl around like sex-crazed feral cats in erotic cavewoman garb.

"You know," Devlin said, "being Catholic, I have enough generalized guilt to cover three lifetimes. I wish there was something, or someone, who could have helped you."

"Well, that's a nice sentiment. Thank you. But you know what they say about fighting City Hall."

"Fuck that. My entire career is built on fighting City Hall. Big government, big business and big medicine. Like you said: 'They can run...' Give me the case, and I'm a wolf. I will depose Little Red Riding Hood's grandmother and put her in a body bag, if it will help my client's case. I'll use any tool that might help."

She sat back, impressed by his passion. "Example?"

"I just started using a new research methodology called a 'focus group.' Not many attorneys are using them."

"Focus group? Sounds like a meditation cult."

"It's a way to try to understand a case as the jurors might."

"So, no burning incense, pentagrams or sacrificial lambs?"

"No, we bring ten or twelve people to the office on a weeknight, feed them pizza, pay them thirty bucks each and present the case. Then we take a hand vote for plaintiff versus defense and talk about the merits and weaknesses on each side."

"Sounds expensive."

"It is, but that's what I mean. I go all in on each case. I would have done the same for you against those cockroach cops. And we would have squashed 'em."

"Unless they *quashed* you first," she said, smiling.

Devlin laughed and raised his glass. "Hear, hear." They clinked glasses.

"Seriously, it's nice to hear. I guess despite what they say, chivalry isn't entirely dead."

BY the time they rolled up to the Good Night Motel, neither noticed or cared about the *COOL AC!!* awaiting in their respective rooms. She was wondering about what happened next. Devlin, despite dating a Playboy bunny in the seventies, was also sometimes still naïve to the moment. Somehow he could read a jury of twelve strangers like the Amazing Randi, and yet, simultaneously miss a woman showing a strong interest in him. This connection, however, was obvious. He killed the engine and climbed out to open her door, but she had already gotten out herself. Sloane Monae wasn't waiting around for any man to do what she could do herself. At the stairwell, the fork in the road, they both paused.

Waiting.

Wondering.

Monae thought it was probably too soon, but the combination of good laughs, margaritas and the freedom of being out of town had left her wondering if he was going to move in for a goodnight kiss.

"Haven't laughed that hard in a long time," Devlin said. "Thank you."

"I'm glad the details of my sexual harassment are so entertaining," she said.

"No, I mean—"

"It's OK," she said, smiling and touching his arm. "I'm kidding. I needed a good laugh, too."

Despite her obvious appeal, Devlin's attention was split. He had an uncanny ability to visualize the totality of each case within minutes of listening to someone's story. He could see the path of facts and exactly where it would all lead: the case themes and theories, and the best way to present it to the jury. It was an almost out-of-body experience that happened with every new case, a process he couldn't quite explain. With everything he could muster, from this point forward he would never stop thinking about creative ways to do his best by Mickey Conrad and all his other clients, which is why he woke up every night thinking about his cases. The lingering silence ended as it often did for Devlin in these situations, with a half-hug and an odd handshake of sorts.

"OK, well, good night," Devlin said.

"Good night," she said, turning and starting up the stairs.

Devlin savored one final glance as she ascended. Then they each went to their separate rooms. Once inside, Monae pulled the revolver from her handbag, opened the cylinder to see six butt ends of brass, snapped it shut and set the gun in the top drawer of the nightstand. Then she took a cold shower and slipped on her burnt-orange UT shorts and a white "Hook 'Em Horns" T-shirt. She turned out the light and crawled under the covers. She was thinking about Devlin's smile, and wondering why he hadn't tried to kiss her, as she fell asleep.

Devlin should have been exhausted, but he was visualizing the mayor's case and methodically walking through each step. He pulled out the yellow legal pad, which was also gradually becoming the Bobby Swift Rule 32 petition, and detailed his sequence for the mayor's defense. He flipped on the nineteen-inch GoldStar TV for some background noise. The grainy image was of Steve McQueen telling Ali McGraw it wasn't a game in *The Getaway.*

To which she replied, "It's all a game."

Chapter Seven

TEN DAYS LATER, JUST BEFORE THE 4TH OF JULY HOLIDAY, Devlin and Monae went north for the marijuana mayor's hearing in Kingman. After their awkward encounter on the first trip, Devlin had had every intention of finding a way to see Sloane Monae up close again before the hearing, to attempt to get a fix on what might be happening—or not—between them. Instead, duty had swamped Devlin as he logged fifteen-hour days. They had talked on the phone, as lawyer and investigator, multiple times about Mickey Conrad's approaching hearing, but never saw each other in person.

Devlin had been immersed in his fixed grind. With too much to do and too little time, at best he was getting four hours of sleep each night. Regardless, he was in the office early every morning and normally skipped lunch or gobbled a quick sandwich or protein bar at his desk, unless he'd scheduled a useful networking meeting. For those, once or twice a week Devlin used the lunch hour to meet with judges, other lawyers (both criminal and civil), cops in his group legal plan, and potential expert witnesses.

He only took a break at six each night to play basketball, where Goldie mentally beat down Lamont the Dummy like he had stolen something. Devlin was also practicing kung fu, which he had been doing three times a week for a year with instructor Gus Housman. The short, stocky master, who had studied in China, was the only human being Devlin had ever encountered who had some sort of internal armor plating covering both shins. Devlin always wondered whether it was scar tissue or just a genetic anomaly, but Housman could endure repeated kicks to the shins without so much as a grimace. He could also jump up, muster a 360-degree spin in midair and kick Devlin in the face on the way back down. He had demonstrated this more than once. One of Housman's favorite character-building activities was instructing the entire class to lie down in a row, face-up and shoulder-to-shoulder; then he would walk across the line of bodies, stepping on each student's throat. Housman never revealed his motivation for such a cruel exercise, but Devlin had decided it was an extreme form of stress inoculation in preparation for being struck in the throat and not losing faculty.

He was also continuously enrolled in night classes at Phoenix College. He had completed a course in vehicle-accident reconstruction, and was now taking human anatomy, which would be invaluable in better understanding the intricacies of medical malpractice. After basketball with the yeti, kung fu with Housman or night class, Devlin always returned to the office to take a shower. For the remaining hours of the day, Devlin dressed in shorts and a T-shirt to work until midnight or later, when he could finally go back to the condo and collapse. But most nights the specters of his cases summoned him, usually around 2 a.m., to start the ritual all over again. Devlin had clung to the hope that the resolution of the appeal in *Kay Pearson v. Flynn Enterprises* would have been the magical key to end his nightly torment. But, alas, the sheer volume of work was the deeper underpinning. Eventually Devlin always just gave up and, instead of trying to go back to sleep, went back to the office regardless of the time. Some mornings he was back in his suit and tie and climbing into the Blazer at 4 a.m. Other days it was 6 a.m. Lack of sleep, at least, made it easy to adhere to his father's mantra.

Your work is to serve. Service is your work.

Even with such an enviable work ethic, Devlin was never big-law-firm material, nor was he really small-law-firm material; Devlin was a soloist who, like many of his clients, liked to live and work around the fringes of normal conventions. He had set up Devlin & Associates under that context of individuality. Unwilling to pay high office rents, Devlin found a vacant plot downtown, on Third Avenue, and had a single-story red-brick building constructed from scratch. The land and structure set him back $875,000. He was able to pay a hundred grand upfront from a case settlement, and got a fifteen-year note for the balance. The building had a spacious lobby and six offices, each with a separate receptionist post. At various times, the associates he brought in paid Devlin monthly rent and shared office costs, but each retained the respective case fees. Each lawyer was free to sink or swim completely on individual merit. Figuring they'd all be spending most of their waking hours at the office, Devlin spared no amenity. There was a Jacuzzi, a full steam room and a single shower facility, and each of the offices had a brick fireplace, which was mostly for effect. There were maybe ten or so days every year in Phoenix cold enough— barely—to warrant the use of a fireplace. Devlin had moved into the new building on one of those days, in January 1974. With a high that day in the low forties and ash-gray skies that conjured the drudge of winter in Buffalo, Devlin had built a fire and unpacked boxes all afternoon. He'd only lit a handful of fires in the near-decade since, because some magical lodestar warmed the desert in ways Devlin could only have dreamed of as a child.

With the rent from the various other attorneys who had set up shop at Devlin & Associates, plus a few sizable settlements over the years, Devlin paid off the building note early and now owned the property free and clear. At that point he had also decided to go it alone temporarily as a break from having tenants, who each came with their own various dramas, water cooler chit-chat and personal challenges. As of 1984, Devlin & Associates comprised its namesake, Nadia Flores as the woman who made it all run, and five available offices that each had a brick fireplace.

In the ten days since going to Kingman, Devlin had drafted CandyMan's initial complaint. In the long hours before midnight while alone at the office, Devlin loved the solitude of writing. The formal complaint, boiled down to its essence, was a story telling the plaintiff's version of events. Every story had a point of view, so of course the defense would have a different story with their take on the events. The jury was the audience for this stage play. In this case, Devlin wrote about how CandyMan ended up with a shattered hip that needed to be replaced because the other driver had inexplicably pulled directly into CandyMan's path when he was minding his own business and humming along at fifty miles per hour on his motorcycle.

The next morning, after a few hours of sleep back at the condo, Devlin arrived at the brick building and gave Flores the yellow legal pad filled with twenty-two pages of his barely legible scrawls. Oddly, her typewriter was gone, and she was pulling what looked like a TV from a box. In addition to her tireless work ethic, Nadia Flores was a forward thinker who wasn't afraid to try whatever new tool or technology might make Devlin & Associates run more efficiently. Like Devlin, she was an East Coast transplant (from Media, Pennsylvania) who took initiative, including spending Devlin's money as needed for the business.

"The hell's that?" Devlin asked.

"IBM PC," she said.

"PC?"

"Personal computer."

Devlin looked around. "How are you going to type without a typewriter?"

"I'm not. I'll use the computer."

"Are you sure that's a good idea? I heard these things are just one big headache, right?"

"Those were the first models. That was two years ago."

"Still... I don't know," Devlin said. He felt uneasy and displaced: there had always been comfort in the constant click-clack of Nadia Flores' typewriter over the years—the white-collar equivalent of heavy industry and an assembly line churning out product and generating revenue. Flores was inextricably linked to Devlin's first official job with Grant & Ross, where she was the office manager and Devlin had hustled wills, taken on traffic violation cases and handled messy divorces at $20 a pop, from his office that was the size of a janitor's closet and his old gray desk that looked like an extremely small retired battleship. When he'd started his own firm, he recruited Nadia Flores away ostensibly for her no-nonsense approach and ruthless efficiency. But really, although she was only five years older than Devlin, Flores was a nurturing presence who reminded the lawyer of his mom. And Claire Devlin, the daughter of a retired New York City firefighter who ran a 1920s speakeasy that employed Claire's mother, was the ultimate nurturing presence: kind-hearted, protective and completely devoted to her three children. She was beautiful, elegant and a talented swimmer, too, who competed in a U.S. Olympic Trials meet.

In her role as surrogate parent, Nadia Flores had access to every facet of Devlin's life—professional, personal and financial—and Devlin knew in his gut she would never betray that trust. Like his mother dropping him at Notre Dame to start college, Flores was there every day as a comforting backstop to whatever might arise. With that important bond, Devlin didn't like that a part of the equation tied to his own gradual ascension, that integral and reassuring click-clack sound, was being replaced by... what, exactly? An evil cathode-ray glow, sputtering electronic silence? *No thanks.*

"How much did that thing cost me?"

"Two thousand dollars. Plus another $800 for the printer."

"Jesus Christ. Two grand for a fucking typewriter?"

"It's not a typewriter, Connor. It's a computer."

"And what happens when it breaks? Then what?"

"Trust me. It will be better. Much easier to make edits. No more Wite-Out."

"Well, I don't like it. I'm sticking to legal pads."

"Tell that to the lamplighters," she said.

"Don't forget court jesters and pin setters."

"Pin setters?" she asked.

"Yeah, back in Buffalo the first Connor J. Devlin, my grandfather, was a pin setter at the bowling alley. He got ten cents a game to reset the pins manually."

"Well, there you go. Times change. In ten years, all the typewriters will be gone."

Devlin laughed. "All the typewriters will be gone? Do you know how crazy that sounds? Where are they going? Everyone's just going to throw away their perfectly good typewriters and drop two grand on these contraptions? That will never happen."

"OK, well, we'll see."

Devlin walked away, laughing, "All the typewriters will be gone. Yeah, right."

Once she had her new PC set up, Flores created her first Microsoft Word document, CandyMan's formal complaint. She printed three copies, including one for Devlin and one to send by courier to the defendant, who was the attorney for the driver's insurance company. For the third, she drove south and five minutes later parked in the fifteen-square-block area of the court complex in downtown Phoenix. She had to hand-carry the CandyMan complaint to be filed with Maricopa County Superior Court. Where Shakespeare had the Globe Theater, Devlin's stage complex was here, north to south from Washington Street to Jackson Street, and east to west from First Avenue to Seventh Avenue, where the rule of law and its attendant human dramas, both civil and criminal, played out daily in various buildings, offices, conference rooms, cafeterias, jail cells, courtrooms, hallways and judges' chambers.

With CandyMan's formal complaint filed, Devlin put his attention to several of his other forty or so cases while he awaited the response from the defense attorney. One of those cases was Darcie Savoy, with her upcoming pre-trial settlement conference scheduled this month. Six months ago, her aunt had wheeled Darcie Savoy into Devlin & Associates—a 20-year-old with cerebral palsy, which had struck her down physically but had most certainly not diminished her razor-sharp cognitive abilities. Now confined to a wheelchair, Savoy explained what had happened when a well-known orthopedist botched her surgery. Actually, as it turned out, Devlin's sleuthing had uncovered that the orthopedist had passed the procedure off to a resident who performed the surgery in an attempt to release some of Savoy's painful muscle contractions. Despite an already overloaded slate of cases, Devlin couldn't deny the young woman's large brown eyes, and her persistence in spite of her challenge. He had told her at the outset that he would do whatever he could to get the doctor's insurance to cover her $13,000 in unpaid medical bills. The doctor Devlin had sued, Henry Wong, had a consent clause in his liability insurance that required him to settle any case brought forth. Wong, however, had so far refused to settle. As part of his preparation for the settlement conference, Devlin needed to reread all the case materials, including every deposition transcript, as he tried to map out a plan to close the case. An hour later, satisfied with his plan, Devlin dug in his top-right desk drawer, got up and vaguely told his right-hand ally he had an errand to run and that he'd be back within the hour.

Fifteen minutes later, Devlin rolled up to a depressingly shabby apartment building on the west side of Phoenix and, with the Blazer idling, dug in his pocket for the address Flores had written down the day of the call. Unfortunately, it looked like he was in the right place. Devlin sat and listened to the radio for a minute or so, bracing for the heat blast.

Then he killed the engine and the music, and stepped into the searing June day, the temperature already topping 110 degrees under a cloudless, blazing dome. The heat stilled everything into a semi-molten blur. Dozens of distributary channels of sweat immediately formed and trickled across Devlin's body as he walked toward the slumped two-level building, across a long-forsaken stretch of charred brown grass. While he was sidestepping a toppled shopping cart, a rusted muffler and a dog-pissed twin mattress, one of Walsh's classic admonitions rang in his head, and made Devlin laugh.

Fuck the witness: you're the one in charge. Your job as a lawyer is to get the right questions into the minds of the jurors, because they'll retain the questions much more than the answer the witness gives. In the jury room, jurors recall the essence of things, not particular "yes" and "no" answers. Load your message right into the question, and then who gives a fuck how they answer.

Devlin had to search a bit to find unit #12. He knocked on the dented aluminum door, flecked with at least four different colors of paint. No answer. Devlin rapped again, three times, with a closed fist. Finally, the door cracked open.

"Walsh, you old bastard."

"Well, if it isn't The Kid himself."

"Yeah, well, fuck you, too."

"Back at you, kid."

Walsh squinted into the candescent light, his thinned and graying hair mussed. Clearly, he had been dead asleep at three in the afternoon. For the sleep-deprived Devlin, the darkened cocoon looked especially inviting. Walsh had always been slender and fit, but now he looked positively gaunt in his baggy gym shorts, no shirt. A white five-day stubble covered his face and neck. He might have been officially freed of his shackles, but Walsh's personal insolvency was complete.

"Come on, fucko: are you going to invite me in out of this heat, or what?"

"Kid, look... what do you want?"

Devlin sighed. From the moment he had found the totem on New Year's Eve 1979, he had always envisioned this moment as something special, even triumphant. It had been Walsh's triad of power—his inherent spark, precision and unshakable confidence—that had helped hone the young Devlin into the lawyer he was now. But instead, this was starting to feel like an unintended hit job that would only serve to remind Walsh of how far he had sunk. Devlin dug it out of his pocket—the Rolex he had plucked from the pawn shop for $300 after seeing the inscription on the back: *To Trevor, Congratulations! Love, Mom.* Finding the watch had come in the immediate afterglow of Devlin's seminal victory in the nursing home case, a victory that had since been mostly unraveled.

Devlin dropped the watch into Walsh's upturned palm. Walsh studied the crystal, which was free of scratches, and the smooth band free of nicks. He turned the watch over and ran his thumb over the back as he read.

"Well, fuck me, kid. How the hell did you get ahold of this?"

"How doesn't matter. I just wanted you to get it back."

For Devlin, returning the watch had always been meant as a celebratory gesture for Trevor Walsh. But this was not, in any way, a crowning moment. Devlin watched as Walsh slid the watch on his wrist with a careful reverence, snapped the clasp and polished the crystal on his cotton shorts. Then Devlin watched Walsh wiping at his eyes.

"I don't know what to say, kid."

"You don't have to say anything, old man." Devlin, saddened, realized in that moment that the once-cagey legal superstar was never coming back. Walsh reached his hand out and leaned forward. Devlin took Walsh's hand and pulled him in for a hug that never fully materialized.

"You take care, old man."

Walsh only nodded, his eyes still teary, and then looked away. He closed the door without saying another word. Devlin's undershirt was soaked through with sweat as he turned, walked and climbed into the Blazer. He started the engine and leaned his face toward the AC vents. There was nothing more to say, or do, or process. Since he'd spoken to Walsh by phone, Devlin had initially lingered in sentiment and then prepared himself for this eventuality. Plus, he was flat out of time. Before going back north with Sloane Monae, he had three other cases to work, all originating from Devlin's group legal plan. He eased the Blazer into gear and drove away, already thinking about next steps in each of the cases—all efforts to reverse wrongful terminations of law enforcement officers. Further recollections of Trevor Walsh's legend would have to wait.

The first case was the M&M'S Caper. Two City of Phoenix police officers had sought Devlin for representation in a case that was almost laughable, except that their careers had been shit-canned over it. They had responded to a 961, a garden-variety traffic collision with no serious injuries. The two officers arrived in separate units to find an overturned delivery truck that had spilled its load of candy across an intersection. After they helped clean up the mess, the driver gave each cop an unopened box of the candies as a thank-you. Some humorless civilian with no life had watched the scene unfold and then anonymously reported the two cops for accepting unlawful gratuities. With the end result being a trial scheduled to begin tomorrow, Devlin would be up and preparing into the wee hours tonight.

By some perverse confluence of timing, he had two other cases going to trial in the next couple weeks. In one of those cases, which he'd dubbed the Parker Seven, seven 20-something highway troopers got busted—and later fired—for being on duty and partying with a bunch of college girls on spring break in Parker, Arizona, a binge-drinking hub on Lake Havasu that offered reliably warm weather, sandy beach areas, girls in bikinis, shirtless guys and a free-flow booze nightlife. The cops were young and single themselves, and had been caught red-handed drinking on duty with the bikini-clad girls. Two of the cops actually had sex with their respective coeds right on their patrol motorcycles, which was no easy feat. Devlin was enormously relieved, at least, that during his investigation he was able to establish that the two girls on the motorcycles were both 18—so there would be no criminal charges. Since this was a misconduct case, a police department supervisor was overseeing the investigation internally. Devlin made a mental note to call the supervisor to discuss a few points.

In the third, the Coffee Cup case, Devlin had a Phoenix police-officer client who allegedly had a real jerk for a sergeant—so the cop, in turn, unzipped his pants and rubbed his unit all over the sergeant's special beverage cup one morning before coffee. Try keeping that a secret in a cop shop. Had it been a disgusting act? Of course; no argument there. However, as Devlin planned to tell the jury, a man should not lose his entire career and future pension over one sophomoric lapse in judgment. Devlin had to prepare for the two depositions already scheduled in that case. With that thought, he rolled up to the red-brick building on Third Avenue, parked in his covered space, cut the engine and climbed out into the unrelenting heat. Before he reached the air-conditioned safety of Devlin & Associates, a man he didn't recognize climbed out of his car and called out as though they were old friends.

"Connor Devlin! Rapscallion and legendary bon vivant."

Devlin stopped. He could already feel the sweat beading across his body.

"You don't remember me," the man said as he approached and extended his hand, which Devlin shook. Devlin was stalling, waiting for a flicker of recognition to bubble up. Nothing. The sheer volume of his career caseload—and each case with its own cast of clients, relatives, lawyers, court staff, endless to-dos, depositions, motions, filings, settlements, juries and all the rest—multiplied by fourteen years meant the names, faces and details blurred. There were times Devlin would get a call from a *current* client, and it would take him a few seconds to connect the name and specifics of the case.

"Five years ago," the man said, his red face shiny with sweat, "you cross-examined me on the stand."

Devlin's mind was swimming: he was thinking about Darcie Savoy, and her upcoming pre-trial settlement conference; Bobby Swift and his jailhouse lawyer Leander Farley; CandyMan and Sunshine; the Parker Seven and the Coffee Cup cases; the mayor's hearing in Kingman; and, to top it off, the trial starting in eighteen hours for the M&M'S Caper. Whoever this guy was, his timing was suboptimal. Not to mention the fierce July rays now strafing Devlin's vulnerable complexion.

"Let's get out of this heat," he said—more an order than a suggestion.

They stepped into the lobby where Nadia Flores sat, quietly tapping away on her new Orwellian contraption. To her right was a curved white stucco wall with polished chrome block lettering affixed: Devlin & Associates. Behind her was Devlin's spacious office, the largest of the six. The babble of water from the fountain in the corner infused the space with a sense of cooling calm… or at least that's what

71

the red-headed interior designer Devlin had hired told him one morning in bed. And that was only after she'd scheduled a third consultation, which was when Devlin finally got the clue to her baser intentions.

"Nice digs, counselor. I knew you were the real deal. You still don't remember?"

"Look, I'm booked solid today and have a trial tomorrow morning. Could we schedule for next month?"

"Five minutes. I really need your help."

Your work is to serve. Service is your work.

Devlin's old man still lived in Buffalo, but he was right there every day with the kid, whispering his maxims. Dad was also available by phone, any time to discuss any matter, a comforting go-to source he regularly tapped. Along with Mom and Nadia Flores, Dad rounded out the power trio Devlin called on for whatever challenge he faced. During those calls Dad always reminded his only son of their fallback position, to out-Irish any opponent, which meant there was only one acceptable response even though Devlin knew this potential client's five minutes would turn into at least half an hour or more.

"Sure," Devlin said. "Let's step into my office."

Two minutes into the story, it all came back for Devlin: five years ago he represented a client in a medical malpractice case for a botched back surgery. His client was an otherwise vibrantly healthy man who owned a construction company. The screwed-up surgery ended his career, because he couldn't walk job sites, climb ladders or pick up anything heavier than a screwdriver. The man now seated in his office, a Greek doctor named Westin Giannopoulos, shared a practice with the defendant but had not actually performed the surgery. During cross-examination, Devlin essentially shredded the Greek's testimony and sent him out of the courtroom in a zippered black body bag.

"So, wait," Devlin said. "I sued your medical practice, killed you on the stand and cost your insurance carrier some serious loot."

"Exactly," he said.

"OK, I'm confused. Why are you here?"

"That's easy. When I saw what you did to me on the stand it made me respect you. I was thinking that if I ever got in a jam, you're the guy I'd want in my corner."

Devlin nodded, but he was mostly focused on what he needed to do next: re-read all the depositions in the M&M'S Caper. "So, you're in a jam?"

"You could say that."

"Tell me what happened."

"Along with being a doctor, I'm a consultant for the Arizona Medical Board. They hire me to evaluate other doctors caught up in various scandals. I do my interviews and investigation, and write an unbiased, third-party assessment including my recommendation for a suitable punishment, up to loss of licensure. It's serious stuff. My input can save, or end, a doctor's career."

"I'm with you, but not following where you need the services of a lawyer…"

"Well, one of the female doctors they referred to me for assessment was, how shall I say this…? She looks like Christie Brinkley."

Devlin suspected he knew where this was headed. "A real, Uptown Girl."

"Exactly."

"So instead of assessing her own scandal, you and she have become the new scandal."

"Exactly," the doctor said. "Needless to say, we ended up in the sack."

Needless to say? The guy wasn't exactly Adonis, a god of beauty triggering rabid desire in women. Devlin was morbidly curious how the Greek had connected the dots, from meeting this woman to knowing her in the biblical sense, but he let it go.

"Look, I know I crossed the line," the doctor said. "Total professional misconduct. We were intense for, like, two weeks. Did it every day, twice a day sometimes; my office, her place, my place. My car, her car. I think one day we did it three times— you know, breakfast, lunch and dinner kind of deal."

"I get the idea."

"Right, but here's the thing: I'm married. To a doctor. And so is she—get this, to another doctor!"

Devlin suppressed a smile: *what a bunch of fucking doctors.*

"So, naturally, I had to cut it off, and she goes nuts. Started calling constantly, showing up at my practice, threatening to tell my wife. I need your help."

Devlin shook his head. "Sounds tricky. I'm not sure there's anything we can do legally."

"Well, here's the thing. Now she has this weird lawyer who's trying to extort money from me. If I don't pay up she'll blow the whistle on me to the Arizona Board. I just want to keep my marriage and my job. I'll pay her to make it go away, but I need someone to make sure it's done right, once and for all, so she can't come back for more. I don't trust her."

Trust, Devlin thought, was in short supply on both sides here. One thing in particular piqued Devlin's interest: "What did you mean when you said she has a weird lawyer?"

"I don't know. I only talked to him once, but he's just... hinky."

"Hinky?"

"Yeah, you know, like he's got crossed wires in his brain. You'll see."

"Well, let's not get ahead of ourselves. You want me to represent you, talk to this weird lawyer, and see if we can work out a confidential settlement?"

"Yeah. With a heavy emphasis on 'confidential.'"

"OK, here's what we'll do. Leave his name and number with Nadia, my assistant, before you go. I'll talk to this hinky lawyer. No promises, but if she hasn't gone public yet and is just after money, then it may only be a matter of nailing down the amount and making it official. We'll have to see if they can be reasonable. Did she mention an amount?"

"Not really. Maybe a hundred grand? I don't know."

"Which is it: 'not really,' or a hundred grand?"

"I don't know. Can you just talk to the guy? I'm freaking out here."

"All right. Slow down. Take a deep breath. I'll talk to him, OK?"

"Yes, thank you. What's this going to cost me?"

Devlin's phone rang. He picked up to hear Flores say, "It's Leander Farley on the phone from Arizona State Prison."

What was it with this guy and his personal prison phone? Devlin motioned to the Greek doctor. "Yeah, put him through... Leander, I'm actually with a client right now. Let me get back to you."

"Just wanted to see how we're doing on the Rule 32 petition for Bobby."

"Yeah, I'm working on it. Let me get back to you."

"Any idea when you'll file?"

"Soon. I'll get back to you."

Devlin hung up without waiting for a response. "Sorry. Where were we?"

"The bad news. How much?"

"Right. OK, let's see how the meeting goes. I'm thinking for fifty grand she'll stay quiet and leave you alone. Hundred tops. But we shouldn't lowball. You're not getting out of this for five or ten grand, unless you want her coming back to the well."

"OK. How about your fee?"

"You've got enough on your plate without worrying about how to pay me. So, for now the first meeting is on me. If that's all it takes, consider it *pro bono*."

The Greek started to tear up, and he nodded his head slowly. "Thank you. Thank you, thank you. My wife and kids... I can't..."

Devlin stood, as a cue that the meeting was over, wondering where this emotional construct had been when Dr. Swimsuit Model and the Greek were riding each other like rented mules.

"Leave that name and number. I'll have Nadia set the appointment, but it will have to be for next month because I have a trial tomorrow and then an out-of-town hearing. But rest assured, once we have the meeting on the calendar, that should put any of her antics on hold. In the meantime, no contact with either her or the lawyer. From now on, everything goes through me, got it?"

"Yeah, of course."

Like Monae, Devlin knew the truth about clients: they lied, too, to serve their self-interests, which included sating the libido. Especially sating the libido. "I'm serious. If I find out you're *shtupping* her again—"

"Oh, no way," he said. "There's no way. Not ever again."

Devlin just gave him the hard look.

"You have my word. I won't go there."

"No matter what."

"No matter what."

Devlin spent the next six hours at the office, until 10 p.m., re-reading depositions in the M&M'S Caper. Then he drove home and spent three more hours writing out his opening and closing statements. After practicing both scripts until he could recite them by memory, he tumbled into bed around 2 a.m. for a few hours of sleep. Back up at 6:30 a.m., he was in a tailored brown suit and green silk tie with brown-and-cream-colored wingtips, waiting outside the courtroom before 9. Even after fourteen years, going before a jury had not lost its adrenaline-pumping allure. In fact, it was the greatest thrill Devlin had found in life, as he poured heart and soul into advocating for justice in cases big and small.

The ideal trial lawyer brought a bit of flair and bravado to the stage. From the first step of selecting the jury, which was like trying to pick the right card in a swift street game of three-card monte, being a player in a courtroom trial was a grueling, sometimes exasperating and always exhilarating process. In many trials there were no clear winners. As Devlin quickly learned, substantial winning verdicts immediately went on appeal, which meant more years of uncertainty. Ultimately, a trial always represented the final branch of the law, wherein all other reasonable efforts had been exhausted. Instead, the two warring factions would clash in the arena and let a third-party panel be the arbiter of their respective efforts. And in this particular case, another quick and anonymous affair on the court's docket that would go unnoticed outside the courtroom, Devlin's preparation once again won the day. Like most trials, there were only a few witnesses, no one in the gallery, and the jury was deliberating by mid-afternoon. In the end, Devlin was able to demonstrate that others had committed much worse offenses with lesser consequences. He got both M&M'S Caper defendants reinstated into their jobs, with back pay for the missed time—for the tidy fee of $475 each.

Chapter Eight

FOR THE TRIP NORTH THE NEXT DAY, Devlin picked up Monae in the Blazer at 8 a.m. Monae once again looked resplendent in a simple blue summer dress that tastefully accentuated her toned, athletic frame. Devlin had opted for a similarly blue dress shirt, with tan slacks and case-winning wingtips for a classic look. When she climbed up and into the high Blazer, Devlin felt the strong urge to lean across and kiss her. He could smell her sweet floral perfume. Instead, they fumbled through the odd handshake again and then leaned in for a half-hug that felt awkward for both.

"Looks like you got the memo on attire," Devlin said, pointing to his shirt.

"As did you," she said. "Looking sharp, counselor."

"Likewise, detective. You ready to do this thing?"

Monae's mind temporarily detoured back to the gutter, but she played it cool. "Hell, yeah. Let's go spring the mayor."

THREE hours later, they rolled into Kingman. Monae had booked two rooms again at the Good Night Motel, which had removed *COOL AC!!* as its prime attraction and replaced it with the latest-and-greatest twin amenities sweeping the nation (as indicated by the addition of a third exclamation mark): *FREE cable TV + HBO!!!* They retreated to their respective rooms to change into their official business attire for their meeting with the county prosecutor at noon. Devlin had already spent several long sessions on the phone with Ben Appleton, an affable University of Chicago law graduate who'd apparently chosen the big-fish/small-pond career track. From the start, Appleton had wanted to throw the book at Mickey Conrad by charging him as a drug trafficker. Through those early phone calls Appleton never budged: the state wanted trafficking, a first-degree felony with a minimum of five years in prison and up to twenty-five years. Twenty-five years for transporting plants! Devlin earned every penny of his cut by convincing the prosecutor to allow Conrad to plead to the lesser offense of possession, which might include prison time but would also make Conrad eligible for probation. It wasn't until their last phone call that Appleton had hinted at the possibility of considering a lesser charge.

"We've got him dead to rights on drug trafficking," Appleton said now at the meeting, leaning back in his chair and eyeing the investigator the lawyer had brought along. "The amount of the narcotic involved, three hundred pounds, is way beyond simple possession."

"Understood," Devlin said. "But there was no evidence of my client's intent to sell. No scales, no plastic baggies for packaging, no large amounts of cash on his person or in the plane at the time of arrest. He was just the delivery guy caught with a big shipment. And the only reason he was the delivery guy was his skill as a pilot that he learned in Vietnam courtesy of the U.S. government. I've researched his war record, which is exemplary. The probation program I've detailed will include public service, no drugs and/or alcohol, and resigning his office as mayor. We're recommending one hundred hours of community service, to include lecturing children about the ills of drugs and sharing his cautionary tale with veterans' organizations."

"Yeah," Appleton said, "I'm pretty sure Judge Hartwell is ex-military, but I guess that could go either way for you." He tapped a number-two pencil on his knee, because he was distracted by this investigator who smelled good and looked even better. She was wearing a tight gray suit with big shoulder pads, and her white silk blouse revealed just a hint of cleavage. She had the hair and long legs, crossed and slowly bouncing, the spiky black heel clicking on the desk front a couple times. It was easy for Appleton to conjure up a fantasy—if this other lawyer would just get gone…

"So, you'll allow it?"

"Allow what?" Appleton said, wondering what exactly *would* be allowed in his fantasy.

Devlin and Monae exchanged glances. Appleton's mental salivation was impossible to miss. Monae noticed and sloughed it off as she always did. Devlin was a little surprised to recognize a small pang of jealousy—and a protective urge, knowing what she had shared about the police department. Devlin said, "To plead to possession."

"Sure. Whatever. Just don't be surprised if the judge tells you to go pound sand. What time we scheduled?"

"Mitigation hearing starts at 9 a.m.," Devlin said.

"How many witnesses you calling?"

"Four."

"Jesus, really?"

"Is that a lot? We'll call the defendant, two Vietnam vets who were also pilots, and his wife."

"Just don't bore me."

"That," Devlin said, "will be top of my list."

That afternoon, Devlin and his partner spent a couple hours in his motel room preparing the three witnesses for their testimony. Monae role-played as prosecutor and offered some excellent pointers. Then the five squeezed into Devlin's Blazer and drove a few minutes to meet Mickey Conrad and the Wookiee at a steakhouse. On the way up from Phoenix, Devlin and Monae had discussed the importance of Mickey Conrad understanding exactly what would happen and how it should all play out. The eleventh-hour agreement by the prosecutor to allow Conrad to plead to possession was a point for cautious optimism concerning the potential for probation. Still, the lawyer's job was to relay that everything still hung in the balance for his client, which meant the strategy was that Conrad was to keep his mouth zip-tied unless asked a specific question by the judge or the lawyers. Collectively, everyone was tense about how it would unspool in court, and they only picked at their food— except the Wookiee, who fully enjoyed his prime rib, savoring each bite he dipped in spicy horseradish.

After dinner, the group chatted in the parking lot and then parted ways. Mickey Conrad left with his wife and bodyguard. Devlin offered to drive the two veterans back to their hotel. Then it was just Devlin and Monae alone in the Blazer for the short and awkwardly silent drive to the Good Night Motel.

Out of the vehicle and back at the stairwell, Devlin and Monae faced a second fork-in-the-road moment under the moonlight. Except this situation had a wholly different feel than the last time. On the first trip here, the moment of truth had been preceded by one-on-one time, laughter, intimate conversation and, of course, multiple rounds of tequila. Conversely, this trip and the various meetings were all sober business designed to keep Mickey Conrad from screwing up a hearing that would begin in less than twelve hours. Although it wasn't a full trial, Devlin was feeling that familiar combination of restlessness, excitement and anticipation about the outcome. Monae, too, didn't want to do anything that might somehow jinx their efforts tomorrow in court. Both sensed that the time to celebrate, whatever that might come to mean, would be *after* a resounding victory in the courtroom. Not before. Not now.

When it was time to part ways and retreat to their respective rooms, the sexual chemistry had already been turned to a low simmer. They had just stepped from the Blazer and were standing in the dim parking lot. Devlin wore a gray suit and tie, and Monae still had on her gray suit with big shoulder pads, white silk blouse, stockings and spiky black heels. The moonlight glinted off the chunky gold "X" at the clasp of her handbag. Separately, they were both focused on whether they had done everything in their collective power to prepare for the hearing.

"Good night, counselor."

"Good night, detective."

"You'd better break a leg tomorrow."

"You know I will."

With the casual exchange lowering his guard, and without thought, Devlin leaned in, stopping briefly within an inch of Monae's lips, and then kissed her lightly. Monae was taken aback, but certainly not disappointed. She felt a hot rush of blood. The man knew how to kiss: slowly, then a little more deeply. Then slow again. Devlin slowly clasped his hands at her lower back, gently pulling her closer. Then their bodies were touching, and she could already feel him pressing into her taut Vivienne Westwood skirt. It was the age-old clash of spirits: minds probing, bodies bonding and hearts assessing in a coursing concoction of pheromones and unleashed biochemistry.

Under the watery sheet of gray light in the motel parking lot, where the familiar traffic thrum of the city had been replaced by a sprawling din of small-town silence, Devlin fully squared his hips to hers. Then she eased back ever so gently, almost imperceptibly. She wondered how far this might go tonight, holding her eyes shut tight and being careful not to let her hands go astray. She could feel the heat building inside. Then, slowly, they paused the kiss.

"Well," he said, gripping her now with both hands at the hips, pressing into her below her waist.

"Well."

Fully clothed and standing in a public parking lot, an unspoken eroticism triggered primal urges in both, male and female separated from connection only by layers of fabric.

"The mayor's mitigation hearing," Devlin said.

"Of course," she said. "That's a reality check."

"I guess we should…" Devlin offered.

"Right. We should."

Devlin still had his hands on her hips, their bodies still pressed together in dangerous places. Neither spoke of what they knew. She had her hands at the small of his back, clasped, to keep him drawn into her. It was too soon, but she didn't care. From that first trip up here, he had triggered something in her, an abandon she wanted to give in to and experience without over-analyzing it. No holding back. Now she wanted him to just sweep her up into his arms and carry her off into his den. Except it was too soon, so she revised: she wanted him to keep kissing her. She liked the feeling of closeness and connection. She could take a cold shower later if she needed to.

Devlin looked at her in the dimmed light, vulnerable and disarmed in a way he hadn't seen. He gently took her hand and walked toward his room, both of them moving with an ease neither had anticipated. Monae's heart raced, and she wondered again if it was too soon. *No, it's not. Yes, it is. Shut up and just go with it. No, it's too soon.*

"Wait," she said, stopping. "I like you."

"I like you, too," he said with a faint grin.

"I don't want to just be this week's girl. I'm not like that."

"I don't want to just be this week's girl, either," he said.

"Seriously."

Devlin pulled her in and kissed her again.

"Look," she said. "You're… all right. And smart."

"Don't forget funny," he pointed out.

"I want to," she said. "But I think we should wait. The hearing?"

Oh, fuck—yeah, the hearing. Amazing how a first kiss had the power to warp time, space and dimension. "You're right," he said. "We should wait."

He kissed her again, reaching around to the curve of her skirt. Monae's arousal met his. Devlin heard a thunder roar, drawing all blood to center. She let her hands fall lower. One second she was telling herself to stop, for the mayor! The next second she had slipped over the cliff's edge in a hushed delirium as they went over the waterfall together.

Things blurred as they moved to Devlin's room, pulling at each other's clothes, tumbling onto the full-size bed. Suit jackets tossed aside. Tie undone. Silk blouse unbuttoned. Black bra discarded. She got his pants undone and yanked them off.

"Are you sure?" he said. "Like you said, we should wait, right?" He slid her tight skirt down her sculpted legs. "Stop talking," she said. She had a momentary thought: *Hang the skirt so it doesn't wrinkle?* Then she was naked except for the panties she had chosen with considered intent before dinner—*highly unlikely... but just in case*—and then those were gone, too. The neon light around the edges of the window curtain cast a translucent glow across everything. Devlin saw a sharp resemblance to Jaclyn Smith, the most elegant of *Charlie's Angels*. Monae's effect was a powerful juxtaposition of soft innocence and sultry energy. There was an easy flow to their connection. It all happened quickly, beautifully, until they were side by side on their backs, a warm sheen of sweat covering them both.

"Well," he said, through heavy breaths.

"Well," she said, giggling.

"The mayor's mitigation hearing," Devlin said.

"Of course," she said.

"I guess we should..." Devlin offered.

"Right. We definitely should."

"I knew you were you going to get us into trouble."

"Me?!" she said. "You started it."

"I guess I did. And you know what?"

"What?" she asked.

"I'd say this is a good omen: we're going to kill it in court tomorrow."

"Agreed."

They kissed again, slowly. Another long and lingering kiss, with the entire world a million miles away. For a brief moment, they were the epicenter of all existence. Nothing else mattered, because they were the only sentient beings in the totality of the universe. Then Monae slipped from the bed, went to the bathroom and partially closed the door. Devlin thought about getting up to find his boxers, but instead just pulled up the motel bedspread. He thought about Sloane Monae's eyes and her toned torso, how exquisite she had looked arched before him in her black underwear, a graceful being sent from some other world.

Then, still early in the evening and without warning, a comforting peace enveloped him completely and he drifted into an expansive netherworld. Monae flushed the toilet and stepped back into the room to the sound of light snoring. Devlin slept until it was light again outside.

AT 8:30 the next morning, the group—Devlin, Monae, the mayor and his wife, the two veterans and the Wookiee—walked into the Mohave County Superior Court building. As instructed by Devlin, the Wookiee had left his pistol in a lock box cable-tied to the bed in the motel room. Court or no court, the Wookiee had not deviated from his standard wardrobe of black leather jacket, jeans and boots. Mickey Conrad had dusted off his only tie and suit, a dark-brown number with jacket sleeves that were too short. He had shaved, too, and with his hair cut and slicked back, he looked much better than he had in Gallup months before. Having his wife Marla at his side seemed to calm him further, too. Monae was pleased that he had so closely followed her instructions, although she wondered again about the wall-cavity situation.

The proceedings began promptly at 9 a.m. as the bailiff announced the judge, who then ordered everyone to be seated. He read the case number. The mayor sat nervously in the courtroom between his investigator Sloane Monae and his lawyer Connor J. Devlin. There was a little buzz about the case—*Marijuana Mayor Goes Before Court*—and subsequently a curious gallery had turned out: a few retired folks; some factory workers and restaurant staff who worked nights; the mayor's friends, political supporters and opponents; reporters from three newspapers; and several homeless people who had simply followed the crowd. The prosecutor Appleton, a thick, sullen man, introduced himself. And then the other side.

"Your honor, Connor Devlin for the defense."

"And how does your client plead?"

"Your honor, Mr. Conrad pleads to possession, a non-designated, open-ended offense."

Monae and Devlin were thinking the same thing: it was the right strategy, but speaking it in court highlighted the risk. If he got probation and then slipped, Conrad was looking at a felony charge. Devlin's cards were all face-up on the table.

"And the state?" the judge asked.

"Your honor, the state stipulates to the plea agreement." Appleton unconsciously glanced at Monae.

"OK. We will proceed with the mitigation hearing and, depending on our timetable, I will make my decision at the conclusion. Mr. Devlin, you may call your first witness."

"Thank you, your honor. I call the defendant, Mr. Michael Conrad."

Devlin's strategy was to eliminate any high drama and just have the mayor speak on his own behalf. Then Devlin would use each witness to corroborate and bolster everything Conrad had established. Devlin spent the next hour and a half carefully walking the mayor through the testimony they had planned. By the end, Devlin's messaging and strategy had shone through clearly. Mickey Conrad was a first-time offender with no previous record of, nor proclivity toward, violence or impinging on another person's well-being. He was also a decorated helicopter pilot who fought for the United States of America in Vietnam and was awarded a Purple Heart. He was gainfully employed as the mayor of a thriving and prosperous U.S. municipality, a post that he would sadly relinquish as a condition of making amends. And while there was certainly no such thing as a victimless crime, this offense involved risk and potential injury, or death, only to the defendant. Devlin asked his final question: "Mr. Conrad, can you assure this court that this was your first, last and only offense?"

"Yes, I can," he said humbly.

"And how can you make such a claim?"

"I would do so by borrowing from the final lines of the Soldier's Creed that I learned in the U.S. Army."

"And what is that Creed?"

"'I stand ready to deploy, engage and destroy the enemies of the United States of America in close combat. I am a guardian of freedom and the American way of life. I am an American soldier.' In other words, sir, you have my word of honor."

Monae thought again about the wall cavity at Conrad's house, and decided right then that he had emptied it as promised.

"Mr. Appleton, cross-examination?"

"Thank you, your honor. Mr. Conrad, you stated in your testimony that this offense involved risk and potential injury or death only to the defendant, yourself. Is that correct?"

"Yes, sir."

"But isn't it true that flying an aircraft in any U.S. airspace, without a registered flight plan and without coordinating with other aircraft, is inherently dangerous to others, both in the air and, potentially, on the ground?"

"Objection," Devlin said. "Calls for speculation." While Appleton had gone along with the plea deal for possession, it was still his job to remind the judge he could drop the hammer.

"You raised the point, counselor, so I'll allow it."

"Sir?" Mr. Appleton said.

Mickey Conrad nodded. "Yes, sir. What I did was dangerous and stupid, and could have ended a lot worse had I crashed into a building rather than out in the sticks."

"Thank you," Appleton said. "Nothing further, your honor."

"Mr. Devlin: next witness."

By 3 p.m., Devlin had walked the two Vietnam veterans and Marla Conrad through similar testimony to establish the mayor's good character, notwithstanding the gross error in judgment to start transporting marijuana. Devlin concluded with, "Your honor, Mr. Conrad has willingly suspended all flight activities as a pilot and will continue to do so as part of the conditions of his probation, and he poses no risk to anyone if allowed to serve his time through probation. Thank you, your honor."

The judge looked at the paperwork and flipped back and forth between pages. Devlin was confident, but could still feel his palms sweating up. Monae, too, could feel her heart racing. She turned and looked at Devlin, who smiled and nodded at her ever so slightly. The man definitely pushed her buttons.

The judge didn't look up as he spoke. "Today we have heard testimony that the defendant is a gainfully employed public figure and first-time offender with no previous record. There was no bodily injury or property damage during the commission of this act, although there was the potential, as the state points out, for such. The court is mindful of the sacrifices this defendant made in serving his country during a time of war." Monae wanted to leap for joy: she had pegged the military bond as key. Then the judge sighed and said, "But military service alone in no way absolves this defendant of his actions, nor curries special favor in this courtroom."

Monae felt the gut punch. Devlin squeezed his fists. The prosecutor leaned forward slightly. Mickey Conrad closed his eyes, let out a long, slow, silent breath and said a mental prayer. One of the homeless men in the gallery, not really following what was happening, got up and shuffled out of the courtroom, creating a momentary stir. The bodyguard was thinking about where they would go for dinner.

Once the courtroom settled back into complete silence, the judge spoke: "The court is not yet ready to render a decision in this case, and will recess on this matter until 9 a.m. tomorrow."

Gavel. Next case on the docket. Devlin had only one overriding thought: this cannot be good for Mickey Conrad.

That night, Devlin took the group—Monae, the mayor and Marla Conrad, the two veterans and the Wookiee—to the Mexican restaurant for dinner, which was an initially somber affair with the uncertainty of Mickey Conrad's fate looming. To break the tension, Devlin told a story about getting dragged into an Army physical, in a gritty area of San Pedro during his law-school years in California, at the height of the Vietnam War. Devlin, 24, found himself at a recruiting center in a cavernous room with hundreds of other guys, most age 18 to 20, seated at small tables filling out the paperwork. While they were writing on the forms, an Army sergeant major marched onto the stage at the front of the room. Gunny sported the requisite shaved dome under his round brown hat, a bulging neck the size of a log, and a uniform starched to the hardness of Formica. He didn't speak; he screamed.

"You fucking maggots! Your mamas aren't here to help your sorry asses, so fill out your application correctly, or I guaran-goddam-tee you I will ruin your day myself. Is that understood?"

A non-unified smattering of "Yes, sirs" went around the room.

"I goddam said 'Is that understood,' you maggot spunk!"

The second "Yes, sir!" was louder but still not Army-certified, though none of the assembled were even yet in the employ of Uncle Sam.

"I can't HEAR you!"

"Yes, SIR!"

"Any questions, you maggots?" A hand went up near the stage. "What's your question, son?"

A Hispanic kid said, "Sir, I didn't finish eighth grade. Do I put '7' or '8' for education?"

Gunny jumped from the stage and got so close the kid could feel the warm spray when Gunny yelled, "You fucking maggot, you're not smart enough for the Army, you low-grade shitball."

The poor kid just stared at Gunny, afraid to speak.

"Goddammit, son, last grade completed. Do you know how to write a '7'? Let me explain this so all you other Einstein-maggots don't get confused. One through twelve, pretty self-explanatory. Last grade completed. If any of you geniuses went to community college, add "one" for each year completed. One year of community college, that's twelve plus one equals thirteen. Still with me, dipshits?"

"Yes, sir!"

"Now, if you finished college—of which there's a better chance the ghost of Ho Chi Minh will float out my ass in the next three seconds, drinking a Budweiser—then you put '16.' Now, any you other dumb motherfuckers don't understand simple math?"

Devlin, a few tables from the kid who just got reamed, raised his hand. He already knew the answer to the question he was about to ask, but he didn't like the way Gunny had demeaned that poor kid. And, of course, it would be fun to poke the tiger to see him snarl.

"Good Lord in heaven, what now?"

"Sir, I've completed two years of law school. What number is that?"

From where he had been standing until he was right in Devlin's face, Gunny let out a long "Oooooooooooooh." Then, with platinum-standard mockery: "We got ourselves a smart college boy. College boy's going to *law school*. Oooooooooooooh! Can we all kiss your tight-white ass, fancy boy, 'cuz you're *soooooooo* smart? College boy thinks he's the smartest guy here!" Then, on a dime, Gunny switched back to his full-throated theater-of-war bark: "Well, I'll tell you where you can go, college boy: straight to the goddam rice paddies, where Charlie is going to shoot your balls off with Soviet-issued carbines. Do you goddam understand me?!"

"No, sir," Devlin said. "You still didn't answer my question."

THE story got good laughs from everyone, and hit the mark in piercing the somber mood. Because the lawyer knew his client would be unable to sleep much anyway, Devlin ordered another round and held court for two more hours. He regaled the group with more stories about growing up in Buffalo, his laughable attempt to promote a boxer (with Trevor Walsh) they billed as "The Hawaiian Champ," and working on the Organized Crime Strike Force in the early seventies, which was an operation to take down Mafia kingpins who had waltzed into Arizona as a Western outpost for their criminal operations.

By the time Devlin and Monae got back to the motel— *FREE cable TV + HBO!!!*—it was after midnight. They faced yet another moment of truth under the moonlight. They embraced and kissed—a long, lingering connection. They broke off the kiss and held each other, both smiling.

"Helluva day," Devlin said.

"What do you think the judge will do tomorrow?"

Devlin shook his head. Then he offered, "I guess we should..."

"Right. We should."

They laughed.

"We both know where that thinking got us last night," Monae said.

"Last night was spectacular," he said, kissing her again.

When they paused she said, "Truly. You have *no* idea." Their bodies were pressed together, her hands around his waist and drawing him into her. "Tomorrow's a big day—today, actually."

"That it is," he said.

"So I think I'm going to be the good girl tonight and send you to your room. You need your beauty rest." She smiled, looking particularly stunning under the gray cast of light in the motel parking lot, a bargain-rate backdrop to all their sexual tension and intimate turning points.

"That I do," he said. "You're right. We should get some sleep."

Then they started kissing again. Once again, things quickly blurred as they moved to Devlin's room, tumbled in and closed the door.

Chapter Nine

ONCE AGAIN THE MAYOR STOOD IN THE COURTROOM, fidgeting between Sloane Monae and Connor J. Devlin, as the judge read the case number. The gallery size had diminished as the proceedings spilled over to a second day in court. The machinery of the jaws of justice, for Mickey Conrad, was spring-loaded to full tension, everyone craning forward in unison like buzzards smelling blood and circling the mortally wounded.

"Let me repeat parts of what I said yesterday," the judge said. "The defendant is a duly elected and public figure of a municipality, and a first-time offender with no previous record. There was no bodily injury or property damage inflicted during the course of this felony, although the state points out that there was the potential for fatalities. The court is mindful of the sacrifices this defendant made in serving his country during a time of war. However, that fact alone cannot simply absolve this defendant of the consequences of his actions. After careful consideration I was able to come to my decision, which includes an acknowledgment of the tremendous sacrifice American military personnel in all branches of the U.S. military made during the Vietnam War. Like Mr. Conrad, I too served in Vietnam. I was in the 9th

Infantry Division. Although they called us the 'Old Reliables,' it was only with the gunship support from the skies by skilled pilots like Mr. Conrad that I am here today to render this decision. Perhaps it was Mr. Conrad himself who whisked me and members of my platoon to safety on one particularly horrible day I can recall. We will never know for sure, but whether it was the defendant or another, I know it was skilled U.S. Army helicopter pilots who saved American lives that day—including my own."

Devlin and Monae were both stunned and moved to tears. Mickey Conrad, too, wanted to hug the judge, a brother in arms who had survived the same horrendous slog.

"Of course, former military service does not provide some sort of *carte blanche* to commit whatever acts one chooses upon conclusion of that service. But we must acknowledge the enormous mental, emotional and physical strain that wars— and the Vietnam War in particular—have exacted on returning soldiers. Did the defendant's wartime service somehow diminish his cognitive skills, thereby leading to his decision to partake in the act under consideration in the courtroom today? Perhaps it did, perhaps it did not. Did the defendant's wartime service provide the very skills he used to partake in the act under consideration in this courtroom today? Very clearly, as we heard, that answer is yes. Does the defendant's sense of duty to honor his oath, the Soldier's Creed, carry any weight in this courtroom? Clearly, the answer is that the defendant's promise to never do this again is to be believed, because he is bound to that oath."

The anticipation was almost unbearable to Mickey Conrad, who wanted to scream. His wife Marla, too, had her eyes closed, as did Devlin. Monae shut her eyes as well as the judge delivered the verdict: "The court finds the plea agreement acceptable, with a probation period of three years to be served, as outlined in the agreement."

As the thick tension broke, Mickey Conrad could not hold back the tears. He leaned into Devlin and wept as Monae joined the hug circle. Outside the building, the red-eyed mayor took a deep breath that felt like the first one since he'd been arrested. It seemed he would never let go of Marla, who was still in tears herself.

"He actually came down hard," Devlin said. "Usually they'll give a first-time offender one year of probation. Three years is pretty stiff. But no prison time. Hallelujah."

"That's three years you have to keep your nose clean, Mr. Mayor," Monae said.

"Still, as we've said from the start," Devlin offered, "*not* going to jail was always the goal. Let's not lose sight of that. At least you're free to do as you please now. Within the limits of your probation."

Monae threw a little jab: "We good on the freezer, Mr. Mayor?"

"Oh yeah. Clean as a whistle. Nothing but TV dinners and Rocky Road. And yes, I took care of the other, if that's what you're asking. Damn shame, though."

"The other what?" Devlin asked.

"Nothing," Monae said. "Just a little understanding the mayor and I have."

Monae thought about the entire progression, from the back of the limousine on that cold day to finding Devlin and now Mickey Conrad being a free man, at least within the limits of his probation. Just as she'd suggested: she helped him beat the house.

Mickey Conrad sighed again. "Well, I guess this outcome means I sure as hell got my twenty-five grand's worth." He laughed as the two other Vietnam vets joined the confab and took turns hugging the mayor. Even the Wookiee cracked a smile and patted his boss on the back.

Devlin eyed Monae, his mouth partly open in feigned shock and begrudging respect for the savvy negotiator. He spoke to Conrad without breaking eye contact with Monae. "Twenty-five thousand is indeed a small penance for your freedom."

The mayor wasn't really listening, because all he could think about was that he was not going to prison. "You and your Rolex, Ms. Monae. Looks like I just bought you another one, right?" He laughed and patted her on the back, and they started toward the gleaming red Blazer.

"You two lovebirds should come up to Silverton," the soon-to-be-former mayor said. "I'll give you the full red-carpet treatment."

"No, we're not—" Monae said.

"—a couple," Devlin finished.

"What?" Conrad said, staring at them both for a good five seconds. "You sure about that? Because the energy here... I just assumed, right, Chacho?"

The Wookiee was back to thinking about dinner. "Sure, boss."

"Marla?" the mayor asked.

"I plead the Fifth," his wife said, smiling.

Monae could feel her face flushing; Devlin was perplexed that they were telegraphing their affection so openly.

"Anyway, I can't believe my attorney drives a red Chevy Blazer."

"Just like I can't believe my client flew a planeload of dope up from Mexico," Devlin said, laughing.

"Yeah, on second thought," Monae said, "You're not paying us nearly enough."

"You got that right," Devlin said, eyeing Monae again and smiling.

"Well," she said. "Hats off to the best negotiator."

Then they both turned and looked at Conrad, who shook his head, looked at Marla and laughed. "Not a couple? Yeah, right."

EARLY August in the desert was especially brutal, as moist air swept up from the Gulf of Mexico and lingered across the desert-basin metropolis. The annual phenomenon, known locally as Monsoon Season, brought cloyingly high humidity that combined with brutal daily temperatures of 105 or more. Accordingly, Devlin had spent the last month ensconced in air conditioning, whether at the office, at home or in the Blazer.

Since the mayor's hearing, Devlin had ground out a full draft of Bobby Swift's Rule 32 petition, which illustrated just how complex and nuanced the arena of appellate rights could be. Devlin had known for weeks that the best expert available for guidance in this difficult area of law was already within his personal network, but he had avoided the fact all the same. Finally, he resigned himself, walked outside into the inferno, climbed in the Blazer and headed downtown to The Bunker.

Devlin found a parking space on the street in front of Phoenix Municipal Hospital and walked across the sizzling pavement to the squat brown building with two façade windows. Devlin carried a single file folder. Based on what he'd heard about the legendary Goldie, before pulling open the door Devlin looked skyward and paused, knowing this would be his last taste of natural light and fresh air. Even outside, the dingy stench of cigars was already nauseating. Inside, whatever color the wallpaper had originally been thirty years ago had fused into a rare shade of stomach-churning brown. The secretary just smiled and pointed across her shoulder to the windowless office where Phil Goldberg, aka Goldie, held court and was no doubt penning another brilliant legal treatise at age 60. Perhaps Goldie would add another notch to his belt by helping Devlin craft his own winning appellate decision. As Devlin stepped into Goldie's office the cigar smoke was thicker, and the smell more rancid. Without any windows, the only light came from two overhead panels of fluorescent tubes covered by Lucite that had turned another unique shade of flaxen brown. The overall effect was of Goldie working under the dim light of perpetual dusk, like some hulking, nocturnal creature shunning daylight.

"Lamont, you big dummy. Welcome to The Bunker."

"Goldie."

"Decide to ditch your loser lottery practice and learn some actual law, huh?"

"Something like that."

Bookshelves adorned every wall, floor to ceiling, each stuffed with statute volumes, reference books, the two most recent sets of encyclopedias (Britannica and World Book), novels, poetry anthologies and endless dusty stacks of magazines including *MAD, Popular Science* and *Penthouse*. Two identical Mr. Coffee drip makers sat side by side on the credenza behind Goldie. The machines had once been white; now, after years in the smoker, both had the same dirty hue as the walls. One was always percolating, while the other was a redundant backup to prevent any catastrophic interruption to Goldie's steady intake of oily goop. On Goldie's desk, a charcoal mound of ash filled a wooden ashtray the size of an overturned hubcap. A single plume of smoke trailed upward from the stub of a lit cigar.

"So, what do you need, Dummy? As you can see, actual law is being practiced here, not that ambulance-chasing, flunky bullshit. Time is money: you're already burning both."

Goldie picked up the cigar, took a couple deep puffs and blew the carcinogenic vapor straight at Devlin's face. Goldie's mug was broad and thick-lipped, with a pug nose and endless forehead. The whites of his eyes, behind the thick black Coke-bottle reader glasses, were perpetually red-veined from the toxic veil hanging in his office. Devlin's eyes, too, watered from the smoke as he opened the file folder and handed the handwritten document to Goldie, a cluster of yellow legal pages stapled at the top left corner.

"I have a client in the state lockup. We're going for a Rule 32. I wanted you to give it a look, let me know what you think."

Goldie took the document and eyed it suspiciously, as though he'd just been handed stolen merchandise. "What I think is I'll wipe my ass with this, and you'll start from scratch."

Goldie was definitely an acquired taste. Devlin smiled, but Goldie did not.

"Seriously," Devlin said.

Goldie took another long drag on the cigar—which burned it down to a dangerous nub, forcing him to hold it like a joint between index finger and thumb. Then Goldie made eye contact and a protracted silence ensued, neither looking away. Devlin did not let on that he was choking on the smog and felt increasingly nauseous. He'd been in Buffalo pool halls that, compared to this office, could have been billed as health spas. And was the staring contest some kind of test? If so, perhaps Devlin had passed, because finally Goldie nodded and broke the impasse.

"A petition for post-conviction relief." Then Goldie yelled, "Ladies and gentleman, Dummy has entered the domain of real law!" Back to a normal voice, he said, "Did this client of yours take a plea?"

Devlin nodded.

"That's a steeper mountain to climb. You will have to articulate the client's appellate rights that are non-waivable. What elements are you raising in your Rule 32?"

And with that, Devlin walked Goldie through his strategy. He knew his elements. He knew his case. He knew how to articulate it. Still, Goldie's intimidating, squat presence could, and often did, dumbfound even the most brilliant lawyers. Not Devlin, however. He respected the hell out of Goldie, but he did not fear him.

"My foundation is an element not available at trial," Devlin said.

"Supporting evidence?"

"Based on new U.S. Supreme Court precedent."

"To what end?"

"Resentencing. At the time of his conviction, sentencing guidelines did not include the possibility of parole. With this new precedent, we will argue that he's now available for resentencing and, hence—"

"Parole. What, exactly, did this client of yours do to get locked up?"

"Attempted second-degree murder." Devlin braced for Goldie's blowback, but none came.

Goldie started to read aloud what Devlin had written: "'Petitioner was convicted of attempted second-degree murder in violation of Arizona Code Section ... blah blah blah ... Pima County Superior Court on March 18, 1978. A sentencing hearing was held on September 25, 1978, where Petitioner was sentenced to thirty years' incarceration without the possibility of parole.' Well, congratulations, Dummy. Two legible sentences without any obvious mistakes. Shocking, that with such refined brilliance, you're not already seated on the Supreme Court."

"Would you read it, and let me know?"

Goldie took the death-knell drag on his cigar. A voluminous pillow of black and gray chest hair rose and fell with each breath through the opening at the top of his shirt. "Yes, Lamont. I will read your fifth-grade civics report. And then tell you the truth, which will be that you should be driving a cab. Or better yet: drilling holes in sheet metal."

"What will that cost me?"

"You serious?" Goldie said. "Don't insult me with that. You can't even afford the time you've already wasted, so I will entertain this folly strictly through a duty-bound sense of empathy for the woefully incapable and pathetic. Like I'm helping a retard cross the street so he doesn't get flattened by a truck."

"Well, thank you."

"Yeah, thank you, Dummy. You've basically obligated me to do this because I can't let you put another stain on our profession with your sprawling incompetence." Then Goldie muttered an odd non sequitur: "Fuck a shifty witch." And with that he chuckled, lost in the labyrinth of dark hallways in his own unique mind.

"Well, again—"

"Stop talking." Goldie stared through the smoke and shook his head. "OK, Dummy not understand, because every time I insult you, you thank me. Try this: walk out of here so I can get some real work done."

Devlin smiled, stood and turned to walk out. That he'd survived his first professional encounter with the legendary lawyer was reason enough to celebrate. However, that Phil Goldberg, Esq., himself was willing to read and advise on one of Devlin's cases basically ensured the best possible outcome. All Devlin cared about was using every possible creative angle to help his clients. And there was no more creative angle than tapping Phil Goldberg's mad-scientist genius. Before Devlin reached the doorway, Goldie called out.

"Oh, shit. Sit back down, Dummy. One more thing."

Devlin turned and asked, "What is it?"

"I said 'sit,' so sit, Dummy."

Devlin returned and sat in the chair again. "To be frank, I'm not sure I'm ready to start a practice together."

"Yeah, right. Over my dead body that would ever happen. This is me tossing a seal a fish. And in that scenario, you're the seal, and here comes the fish: a case that stinks, which makes you the perfect lawyer to take it. And you will take it, understand? Plus, it's in your arena of flunky law so it all works out."

Devlin had never been referred a case in this way, which felt more like a mafia boss ordering a hit. But if Devlin was the triggerman and didn't have a choice in the matter, at least he had Goldie in his corner on Bobby Swift. Still, not the best timing to be adding another case to his workload.

"Sure, Goldie. Whatever you need."

"Good, Dummy. Toots will give you the file on the way out. Read it, and when you come back to get the bad news on your baby-shit Rule 32, I want to hear your strategy on the new case."

"Sounds good."

Goldie coughed, sending flutters of ash from the hubcap into the air, floating toward Devlin and fluttering down like a miniature desk-volcano had just erupted. Then Goldie said, "Friend of mine from way back was a criminal defense guy who did a stint in the prosecutor's office in Brooklyn. One time they had this rabid-eyed defendant with four words tattooed on his arm: 'Fuck a shifty witch.' My friend asked why he got that tattoo, and the guy said it was his personal creed to watch out for wily women who might stab you in the back. This tattooed mantra was his way to always be alert and get the jump. You believe that fucking guy?"

Devlin smiled.

"Now, Dummy. Why in God's good name are you still sitting here? My dogs are quicker on the uptake. Go."

Devlin nodded, stood, walked out and stopped to get the file from Sheila Anderson, not Toots, according to the nameplate on her desk. Devlin smiled, took the folder and walked back out into the suffocating August heat and humidity, a delirium-inducing paradise compared to The Bunker. Then he laughed: *fuck a shifty witch.*

Chapter Ten

AT FIRST GLANCE, DEVLIN COULD SEE exactly why Goldie had tossed the rotten-fish case at him. After meeting with Goldie, Devlin had finished out the day at the office, survived a round of Gus Housman's throat-walking at kung fu class, ate Thai food with Sloane Monae and then retreated to the Scottsdale condo with a stack of paperwork. After having her over the last four nights in a row, this would be the first night Devlin would go to bed alone. The last six weeks with her, since the mayor's hearing, had been a sweet slice of pure heaven. She was tall, athletic and beautiful. But more important, she was educated, smart and savvy. There was nothing better than the early months of a budding romance, when two people were on their best behavior, the future was a distant concern—if even considered—and everything revolved around lightheartedness, fun and discovery, with the biggest issue of the day being "My place or yours?" Devlin was savoring every second. But now he had to get caught up.

The "file" Goldie had given Devlin was exactly three short documents. The first was a grainy photocopy of a Phoenix Police Department incident report with a one-paragraph description of events written in block capital letters. Dated eight months ago—December 25, 1983—the report was rife with spelling and spacing errors throughout:

ON DECMBER 24, 1983, AT APPROXMITELY 23:55 HOURS I WAS DISPATCHED TO THE AREA OF CENTRAL AVENUE NORTH OF THOMAS ROAD NEAR EAST CATALINA DRIVE AFTER RECIEVING A CALL ADVISING THERE WAS A NON-RESPONSAVE PERSON IN THE STREET SOUTHBOUND #3 LANE. UPON ARRIVAL I CHECKED FOR A PULSE AND DID NOT FIND ANY SIGN OF LIFE. VICTIM WAS AN ASIAN MALE APPROXMITELY 50-YEARS-OLD. I RADIOED DISPATCH FOR A SECOND UNIT TO HELP SECURE THE SCENE AND ADVISED TO ALERT DETECTIVES TO A POSSIBLE SUSPISCOUS DEATH EITHER HIT AND RUN OR OTHER. ALSO ADVISED MAY BE MEDICAL ISSUE. WITH THE HELP OF OFFICER MILOVICH WE SECURED THE SCENE USING YELLOW TAPE. WE NOTED THE DECEASED WAS POSITONED ON THE WEST SIDE OF CENTRAL AVENUE IN THE #3 LANE IN A MANNER INDICATING HIT AND RUN BY SOUTHBOUND TRAFFIC. ORIENTED DIRECTLY IN FRONT OF "EZ PARKING" STRUCTURE. BODY POSITION DID NOT LOOK LIKE NATURAL FALL. NO VISIBLE SIGN OF INJURY SUCH AS A KNIFE PUNTURE OR GSW. NO SHELL CASINGS FOUND AT SCEANE. THE ROAD SURFACE WAS VERY WET AS THE AREA WAS UNDER CONTINUED STEADY RAINFALL FOR THE PRECEDING 7 HOURS. THE ROAD SURFACE WAS FREE OF ANY VISIBLE SKID MARKS OR INDICATIONS OF IMPACT WITH ANOTHER VEHILCE SUCH AS BROKEN GLASS OR PLASTIC. NO INDICATION OF ANY PAINT TRANSFR FLECKS ON ROAD SURFACE. AFTER DETECTIVES ARRIVED THEY INSTRUCTED US TO CANVAS A ONE-BLOCK PERIMETER FOR WITNESSES. WE WERE UNABLE TO LOCATE ANY WITNESSES. COUNTY ME ARRVED AT APPROXMITELY 0300 TO TRANSPORT THE DECEASED. I LEFT THE SCEANE AT APPROXMITELY 0310 TO RESUME REGULAR PATROL. THAT CONLUDED MY INVOLVEMENT WITH THIS CASE.

Interestingly, the scene described was only a few blocks east from Devlin's office. The next document was an autopsy report written by Devlin's genius pal Ford Rockwell, who had climbed to the top spot as director of the Maricopa County Office of the Medical Examiner. Not surprising. Devlin had hired Rockwell as an expert witness on a long list of cases, because the man was a rare combination of brains and beauty. On the brains side, Rockwell's academic credentials were prodigious: Dartmouth University for undergraduate, Harvard Medical School, and triple board-certified in pathology, dermo-pathology and neurology. Rockwell was a pathologist who could deftly unravel the medical vernacular on malpractice and wrongful death cases and, equally important, appeal to jurors. And that was the beauty part: Rockwell looked like a more angular Burt Reynolds from *Smokey and the Bandit,* right down to the thick moustache.

The name of the deceased was Ho-Chan Park, a 57-year-old man. Devlin skipped the introductory description of the corpse and the medical minutiae, and scanned down to the heart of any wrongful death case:

> **DESCRIPTION OF INJURIES SUMMARY:** *Multiple blunt force traumatic injuries with multiple fractures on LT side. LT coxa subdural hematoma approximately 6-inches x 5½-inches. Fracture to LT pelvis and LT femur with dislocation of LT hip joint. Fracture to LT femur. Subdural hematoma to LT scapula approximately 3-inches x 2½-inches. Subdural hematoma to LT glenoid approximately 2-inches x 2-inches. Numerous bone fragments from fractures penetrating the muscle tissue. Depths of penetration range from ½-inch to 1-inch.*

> **OPINION:** *Injuries appear to have resulted from a forceful blow administered to the LT lateral body at an approximate 90° angle.*

> **TIME OF DEATH:** *No witness statements. Body temperature, rigor and livor mortis and stomach contents approximate time of death 23:50 on 12/24/83.*

> **CAUSE OF DEATH:** *Blunt force bodily trauma.*

> **MANNER OF DEATH:** *Likely vehicular hit-and-run.*

The last document in the "file" was a single piece of lined paper ripped from a spiral notebook with hanging scraps and handwritten notes, presumably from the blue-ink pen of Goldie:

> -*Park signed in building log 08:01 and signed out 23:48. Going Home! His direction of travel determined: had to be walking north from office and then across Central west to parking garage.*

> -*Heavy rain/dark: didn't hear/see vehicle?*

> -*Blunt force trauma all to left side (northbound traffic) — hip, leg, shoulder. Body found west side of street in far-right lane near curb (southbound traffic). Why?*

> - *Clear hit and run. Probably drunk driver. Must find Defendant!*

Devlin would have to agree: if Ford Rockwell himself had assessed the injuries and determined the manner of death was not a heart attack or some other medical calamity, then those facts were straightforward. Devlin looked up at the TV, which was on low volume: a rerun of an old *Sanford and Son*. Devlin chuckled at his doppelgänger Lamont the dummy.

But this didn't really make sense, either, because Goldie operated solely in the rarified legal air of arcane appellate law. Why would he care about a random drunk-driver hit-and-run with no defendant? And if there was no defendant—i.e., no case—why would he even bother to refer it to a plaintiff's attorney? Perhaps it was nothing more than Goldie playing a game of "Watch the Dummy Chase His Tail."

Devlin got off the couch and walked to the sliding glass door in his blue Notre Dame shorts and white T-shirt, and stared into the midnight blackness of the golf course beyond his back wall. The August heat meant he'd be unable to open his sliding door, not even at night, until the firestorm finally relented in October.

There was something more here Devlin was not seeing, something that would compel Goldie to refer such a flimsy case. It also meant Goldie was testing Devlin to see if he could figure this out without Goldie having to lead the dummy by the hand. Devlin was always ready for a challenging case, and the bonus would be staying in Goldie's good graces at least until he advised him on the Bobby Swift filing. He grabbed a blank yellow legal pad, sat back down on the couch and sketched out a scene diagram using the police report and Goldie's notes. Then Devlin used his pen to re-trace Ho-Chan Park's movements on Christmas Eve 1983.

The guy walked north from his office building on the east side of the street and then crossed west across Central Avenue to the parking garage. Goldie was already making one assumption to determine the direction of the pedestrian's travel: that after putting in a sixteen-hour day (Devlin was impressed that this lunch-pail worker, whoever he was, hadn't even left the building to eat), the guy could have *only* been going north and then west to go home. Then again, there was the possibility he got to his car and realized he'd forgotten something—or decided to work some more (unlikely)—and attempted to return to the office. In that scenario he could have been hit on his left side in the southbound lane, which would match the injuries and position of the body when found by the police officer.

But if Ho-Chan Park's direction of travel was established, then Goldie's question was a good one: if the victim's injuries were all to his left side, why was the body found near the curb in the southbound lane? The laws of physics would only allow that someone struck in the northbound lane would remain there in that path of travel, not thirty feet *lateral* to the impact. Devlin had done so many vehicle collision cases that he knew the average lane width on city streets was ten feet, so the six traffic lanes on Central Avenue plus the center turn lane totaled roughly seventy feet curb-to-curb. Devlin looked up at the TV, laughed at one of Fred Sanford's witticisms and then made his own note, in black ink, on Goldie's spiral notebook page:

-Drunk driver northbound crossed center line and struck victim in southbound lane.

Case closed. Or at least that was the most obvious conclusion: a drunken Santa Claus case—with no Santa Claus—which is why the cops hadn't pursued it. But again, why would Goldie be so hot to find this defendant in a run-of-the-mill criminal matter? Tragic as it was, a drunk driver killing a pedestrian in the late hours of Christmas Eve was not exactly Goldie's domain of precedent-setting appellate law. Devlin wrote more notes:

-Who is / are Defendant(s)? Who is / are Plaintiff(s)?

With no apparent skid marks at the scene, the drunk driver never made any attempt to stop, swerve or avoid the victim. Then again, Devlin knew the unusually wet streets could've prevented any indications of a driver's attempts to stop. Regardless, the drunk driver had not stuck around to offer help or wait for police to arrive. Devlin knew he couldn't go back into The Bunker with more questions, so he'd need to bring in an expert. Despite a dearth of helpful facts, a good gumshoe could start digging around to see what they might piece together. With that thought, Devlin smiled and felt a warm pulse of energy through his body.

Fortunately, he knew just such an investigator.

Part II

The Investigation

Chapter Eleven

IN EARLY SEPTEMBER, A HEAT SCRIM of disorientating haze encased the entire city. Like some separate entity, the muggy desert heat cast a blinding afternoon glare marked by the loud machine-buzz of cicadas. That sound signaled a storm gathering off to the west, a desert-monsoon concoction that would soon push black thunderclouds and a towering wall of dust across the city. At Devlin & Associates on Third Avenue, withering trees lined both sides of the sidewalk leading to the double glass doors, casting wispy shade onto the sun-flamed concrete. A red fire-burst of delicate bougainvillea blooms framed the entrance to the brick building. Mercifully, Devlin was safely ensconced inside his air-conditioned hub.

After a month delay, he was finally seated with Darcie Savoy for her pre-trial settlement conference. Thankfully, Devlin had already prevailed at trial in both the Parker Seven and Coffee Cup cases: all eight defendants exonerated and reinstated to their jobs with only standard internal disciplinary marks on their records.

At the conference room table were the client and her mother. The doctor's insurance carrier representative was a rotund Hispanic man waiting in one of the empty offices, wondering why it had a fireplace. After a grinding half-day of back-

and-forth negotiations, Devlin was huddled in his office with his hired mediator, David Nash, a retired judge in his early 60s with his trademark white Abraham Lincoln beard—i.e., no moustache. Devlin had known him for years, and had originally met him when Nash was still on the bench. Devlin had come through his courtroom during the early days with Trevor Walsh. Nash immediately liked the kid's pluck, flair and style, and his clear respect for the rule of law. Once Nash retired, he became Devlin's go-to mediator and had now helped settle dozens of cases. Throughout those years the two had developed a deep fondness for each other that manifested in their ongoing banter of sharp and vulgar insults. Today, the most Nash had been able to wrangle out of the corporate suit was $15,000.

"That will barely cover her medical bills," Devlin said.

"Yeah, and with barely anything left over for you," Nash offered. "Once again demonstrating your crap abilities as a lawyer."

"Or your complete ineptitude at negotiating."

"Hey, you're paying me the two bills an hour either way."

"You really think there's no more juice to squeeze?"

"Not a single drop of blood left in this turnip."

Devlin pondered, knowing he'd be too embarrassed to tell his client that this was the best they could do. He wanted Darcie Savoy to be able to pay off her medical bills with enough left over to help her finish her college degree. She was studying to be a nurse, which Devlin admired given her wheelchair-bound reality.

"All right," Devlin said. "Tell them we agree to the settlement amount of fifteen, but tell that fat fuck I want to buy a $20,000 annuity for Darcie Savory to cover the cost of her college education. I want the extra twenty kept confidential and rolled in with their fifteen as the full settlement."

"You running a law practice, or a charity?"

"Today, both."

"You really want me to go back to him with that? Sure you don't want to sleep on it?"

Devlin rang Flores while staring at Nash: "Please bring in the checkbook."

"OK," Nash said, standing. "You are one bat-shit-crazy ambulance chaser."

Back across the hall, the insurance company representative carefully listened to Nash, leaned way back in his chair—to a precipitous fulcrum where Nash was certain he was going to topple backward—and eyed the old judge. The entire concept was still needling him: what kind of Phoenix law firm has a fireplace in every office? It was all very suspicious.

"Wait, he wants to write *me* a check?"

Judge Nash nodded. "You still pay out the fifteen, and he's ponying up twenty."

"He's putting in more than us? That... doesn't make any sense. A plaintiff's lawyer wants to write *me* a check?"

Judge Nash shrugged his shoulders; he thought Devlin was off his meds, too. "He has his own way of doing things. Whatever he has to do for his clients."

"But he won't make anything on the case. He's losing money."

"Right," the judge said. "Helluva way to run a law practice, eh?"

"Well, this would certainly be a first. What's the catch?"

"No catch," Judge Nash said. "He just wants to do the right thing."

"Bullshit," the defense lawyer said. "I don't believe you. I've never met a plaintiff's lawyer who wanted to do the right thing. I don't think it's possible."

"While it's not for me to decide, one might argue the same about corporate defense attorneys," Nash said.

"I just can't believe there's not a catch here somehow."

"A cynic," the retired judge said, "is a man who knows the price of everything, and the value of nothing."

"Vince Lombardi?"

"Oscar Wilde," Nash said.

The insurance representative asked, "Why are there fireplaces in every office?"

Nash shrugged his shoulders.

"He's going to give blood-sucking leeches a bad name."

Judge Nash nodded again. "Well, what can you do? And once again, he wants it to remain confidential. He doesn't want his client to know he's sweetening the pot."

"It still seems fishy. I'll need to make a call just to be sure."

"Sure. I'll leave you to it."

Although an odd request and one that had to be vetted by the insurance company's top brass simply out of principle, plus deep suspicion and galvanized distrust of Devlin's entire specialty— *A plaintiff's attorney wants to write us a check?*— the insurance carrier agreed to the unprecedented and clandestine terms. When Devlin walked back into the conference room he was able to tell Darcie Savoy and her mother the good news: she would receive $35,000, which would cover all her medical bills with enough left over to pay for her remaining college expenses. Devlin watched his client's eyes well up with tears. Then her mother started to tear up, too, neither of them able to speak. Devlin wiped at his own eyes, too. Darcie

CHAPTER ELEVEN

Savoy opened her arms and motioned from her wheelchair for a hug, and the lawyer huddled with the mother and daughter in an awkward embrace.

HIS name was Ho-Chan Park," Devlin said. "Cops found him dead in the road late on Christmas Eve."

"That's horrible," she said, chilled by both that news and the whirling ceiling fan. She pulled the sheet over her naked lower half. She glanced at Devlin: the man just had a certain air that made her pulse quicken. She and Devlin were each propped on a pillow, leaning against the headboard of the matching bedroom set Monae's parents had bought her as a college graduation gift. Her apartment was downtown, near Devlin's office, and her living room doubled as the office for her private investigation firm. The proximity to Devlin's firm greatly facilitated this rare midday meetup. Devlin was the first man she'd ever brought here to the inner sanctum of her career and new life in Phoenix.

"Drunk driver?" Monae asked.

"That's the case theory. You read the file. What do you think?"

"Not much of a file, right?"

"Exactly."

"Based on the drawing you sketched, injuries all to the left side of the victim and the position of the body in the southbound lane..." Monae drifted into thought and then offered, "It's very unlikely he was hit in the northbound lane. I've done a shit-ton of crash investigations; a body is not going to travel thirty or more feet lateral to the point of impact."

"My kind of girl."

"And what kind is that?"

"You put 'shit-ton' and 'lateral' into the same sentence," Devlin said.

"Yes, meaning this is strong circumstantial evidence that it was a hit-and-run by an inebriated northbound driver," she said.

"Unless our victim was going back to his office and got hit in the southbound lane. Then the impact would have been to his left side."

"No," she said, shaking her head.

"No?"

"Because no one goes into work at eight in the morning, stays in the building until almost midnight and then, five minutes later, decides to go back and do more

108

work. The only way he was walking was east-to-west, *toward* that parking garage."

"Maybe he forgot something," Devlin offered.

"Like what?"

"I don't know. A file he needed?"

"After working sixteen hours?" she asked. "Leave it for the morning. What about his car keys?"

Devlin shook his head. "I already checked. Inventory log included his keys."

"Well, then it seems pretty clear-cut, except you need a defendant, right?"

"There are no witnesses," Devlin said. "No one saw anything."

"There are always witnesses. You just have to find them."

Monae reached to the nightstand, grabbed the slim file folder and flipped to the autopsy report.

"OK, ME says approximate time of death 11:50 p.m." She grabbed the police report. "Cop on scene five minutes before midnight. But we know by the building sign-out log he didn't leave until 11:48 p.m. That leaves a body on Central Avenue for up to five or six minutes, and no one saw it?"

"It was late on Christmas Eve. Almost no traffic."

"Still. Someone saw something."

"It was pouring rain, too. It would be possible to drive by and not see anything in that downpour. Foggy windows. People freak out here when it rains."

"Maybe," she said.

"Even if someone did see something, no one called it in. No way we're finding these people."

"No way? Are you serious? You need to put a crack investigator on the case," she said, leaning in and breathing in Devlin's ear. "You need *Police Woman*."

"What I need is a defendant so I can tell Goldie who we're going to sue for wrongful death. Then I'll get my revised Rule 32 for Swift. Obviously I want to help this victim, but I can't work a phantom case, because we don't have a plaintiff, either. There's not a single relative listed in the follow-up report. No one to bring action. No beneficiary, no case."

"Like I said, you need *Police Woman*."

"Well, Hot Fuzz, can you go find me the Santa Claus *and* a relative of the victim?"

"Makes me wonder..."

"What?"

"If I'm 'Hot Fuzz,' who are you?"

NINE hours later, near midnight, Monae was squatting on the sidewalk in front of EZ Parking, staring across Central Avenue. She had been in that position for several minutes, just silently staring ahead like a catcher waiting for a curveball. Even at this hour, the steady heat transpiration from the cityscape was roiling the night into a 110-degree kiln. She ignored the heat waves pulsing off the concrete and stared as though in a trance. Knowing it would still be this hot, Monae could have donned her burnt-orange UT shorts and a T-shirt. However, she was old-school when it came to work attire, and right now, despite the late hour, she was working a case. She wore a billowy burnt-orange jumpsuit (always the color of her beloved alma mater) with a thick brown belt and matching brown heels. Devlin had wanted to tag along as her late-night protector, but Monae had declined the offer because she didn't need a man to protect her: three years patrolling the mean streets of Dallas had taught her how to handle herself. More importantly, having to explain her investigative processes and methodologies to the lawyer would only slow her down and interrupt her flow, such as now as she stared at the empty street, visualizing what had happened on Christmas Eve.

She carefully "watched" Ho-Chan Park leave the office building across the street, about twelve minutes before midnight, probably pausing as he stepped into the heavy downpour. She pictured him looking to the sky and thinking, *WTF?,* which was what everyone who lived in the greater Southwest did when it rained. Then he walked northbound, on the side of the street away from her. He was already looking across the street, this way, to the spot where she crouched in front of the garage where he had parked every day. Given the heavy rain, he was moving quickly. There wasn't much traffic just before midnight on Christmas Eve, almost none. But by now, a car traveling northbound had entered the scene. Monae made notes on a small pad as she played it out. *With no other vehicles, why didn't he see/hear car? Drunk driver didn't turn on headlights? And/or heavy rain.*

Ho-Chan Park started across the street toward Monae, hustling to get out of the downpour. Now he was across the center turn lane, more than halfway to safety. Monae almost felt compelled to yell out a warning: *look out!* The northbound car was drifting. *Maybe truck? Commercial vehicle best defendant for civil case.*

Ho-Chan was almost to the curb near Monae. Then the vehicle drifted all the way across and struck him on his left side, sending his body up, forward and then onto the pavement in a horribly unnatural clump just feet from where Monae crouched. Someone saw the body and called police. *Who? Find that witness. If no plate, check body shops for vehicle repairs to hood and front/left.* The cop arrived to find the deceased five minutes before it turned to Christmas morning.

Monae turned to her left and peered north, noting every building, storefront, restaurant and retail establishment on both sides of the street. She knew the cops had missed a boatload of potential witnesses if they had only tried that night, when everything was closed. *Canvass all.* She stood and stepped off the curb into the empty street, leaning over and peering at the hot asphalt. Turning back to EZ Parking and checking the diagram in the police report, she found the approximate spot where Ho-Chan Park had died. She looked closer. There was nothing visible to mark his final resting spot: no blood, no tire marks, no impact gouges. She squatted down again and surveyed the scene one last time from that level. Then, with cars approaching, Monae hustled back to the safety of the sidewalk and wiped her brow.

"Holy shit," she said, aloud, realizing now that she was sweating across her entire body, right through her orange jumpsuit. Even to an initiate accustomed to sultry college summers in Texas, the unrelenting desert heat had the power to generate shock from its sheer levels of intensity. Monae brushed aside the discomfort and continued her probe into the sticky night, walking north and writing down the street number atop every doorway. When she got to the first cross street, she stopped. *First exit point.* She looked to her left and then to her right, making another note: *Most people go right.* Women's intuition: this street was too small and too close to the crime scene. She continued clicking her way north on the sidewalk, a solitary hunter tracking prey, her senses heightened to the hunt. She decided the next three side streets were also too small and too close to the crime scene—just little feeders that would not provide a clear escape route for someone with a heart potentially blackened by guilt. As she approached a small homeless encampment of cardboard boxes, shopping carts and ratty blankets, Monae was immediately buoyed by the huddled collection of potential witnesses. Ten minutes later, however, Monae had only established that each of the eleven people was having difficulty with the concept of sequential time, that she was asking them to remember something that happened *last year* on Christmas Eve. A few challenged Monae that it was currently 1984, including one who asked her to prove it. One refused to speak to her until she showed her badge. Another came to Monae's defense, saying she was not required to show her badge because it was her First Amendment right. Then the others started arguing among themselves about what year it was and who was the president, with Jimmy Carter and Ronald Reagan garnering all but one vote. The lone holdout was a woman vehement in her conviction that the president was, in fact, that young man from "up north, probably Canada, Walter Mondale." Monae smiled sadly, dug in her Paloma Picasso, handed out all the cash she had and thanked them.

She continued moving north from East Lexington Avenue to a larger east-west artery, Osborn Road, two lanes in each direction. She paused like a bloodhound sniffing the air for the scent. She made a note that this would be the first viable escape route, and again: *Most people go right.* She peered east into the night and pondered. The street was quiet, without any visible places where witnesses may have congregated—the neighborhood watering holes, restaurants and nightclubs that might be open late on Christmas Eve. She also knew that straight ahead on this stretch, starting at Seventh Street, was the Phoenix Country Club golf course that bordered Osborn Road, a large tract of urban land rendered pitch-black and devoid of people on Christmas Eve. Still, she would have to walk this route just to be certain. She wiped her brow and persisted north, the lone pedestrian in a typical Western U.S. city ruled by wanton solo drivers guzzling buck-a-gallon gasoline. She passed a succession of small streets that fed east into Seventh Street and either dead-ended or jogged. *No good.* Then she got to the first major intersection, at Central Avenue and Indian School Road, and paused under the murky glow of streetlights. Then an intuitive blast hit her, and Monae was one hudred percent certain: whoever had hit Ho-Chan Park barreled north at a high speed, in an adrenaline rush, and then took this right turn onto a major thoroughfare to make their escape. During pursuits, fleeing suspects almost always went right, right, right. There was just something more unconsciously comforting about a quick right turn, rather than left across lanes of traffic. She turned onto what she believed to be the escape route, east along Indian School Road, walked slowly and repeated the process of writing down every address of every business where her witness might be lurking. Along with all the addresses she had written down from Central Avenue—and anything she would find on Osborn Road—it was going to be, in her vernacular, a shit-ton of places she would have to vet. Not to mention all the body shops in a sprawling city.

Along with that thought, she had to grudgingly admit that her original enthusiasm had already dimmed to disheartenment. Even on this night, which would be far busier than Christmas Eve, midtown Phoenix was a bone-dry ghost town: there was little to no traffic, and every address she jotted down was shuttered for the night, which meant no patrons who could witness a crime. Monae exhaled audibly and wiped the sweat from her forehead: she was standing square at the center of a far-flung desert metropolitan haystack, looking for a single needle.

Chapter Twelve

"GET ON THE KNEELERS."

"What?" Devlin asked.

"Get on the kneelers."

"Why?"

"We have to pray on it."

Devlin obliged the unorthodox request and, on an October Wednesday in the middle of the afternoon, slid forward to kneel behind the oddest of odd attorneys he'd ever encountered. The two lawyers were the only ones inside the Church of the Immaculate Conception of the Blessed Virgin Mary, better known locally as St. Mary's Basilica, at Third and Monroe Streets. It was the oldest Catholic parish in Phoenix, an adobe structure with a steeple-pitched, shingled roof, dedicated in 1881. Devlin never had any reason to consider such a revered spiritual site a suitable venue for a legal mediation.

Yet, 103 years after construction, Devlin was studying the back of the ratty-looking lawyer kneeling one row in front of him: disheveled hair, *orange* polyester suit jacket, brown polyester pants and scuffed white shoes. The guy's fashion sense, at least, aligned with his approach to the law: nutty as a fruitcake. He had insisted the only place he would meet Devlin was here, in church, in the middle of the week when they would have quiet, privacy and, as he had told Devlin, the comforting spiritual balm of resolution… whatever the fuck that was.

Devlin had agreed to the bizarre meeting place and then performed his due diligence. He was able to confirm that Tom Scarsdale, Esq., was a sole practitioner and a member of the Arizona Bar Association. Scarsdale represented the nubile playmate Westin Giannopoulos had been cavorting with nine ways to Sunday—who was now extorting the Greek.

Devlin exhaled audibly. Clearly this was not the sort of human entanglement Aristotle had envisioned when he wrote "It is more proper that law should govern than any one of the citizens." Devlin was here, duty-bound to uphold the rule of law lest it decay through insufficient corrective mechanisms. Even this sordid legal tale of two cheating doctors had a thin thread back to arguing against the divine right of kings and queens.

"Tom?" Devlin had said as he walked up behind the man who would immediately prove to be the kookiest lawyer he had ever met.

Scarsdale admonished with a loud, "Shhh!" And then he whispered, "Get in the pew behind me." And if that wasn't enough, now Scarsdale had ordered Devlin onto the kneelers, where his face was six inches from the back of the peculiar attorney.

"We'll be performing a miracle if we put this together," Scarsdale said.

Right, Devlin thought. There was feeding the five thousand, raising Lazarus and now this one: getting the wayward Greek to pony up to keep a hot-and-horny fellow practitioner from destroying his marriage and career through extortion. A true miracle! Then Devlin asked, "Why are you whispering?"

"Shhh. I don't want anyone to hear me."

Devlin looked around: no chance of that even if the guy had a megaphone and three sticks of dynamite. The place was barren.

Scarsdale whispered, "If your guy will pay her $250,000—"

"That's not going to happen," Devlin replied at a normal conversational volume.

"Shhh!"

"He doesn't have that kind of money."

"Shhh!" Scarsdale scolded again, like a befuddled parent with whining toddlers during Sunday mass. After a long silence, he whispered, "Let me repeat: $250,000."

Devlin thought of Monae and couldn't resist. He whispered, "That's a shit-ton of dough, my friend."

"Are you serious?" Scarsdale whispered, "In the sacred house of our Lord and Savior, Jesus Christ the Almighty?"

Devlin continued whispering: "Yeah, I'm serious; that's a lot of loot."

Scarsdale just shook his head.

"Look," Devlin whispered, "I can't go back to him with that amount." Devlin had wanted to say "my client," which he could not because elevating the Greek to "client" status would be to normalize what Devlin could not. Instead, this was a one-off attempt and reluctant favor for the doctor, a sordid dealing done off the books. "It's just not doable," Devlin said and then, tired of whispering, said, "Let me try half that, $125,000."

"Shhh!" The angry parent was losing any lingering patience. "Let me repeat: $250,000."

Devlin realized this weird negotiation, conducted on church kneelers with the fashion-misfit lawyer, was going nowhere.

"OK," Devlin whispered. "I'll take it to him and see what I can do."

"Keep in mind that's an easy price to keep his medical license and his marriage."

"Yeah, a real bargain for sure."

A week after the church-pew negotiation, Devlin was in his tailored suit in the venerable building where he had tried the big nursing home case, the Maricopa County Courthouse and Old Phoenix City Hall, which everyone just called the Old Courthouse. This historic structure on Jefferson Street consisted of two conjoined buildings. In the summer of 1927, a board of supervisors from Phoenix traveled to numerous states to evaluate the latest in new courthouses. Then they designed a new building borrowing the best of all they'd seen. The end result, in downtown Phoenix, was a two-story red brick structure that occupied an entire city block, at a total cost of $1.2 million. The first city and county employees moved in on June 23, 1929. As the size and stature of Phoenix expanded in the fifties, the growth eventually necessitated the building of a new city hall farther west on Washington Street, as well as an $11 million government complex completed in 1964. But Maricopa Superior Court still used the stately courthouse where the first trial of Ernesto Miranda had unfolded and eventually led to the landmark *Miranda v. Arizona* case taken up by the U.S. Supreme Court in 1966. Devlin regularly traversed these same halls as the echoes of Miranda warnings reverberated every minute of every day in all fifty states, a warning Sloane Monae herself had uttered hundreds of times to handcuffed people in her custody she wanted to question.

All noble legal precedent aside, Devlin was here on behalf of the drunk stripper he was representing. She had been driving down Mill Avenue in nearby Tempe, the Arizona State University college town landlocked by the urban sprawl of greater Phoenix, and hit another car driven by a pregnant woman. The drunk stripper panicked and drove off, elevating the charge against her to hit-and-run when the cops found her ten minutes later at her house, thanks to a witness who got the plate. And when they did, the blind-drunk stripper had blurted, "I hope I killed her and the baby." This was one of those civil cases that put Devlin on the opposite side, as her defense attorney representing her insurance company. He had only agreed to take the case because the injuries to the pregnant woman were minor bumps and bruises. And he saw a way to essentially put his own client on trial for her rank stupidity. Upfront, Devlin had offered the plaintiff's attorney on the other side $100,000, which was the policy limit and a big payday for minor injuries. Devlin was actually advocating for the plaintiff by making it a no-brainer: take the money and run. Instead, the plaintiff's lawyer was overplaying his hand by going to trial. For Devlin, it was tantamount to legal malpractice that the other side had turned down the offer.

Given the facts of the case, Devlin had never wanted to dignify his client or her case by allowing her in the courtroom, even sober. She was all bravado, mascara and hair spray, with a rocket body and a haughty air that the world owed her everything because she had a gritty sex appeal. Per his original case strategy, Devlin came into the courtroom alone, commanding the space with his typical confident gait.

"Where's your client?" asked the plaintiff's attorney, a guy about Devlin's age in an off-the-rack suit.

"She's not coming."

"What?" the attorney said, as though he'd just been told aliens had landed atop the courthouse. "What do you mean she's not coming?"

Devlin looked around for effect. "Just me."

"I want her on the stand. This isn't fair."

Devlin shook his head. "My dad used to tell me there's two kinds of fair: state and county."

"This is unacceptable," the flustered attorney said. "We need to take this up with the judge."

"Great; let's take it up with the judge."

Minutes later they were both seated in the judge's chambers, like two schoolboys before the principal. Devlin went first: "Your honor, we're admitting liability. I offered the plaintiff the policy limit of $100,000 upfront to avoid a trial altogether. This should never have gone to trial. Further, the plaintiff's attorney did not subpoena the defendant."

The judge, a woman in her fifties with her blonde hair pulled back into a precise ponytail, peered over her glasses at the plaintiff's attorney.

"With all due respect, your honor, we would like the opportunity to put the defendant on the stand."

"Did you subpoena her?"

"Well, no, ma'am."

The judge was already shaking her head. "Counselor, Mr. Devlin never made any representations that she'd be here. And you didn't subpoena her, so that's on you. We will proceed with selecting a jury and trying the case minus the defendant."

"But, your honor—"

"No sir," the judge said. "We are moving on to jury selection, and the defendant will not be in this courtroom. Period."

Devlin didn't gloat, because he'd been on that side many times. But he did smile at the notion of one of his dad's old-school witticisms.

State and county.

The trial was a half-day affair. Devlin stole any thunder the plaintiff might have planned by telling the jury he was admitting liability by the defendant, Devlin's client. Further, Devlin told the jury he would not insult them, nor the judge and opposing counsel, by even allowing his client into the courthouse since she had done and said despicable things. Her conduct was simply indefensible. Devlin took all the energy out of the case by essentially putting his own client on trial. Devlin admonished the jury that they should not open the floodgates to hundreds of thousands of dollars in a case he had offered to settle for $100,000. The jury agreed and awarded the plaintiff $15,000 with no punitive damages. Devlin did not celebrate because his original offer would have given the pregnant woman more than four times the jury award, which Devlin was thinking could have been earmarked as a future college fund for her impending arrival. As the two lawyers packed up their bags, the plaintiff's attorney said, "Well played, Mr. Devlin."

"I was trying to get your client as much as possible. You could have just settled for the hundred grand. Take the sure thing instead of going for the home run."

"Seriously? You going to lecture me now?"

"I offered you the policy limit," Devlin said. "Upfront. No strings attached. Look, I get it: when I'm on that side, I'm always dealing with insurance company defense attorneys who grind you. If these stiffs have authority to a hundred, they'll offer five or ten grand. Then we wrangle all day and settle at forty. What a noble pursuit they've undertaken to be chiseled on their headstone: 'Here lies an insurance company defense attorney who made it his life's work to withhold money from victims.' Not me. If you would have settled I would have gladly given you the hundred upfront, to help your client, and that would have been the end of it. No jury and no trial."

"It's not that simple," he said.

"It can be," Devlin offered.

"Bullshit," he said, shaking his head. "This case was worth more."

But it wasn't, Devlin thought. He also saw it wasn't worth debating. "All right. Believe what you want. But you don't always have to pole vault over mouse turds."

"I don't know what that means," he said, walking away.

Devlin smiled. *Rule #9: The side that makes the fewest mistakes wins.*

TWO weeks after the drunk stripper case had concluded, Devlin and Westin Giannopoulos were seated in Devlin's office. The Greek doctor had agreed to pay the quarter-million to keep a lid on his sack time with his supermodel fantasy. It was a move that took a big chomp out of his liquidity. In turn, the other good doctor had stopped all contact and signed an affidavit pledging confidentiality and silence on any and all matters that had transpired between the two parties. With one bizarre meeting held on church kneelers, Devlin had saved the Greek's medical license, career and standing with the medical board. Devlin decided the Greek was on his own as far as how he squared this all with his wife, including the absence of a quarter-million from the family ledger.

He'd instructed the doctor to deposit the $250,000 into a trust account, which Devlin then forwarded to the odd-duck attorney.

"What do I owe you?" the Greek asked.

Devlin shook his head: "Like I said, nothing. This one's on me."

"You saved my bacon," the doctor said. "I have to pay you something."

"Look," Devlin said, "it was one meeting. But if you insist, then just pay me what you think it's worth."

"That's a deal."

"And one more thing you have to promise," Devlin said.

"What's that?"

"Not another Uptown Girl. Ever. All right?"

The doctor smiled and nodded. "Agreed."

"Or Downtown Girl, for that matter," Devlin said, standing and shaking the doctor's hand. "The downtown ones are even worse."

As the Greek turned and left, Nadia Flores put a call through to Devlin. When he picked up the receiver and heard the voice, he could almost taste the cigar smoke, too.

"Jesus Christ, how long does it take Dummy to read a simple case file?" Goldie asked.

"Goldie," Devlin said. "I've been meaning to get back to you."

It was a stretch: Devlin had actually been stalling. It had been three months since he had passed into the smoky depths of Goldie's legal netherworld, The Bunker. Monae had been canvassing every business and storefront for weeks, along Osborn Road and now Indian School Road, without turning up anything. So, still no defendant. She'd been checking all the body shops, too. Nothing there, either. There was at least some progress on the case: Monae had tracked down every possibility only to confirm that, at age 57, Ho-Chan Park had been woefully alone in life. No wife, no children and no relatives living anywhere in the state. Just a guy whose sole purpose seemed to be working around the clock, which helped explain why the final day of his life had been a sixteen-hour grindhouse session without even a lunch break. However, Monae and Devlin had teamed up to track down—through the deceased's dental records and an off-the-record meeting with a police contact—the only living statutory beneficiary to any claim. Ho-Chan Park's mother, a slight Korean woman who spoke no English, lived near MacArthur Park in Los Angeles. Devlin, at least, now had a potential plaintiff. And with that, the case became more real. The foundation of Devlin's entire career was his sense of justice. Whenever someone had been wronged, it gnawed at him. That's how Devlin saw himself, as a disciple of justice trapped in a lawyer's body. Assuming they could find a defendant, Devlin would learn everything there was to know about Ho-Chan Park's mother, and he would be her voice in a world that might otherwise not care about her.

Devlin and Monae, too, had been to see Ford Rockwell—who still loved his grape Nehi—at the Maricopa County Office of the Medical Examiner. The Burt Reynolds double, however, couldn't offer anything new beyond what he had already stated in the autopsy report: Ho-Chan Park had died from blunt-force bodily trauma as the result of, Rockwell believed, a vehicular hit-and-run. Rockwell shared Devlin and Monae's drunk-driver case theory and also lamented their inability to produce any evidence about the driver. How many more businesses and body shops could Monae canvass before the lawyer and investigator had to admit they were holding a cold case, at a dead end?

"Anyway, that's not why I'm calling," Goldie said, audibly taking several sloppy puffs from his cigar. Devlin wanted to ask about the Rule 32 petition and whether Goldie had read it. But he was also playing a strategic game with Goldie, who was a rhinoceros at high tea and liked to see himself as in charge of everyone and everything. Of course, Goldie was a legal purist, a lawyer's lawyer with an enviable intellect. Because Devlin was Goldie's legal peer in a different way, Devlin knew it was important to Goldie's psyche to let him believe he held the reins. Goldie might have thought he was pushing Devlin around when, in fact, the younger lawyer was actually choreographing their play.

"What's up, Goldie?"

"I have another case for you," Goldie said, puffing away.

Another case? Devlin thought. That meant Goldie already believed he'd officially passed off Ho-Chan Park to Devlin and had no intention of taking it back. "My caseload—"

"Did I tell you to talk, Dummy? No. Shut up and listen."

Silence.

"Good, Dummy," Goldie said. "We'll call this piece of shit the 'Defective Manhole' case. And when I say 'piece of shit' I'm being overly generous. This case gives piece-of-shit cases a bad name. The only reason I'm referring it to anyone is that the client is an old family friend of my father's who, despite my blunt missives otherwise, believes he has a payday coming from the City of Phoenix, which he does not. As you will see."

"What do you want me to do?"

"I want you to take the case, humor the client, hold his hand and then kick him to the curb when you lose. Then I can at least tell my father we gave it a shot. Think you can do that, Dummy?"

Devlin thought about Bobby Swift cooling out in his six-by-nine. Maybe he should cut Goldie loose and just go with his Rule 32 petition as-is? Except Devlin was intrigued to hear Goldie's take, which might be worth taking this unwinnable case.

"You still there, Dummy?"

"Yeah, I can do that. Just give Nadia the contact information, and I'll get started on it."

As soon as Devlin hung up, his assistant buzzed.

"Yeah?"

"I have Sunshine holding. She'd like an update on their case."

"Hold on." Devlin had to dig around to find the CandyMan complaint because he couldn't remember when they had filed it: July. Seriously? It was now November; how had four months passed already? "Tell her I'll have to call her back."

Devlin was thinking about the Defective Manhole case when, less than thirty seconds later, Flores buzzed again. "I have Leander Farley from the state prison in Florence."

"Not today. Tell that jailhouse lawyer I'll have to call him back."

"Will do."

This was a typical day in Devlin's life as a trial lawyer: juggling too many balls, best described with the go-to maxim: *What...the...fuck.* Depending on volume and rate of speech, along with the respective emphasis, inflection and energy placed on each of the words, this phrase was critical and facile Buffalo parlance that every teenager had learned by high school to nuance in numerous different directions:

- Inquisitiveness (rising inflection on each word): *What the fuck?*
- Exclamation (spoken with levity in a sing-song): *What the fuck!*
- Resignation (flat intonation with shoulder shrug): *What. The fuck.*
- Excitement, joy, happiness (spoken rapidly in a single blurt): *Whatthefuck!*
- Anger (big emphasis and volume increase on second word): *What THE fuck.*
- Complete and utter shock: *What the...?*
- Disbelief (pause between each word): *What...the...fuck.*

Devlin had applied the last one to mark this day when Flores buzzed again: "I have an urgent call."

"What now?"

"It's Sloane Monae. She said to tell you she got a hit."

"No shit?"

"What does that mean?" she asked.

Devlin couldn't believe it himself: it meant Monae had found a witness.

Chapter Thirteen

OVER THE LAST TWO MONTHS, Sloane Monae had followed twin tracks in her investigation. First, she and Devlin visited every automotive business in greater Phoenix—almost fifty in all—where someone could get dents repaired, body work done and cars painted. She took most of them, but asked him to help with a dozen so they could get through them all more quickly. They didn't have a make or model of vehicle: they just asked if anyone had come in last December, after Christmas Eve, or in January. Devlin and Monae figured anyone wanting to hide the damage wouldn't wait any longer than that to get the vehicle repaired.

However, because they were asking about something that might have happened ten or eleven months ago, mostly what they got were blank stares. Monae alone got a second category of looks, machineheads and knuckle-draggers sizing her up like fresh prey. A few of the guys, at maybe ten of the auto body shops Monae visited, perhaps under the spell of her overall allure, were willing to go back and look at invoices for the two months in question. Those, too, didn't turn up anything. Monae and Devlin talked it out and decided that whoever had hit and killed the victim either didn't get the vehicle repaired—which could be further evidence if they could get a plate and see the still-damaged vehicle—or the suspect got the repair elsewhere in Arizona, out of state, or at some underground garage off the grid. This track had run dry.

The second track was one that Monae pursued all on her own, which was to methodically visit every retail business, office tower, restaurant, bar, alley nook, OTB hole-in-the-wall and storefront along Central Avenue, and then east on Osborn and Indian School roads. Through the searing heat of September, into October when the summer pulse of fire finally eased, and now into balmy November, her spiel had been unchanged: she was investigating a possible homicide, and had anyone seen anything late on the night of December 24, 1983? Anything suspicious at all might be helpful, such as a vehicle traveling northbound—possibly with a cracked windshield and body damage to the left front—on Central Avenue in the southbound lane, possibly with no headlights. Along the way, she had talked to building security officers, employees going in and out of high-rises, restaurant workers and managers, bartenders and patrons, sandwich shop owners, guys with black fingertips from changing tires all day, more homeless people, kids on bicycles, random pedestrians, teenagers smoking cigarettes in doorways, prostitutes and yellow-cab drivers. No one, it seemed, had even been in the area late on Christmas Eve. And the few who had been around had sought shelter from the downpour.

By the time she pulled open the door on a Walgreens store a country mile from Central Avenue, she had already admitted defeat. She had reached the limit of the perimeter she and Devlin had originally set: she couldn't spend any more time, or any more of Devlin's money, endlessly wandering the urban haystack. This would be her last stop before breaking the bad news to her boyfriend. And, really, she had come inside just to get a cold drink from the cooler, because even in November it was 82 degrees outside and she was thirsty. She grabbed a frosty bottle of lemonade, walked to the register and dug in her black handbag. She pulled her wallet, which was tucked beside the oily steel of the Detective Special revolver. Monae paid for the drink and asked if she could speak to the store manager. She'd decided that since she was already here, she might as well ask. The clerk called it out over the loudspeaker, and Monae waited a few minutes, drinking her cold lemonade.

"Help you?" said the manager, a soft-spoken man with tinted glasses and hair graying at the temples.

"I'm investigating a possible homicide, and was just wondering if you happened to be here last December 24, around midnight?" She took another swig and prepared to leave because, of course, he had not been here and had not seen anything. No one in this teeming city had seen fuck-all.

"Yes, I was," he said. "At 23:53."

Monae nearly spit lemonade on him. "Excuse me?"

"Yep. Like I said, Christmas Eve at 23:53."

"You remember the exact time?"

"Retired Air Force. Old habits die hard. I was military police. I've used the twenty-four-hour clock ever since. Just makes more sense, right?"

An ex-military cop! Are you kidding me? Monae set her bottle by the register, maintained her poker face and retrieved her small notepad and a pen. "And you're certain of the date?"

"Dead-nuts certain. My wife was none too happy I had to close Christmas Eve. But I'm the low man on the totem pole, assistant manager, so there you go. Air Force or retail: can't buck the chain of command."

"Tell me what you saw."

"Are you Phoenix PD?" he asked.

Shit. Don't shut me down. "I'm former PD, Dallas. Now I'm an investigator for a law firm here in Phoenix."

"Ahh, so I guess you can't show me a badge. Just so I know who I'm talking to."

"No badge, but the firm is Devlin & Associates, and we're trying to find out what happened here, for the mother of the deceased."

"Gotcha. That makes sense."

"Can you tell me what you saw?"

He paused briefly before saying, "Yes. Yes, I can. We closed that night at twenty-two hundred. Once I'd signed everyone out, counted the drawer, done the inventory and finished everything up, it was just before midnight. I turned out the lights and stepped outside to lock the front door. Another reason I remember this night was because it was pouring rain. Rare here, right?"

Monae nodded. *Yeah, about as rare as an ex-military-cop-turned-witness who was reciting a time-stamped account of his actions the night of the crime.* She was ready to burst, but played it like she was holding a pair of twos.

"I locked the door, double-checked it and then turned to go to my car. That's when I heard a loud sound coming from the west, right there on Indian School. When I looked up I saw a car with its wheels locked up, sliding toward the stoplight out front, which was odd since there was no other traffic. The car was able to stop at the light. The sound of the skid was different because of the wet street. That's why I didn't realize what it was at first. The sound, I mean."

"Do you know what kind of car it was?"

"It was an orange Trans Am. The one with the bird on the hood."

"How can you be so sure?"

'Smokey and the Bandit.'

"Excuse me?"

"The movie? Loved that movie. Jackie Gleason… just great."

"So, what about the car?"

"It was the exact same car Bandit drove, except orange."

Monae pondered this information: certainly the gearhead demographic she and Devlin had visited at all the auto body shops would remember a glaring orange Trans Am with major front-end damage including a likely busted windshield—an American muscle car the boys would all celebrate returning to its full glory as the ultimate babe magnet. She and Devlin had decided that whomever had committed the crime was smart enough to get the car repaired way below the radar or, perhaps, dump it altogether. The driver could also have been someone from out of state who drove home. "What else?"

"While I was watching the car sit at the stoplight, the headlights clicked on."

"So, it had been driving with no headlights?"

"Correct."

"Did you see the driver?"

"Nah, not with the rain. Windows were fogged. But that's when I glanced at my watch: 23:53."

God bless this man. The timeline fit perfectly: the cop was dispatched to the scene two minutes later. Monae's mind was racing as she played it back. The suspect had been driving fast and, in the adrenaline rush, sped north on Central Avenue, turned right at Indian School Road and then realized they needed to dial it down and obey all traffic laws, like stopping at the red light, which sent the car into a skid on the wet street. Then, sitting there, they realized the headlights were off and clicked them on. Monae had no doubt: this was their mystery driver, the needle in the neon-jungle haystack.

"Did you happen to notice the condition of the car?"

"Condition?"

"Anything about the car you noticed?"

"Well, nothing specific."

"No body damage? Cracked windshield?"

"To tell you the truth, the street light right there had been out for a while. So once it stopped, the car was in the shadows. Plus the rain, you know?"

"But you're still certain on the make and model?"

"Oh, hell yes. No doubt there. I could I.D. that body shape anywhere."

Except it was all worthless until she asked the million-dollar question and got the answer she needed. She was afraid to go there. She took a deep breath and the last swig of lemonade to kill a few more seconds.

"You didn't, by chance, get the plate?"

"Because all this struck me as suspicious, I actually walked toward the street in that downpour with that in mind, that I should see what this was all about. Cop's curiosity; you know what I'm saying. It all happened pretty quick. Then the light turned green, and the car drove away at a normal speed."

"So...," Monae said, waiting.

"So, what?"

"The plate? By chance?" She cringed.

He shook his head, a sudden grave look weighing down his face. "I'm sorry. It was really hard to see that night. Like four inches in parts, I read."

Monae slumped. Of course it had all been too good to be true. She had come so close. She knew the make and model, so maybe she could look into that. Except a gust had swept in, picked up the precious needle and sent it swirling back into a smaller haystack of orange Trans Ams.

"Well, thank you," she said, turning to leave.

"Awww, come on," he said, grinning widely. "You're killing me with that face."

"Excuse me?"

"I'm just goofing around. I got it."

"You got what?"

"The plate."

What was he saying?

"Sorry," he said. "That was stupid of me. You looked like you were going to be sick."

"You got the plate?" Why would he do that to a woman who had been wandering the city streets, alone, through hellfire and beyond?

"Wait here. I even wrote it down. Let me go find it."

WITH the license plate number in hand, Monae needed to go see Sir Larry. On a previous case, Monae had needed someone who could tell her the registered owner of a vehicle. She knew a few cops who could do it if she asked, but they ran a risk:

the police were not authorized to randomly run license plates for civilians, and especially without any reasonable suspicion or probable cause. She'd asked around, made some calls and tried developing several different contacts that didn't pan out. Finally, she'd landed on an MVD office with someone who was willing to help her for a few extra bucks under the table. Lawrence Granger was discreet, low-drama and reliable. From the outset he also had a crush on Monae, but that was a minor complication, an occurrence she had been navigating her entire adult life.

"I'm Sloane," she had said when they first met.

"Larry Granger."

"I like 'Lawrence,' better" she said. "It makes you sound... regal."

"Yeah, I'm the viscount of perfidy."

"I like that, too," she said. "Sir Larry it is."

On this immediate mission, she sped east toward the Motor Vehicle Department on Van Buren Street, the notorious go-to strip for all illicit needs: drugs, untraceable ghost guns and prostitutes. Even today, under the harsh midday glare, Monae passed women wearing stiletto heels and impossibly short skirts, leaning into vehicles to negotiate. She parked behind the MVD, by a long block wall tagged with graffiti and topped with razor wire, rolled up the window and climbed out. She eyed her reflection in the car glass. She was wearing her power suit, which was a red blazer with thick shoulder pads over a white silk blouse, with a wide black belt, loose-fitting dark grey pants that flared at the bottom, and black pumps. She undid two more buttons on her blouse to reveal her black bra from certain angles.

Inside the government building, Monae pulled a numbered tab and stood until she made eye contact with her guy, who looked like an unshaven and overweight version of Steve Guttenberg, the lead from *Police Academy*. He nodded at her almost imperceptibly. Then she retraced her steps back to her car, where she reached inside her purse and grabbed a single bill. She stood waiting for a few minutes under the hard beams of sunlight. A gray metal door opened at the back of the building, and chubby Steve Guttenberg ambled over.

"Sloane."

"Sir Larry."

He snickered and took out a yellow-and-white pack of Kent III cigarettes: *When you know what counts.* He offered her one, which she declined, and tapped out his own. He lit up, snapped his silver metal lighter shut and took a deep pull. "In a parallel universe you'd be the viscountess on my arm. At the grand ball or some shit, right?"

She smiled and touched his arm, certain he was getting a good look. "You're a sweet guy."

"That's the problem."

"Problem?"

"Yeah, apparently I need to be a superficial jerk to get a girl like you. And rich, of course. A rich jerk. Or at least have an ass like George Michael. My ass is bigger than his and Andrew Ridgeley's combined." He took another pull, reflecting on the life that might have been, if only he'd been someone else. "I now realize that knowing and stating who comprises Wham! is strong evidence against me. So there you go."

Monae handed him a slip of paper with the license plate number of the orange Trans Am. He took a puff and squinted through his own blown smoke. "What'd this one do?"

"I need to know who owns it."

"Can do. You know it's my wannabe Wham! ass if I get caught."

"I know. That's why I appreciate you." She pressed the $100 bill into his palm and let her hand linger. He squeezed her hand gently. Even in that brief touch she could sense the voracious longing for female contact.

"Any chance we could do trade this time instead? Just dinner? Nothing funny. Promise."

She smiled and then slowly pulled her hand away. "You know I can't. My boyfriend wouldn't like that."

"Boyfriend, duh." He nodded, taking another pull, resigned to his station in the human hierarchy of DNA, net worth and general downward trajectory. Doing favors for Sloane Monae, at the risk of being fired, and ogling her black bra was as close as he was ever going to get to someone like her. "Well, my lady, my court awaits," he said, bowing.

"How long?"

"Tomorrow. Not going to tell me what he did?"

"It's not really important."

With that Sir Larry stubbed his cigarette on the ground and walked back toward the building. Without looking back, he said, "You take care, Sloane."

The next day, Monae returned and repeated the process for the meet-up. When Sir Larry came out the door and lumbered over he was already lighting up his Kent III and snapping the lighter shut. He handed Monae a sheet of paper folded in half. She unfolded it and read aloud: "Nineteen eighty Pontiac Firebird Trans Am Coupe

400. Registered to——" She looked up. "What's this?"

"Fleet registration account. I checked: there's twelve vehicles under the same account."

"So there's no way to know who was driving?"

"Unfortunately, no. Sometimes they'll add a fleet manager's name, but that still doesn't help you much. Archard Holdings must be up to no good. What'd they do?"

Monae shook her head and tamped down her disappointment. "General villainy."

"Sounds mysterious," Sir Larry said, kicking a rock with a scuffed brown wingtip that had never been polished. "We going on that dinner date now?"

Monae didn't really hear him as she passed him another $100 bill. She'd managed to find the single vehicle, in a city of millions, that she believed had hit Ho-Chan Park. And now she'd reduced the potential pool of drivers to those employed by this company called Archard Holdings. All of which felt like progress and defeat simultaneously, because she still couldn't tell Devlin who, specifically, was driving the car on Christmas Eve.

Chapter Fourteen

"THIS IS FOR YOU."

Westin Giannopoulos dropped a small, ratty gym bag on Devlin's desk and stood there smiling. The Greek doctor had showed up at Devlin & Associates, unannounced, a month after he'd ponied up the quarter-million to save his bacon.

"What's this?" Devlin asked, eyeing the bag suspiciously.

"Christmas present," the doctor said.

"I said you don't owe me anything."

"Actually, you said to pay you what I think it's worth."

"So I save your career and get this piece-of-shit gym bag?" Devlin said, smiling.

"I'm forever indebted."

"Well, you want me to open it now, or later?"

"Later. I just wanted to thank you again in person."

Devlin stood and shook his hand. "Keeping your powder dry like you promised?"

"Dry as the day a rummy goes on the wagon."

"Good man."

The doctor smiled, turned and left. Devlin sat and started to pull the zipper on the gym bag, when Nadia Flores buzzed: "I have Maria Ramirez from the City of Phoenix."

Shit, Devlin thought. The Defective Manhole case. He had gone to meet her the day before Thanksgiving, and now it was December. He had been struck by both her legal savvy and brusque confidence. She was a Yale Law School graduate and now a rising star with the City of Phoenix. Devlin knew what was coming next. He set the gym bag aside and told Flores he'd take the call. During the requisite pleasantries, Devlin ran a finger over his shirt's custom monogram a couple inches above the belt line on his left side, which is where he had his tailor stitch it because no one else put a monogram there.

Maria Ramirez laid it out for Devlin: "There will be no settlement discussions in this case, because you have no case."

Devlin, like Goldie, would have to agree one hundred percent. "No case? I'm offended."

"This is clearly the kind of case that gives your profession a bad name and should never be brought before any U.S. court."

Again, Devlin agreed one hundred percent. He could only offer flimsy statements of fact: "His injuries are real, counselor." Devlin had been able to corroborate that part of the story with medical records and insurance paperwork.

"Let's see what the jury has to say," she said.

"Are you sure that's the path—"

"This discussion is terminated," she said. "I'll see you at trial. Good day, Mr. Devlin."

Devlin hung up. This dog-shit case involved an allegedly askew manhole cover wherein Devlin's new client supposedly got his foot tangled in the gap between the metal disc and the steel ring, fell at an odd angle, and on the way to the ground blew out a ligament and tendon. However he actually sustained the injury, it required an expensive surgery and a full leg cast for months, and ultimately the man lost his job as a delivery truck driver given that he couldn't make his route without his right leg to work the pedals. The liability aspect was easily dismissed because there was no evidence—no photographs, no corroborating witnesses, no documents—to establish that the manhole cover was ever, in fact, ajar and that the City of Phoenix, therefore, had caused the injury. Maria Ramirez, rightly so, told Devlin that this man could have fallen down in his backyard and simply made up the story about the manhole cover. Again, Devlin agreed with his opponent: the man had somehow injured his knee, but there was zero causation linking the City of Phoenix to those injuries. Devlin wondered, too, if this guy had concocted the manhole scheme as a potential payday.

Further, unrelated to anything legal, the guy had questionable jury appeal through no fault of his own. He had thick black hair that spiraled out from his shirt collar in a 360-degree growth, forming a dark, organic turtleneck. Similarly, the growth of his beard extended up his cheeks to just below his eyes, as though he were peering out from behind some sort of dark-hair camouflage. Beneath the hair on the man's face and body were large boils, which created a frightening countenance of hairy lumps. He looked like a mutant G.I. Joe. The pants and shirt he wore to meet Devlin looked one size too small, which only accentuated the lumpy landscape of his skin. Further, the man carried a perpetual grimace of irritation at every question Devlin asked. The overall effect was that he was off-putting without intending to be. For all his legal talent, even Devlin couldn't find a suitable light to shine on this guy. And now he had to go to trial and represent him in open court.

When Devlin realized he was late for a meeting, he jumped up and left without looking in the gym bag. Later, while tidying up, Nadia Flores peeked inside, thinking her boss had left sweaty basketball clothes that would soon be rancid. When she saw the bundled cash, her curiosity demanded that she count it. Surprised by the amount, she zipped the bag, carefully hid it in the credenza behind Devlin's desk for safekeeping and, out of discretion, never mentioned to her boss that she'd even seen the bag, let alone nosed around inside. Out of sight, out of mind: in the swirl of his chaotic caseload, Devlin still hadn't checked the mystery bag.

"IT was an orange Pontiac Firebird Trans Am that hit our victim," Sloane Monae said, slurping up a Pad Thai noodle amid the loud chatter of the lunchtime crowd at their new favorite downtown haunt, Ong Lek Thai Kitchen. They always shared the Tom Kha Gai soup and one plate of Chicken Pad Thai, and each had iced tea.

"And you know this how?" Devlin asked.

"I told you: I found a witness."

"Right. The Walgreens manager."

"Assistant manager. It's registered to a company called Archard Holdings."

"But no driver?"

Monae shook her head. "Fleet registration."

"Interesting," Devlin said. "What do we know about the company?"

"I haven't had a chance to look into that yet."

"If we put ourselves on the defense side, the first issue is causation: did this purported witness actually see the vehicle strike the victim? Plus, how many people have access to a company vehicle? Maybe dozens."

Monae slurped another spicy noodle. "We know it was that vehicle."

"We know?"

"I know. *You* know."

"We know what we can prove. We need a witness who actually saw the crime. Your guy saw a car sliding around on a wet street *after* the crime. There are more crap drivers in Phoenix than Carter had liver pills. Can your witness put someone behind the wheel?"

Sloane Monae silently took a drink of her iced tea.

"What we have is a drunk driver on Christmas Eve, perhaps dressed in a red-and-white suit. If the car's connected to this company, that's what their lawyers will say. Disavow any knowledge or involvement."

"We need the driver," she said.

"Yeah, because I don't care if our mystery Santa was selling cocaine to his elves and pimping out the little women: we can't put him at the scene."

She laughed. "That's... twisted."

Devlin smiled. "The nadir of decency: pimping out elves."

"Look," she said. "I'll find a connecting link. Whoever was driving that car did the hit-and-run. Guaranteed."

"I'm not disagreeing with you. My career is fighting for David, but I need a Goliath."

"Oh, ye of so little faith. Just give me a little more time to see what I can find. Are you going to reach out to Park's mother?"

"I want to. I want to know everything about her. But I also don't want to build false hope if we don't have a case. She's already lost her son. If I can't amend that pain then I'm worthless to her. I need a case first."

"All right. Just leave that to me."

Chapter Fifteen

THE JURY WAS OUT FOR LESS THAN TEN MINUTES before returning a verdict for the defense. As predicted by Goldie and Devlin, the Defective Manhole case was unwinnable. On paper it was a loss, but Devlin had represented his client to the best of his ability and done Goldie a solid on one of his two referral cases. Regarding the other, as 1984 turned to 1985 and a welcome January chill settled across the valley, Devlin was frustrated at not being able to do anything yet with the Ho-Chan Park "case." It had been six months since Devlin had gone to Goldie for feedback on his Rule 32 petition, and as much as he valued Goldie's rarefied assessment, he was wondering if the legend's stamp of approval was worth the delay. Devlin's client, after all, was sitting in prison. And while Monae had already proved herself exceedingly capable as an investigator, she had not been able to make a court-ready evidentiary connection between the orange Trans Am, the crime scene and the victim. Devlin pondered all this while seated behind his desk at Devlin & Associates. As he reached up to buzz Nadia Flores to ask her to call Goldie, she beat him to the punch: "Connor, I have a call for you."

"Who is it?"

"She won't say. But she said you'll want to take her call."

"Put her through."

After a short pause, Devlin heard a voice he didn't recognize, along with a lot of background traffic noise. "I know about the case you're researching."

"Which case? Who is this?"

"There's more to it than you think."

"More to what?" Devlin asked.

"Ho-Chan Park."

That got Devlin's attention: How could anyone know about that? "Who is this?"

"Follow the crumbs: you need to look into what Ho-Chan Park was investigating."

"Investigating?" Then Devlin remembered. "Was it Archard Holdings?" No response. "Hello?"

"Follow those crumbs." The line went to a dial tone. What an odd exchange, Devlin thought. As soon as Devlin hung up, Flores buzzed through again: "Connor, I have your mother holding."

"Put her through."

Devlin's mother was Jewish. Her father had been an orphan raised by nuns. Devlin had forgotten most of the Yiddish phrases he'd heard growing up, as he and his two sisters primarily followed their Irish patriarch's Catholic spiritual beacon.

But Devlin did remember his grandfather saying that anyone who could clear their throat could speak Yiddish. There was a slight pause before Flores said, "She's calling about your father. It's not good."

THE second Connor J. Devlin, the lawyer's father, was a hard-driving, first-generation American who had played professional football for the Canton Bulldogs in the 1920s. As a boy, Devlin's dad had climbed onto a boat with his parents and left Ireland for America. He only ever got through eighth grade, but brought an iron-will work ethic he would one day imprint on his only son. Through his unrelenting zeal, the senior Devlin had found early success running illegal hooch with Joe Kennedy. Then he married a Jewish woman, making Devlin officially Catholic and unofficially Jewish. Devlin's old man eventually went legit with a profitable chain of grocery stores across the Northeast. Devlin grew up bonding with his father at Buffalo Bisons minor-league baseball games during the summer. On their way to Offermann Stadium, they'd walk past Freddie's Doughnuts on Main Street. The namesake proprietor was Frederick Maier, an immigrant from Ukraine via Canada in 1913, who churned out the warm doughnuts and their sweet aroma that became a fixture in Devlin's boyhood.

For grammar school, at his father's insistence the younger Devlin had attended the private Mount Saint Joseph Academy, which was run by an order of French nuns. The nuns lived on the upper floors of the four-story building and taught on the first floor. Speaking to a room of first-graders, each in a coat and tie, the nuns conveyed a loving acceptance and a nurturing attitude toward learning, along with a firm sense of quiet discipline that was never heavy-handed. Devlin, along with all the other boys, had to learn the Catholic mass in Latin.

If the senior Devlin was a success in business, he was also beyond comparison in his dedication to helping others. It was the former, the well-moneyed reputation, that made Connor Devlin a constant target of his classmates at his next school, St. Joseph's Collegiate Institute. The whispers— *Here comes little Paddy Devlin with his money-bags old man*— would eventually devolve into verbal jabs and relentless taunts. Further, Devlin's low entrance exam score immediately relegated him to Room 103, more aptly known as "The Zoo." If anything, Devlin actually had an uncanny ability to rise up on test days, as he would later demonstrate spectacularly during the two biggest sit-downs of his life, the LSAT and the bar exam. This early poor showing was an outlier, and one undergirded by disinterest and distraction rather than any lack of faculty.

From the truly stupid to the undeniably brilliant, "The Zoo" was an oddball collection of misfits, dim bulbs and boys who needed Ritalin long before anyone had ever heard of attention deficit-hyperactive disorder. Tommy Weston did nothing but sleep all day, and earned the apropos nickname "The Sloth." Billy Fowler, brilliant but bored, learned to throw his voice and would have two-sided conversations with flies buzzing outside the window. Vito Puccini, whose father owned a flower shop, was already shaving in grammar school, and went home after final bell each day with a five-o'clock shadow. He also couldn't figure out how to use a telephone, so the boys called him "Einstein." Vito was always muttering *minga*, a Sicilian slang word for penis that Vito used to describe both good and bad emotions—"*Minga*, that's a good looking girl," and "*Minga*, I hit my thumb with a hammer"—as well as to denigrate ("You are such a lousy *minga*") and compliment ("*Minga*, you done good, *minga*.")

More than half this crew would fail out that first year. By his sophomore year Devlin had survived the attrition rate with the highest GPA in "The Zoo," and graduated across the hall to the "Brain Room."

To his credit, Devlin made no apologies for who he was, which was inextricably linked to who his father was in Buffalo. Rather than shrinking from the spotlight cast by his father's success and charitable efforts, he faced it head-on and wore his heritage proudly as he progressed through high school. Instead of making a low-profile entrance each day, Devlin drove to school in a sparkling new 1959 Cadillac convertible, a gleaming symbol that only raised the ire of jealous classmates. Without him realizing it at the time, that inner anger at being disliked would be the perfect seed to Devlin's eventual gladiator passion and drive in the courtroom.

FROM his airplane seat, Devlin peered back through time to the blanket of snow covering his hometown of Buffalo. He was immediately suffused with that old sense of camaraderie he'd always felt growing up. Devlin came of age, along with his two older sisters, during the Eisenhower post-war years, an era of boundless opportunity as America flourished in the fifties. Buffalo itself was an everyman, ethnic, blue-collar, bar-stool community with a Catholic church every half mile. Entrenching itself in hardened realms, the heart of Buffalo's economy had been anchored by Bethlehem Steel and automobile manufacturing, with both General Motors and Ford churning out two-ton highway barges. As a Great Lakes port city, Buffalo's grain industry did a brisk trade as well. Although Buffalo's halcyon days had come and gone with the Pan-American Exposition, a World's Fair, in 1901—where an assassin's bullet felled President McKinley— the city's core was ethnically diverse and middle-class. There was the Polish neighborhood on the east side, the Irish on the south side, and the Italians to the west. There was a modest Black population and, throughout, a sprinkling of Germans and Eastern European nationalities. But most, regardless of creed, color or religion, were in the same economic boat—and that meant the men carried lunch pails and the women did everything else.

In 1959, when Devlin was 14, his gentle giant of a father cemented himself in Buffalo lore by being instrumental in bringing Ralph Wilson's professional football team to the city as the American Football League's (AFL) seventh franchise. Wilson named the team after the original Buffalo Bill, the colorful figure of the 1880s American Old West.

After graduating from law school in 1970, Devlin had wanted to return to Buffalo to begin his career under his patriarch's sprawling legacy in that community. This was just one year after the Bills had taken O.J. Simpson with the first pick in the 1969 AFL-NFL draft after finishing 1-12-1 in 1968. However, instead of welcoming his son back to his hometown, the senior Devlin told the 25-year-old lawyer that if he came back to Buffalo, he would always be known as the second Connor J. Devlin's son. His father told him to stay in the Sun Belt instead, where he could make his own name.

As Devlin launched his legal career in Phoenix in 1970, his father became the de facto leader of the Democratic Catholic community and the sports coordinator for the City of Buffalo. That position and his spot on the city council were the perfect platform from which the senior Devlin, who stood six feet, three inches and weighed 250 pounds, dedicated himself to community causes.

Your work is to serve. Service is your work.

When Devlin went back to Buffalo each year for Christmas, there were family dinners with Buffalo Bills luminaries. Likewise, throughout the seventies the senior Devlin would visit Arizona every winter after the football season ended and stay at the Arizona Biltmore with close friend George "Papa Bear" Halas, owner of the Chicago Bears, and other NFL royalty including Art Rooney, owner of the Pittsburgh Steelers, and Art Modell, owner of the Cleveland Browns.

The plane touching frozen asphalt jolted Devlin from his reverie as the reverse thrust of the engines roared.

"WHAT the hell are you doing here?"

The younger Devlin smiled; despite being laid up in a hospital bed, his dad hadn't lost his work-boots grit.

"I'm fine," his dad said, shaking his head.

"I know, Dad," Devlin said. "I just came because I know how beautiful Buffalo is this time of year. Who doesn't love seven feet of snow?"

The son knew his father was not fine, because he had been diagnosed with lung cancer. And the prognosis was not good. As soon as he'd talked to his mother, Devlin had called Sloane Monae to tell her he needed to leave immediately for Buffalo. There was an awkward tension on the call, because Devlin wanted to invite her along to meet his family for the first time, but it didn't feel right under this dark cloud of uncertainty.

The next day Devlin drove his father to his first chemotherapy treatment, in his 1976 brown Cadillac Fleetwood Brougham replete with a brown vinyl top. Being back in Buffalo in February reminded Devlin how much it snowed there. Six inches of snow in Buffalo was a light dusting; a foot or more was standard fare. Although it hadn't snowed for days, there were mountainous piles of accumulated snow.

During the chemo treatment, a nurse mentioned that some of the patients drank Coca-Cola, which seemed to lessen the severity of the pain. Or maybe it was a placebo, a sugary distraction that took people's minds off the process. After she left Devlin's father said, "I might try that. I've never had one."

"What are you talking about?"

"I've never had one."

"You've never had a Coke?"

Devlin was stunned and amused by this odd revelation of fact, that his silver-haired 80-year-old father had somehow grown up in the golden age of advertising in America without once trying Coca-Cola. There were probably isolated tribespeople in the Amazon rainforest who had tasted Coca-Cola. But Devlin himself had never tasted it until he went to Notre Dame, because his mother had banned soda from the household.

"I'll be right back," Devlin said, getting up and wandering away to look for a vending machine. Minutes later he returned with two mildly cold cans of Coke and depressed the Sta-Tabs on both. Everywhere he looked, Devlin saw the machinations of law. This new can design, which used a connected flange of aluminum on the lid as a lever to press down the sealed opening, eliminated the ring-tab design phased out in 1975. Just before he got the big nursing home case, Devlin had looked into representing a client whose kid had suffered throat injuries when she swallowed one of the metal ring-tabs from a soda can.

The senior Devlin studied the bright-red can and then took a drink. Then he nodded and said, "This stuff is pretty good."

Devlin rarely drank soda, but he savored this one as he tried to hold his emotions in check. The doctor had said three to six months, tops. Devlin knew that even though his dad would defy that estimate by at least double, that meant at best they were in the final year of a life well-lived. His dad was a throwback, the man who was your father, not your pal. He was a giant in his son's life, and in the lives of an entire community. Devlin would be losing his most reliable advisor. In his mind he could see the family plot here in Buffalo, piled high under snow right now, where they would lay his father to rest. Devlin took a drink of Coke.

"What else haven't you done, Dad?"

"What?"

"You've never had a Coke until today. What else do we need to cross off the list?"

"Ah, hell. I'm not dying. Stop it."

"I'm serious. What else?"

"Well…" He pondered for a moment. "I've never had a fast-food hamburger."

Again, Devlin was floored and started laughing. "You're kidding me, right?" Devlin never swore in front of his father, not even as an adult, or it would have been stronger: *You're fucking kidding me!*

"No, I'm serious. Never."

"You've never had a McDonald's hamburger?"

"Nope. Or at Insta-Burger King either."

"You mean 'Burger King'?"

"No, that's what I still call it. When it first started, that was the name."

Devlin just laughed again: his father never failed to surprise. And if he'd never eaten a fast-food burger, how did he know such an arcane backstory on the lineage of Burger King?

A day later, Devlin piled his father, mother and both sisters into the brown Cadillac Fleetwood and drove the snow-packed streets to the drive-through at McDonald's. Mom sat up front; Dad sat in the backseat between his two daughters and was straining to look at the menu board when Devlin started to order.

"Who the hell is Connor talking to?" his dad asked.

"He's talking to the Hamburglar," Kate said, smiling.

"Who?"

"Dad, there's a speaker inside the menu," Carol said.

"Dad?!" Devlin said. "What do you want?"

"I want a hamburger," he said.

"OK," Devlin said.

"No, wait," his dad said. "I'd like it on a toasted bun, medium rare, with some pickles."

"What?" the voice emanating from the menu asked.

Devlin shook his head. "Just give me a hamburger."

Devlin paid at the window and pulled away with the bag in hand. He drove on and passed the food to the back seat, turning to go back home. He could hear the paper rustling as his dad unwrapped his first fast-food hamburger.

"What in the hell did you order me?" his dad yelled. "This has mustard, ketchup, mayo, tomato. I said 'pickles.' What in the hell?"

All three kids and their mother Claire were laughing.

"This bun's all smashed," Dad said, the old Irish bootlegger who'd met Claire at her father's speakeasy. "And where the hell is the burger? I said 'toasted,' too. Is this it? Are you kidding me? This burger is about the size of my thumbnail, and looks as dry as the heel of my shoe."

"You want a Coke with that, Dad?" Devlin said, laughing.

"Yeah," Carol said. "The second in your life, right?"

The chorus of chuckles from the other four erupted until they were all in tears, no one certain whether they were laughing or crying.

Chapter Sixteen

SLOANE MONAE DIDN'T KNOW ANYTHING about the savings and loan industry when Devlin dispatched her to learn more about what Ho-Chan Park had been investigating. The anonymous call tipping Devlin might not have had any credibility, except that the mystery woman had to be someone who could make the connection between the Christmas Eve driver, the name of the victim and what Devlin was trying to put together. Who else could that be but an insider? Devlin figured it was worth a look.

Monae started by asking around at the building where Ho-Chan Park had spent the last hours of his life. She learned that Park's closest associate was another accountant named Omar Sidi, a lanky and attractive African emigrant man. Park and Sidi were federal bank examiners, de facto partners who worked in the same office. And, in their chosen profession, each earned a princely salary of $15,000 per year. To arrange a lunch meeting with Sidi at Ong Lek Thai Kitchen, Monae told him she was investigating Ho-Chan Park's death for a law firm. Sidi would have been reluctant to speak to anyone, except that he was frustrated that the Phoenix police had not done anything, as far as he could tell, to figure out what had happened to his friend. He had started the lunch meeting at Ong Lek Thai Kitchen by walking this investigator through the dull and dry economic backdrop to their current work, all of which Sidi found deeply thrilling.

Sidi went back to 1979, when Federal Reserve chairman Paul Volcker doubled interest rates in an attempt to stop runaway inflation. Then Sidi talked about Ronald Reagan promising to cut taxes, increase defense spending *and* balance the budget. Enter the savings and loan institutions, which Americans loved because the entire industry conjured a fictional *It's A Wonderful Life* fantasy; i.e., Jimmy Stewart making loans to the little people so everyone could realize the American Dream. Problem was that by 1982 the S&L industry was insolvent on a market-value basis—by $150 billion, a deep sea of red ink the Reagan administration had to hide given its earlier impossible promises. Then Reagan cut the budgets of the federal regulators—people like Ho-Chan Park and Omar Sidi who were supposed to investigate bad loans.

"What was he working on when he died?" Monae asked.

"H.C. was such good man," Sidi said, with a thick accent. "We were the two token minorities, and just bond immediately. I always call him 'H.C.' He just call me 'O.' I miss him calling me that. You will find who did this?"

Monae knew better than to make such promises. "We're going to do everything we can."

"And you are also police? Better police?"

"No, no. I was. Now I work for a law firm as an investigator. We're looking into Mr. Park's death as a civil matter, for a wrongful death action."

"Yes," he said, nodding solemnly. "It is very wrongful. I am so angry the police do nothing. My friend dies, and they do nothing."

"Can you tell me more about your work?"

Sidi looked around as though they were being monitored. "I cannot talk about my work."

"No?"

"No. Officially, no. You are seeing my meaning?"

"I think so. Your work is confidential, and you also want to help figure out what happened to your friend."

"For one hundred percent."

"OK. Whatever you tell me about your work is off the record. I'm just interested in learning what happened to your friend. And why."

"I try explain. Savings and loan big mess right now. Easy entry, weak policing and high profit potential. And very bad accounting standards. Ho-Chan figure this out and come to me. He tell me: 'We got real problem, O.' We start digging around. Not even quite sure what we uncovered. In 1980 S&Ls make profit of $781 million. By 1982, S&Ls losing $4 billion a year. Why can this be, in two years? Then we see S&L assets increasing; why can this be, if they lose so much money? New laws in California, Texas and Florida allow S&Ls start speculating in real estate. How crazy can this be? In Texas, forty S&Ls triple in size. Triple! Too much crazy happening, so we work around the clock to figure it out. H.C. is point person on investigation."

Monae had a college degree, had gone through a rigorous police academy at the top of her recruit class, and considered herself intelligent, but she wasn't really following the thread here. She instinctively fell back on her police interview training. "How would you explain what was happening, to your kids?"

"No kids."

"No, I'm just saying, if you did. In simple terms."

"I like have family one day," he said, smiling and taking a spoonful of Tom Kha Gai soup. "Just not meet right girl yet."

"So, what, specifically, were you investigating?"

Sidi looked around the packed restaurant and, despite the din, lowered his voice to a barely audible whisper. "No one know, this so secret-secret."

Monae nodded.

"H.C. tells me this, too, that about one-third of S&Ls now unprofitable. State and federal insurance running out of money to refund depositors. However, S&Ls still open making bad loans. Ticking time bomb."

Omar Sidi may as well have been speaking French, in which he was fluent, with that revelation. He was born in Dakar, Senegal, and brought to the United States by his parents when he was a teenager. Although he had learned English quickly in his new homeland, he retained a thick accent and a unique syntax Monae found endearing.

"I'm sorry," she said, thinking how far away this all seemed to be drifting from Devlin's hit-and-run civil case. "I'm not really following."

"Let me explain different way. You have husband, yes?"

Monae smiled, thinking of Devlin and how that possibility had floated in her mind. "No husband."

"OK, definitely boyfriend, yes?"

"Definitely boyfriend."

"OK, let us say boyfriend pretends he is rich, so much money he says, fancy car, fancy dinners, fancy house, he buys you diamond ring and beautiful gold necklace." Monae liked the example. "Except really, this boyfriend?" Sidi's face turned to a scowl as he slammed the table with an open palm, which was so loud Monae jumped. People on both sides of them glanced over. Sidi was enraged by the fraud. "He has declining assets. No money. Everything put on credit cards. Except then you find out. You should tell him to stop spending, yes?"

Monae nodded.

"You are the girlfriend, the U.S. government. Except what do you say instead?"

Monae got it now. "Keep spending. Keep making bad loans. Keep the scheme going."

"Yes!" Sidi shouted, again attracting the eyes of the other diners. Then, back at low volume: "You allow bad S&Ls to remain open and keep big losses growing. You are like casino who lets gambler bet, bet, bet with house money and no cutoff. Very bad. The hole can only get deeper. My father always tell me: 'Omar, you cannot borrow your way out of debt.'"

"How does this end?"

"Very bad," Sidi said, lowering his voice again to almost a whisper. "When the bill come due, billions and billions. Please, secret-secret."

"Secret-secret," she said, nodding.

Sidi was whispering again: "We look especially at Archard Holdings."

It was like someone had dropped a bomb on their table. "Wait, hold up? Say that again."

Sidi looked confused, wondering what he had said. "I say 'secret-secret.'"

"No, after that."

"'We look especially at Archard Holdings'?"

"That's the company you and your friend were investigating?"

Sidi nodded.

OK, Monae thought. Another puzzle piece fits together. "Please continue."

"Archard Holdings very bad. Run by Adalius Becker. He order cover-up, from top down. Even my superiors on FHLBB know——"

"FH-what?"

"Federal Home Loan Bank Board. They create crazy new accounting like 'loan loss deferral.' How crazy can this be? I tell you: to delay any accounting of losses! Inflate net worth and net income to hide so much red ink."

Sidi leaned back, nodding, as though he'd just told Monae the identity of the "Subway Vigilante," Bernhard Goetz, before the world knew, before New York City media outlets had run wild with the story to start the year. The picture was forming: if this is where they were nosing around, Monae could see the hornet's nest Sidi and Park had poked—repeatedly. Monae leaned close and whispered, "So you and Mr. Park uncovered criminal activity that even your superiors knew about, but everyone wanted to keep under wraps. Is that about right?"

"That you are exactly right."

"What else do you know?"

"I know everything you will want to know. This man Becker was born 1930. Enlisted the U.S. Army. He goes to Korean War but never combat. After war he return to study business at University of Wyoming. Then law school at University of Illinois and his own successful legal practice in the fifties in Atlanta. In 1968, he left law firm to become executive at small bank. In 1972 he is already common criminal. He and the head of the bank charged by SEC with defrauding stockholders. You can believe they approved $6.5 million in loans to themselves and other officers of the company! Except Becker gets only a fine and no jail time."

Monae was writing it all down on her notepad.

"In 1974, Becker moved here to start real-estate development company, Archard Holdings. Then he acquire Estate Savings & Loan, based in Omaha, Nebraska. We've been watching him for years. Already Becker increased the assets of the bank from about half-billion to more than $2 billion. How can this be possible so quick? In reality, H.C. first tell me it's all fictional, using deceptive accounting practices. For just one example, H.C. figure out Becker and his partners at Estate S&L traded empty lots with other companies and listed these as profit-producing sales. So, we keep digging and watching. We fear the S&L risky practices are exposing the government insurance funds to huge losses. Very bad. Now the FHLBB makes new rule S&Ls can hold no more than ten percent of assets in direct investments. No more ownership positions in certain financial entities and instruments. Our bosses at San Francisco office of FHLBB send us here. H.C. tell me in secret that Estate S&L has $105 million in unreported losses and passed the regulated direct investments limit by $400 million. Becker believe the bank examiners are against him. We hear rumors that he tells his staff we are the homosexuals who are out to get him, maybe convert him to the homosexual. For some reason Becker hates the homosexuals. H.C. jokes with me that it's because Becker is the homosexual, and that is why he lash out. I think H.C. is probably correct. Then Becker goes to high-level friends in Washington D.C. to get Becker ally on the Bank Board. This is all why we started getting followed."

"Followed?"

"Yes, H.C. and I both. Becker wants to end investigation. Cars parked close by for really no good reason. Always people watching."

"Are you sure?"

"We are very sure."

"How would they know what you'd discovered?"

"We are federal bank examiners. They know who we are. We only figure this out by studying all their financial statements and documents, which they have to give us because we subpoena power. Talking to their employees in secret, but the cat watches the mouse and the mouse watches the cat."

"So, what, the mouse is trying to intimidate you? Get the cat to stop the investigation?"

"Most definitely. But the cat will always eat."

Monae smiled. She genuinely liked Omar Sidi. His benevolence was palpable, but not to be mistaken for weakness. Like her, he had been called to protect the flock without any regard for his own benefit—including, obviously, his personal fortune, at such a paltry salary. He just knew right and wrong and what had to be done. And he had stepped up to do it.

"So, did the cat get a little too close, maybe spooked them?"

"Most definitely. They start to panic. We even see same car sometimes. One time I almost get hit."

Monae's arms tingled as the small hairs rose up. "Wait, you and Mr. Park discussed seeing the same car tailing you?"

Sidi nodded. Monae could feel her pulse quicken: if Sidi could ID the car that almost hit him it might be another connection to Christmas Eve 1983.

"When did this happen?"

"Maybe one week before Christmas?"

"How do you remember when, for sure?"

"I am thinking of going Christmas shopping, to buy something for H.C."

Monae wanted to hug the man. "OK, where did this happen?"

"When I come out of work late one night. We always working late. Ridiculous late. No wonder I not meet the right girl."

"On Central Avenue?"

"Yes, on the Central Avenue. It scares the holy crap out of me. When I find out how H.C. died—" Sidi bit his lip and fought back the tears. "I know what happened."

"Do you remember what the car that almost hit you looked like?"

"Oh, I remember for one hundred percent. I even tell police but they do nothing. I go to university for accounting and history, not police work jumping away from cars."

"What kind of car was it?"

"Sports car. Very fast. Looks fast even parked."

Monae slumped a bit; she needed more than that. "What color?"

"Orange."

Holy shit. "It was an orange sports car?"

"Yes, orange."

Monae wanted to blurt it out, that she already knew it was a Trans Am. Instead, she locked down her poker face, holding aces. "Do you know what make or model?"

Sidi shook his head. "I am not so good with the cars. What is the difference, make and model?"

"It's OK. Did you see who was in it?"

"Just driver."

"No one else?"

"Only driver."

"Can you describe the driver?" Monae was careful not to use a pronoun, male or female, anything that might sway the witness testimony.

"Just normal white man with thick hair."

"Normal?"

"You know, not fat, not skinny. Just normal."

"So, a medium-build white male?"

"The medium build, yes, this is how you say it. All these years I am still learning." Sidi smiled, proud of his progress in studying the English language.

"And you saw he had thick hair?"

"Yes. Like Han Solo, you know? From the *Star Wars*."

"How so?"

"Thick on sides, covered his ears. Parted in middle. Except no blaster."

"Blaster?" she said.

"You know, like from the *Star Wars*. Luke has light saber; Han has blaster. Why can the stormtroopers fire hundreds of shots and never hit Han, Luke or Chewy? Not once in three movies! But they hit Leia twice: I think maybe they are against the women."

"Back to the driver: you got a really good look at him?"

"Like I said, he's watching us, and we watching him. Then he almost kill me so I make sure to know who is this man."

149

"You could identify him if you saw him again?"

"For one hundred percent."

"Do you think this is the same man who hit… H.C.?"

"I know he is same."

"How do you know?"

"You are the detective. Just like you."

"How so?"

"When you know, you know."

"Did you notice if there was any damage to the car: dents, broken windshield?" Monae wanted to establish the chronology, that the Trans Am should have been clean a week or so before Christmas Eve.

"No damage I can remember. I am very sorry."

"No, no, you're fine. I just have to ask lots of questions."

"I understand," he said. "We are same in our work. Lots of questions."

"Is there anything else you can tell me about the car you saw?"

"Yes, one thing."

Sidi smiled, leaned forward and motioned her to do the same. Then he whispered, "I write the license plate."

AFTER lunch, Sloane Monae slid into her 280Z and tucked her Paloma Picasso handbag between the seats. It was an unconscious habit that kept the Detective Special revolver within quick reach. She had just used the pay phone to call Devlin to tell him two people had now identified the same vehicle, by plate number, in separate-yet-similar nefarious acts. A vehicle registered to Archard Holdings, the company Ho-Chan Park and Omar Sidi were investigating. They had one near-miss and one fatal hit-and-run, within about a week of each other.

A strong circumstantial case was forming, but she and Devlin had never considered any other case theory beyond what looked like a classic drunk-driver incident. Now there was a new, darker likelihood: the Ho-Chan Park hit-and-run was not just a random drunk driver, but rather an intentional act. The thought sent a chill through Monae as she navigated traffic.

Chapter Seventeen

BACK ON FEBRUARY 22, 1976, just as Devlin's nursing home case had been ramping up, a small, seemingly innocuous advertisement ran in the local daily newspaper:

Do you need a lawyer?
Legal services at very reasonable fees.

Two Phoenix lawyers, John Bates and Van O'Steen, who had both graduated from nearby Arizona State University College of Law, placed the advertisement to promote the legal clinic they had formed. Their goal was to provide basic legal services (uncontested divorces and adoptions, simple personal bankruptcies, name changes, etc.) at modest fees for average-income people. The lawyers' ad, clearly stamped as an advertisement, gave the downtown Phoenix address and phone number of the Legal Clinic of Bates & O'Steen, just a few blocks from Devlin & Associates.

However, since the State Bar of Arizona forbade lawyers from advertising their services, administrators initiated disciplinary proceedings against Bates and O'Steen. That action led to a hearing where a disciplinary committee recommended that Bates and O'Steen be suspended for not less than six months. The pair appealed to the Arizona Supreme Court with the contention that the ban on lawyer advertising violated the Sherman Antitrust Act and the First Amendment, claims the court rejected. However, Bates and O'Steen had a partial victory when the state justices reduced their sanction to censure only, because their advertising was "...done in good faith to test the constitutionality..." of the ban on lawyer advertising. Then the U.S. Supreme Court established its jurisdiction over the case and set a date for oral argument.

On January 18, 1977, arguing for the appellants John Bates and Van O'Steen was William C. Canby, Jr., a professor of law at Arizona State University and future judge on the U.S. Court of Appeals for the Ninth Circuit. Arguing for State Bar of Arizona was John Paul Frank, a partner at the Phoenix law firm of Lewis and Roca, and the lawyer who had advocated for the defendant in the precedent-setting *Miranda v. Arizona* case in 1966. Arguing on behalf of the U.S. government was Solicitor General Robert Bork, whose nomination to the U.S. Supreme Court would get scuttled a decade later.

Ultimately, the highest court in the land rejected the traditional notion that every lawyer had an established clientele that would inevitably lead others to seek out the lawyers' services. That outlook, the court noted, was an anachronism that created higher barriers to entry into the legal profession by "perpetuating the market position of established attorneys."

That was the almost-decade-old backdrop that had led to what Devlin saw now: an abomination on an otherwise perfect spring day in the desert. The cloudless sky was cast with a shimmering blue glow. The firestorm of summer, with its mechanical buzz of cicadas and towering walls of dust, was only a vague notion. Instead, everything was resurrected into new life. But this billboard, which had just gone up right across the street from Devlin & Associates, was simply atrocious. Indeed, the playing field had changed.

"Hucksters," Devlin said, shaking his head. He was standing on the sidewalk with Sloane Monae and Nadia Flores. The three-man crew who had just installed the sign was packing tools into a truck. "Lawyer advertising has gone from trying to bring affordable legal services to the common man to this snake-oil hustle. It cheapens a noble profession."

Across the street from Devlin & Associates was a popular, independent sandwich shop positioned next to a small parking lot. The long brick wall of the restaurant angled toward the street, making it a perfect eye-level placard for a painted billboard.

The sign featured Richard Franklin, a local lawyer dressed in a dark suit and wearing a black cowboy hat, pointing an index finger à la Uncle Sam in the iconic 1917 poster. Franklin put on a different spin:

You want Dick!
Personal injury — Get paid fast with Dick.
Call Richard "Dick" Franklin — The biggest and best attorney in town.

"Men," Flores said, shaking her head.

"Doesn't that violate, like, ten different state bar ethical standards?" Monae asked. "He's literally talking about the size of his penis."

"And we know what that means," Flores said, winking at Monae.

"No doubt," she said. "Overcompensating."

"What about his male clients?" Flores asked.

"I guess they want Dick, too," Devlin deadpanned. "Everyone wants Dick. I should call him right now and tell him I want Dick… to take down this godawful sign."

"See, Connor," Monae said, pointing at the billboard and poking Devlin in the shoulder. "That's your problem: you need to put out some advertising that gets anatomical. Seriously."

"'Get paid fast with Dick,'" Flores said. "What does that even mean?"

"How low have we gone in our profession?" Devlin lamented.

"Who is he?" Monae asked.

"He's a bottom-feeder. These guys don't care about legitimate grievances and serious wrongdoing. They run case mills. They hire fifteen or twenty paralegals and then go for volume. Slip-and-falls. Motor vehicle injuries. Every case is fifty grand or less. When an actual big case comes along, they refer it out to someone like me who actually knows what the hell they're doing on behalf of real victims."

"Have you ever taken one of their referrals?"

"Hell, no," he said. "They know better than to even ask."

Monae glanced at her watch. "Time for me to start my shift."

Devlin nodded. "This new information you dug up was gnawing at me all night. A car registered to a corporation is identified in two separate incidents, one fatal, with two guys who were both investigating that same company. If we can connect the dots here, we've got a civil case for wrongful death, and maybe a criminal case we could refer to prosecutors."

She nodded. "We have the vehicle cold. Now we need to identify the driver."

"OK, you two, I've got work to do," Flores said, giving Monae a hug because the investigator was someone Nadia Flores hoped would be around for a long time. She had seen a shift in Devlin since Monae had come along, and it was a change she liked. She turned and walked back inside.

"You know what you've done is beyond impressive," Devlin said. "You pulled the first witness out of thin air, then found Omar Sidi and connected both of them to the car that probably did our hit-and-run."

"'Probably'?"

"Look," he said, "we're on the same side here. But we still don't have any direct evidence. We need to I.D. the driver, which might give us vicarious liability with the corporation. We need to tie the driver to the corporation, and the corporation to the act."

She nodded again. "You'll have your driver."

Devlin smiled. He wanted to say it; he *felt* it. Sloane Monae was a fiery concoction of brains and beauty. But it was her similar gladiator passion and drive that most excited Devlin, a woman as unrelenting as he was in the pursuit of accountability and justice. He pulled her in for a hug. Yes, he wanted to say it, but he didn't.

She looked at him, wondering what that winsome look in his eyes meant. What was he thinking? It had been wonderful since the night at the *FREE cable TV + HBO!!!* motel in Kingman, and they never really talked about what might be next. Not that she was in any great rush, but did he ever want to get married? Have children? Had that thought ever occurred to him? While she was battling her own self-doubts, she was curious if the concept of a future together had started to form in him. Not now, but down the road. Neither had broached the subject. They had each been wonderfully immersed in the freedom and connection of an early relationship, where any disruptive details about life plans and other real-world complications were simply off the table.

One such real-world event was the U.S. FDA approving a screening test for an AIDS antibody for all blood banks. That such a health crisis even existed was wholly off the radar of both, and they had never discussed using condoms. Devlin had correctly assumed that Sloane Monae was taking birth control pills, which was primarily because she'd discovered it helped regulate her cycle. When she met Connor Devlin it was synchronous, rather than planned, that she was already taking the pill. With all that swirling in her mind, she came back to the moment.

"When do you next meet with Goldie?"

"Friday morning."

"Well, that still gives me three days to find our driver."

Devlin smiled. "You are an eternal optimist."

"No, I'm just good. Friday it is. You'll have your defendant."

"Shall we make a friendly wager on that?" he asked, smiling.

"Sure, I'm up for taking more of your money. How much?"

"I'll tell you what. I had this odd case where the guy paid me—oh shit, where did that bag go?"

"Bag?"

"Yeah, it was in my office. On my desk, right? What the hell? I haven't seen it. I completely forgot about that bag."

"What bag?" she asked.

"It was a gym bag. With what I assume is cash. From a case."

"Cash in a gym bag? What kind of law practice you running?"

"Shit, I need to ask Nadia if she saw it. Anyway, I never looked at how much is in there. Assuming we can find it, if you get our defendant by Friday you can have whatever's in the bag."

"A mystery amount in a missing bag," she said. "Sounds intriguing. I'll take that bet. Plus, one more thing if I win."

"What's that?"

Monae hesitated. On the downhill side to one year—that's how long she'd known Connor Devlin. And it had been blissful. So why her vague anxiety about what this all meant? What was there to question? Devlin checked all the boxes—pretty much what she would have constructed if she had a *Weird Science* Build-a-Boy laboratory when she was 14. As she mentally debated whether this was the right time to bring this up—since she didn't know exactly what she was bringing up—she just blurted it out: "We have a talk. A real talk. About us."

Devlin looked surprised. He suspected he knew what that meant, which wasn't necessarily a bad thing. He loved what they had. He'd already roamed far and wide, cut that wide swath through the USC campus, dated a Playboy bunny and played the field enough to know that Sloane Monae was a rare catch. But, of course, it had also been easy to stay buried in his work and just let things ride on the relationship front. He didn't have any reservations about where things might be headed. He nodded. "OK, deal. How about me? What if you can't find him?"

"You get Dick," she said, laughing and pointing at the sign. "You get Dick, because you've already lost this bet. Now excuse me, because I have work to do."

"Don't forget there's another clock ticking, too," Devlin said, unaware of the implications of this statement to a thirty-something single woman in love.

"What's that?"

"Statute of limitations."

"Meaning what?"

"Meaning we only have two years to file a wrongful death suit. The clock on our mystery-defendant case runs out when the clock strikes midnight Christmas Eve."

"That's nine months. Plenty of time, right?"

"Well, we'll need time to prepare it."

Monae stared defiantly at her lawyer boyfriend. "Like I said: you'll have your defendant."

She was thinking about what Omar Sidi had said: the cat will always eat. She had always been the cat tracking her prey. And if the cat was going to eat, she needed to go straight to where the mice holed up to gnaw their ill-gotten cheese: Archard Holdings.

Chapter Eighteen

DELANEY DUNNE WATCHED THE FOXY BRUNETTE in Jackie O. sunglasses, sitting there in her gnarly blue sports car. Dunne had been seeing the 280Z for a couple days, maybe since Tuesday? He knew she was watching him as he sat in the orange Trans Am in the parking lot of Archard Holdings, the parent company of Estate Savings & Loan. Behind Dunne was the three-story stucco building that housed the Scottsdale operation.

If she was a detective, she was either not a very good one or had intentionally tipped her hand. Dunne wondered: why would she do that? Either way, Dunne was a conflicted jumble of anger, relief and an acid stomach raging like a forest fire. Mostly, he was flat-out exhausted by the swindle. If law enforcement was finally onto him, then maybe this could be the beginning of the end. But he also feared what that might mean. Maybe there was some deal he could cut to simultaneously get out of this life and keep his ass from going to prison for what he'd done. It all started the day he took Adalius Becker's lamebrain pitch to heart and ditched law school to come work here instead. All those years, now capped by what he had done that Christmas Eve, which had been eating at his insides 24/7. He hadn't had a good night's sleep since.

He barely ate. He was depressed and sad. Dunne only knew one thing for certain: whatever was happening here with the babe, he sure as hell wasn't going to prison for that corrupt piece of shit Becker.

Over the last eleven years, the desert air had played tricks with his mind. One minute Dunne was on a respectable track, on his way to law school, and the next minute he was back-dating documents. That's how Becker lured him into the tent at first: *just minor bookkeeping details no one will ever notice or care about. Everyone does it.* Then Dunne was shuttling paperwork for unsecured loans and helping move fake assets from one subsidiary to another. Then sculpting the new hires, with after-market boobs and liposuction from a catalog, and dressing them as Becker's Barbies. Then intimidating anyone who opposed the boss. At first Dunne sidestepped trivial rules—the equivalent of innocuous white lies. He became adept at working around regulations using justified reasoning. Eventually white lies became blatant and intentional misdeeds. Eventually Dunne trampled rules, ignored laws and committed crimes at Becker's behest until he was all-in on a sprawling Ponzi fraud, a criminal co-conspirator in felony acts violating U.S. statutes. And now he had fallen into the void completely and was on the hook for the death of that banking examiner.

Before, the pay had made the transgressions seem worth the handshake with the devil. Last year Delaney Dunne had earned $85,000 in salary as a special assistant to Adalius Becker. Dunne also received a separate $50,000 net bonus. The women who worked at Archard Holdings did even better: the shorter the skirt, the bigger the bonus. It had always struck Dunne as creepy, that the supposedly righteous Becker, who zealously espoused his righteous Baptist piety, populated his corrupt empire with a phalanx of twenty-something women in push-up bras, miniskirts, lace anklets and towering high heels. Some of these women, without any college education or other training, earned $100,000 a year at Becker's direction, with an additional $10,000 annual clothing allowance they spent at high-end stores.

Dunne's female work peers were almost exclusively blonde, with gleaming teeth and shapely figures. Dunne ran every new young woman through a degrading gauntlet of tests and interviews. Every potential female hire (never the men) sat for the ninety-minute Minnesota Multiphasic Personality Inventory (MMPI), a psychological test that supposedly assessed personality traits and psychopathology. Not because Becker or anyone else ever read the results, but strictly as a head game and stress-inducing exercise to keep the women on their toes and insecure about their prospective employment. Then every new female candidate had to sit for a one-on-one interview with each of the male attorneys, bankers and advisors who held the power to decide who made the cut. It became an unofficial contest among the male power brokers to see who could administer the best hazing ritual. One instructed a young woman to sit in a chair facing the corner and not speak or get up until told to do so. Not to eat, get a drink of water, go to the restroom or for any other reason. Then he left for a meeting on the other side of Phoenix and told Dunne to monitor her. When he returned five hours later she was still in the chair and, according to Dunne, had not gotten up once or spoken to anyone. Trying to outdo his peer, another male attorney instructed a female interviewee to imitate a circus lion. Others asked ridiculous questions: if you were a farm animal, what would you be? Can you name the planets in the solar system, in order, from the sun outward? What weighs more: a pound of gold or a pound of feathers? What causes thunder? That no one yet had given the simple answer (lightning) to that last question was a point of endless amusement among the men.

From these early gambits the general tenor and expectation were established: that the young women would always present themselves impeccably as objects of beauty, to integrate as another design aesthetic along with the expensive artwork, hand-crafted leather furniture and exotic rugs at Archard Holdings. They would adhere to Becker's three D's—demure, dress and demeanor—and be subservient as they carried out their duties.

Another one of Dunne's official duties was to monitor the female employees and, if any started to gain weight, instruct them to go on a diet. These were not subtle suggestions, but rather blunt orders: *Beck needs you to drop ten.* At Becker's direction, Dunne also arranged for a Scottsdale plastic surgeon to give a series of lunchtime presentations attended exclusively by female employees. Subsequently, the surgeon performed numerous liposuction procedures and breast augmentations, at pre-arranged bulk discount pricing, to "improve" Becker's human accessories. The hallways and offices at Archard Holdings gradually started to look like a Saturday afternoon swim party at the Playboy Mansion.

One day Becker spied an early-20s woman from the limousine as he and Dunne were returning from lunch. She was crossing the street and looked like a model from a Calvin Klein advertisement. Becker pointed to her, looked at Dunne and said, "I want that." Becker ordered the limousine stopped, opened the door for Dunne and dispatched him to start wooing the woman. Soon, with no college education or work experience outside the restaurant industry, she was earning a

$90,000 salary as one of Becker's executive assistants.

In another instance, Becker hired an unusually dowdy secretary and challenged Dunne with, "She's really good at accounting, but do you think you can fix that?" Dunne dutifully took the woman aside and explained the way of things, starting with taking her shopping for an afternoon and spending $7,000 of the company's money on new clothes and seven pairs of high heels. She'd need a new hairstyle, too, and some instruction in the proper application of makeup. And she'd need to lose fifteen pounds immediately, preferably twenty, and should seriously consider plastic surgery, starting with a nose job and bigger boobs, which they could do under the same general anesthesia. Even after everything he'd done up to that point, it was on that day that Dunne finally felt the first twinge of shame—for how he had treated this woman and, suddenly, everything else he'd done on behalf of Becker. Whatever impulse finally triggered an internal alarm, it also filled Dunne with an intense sadness, that he had wasted much of his life in service of a corrupt despot. His sadness quickly coalesced into rage. To quell the rising and confusing discomfort, on one shopping trip with a new female employee, Dunne impulsively grabbed two pairs of alligator cowboy boots—two different colors in his size—and dropped another $6,000 of Becker's money.

From that day forward, the criminal stench and twisted play no longer sat well with Dunne. He hated that he worked in a fraudulent empire staffed by paralegals who were just subservient style accessories in the broader scheme. What a con. Delaney was at Becker's side as the short and portly kingpin dumped depositors' money into speculative real estate, junk bonds and shoddy housing tracts. In just three years, Estate S&L's "assets" went from a half-billion to more than $2 billion. At least on paper. Except Becker was using his federally insured institution as his personal piggy bank to take his extended family to Europe and Asia, where he spent lavishly on five-star hotels and rare carpets from the Holy Land. The only way to keep the scheme going was to attract new depositors. And to do that Becker needed malleable men like Dunne to do his bidding. Dunne himself had been fleeced by the slick Becker to be the one charged with outfoxing regulators. Becker's personal protégé, his fixer Double-D, was his crowning achievement. Becker had plucked him from obscurity in 1974 and, in turn, had paid him the kind of money that made skipping law school seem prudent. But there was a deeper cost. Every big con needed its foot soldiers, and Dunne became the indispensable grunt who knew what, when and how to do whatever needed to be done. The man who had wanted to become an advocate dedicated to upholding the rule of law now operated as though there were no laws. Well, there was one law, and only one: enrich and serve Adalius Becker.

What burned Dunne the most was that he'd gone along as a useful idiot in Becker's big swindle. Sure, Dunne got paid, but in the end he had traded everything that mattered. All he was now was a low-rung hustler, a bag man who had crossed a stark line when Becker ordered him—during a $195 lobster lunch, with three other Archard employees at the table—to scare off the two bank examiners. The first time— targeting "the African fed," as Becker called Sidi—had gone according to plan, and Dunne hadn't given it much thought. But after he learned what had happened after the second—Becker had dubbed that target the "chop-suey fed"— Dunne had been beyond despondent. Something had to give.

So, if this delicious darling in the snappy blue ride was here to slip on the handcuffs and read him his Miranda rights, then let's get it on.

SLOANE Monae stared at the mystery driver, sitting there in his orange Trans Am that was as infamous to her now as Clyde Barrow's bullet-riddled Ford V8, and wondered if he was her guy. From afar, at least, he seemed to fit Omar Sidi's general description as Han Solo; i.e., a normal white guy. She chuckled at Sidi's way with words and musings about the poor marksmanship of stormtroopers.

And if that was their guy in *that* car, he had taken it somewhere off the immediate grid of Phoenix shops for any repairs. There was no obvious body damage and, seeing the vehicle sitting there in the glistening sun, she noted that whoever had done the body work had also matched the paint perfectly. Monae wondered if they'd just re-sprayed the entire car, to avoid any potential mismatch between the original and repaired parts.

She wondered, too, if she was making the right play. With the statute-of-limitations clock ticking, she did not have time to dilly-dally around the edges. She had decided to make sure Dunne knew she was on to him—and that, she hoped, would be leverage to get him to talk. Most criminals wanted to proclaim their innocence and set the record straight. As she'd learned on the force, sometimes this was the only play left. There were numerous times she had solved a case wherein she knew the suspect was guilty, but there was no evidence to support her theory of the crime. When that happened, there was only one way to close it: elicit a confession. If he was willing to talk, then she wanted to go into the critical first conversation with some leverage, *this* leverage, that the cat was stalking the mouse.

CHAPTER EIGHTEEN

She swallowed back the nervous anticipation, started the Z, drove slowly into the parking lot of Archard Holdings and pulled right alongside the orange Trans Am, which was backed into the parking space. She and Dunne were now staring at each other a few feet apart, driver door to driver door. Again she studied the driver's door and the front quarter panel, which she figured had been replaced. The paint was a dead match, and if he'd had the entire car repainted he'd also replaced the screaming-chicken decal and covered every detail right down to the "SD-455" lettering on the air scoop.

Both already had their windows down. Monae touched her handbag, not because she expected a shootout, but because she had been trained to be prepared for anything. She cocked her Jackie O. shades onto the tip of her nose and made eye contact, straight-faced.

Dunne kept his poker face, too. "Can I help you?"

"Perhaps. Or, perhaps I can help you."

"How's that?"

"Nice paint job."

Dunne just stared.

"I know about this car and Christmas Eve. I know all of it." This was one approach: just punch them in the mouth without warning, and see how they react. Dunne looked away and stared at a commercial jet airliner climbing past 10,000 feet, desperately wishing he was in that steel tube, any steel tube, being shuttled away from the life he now inhabited. The life he had chosen, the nightmare of his choice. Instead he was still earthbound, staring at options that were all depressing.

"Am I being arrested?" he asked.

This leap floored Monae. *A guilty conscience.* She'd just picked up the fourth ace on the draw. "You tell me."

Dunne pursed his lips and pondered. "How'd you find me?"

"Same way we always do."

"How's that?"

"Coffee."

Dunne nodded. "Do you know who I work for?"

Monae nodded, thinking: *Yes, the real estate guy.* The one Ho-Chan Park and Omar Sidi were investigating. She just played it straight: "I know people who would find information about your employer very helpful."

"Yeah, well, I can tell you he's a real piece of shit."

"That on the record?" she said.

Dunne gave a half-smile. "The walls have ears around here. Know what I mean?"

"Sure," she said. "I know a good place where we could go. Just to talk."

"Just to talk," Dunne said, staring skyward again, wondering where his steel tube might have been taking him. If he had just left for law school that day long ago, none of this would be happening. *Inches and seconds.* He eyed her again: it wouldn't be the worst thing in the world to spend twenty minutes with this stunner. But no way he was going to dig his own grave, either. But did he even have a choice? Maybe she was just toying with him until she put him in cuffs and hauled his sorry ass downtown.

Monae had seen this thousand-yard stare dozens of times, the vacant gaze of the guilty person weighing their options. And per her Dallas PD street time, she was also already operating with one eventuality in mind: the trial. In this case that might mean two trials, civil and criminal. She knew it was a pipe dream: if Dunne was willing to give it up, not only would Devlin have his defendant for the civil case, but Maricopa County prosecutors might be able to bring criminal charges as well for Ho-Chan Park's death. But she doubted very much that he would just start singing.

With that in mind, everything Monae said and did from this point forward would later be scrutinized and surgically dissected in open court by skilled defense attorneys. She could not misrepresent herself or make any other missteps that might taint what she had uncovered, all the connecting links that had brought her here. Dunne was fluttering in that fragile state she'd seen evaporate away forever in the flash of the next second. So, lest she spook him, Monae didn't say a word. This guy needed to look inside and find his own come-to-Jesus moment.

Chapter Nineteen

THE LUNCH RUSH AT ONG LEK THAI KITCHEN had surged and dwindled. A tangy, ambrosial aroma of garlic, chilis and lemongrass hung in the air. There was a soft clatter of flatware, glasses and silverware as a busboy cleared tables. A wobbly ceiling fan whirled at the center of the room.

Sloane Monae sat with Delaney Dunne in a black-vinyl corner booth. Neither had ordered food, and both had untouched glasses of iced tea dappled with condensation. Monae was still tiptoeing through the minefield of not making any legal missteps. That she'd found the likely driver of the orange Trans Am was miraculous. That she'd gotten him here to talk was even more unlikely. However, none of that meant anything if she couldn't deliver the river card to Devlin: Monae needed to identify this guy as the driver on Christmas Eve almost a year and a half ago. And that was going to be a monumental task even for an adept investigator.

She let the uncomfortable silence hang between them, to see how he wanted to open. Not saying anything was one way to play it whenever they had a suspect "in the box" at the police station, which was cop lingo for an interview room. In those days she learned that detectives wanted the suspect to feel squeezed in, both physically and metaphorically. They'd intentionally put the suspect as far from the door as possible, with the metal table in between as a tangible barrier to freedom. But not here: Monae had intentionally directed Dunne to the side of the booth facing outward so he could see the door and that he had an open path to leave whenever he wanted. No one was pressuring him for this interview.

"So," he finally said, "how would this work? If I help, do I get immunity?"

"We're just two people having a conversation."

Dunne was feeling the full gravity of what he'd done, and it was still a raw point that he'd thrown away his life for someone like Adalius Becker. But he didn't hold it against this one, who was just doing her job and seemed razor-sharp from what he could tell. She was like someone from a TV show or movie, which probably tipped the scale in agreeing to come here to talk when she'd asked.

"Well, just because I've done dumb things doesn't mean I'm stupid."

"Fair enough."

Monae gazed into the future again, maybe two or more years from now, to that criminal trial. A savvy defense lawyer in such a case would be looking to exploit any slight misstep here to create reasonable doubt. Monae tried to sort through what she could and couldn't say, and what she could and couldn't represent or promise. She had to be precise. She wondered, too, if she had already taken this too far. Then she almost panicked. Yes, she should call Devlin right now and take him her findings to pick it up from here. *Deep breath.* She also trusted her gut intuition, which was that the cat had her paw on Dunne's tail right now, and she didn't want to let him scurry off just yet. If she did, she might never see him again. Still, doing this interview on her own was fraught with legal perils. *Stay calm. You've got this.*

"And since you asked: the question of immunity is a formal one that only a Maricopa County prosecutor will be able to accurately answer for you. I have no authority to offer you such a deal. Right now, it's just you and me, two people talking."

Dunne looked around the empty restaurant. "So, wait, who are you exactly? Law enforcement, right?"

Monae's heart was racing. She had walked to the cliff's edge, kicking small stones into a void of potential legalities. If he invoked his right to counsel, she'd have to shut it down. But she also could not misrepresent herself.

"I'm an investigator. Private. I work for a law firm. We're exploring a wrongful death civil action on behalf of Mr. Ho-Chan Park, who died on Christmas Eve after a horrible hit-and-run."

Dunne chewed on a fingernail. "So, wait: you're not a cop?"

She smiled and shook her head. "I was, but now I'm not. I'm a private civilian just like you and, again, we're just talking. You can get up and leave whenever you want. I have no authority here."

He knew it! She was way too foxy to be on the job. "Well, you're good, I'll give you that. I totally thought you were a detective."

She nodded. "Tell me what's on your mind."

"I'm sure you read the newspaper. That's who you need to be investigating."

Monae kept her poker face, but she wanted to scream. She didn't really care about Adalius Becker's white-collar crimes and dirty dealings. That was Omar Sidi's turf. She also knew better than to push. Just try to keep him talking. "How about you tell me what you know about your boss." Not because she particularly cared, but only to diminish any fears about who was really in her crosshairs.

"Well, Ms. Not-a-Cop, I don't know anything about that." He took a sip of iced tea.

She knew she'd already lost him, so she swung for the fence: "Prosecutors would need hard evidence to prove a criminal fraud. Tax statements. And lots of accounting records: balance sheets, land sale contracts, deposit logs, money transfers. All of it."

Dunne eyed her. "I'm out of here." He stood.

Monae thought about Omar Sidi and the potential gift: a witness willing to flip and walk Sidi through all the criminal financial schemes. Nothing would make her happier than to give Sidi a boost in the quest that took his friend's life. But her main focus and intent, the one that had her heart pumping wildly, was putting this guy behind the wheel of the Trans Am. Except there was no way he was going to confess to a hit-and-run that would send him to prison. It was maddening, to have found him in this urban Serengeti, have him here in the box and not have any leverage to get him to spill. As he started to walk away, she figured she had nothing to lose.

"Why don't you just tell me what happened on Christmas Eve?"

He stopped and turned. "I think women like you always get what you want."

"Is that so?"

"Yeah. Except not this time."

She nodded. "Let me connect you with the right people to help you sort this out. People who can help you."

He laughed. "Help me? Whatever."

With that, the cat had no choice but to lift her paw from the mouse's tail.

"It's been real," he said.

CHAPTER NINETEEN

"'Every guilty person is his own hangman,'" Monae said, raising her iced-tea glass. "Seneca. Roman philosopher."

Delaney Dunne grunted and shook his head. He felt embarrassed that he couldn't come up with a snappy comeback, so he just turned and walked out.

MONAE sat waiting in a lobby on the tenth floor of the building where Ho-Chan Park had spent the last hours of his life. Even by the stripped-down standards of the police bureaucracy where she had cut her teeth, this office was spartan and devoid of the slightest comforts or aesthetic touches: brown carpet and beige walls, no windows, a gray metal desk for the receptionist and not a single plant or piece of wall art. A small table had a pile of magazines topped by a six-month-old issue of *TIME* magazine featuring an illustration of the smiling mugs of two actors and the headline: "Cool Cops, Hot Show: NBC's Miami Vice – Phillip Michael Thomas and Don Johnson."

Omar Sidi emerged through the door behind the receptionist, access controlled by a push-button keypad. The work of federal bank examiners was being done behind similarly closed doors across the country in similarly locked-and-minimalist facilities, with the measly paychecks to match. The lanky man, in black pants and shoes, white dress shirt and skinny black tie, smiled broadly when he saw Monae sitting on one of the beige metal chairs against the wall. When she stood he embraced her like a beloved family member.

"You bring the good news?"

"Perhaps," she said.

As they sat side-by-side, with Sonny Crockett and Rico Tubbs peering up between them, Sidi lowered his voice to a barely audible whisper. "Secret-secret. You have found him?"

Monae played it like a pro holding a full boat from the deal. She pulled the six-pack from her purse and explained, "I'm going to show you a lineup. I want you to look at each image carefully. If you see someone you think you can identify, tell me the number. OK?"

He nodded. "I am ready."

She unfolded the page to which she'd taped six similar Polaroid images, one of whom was Delaney Dunne from their iced-tea encounter. Monae had excused herself and asked the bartender to surreptitiously snap the Polaroid once she was back at the table when Dunne would be distracted. A few days before the meeting, as she formulated her plan, Monae had asked the owner if he would keep the camera behind the bar for a case she was working. Monae told him she didn't know if, or when, she would need the Polaroid camera, but she wanted it there and ready just in case. After the mystery driver left, Monae snapped a similar Polaroid of the bartender at the same table, two different cooks who were about the right age, and two willing patrons who had been sitting at the bar and wanted to be a part of the sexy sleuth's investigation. Immediately, Omar Sidi pointed excitedly to the image of Dunne. "He is driver. For one hundred percent."

"Here," she said, handing him a pen. "Circle the number, sign your name and tell me where you recognize him from."

He circled number three. "He almost kill me in that orange sports car."

"You're certain?"

"For one hundred percent. He is the one killed my friend?"

Monae maintained her poker face and took the six-pack back. "I'm still investigating all possibilities. That's all I can say for now."

"But I am confident," he said, smiling. "I can see it in your eyes. The cat will always eat."

Monae could not hold back a smile. "The cat will always eat."

AS planned, on Friday Devlin led Monae into the dense air of the windowless tomb that was The Bunker. Goldie's eyebrows shot up as they took their seats in front of his desk.

"Nice eye candy, Dummy. About time you made yourself useful. And to think, I didn't get anything nice for you."

Devlin glanced at Monae. She sat quietly, but he thought he noticed a slight stiffening of her spine. Devlin had warned her that Goldie's legal genius came at a price, and that he was to be tolerated only because he was an unlikely hybrid: both caveman throwback and articulate member of the intelligentsia. Goldie was puffing on his trademark cigar, intensifying the choking cloud of smoke. The latest issue of *Penthouse* magazine, with subscription sticker, was atop the towering pile in his inbox.

Monae was silently deciding that this had to be the most depressing and disgusting workspace she had ever encountered. And she had seen some doozies, at outlier police substations in Dallas near Five Points and Ross-Bennett Grid, and while out on investigations. She was also trying to quell her rising anger: *eye candy?*

"This is my colleague," Devlin said to Goldie. "Sloane Monae. She's a private investigator." Devlin passed him their report, which they'd stayed up until 3 a.m.

writing. "And this details every aspect of what we—well, mostly Sloane—have uncovered."

"Uncovered," Goldie said. "Strong visual there, Dummy. You're two-for-two today."

Monae's heart raced: *Go along to get along. He's not worth it.*

"Seriously, Goldie, she's done weeks of legwork to dig this up."

"Legwork? So that explains why they look so good. Let's see what you've got here." He reluctantly pulled his gaze away from Monae, held up the report and began to read. Goldie tapped his cigar on the hubcap-sized ashtray overflowing with fluttering ashes.

"A 'private investigator,'" he muttered, thumbing the pages. "Nice of you to throw the little lady a bone, Dummy. And by 'bone,' I mean—"

"No," Monae blurted out, unconsciously, then shifted in her chair in the awkward silence. "Just... no, OK?"

"Just no what?" Goldie asked, sincerely perplexed.

Monae looked at Goldie and then Devlin as she inwardly berated herself for saying anything at all. Except, wait: he was the problem here, not her, and yet she felt sick. She did not walk away from three years of sexism and harassment on the police payroll to put up with the same level of shit in the private sector. She'd left the police force; she couldn't leave the workforce entirely.

Devlin was ready to step in on her behalf, but instead he just nodded and smiled; from his view she was doing just fine on her own. Then Monae tapped some unknown reserve, pushed away her fears and stared silently but directly into the thick black Coke-bottle glasses. Goldie laced his fingers behind his head and leaned back in his chair, his belly rising like a full moon over the horizon of the desktop.

Devlin watched this showdown across the expanse of the desk. He wasn't sure what to make of her blurt-and-wait strategy. He'd already prepped her by outlining his approach of manipulation, rather than direct confrontation, as the best way to deal with Phil Goldberg. But here was his girlfriend, poking the bear right here inside his smoky lair.

"I don't appreciate the references," Monae said, outwardly calm as she tried to push away the self-doubt. Devlin braced for blowback from the Lord of the Apes. Goldie stared impassively at this unexpected foe.

"Honey," he said, "I am truly sorry. Is there anything I can do to make her royal majesty more comfortable?"

Despite her nervous anxiety, Monae was determined to make this stand. "See, that's even more insulting. Treat me with the same respect and dignity you afford men."

Goldie smiled. "OK, then. In that case, will you please shut the fuck up so I can read this drivel?" He held up the report.

Monae finally exhaled, breathed in again, and decided Devlin was right: neither he, she or anyone else was going to reform this troglodyte. Her perception in these first few moments of the encounter was that Goldie was in on his own jokes. He didn't come across as an unaware pig; rather, he was a highly aware pig who gleefully rolled in the mud and tried to drag others down to join him. Although she doubted she'd made her point, she was glad she'd tried. Mostly, she just wanted to steer things back to the comfortable arena of shop talk.

"I've identified the car that hit Ho-Chan Park," she said.

"No shit?" Goldie muttered as he turned to Devlin.

"No shit," Devlin said. "Told you she's the real deal."

"And I met with the man who was the driver."

Monae was feeling less agitated as they moved away from that exceedingly uncomfortable confrontation. Had she really, finally spoken up in the workplace? The change in Goldie's expression was ever so slight, but Devlin caught it. And if he saw it, he knew Monae had too.

"But here's one thing I don't know," she said. "Why did you even care enough about this long-shot case to refer it? Clearly this isn't your cup of tea."

"I have my reasons." Goldie abruptly leaned forward to stub his dwindling cigar in the big wooden ashtray. He picked up a new one, clipped the end with a cutter, struck a long wooden kitchen match and started puffing. "Trust me, missy, good reasons."

"My guess—and you can call it feminine intuition if that makes you happy—is that he was someone close to you."

The direct play blindsided Goldie, like a lightning-fast left jab, and before he could lock it down, his eyes welled up briefly. He immediately wiped away the evidence.

"Ho-Chan Park was a friend of yours, someone you cared about," Monae said, twisting the knife with delicious precision.

"OK, yeah, he was my friend," he said. "A good friend, for many years. He didn't have any family here. So despite the long odds, I had to do something to try to help. I promised myself that much. OK? Now, you want to shut your pie hole and let me read this thing in peace?"

"For a case that means more to you personally than any you've handled yourself, you turn to Connor Devlin for help? What does that say?"

"It says jack shit: when my ass itches, I go to the doctor for hemorrhoid cream. Devlin here is just ass cream."

She crossed her arms and looked over to Devlin, who shrugged. Goldie's taunts were the stuff of schoolyards and locker rooms; he'd been there, outgrown that. By the time Monae looked back across the desk, Goldie had resumed reading—this time without commentary.

When he finished, he put down the report and nodded once. Devlin took the cue and said, "So, we have a no-name driver, likely this guy Sloane miraculously tracked down, in a company car registered to Archard Holdings. Except we have no idea what his actual relationship is to the corporation, if any. And even if he was working in an official capacity—which is another point we'll have to prove—what exactly would he have been doing for a real estate firm at midnight on Christmas Eve? As much as we've done, we still don't officially have a defendant."

"Fuck hell you don't."

There was a momentary pause, until Monae said, "Archard Holdings."

"Give her royal majesty a door prize!"

"Not unless we can prove he was on the clock," Devlin said. "Only then is there agency to hold the parent corporation responsible. And again, we'd have to show that the official company business he was conducting, at that odd hour, was at the behest of his employer. That's a strategy that poses seemingly insurmountable challenges. And then, even if we can connect what happened on Christmas Eve with the scope and course of the driver's employment, there's the issue of collectability. According to Omar Sidi, this corporation is not only under the feds' microscope, but also on the ropes financially. If the ship goes down, then your friend's mother gets nothing."

"Yes, Dummy, no one said it was going to be easy. I see three tiers to your case. First, as you said, you have to establish that someone in the employ of the corporation committed the act. That exposes the entire executive structure to some measure of vicarious negligence. Next, you establish why they committed the act. And, finally, you expose who ordered the hit. You've stumbled into a criminal empire here: it's your duty as an officer of the court to expose the full extent of wrongdoing."

Devlin had already been playing this mental chess match, going back and forth about whether to pursue this case as an intentional act as part of a larger criminal conspiracy as Goldie was suggesting, or to use the more tightly focused strategy of nailing the driver for a negligent act.

The two options felt like a choice that offered no complete victory either way. If Devlin was a lawyer crusading to effectuate the totality of justice, then Goldie was right: he had to use the civil justice system as a tool for remediation, to expose a corporation that was swindling hard-working Americans. Plain and simple, that meant nailing Adalius Becker for ordering the criminal acts—and, on behalf of Ho-Chan's elderly mother, tapping the potential gold mine of ill-gotten gains piled up at Archard Holdings.

However, even if Devlin somehow prevailed in that scenario, Becker's battalion of lawyers would drag out the appeals process, which could potentially bleed into the time frame where Omar Sidi and his brethren swooped in, shuttering Archard Holdings and ending any chance of collecting. How would any of that help Ho-Chan Park's mother? The other choice was for Devlin to represent his client by getting the driver for negligent homicide. While this was probably a better strategy for his client, this tack would also let Becker slip away free and clear even though he had essentially ordered a murder. It also capped the elderly woman's potential compensation at the limits of the driver's personal insurance or, at best, some corporate insurance on the Trans Am. Worse, if there was intent by the defendant, the insurance company would not pay out anything; coverage did not extend to intentional acts. Devlin had already played out each strategy a dozen times in his mind.

"Hello? You still with us, Dummy?"

Devlin nodded. "There's nothing I want to do more than nail this criminal clown. But if we spend two years going to trial and getting a huge verdict that's uncollectable, that doesn't help the mother."

He still didn't know how, but Devlin was determined that, one way or another, he was going to connect the dots here—whichever strategy he pursued—and do right by Ho-Chan Park, which would give his elderly mother some measure of resolution. He was so engrossed in thinking about next steps that he almost forgot to ask about what had initiated this entire scenario.

"Goldie, how about that Rule 32 petition? You said you read it?"

"Yeah, I read it. So what?"

"Can I get your revisions? Suggestions? I'd like to get it revised and filed."

Goldie took a couple puffs and exhaled. "Then file it, Dummy. I don't give a shit."

"You don't have any changes?"

"Did I stutter? File it."

"No changes?"

Goldie looked at Monae. "For such a smart broad, you sure picked a dimwit."

"Same dimwit you picked to help with your impossible and important case," Monae deadpanned.

Goldie snorted and smiled. "Touché."

Devlin was shaking his head: all this time, all the work on the Ho-Chan Park case to get a boost on Bobby Swift's appeal, and he'd never needed Goldie at all. The original draft Devlin penned had breezed through the toughest scrutiny in appellate law, without a single change. Back to *Rule #7: Know the other side's case better than they know it themselves.*

Devlin marked the moment: the kid who had shown up in court clueless in 1970, to utter a string of ill-timed, inappropriate and ineffective statements, had penned a winning document in a complicated area of appellate law, which was only a means to an end: helping Bobby Swift. Indeed, Devlin was Goldie's legal peer and more.

And Sloane Monae? *Holy shit*—no one had ever done that to Goldie. And especially not here, in The Bunker, the hallowed crawl space of legal genius. As Devlin and Monae stood, eagerly anticipating the fresh air awaiting them, Devlin wondered what other surprises she had in store for him.

TWO days later, after Nadia Flores had keyed in and printed the document, Devlin drove a hundred miles south to Tucson in the cherry-red Blazer. Devlin had considered starting his legal practice here after law school, in the Old Pueblo, as locals called it. Those same locals also called Tucson "quaint." More accurately for Devlin, Tucson was an acquired taste, an enigma.

As he took the surface streets to Pima County Superior Court to file the Rule 32 petition, he was reminded once again why he had chosen metropolitan Phoenix instead to launch his new life and career in the sun. Everywhere he looked, in any direction, he saw a town that apparently employed planning and zoning officials who were on a permanent LSD trip. There was a Catholic church right next to a muffler shop, which was next to a hamburger joint next to a neon strip club next to a razor-wired tire store... and on and on the scattered mess went in every direction.

Devlin parked at the court complex, filed Bobby Swift's Rule 32 petition with the clerk and headed north back to Phoenix. He made a mental note to explain to Bobby Swift why things had taken this long—that Devlin had sought the guidance of a nationally recognized appellate lawyer on his client's behalf. As it turned out, the delay wasn't necessary, but Devlin's intention had been well-placed.

Devlin worked his way back through the flotsam-and-jetsam townscape to Interstate 10. He rolled down the driver's-side window and breathed in the month that made all in the desert rejoice. March brought increasingly longer days, gusty breezes and balmy temperatures in the 70s as the mild winter gave way to a backdrop of wispy clouds and radiant blue skies. Devlin could smell the perfumed scent of orange blossoms coming through the open window. After heavy rains in February, the desert floor on both sides of the freeway had exploded into a vast carpet of brilliant yellow and purple from the blooming marigolds, lupines, owl clover and poppies. The forthcoming annual firestorm of radiation, June through September, was not even yet on the radar. For desert dwellers, March was quintessential—a perfect succession of easy days that buoyed and energized the soul. The wider surge mirrored Devlin's growing confidence: he would soon be able to tell Bobby Swift that he had good news on his appeal for relief.

Part III

The Lawyer

Chapter Twenty

FOR THE NEXT MONTH AFTER MEETING WITH GOLDIE, Devlin started working to build his case. Fueling those efforts was Devlin's foundation as a trial attorney, built on his sense of empathy and compassion. He was confident, which was not to be mistaken for arrogance. He was now the voice for the voiceless.

Goldie had mapped out one strategy: establish that someone in the employ of the corporation had committed the hit-and-run; show *why* they had committed the act; and, finally, expose who had ordered the hit. Devlin had not ruled out this approach and, regardless of strategy, one of the first steps was depositions. In a big case like this, Devlin would have to cast a wide net to see what he might uncover, including a long list of witnesses he might depose: the two cops who were first on scene on Christmas Eve, Ford Rockwell, Omar Sidi and his supervisor (who had also been Ho-Chan's boss) and the Walgreens assistant manager. At Archard Holdings, Devlin would start at the bottom and work his way up: the fleet manager, who would have records of everyone with access to the vehicles; the driver of the orange Trans Am (whose name they still needed); all executive direct reports to the CEO; and then the overlord of the double-dealing empire:

Adalius Becker. The thought of deposing Becker energized Devlin. Or, better yet, getting him on the stand at trial: there was nothing better than meeting the rich and powerful eye-to-eye and systematically disassembling their webs of arrogant deceit and wrongdoing. Just *how* Devlin was going to get Becker on record as the man who had ordered the hit was still a bridge too far. One step at a time. And there was the gnawing tension: keeping his focus on collectability for Ho-Chan Park's mother while wondering which way to play this case.

With that chess match grinding away in his mind, Devlin moved on to making a list of the tedium required to build any civil case: documents. Devlin needed certified copies of Ho-Chan Park's death certificate and the full ME report from Ford Rockwell. He'd need employment records, performance reviews and paycheck stubs to establish Ho-Chan Park's work history and salary with the federal government. He wanted documentation on the Trans Am, including VIN, ownership history and all maintenance and repair records. Obviously, it wasn't likely they'd put the hit-and-run repair job on the company tab, but one never knew. Sometimes criminals covered almost every track but missed one critical detail. Devlin would request the same tranche of documents for all vehicles in the company fleet.

The lawyer also had to track down a Los Angeles-based interpreter to facilitate communication with Ho-Chan Park's mother in Korean. Instead of trying to coordinate the logistics of getting the elderly woman to Phoenix, Devlin planned to begin a dialogue—via the translator—to get her officially signed as a client of Devlin & Associates and to walk her through the early steps of the process. Then, in a few months, after he'd had a chance to put more meat on the bones of his case, he would travel to Los Angeles to meet her. He also wanted to be able to tell her in person about the attendant payoffs and opportunity costs of whichever track they chose, and the case strategy he was recommending.

Devlin planned to surprise Monae with the news that she would be accompanying him on the trip, which would include a stay at a luxury hotel. This was about as close to a vacation as Devlin ever got, which was to add some personal moments to the fringes of a business trip. It just wasn't in his wiring to take extended vacations as many of his legal peers did, whether to the ski slopes of Aspen or the beaches of Hawaii. Devlin felt most at home in the daily grind on behalf of his clients.

There were also rare respites such as a late-night work session when Monae arrived after hours and initiated an amorous romp in Devlin's locked office, a hushed affair as they kissed and fondled each other like two teenagers with a parent in the other room. After that encounter, as Monae stood in her black underwear and shimmied back into her Calvin Klein jeans, she asked, "You think we're giving that guy too much leash?"

"What guy?"

"The driver. Whoever he is."

Devlin considered it. "Sure, he might disappear. But neither of us has any authority to do anything about it."

Monae nodded, fastening her black bra and searching for her shirt. "I still worry. Does your case fall apart if he's in the wind?"

"He's the connection between the corporation and the crime, and he's the linchpin of both potential case strategies. And yet, we still don't even know his name."

Then she saw it. "Hey," she said, pointing to the gym bag, now atop Devlin's desk. "I totally forgot: my money! Did you look?"

"Nope," Devlin said. "Turns out Nadia had stowed it, I guess. But I wanted to wait for the big reveal. Open it."

She grabbed the zipper that ran the length of the bag's top, pulled, dug around a bit and smiled. She still hadn't buttoned her jeans; the black lace of her panties was visible.

"How much?" he asked.

She pulled out a stack of $100 bills with a paper band labeled "$10,000."

"Whoa," Devlin said. "I paid you an extra 10 grand to find our driver?"

"Nope," Monae said, shaking her head and grinning mischievously. She reached in and pulled out two more bundles. "There's three. You paid me 30 grand to find our driver."

"Thirty grand?" Devlin couldn't believe the Greek had paid him that much for one meeting on church kneelers—on top of the quarter-million he'd doled out for silence. "That's twice now you've railroaded me on a negotiation."

"Railroaded? No, just admit it: I outfoxed you. I can't wait."

"Wait for what?"

"The next one. Third time's a charm." Then she broke the band on one of the bundles, counted out five hundreds, and handed him the rest of the loose cash along with the two wrapped bundles.

"What's this?" he said.

"I can't take that much. But I will let you buy me a new Fendi."

"Why? You won. Straight up."

"Because I'm a good sport."

"Not in my wildest dreams," he said.

"What?"

"A beautiful woman in unbuttoned jeans and a black bra giving *me* almost 30 grand after sex."

"Just shut up before I change my mind."

Devlin hugged her and tucked the cash, $29,500, in the desk drawer where he'd kept Trevor Walsh's Rolex hidden for so many years.

IN May, Devlin, Monae and Omar Sidi met with two prosecutors from the Organized Crime Division of the Maricopa County Attorney's Office, which focused on complex white-collar crimes, including those involving criminal syndicates. Part of Devlin's strategy in pursuing any civil action, which he only had seven more months to file before the statute of limitations ran out, was to put as much pressure as possible on any potential defendant at the outset. A formal criminal investigation would concurrently and nicely turn up the heat on the very people he might eventually be deposing in his case. Sidi was already investigating Archard Holdings at the federal level, and had to get clearance from his higher-ups to alert local prosecutors to the cause. Sidi's superiors would allow it only if the state prosecutors agreed to keep any investigative work quiet until federal charges were officially filed.

Like Devlin, the two county lawyers were each buried in an avalanche of paperwork, stressed and juggling too many cases. They said taking up a state investigation of a sprawling fraud case, which the feds were already investigating, was unlikely. The prosecutors said unraveling financial schemes was a long slog that rarely led to formal charges. That was the monstrous reality in the white-collar arena: well-heeled executives in $900 suits committed their crimes in broad daylight. That always presented a steep wall for prosecutors to climb in connecting the dots. But they were at least willing to listen.

After Devlin walked them through everything, of most interest to the prosecutors was the hit-and-run, which they would refer to the Vehicular Crimes Bureau. The prosecutors believed their peers might at least task a detective to identify the mystery driver and see what charges might be brought. But again, Monae had only brought a circumstantial case connecting the orange Trans Am to the crime. And with no evidence tying any suspect specifically to the crime, there was not an immediate path forward to file charges.

Monae protested that Omar Sidi *had* identified the driver who tried to scare him, in the same orange Trans Am the Walgreens assistant manager saw on Christmas

Eve. Could that possibly be just coincidence? Of course not, the prosecutor told her, but where was the witness who had seen that same driver hit Ho-Chan Park on Christmas Eve? When Monae looked at Devlin he shook her off: the Walgreens guy was only an observer after the fact. Monae slumped back in frustration. Too many times she had seen the same thing in law enforcement: she knew who had committed the crime, but did not have the evidence to prove it in court. At least not yet.

After the meeting, Devlin, Monae and Sidi stepped from the court complex building that faced Jefferson Street. They walked without talking, deep in thought, and crossed the street at First Avenue.

"The cat will always eat," Sidi said, stopping to hug Monae.

She smiled. "That's right."

Devlin gave her the look that asked, *What is he talking about?*

"I will for one hundred percent always be grateful. To you both. You are honoring the memory of H.C. by pursuing this case for his very wrongful death." Sidi looked toward the cloud-flecked blue sky. "I will sleep like baby tonight. I will talk you soon."

Sidi hugged Monae again, and then Devlin, who was caught off guard. Then he turned and walked up the sidewalk toward his car.

"That is just one decent man," Monae said.

"Fighting the good fight," Devlin added.

She turned, hugged and then kissed her boyfriend, a long, lingering kiss that pushed the world away momentarily for both. Then they pulled back and smiled at each other.

"Can you put a name to the driver of the orange Trans Am?" Devlin asked.

"I was already thinking that."

"I'm going to subpoena him to appear for a deposition."

"Consider it done. Let me borrow your Blazer for a couple hours."

Devlin produced his keys, and they switched sets. Devlin didn't have to ask: he knew she was going on the prowl and that the mystery driver had already seen her in a blue 280Z. He pointed to where he'd parked, and she did the same. They kissed again and walked in opposite directions. At the next stoplight Monae paused when she noticed a parked car, a four-door beige Plymouth Reliant K-car, on the opposite side of the street with two men in sunglasses inside. It was immediately suspicious, and she sensed they were watching her. She looked back up the sidewalk: Devlin was already gone. She had already unconsciously slid her right hand in her handbag and was squeezing the cool grip of the Detective Special revolver. With the barrel aimed forward, she could pull the trigger as needed without ever drawing, a technique she had practiced at the range with an old purse she didn't mind shredding.

"What a shit-box," she said aloud, comparing the ugly car to her road-hugging Z. She couldn't tell if the car was running or not. She turned around and started back up the sidewalk, away from the Blazer. Halfway up the block, she paused and turned, her heart racing: the shit-box was rolling up right behind her. A clear tail. At the next street she turned right and stepped into the alcove of a sports bar. As the car rolled slowly around the corner, the passenger spotted her. The lumpy intimidator tapped his partner, who stopped the clunker. They were only about fifteen feet away, engine idling. Monae's palms were sweating. She didn't figure this was anything more than intimidation, but she was ready for whatever might break loose. Then a horn blasted behind the K-car, which was now blocking traffic. The stare-down only lasted a few seconds, but felt like agonizing minutes. Then the car rolled away, the passenger never breaking eye contact behind his sunglasses.

As the car passed, Monae released her grip on the pistol, pulled out her notepad and wrote the plate number that she had been repeating to herself. The next thoughts sent a chill through her: if they knew exactly where she was going to be today, how long had they been tailing her? And if they'd been tailing her, then they probably had her apartment, too. In other words, they knew where she slept. The encounter only emboldened her to immediately get the name of the Trans Am driver. She'd have to cancel a planned meeting with a new client to do so, but this needed to be done now. She re-traced her route back to the cherry-red rig and drove straight to the building on Central Avenue where Ho-Chan Park had worked. She took the elevator to the tenth floor and waited in the stripped-down reception area, with Crockett and Tubbs right where she'd left them. When Omar Sidi emerged through the door behind the receptionist, he smiled broadly.

"Why are we seeing each other again so soon?"

Monae leaned in and whispered, out of earshot of the receptionist. "Want to play detective?"

Sidi leaned back, smiled again and whispered, "For one hundred percent."

MONAE and Sidi sat for more than an hour, parked in the Blazer across the street from Archard Holdings. From their vantage point they could see the orange Trans Am in the parking lot, glistening like a tainted gem in the sunlight.

"The detective work is very boring," Sidi said.

"This is the part you don't see on TV."

"There," Sidi said, sitting up and pointing.

Monae's pulse quickened: it was the same guy who'd stonewalled her. They watched Delaney Dunne slide into the orange Trans Am and wheel out of the parking lot. That Dunne had somehow repaired the damage without leaving a trail still bothered Monae, but she had to let it go. While he might have put one over on her there, she already had the car, with two witnesses giving the same plate. Now she just needed the driver.

"We are the cat now," Sidi said.

Monae started the Blazer, waited and then followed at a safe distance. They tailed him south through Scottsdale and watched him park at Video World, an independent movie-rental place. Fifteen minutes later, Dunne emerged with three chunky VHS tapes in identical brown plastic cases. Then they followed him to a Chinese restaurant. After he came out carrying takeout, Monae started the Blazer and turned the opposite direction of the Trans-Am.

"He is getting away!" Sidi yelled.

Monae smiled and shook her head. "No, he's not. Now is when the cat will eat."

They returned to Video World, where Monae told Sidi to wait in the Blazer. She walked in and smiled at the twenty-something kid behind the counter, who obviously liked what he saw coming into his shop.

"Hi, my boyfriend was just here. We got three movies. Did he leave his wallet, by chance?"

"Wait, you're Double-D's girlfriend?"

She nodded. "I am." A nickname wasn't going to help.

"He must have money. And now I get why he got *Flashdance*."

"How's that?"

"Chick flick. Doesn't really fit with *Risky Business* and *Porky*'s. You'll like it, but *Risky Business* is way better: 'I have a trig mid-term tomorrow, and I'm being chased by Guido the killer pimp!'"

Monae smiled. "The wallet?"

"Oh, right." The kid dug around and walked the aisle where Dunne had been. "Sorry, nothing."

"Shit," she said. "The receipt was in the wallet. Could we get a duplicate?"

"Sure."

Monae knew it was a flimsy way to get what she needed, but it didn't matter because the kid was distracted and willing to do her bidding. He printed off another dot-matrix copy, which took a full minute. He tore it off and handed her the 8.5-by-11 page with small holes running the length of each side. She smiled.

"You've been very helpful," she said, turning to walk out.

"Hope you find his wallet," the kid offered as she left.

Monae climbed in the Blazer, smiled and handed Sidi the receipt. He read the name at the top of the page right above the account holder's home address: "Delaney Dunne." Then he looked at her, his eyes welling up. "Delaney Dunne is the one who kill H.C.?"

Monae squeezed his hand and nodded as she fired the big-block. "We got him."

Chapter Twenty-One

BY JUNE, THE BRUTAL SUMMER HEAT blanketed metropolitan Phoenix with a successive march of daily highs exceeding 110 degrees. And by desert standards, this was still not the worst: the ravaging humidity headed north from the Sea of Cortez and the Gulf of Mexico would land in July and August.

Concerned by the threat of whomever was tailing her in "the shit-box," as Devlin and Monae exclusively called the ominous K-car, the couple had unofficially moved in together. This was ostensibly for protection but mostly because they were both tired of taking turns driving home at 2 a.m. Now Devlin spent every night at her downtown apartment, to keep her from being alone. She appreciated the gesture—but also knew it was more likely she would be the protector should that need ever arise. She had spotted the K-car again, early in the morning as she left for her daily run, which was always at least two miles and up to ten depending on her mood and energy. At the police academy, the training officers had run the recruits like sled dogs chasing glory in the Iditarod, and she'd been blessed, or cursed, with the running bug ever since. She was still as fit as the day she graduated the academy in 1977.

On the morning she saw the car, there was only one thug. After the first encounter

Monae had driven to the Motor Vehicle Department, where Sir Larry covertly ran the shit-box plate and, the next day, handed her the information on a scrap of paper in the parking lot. She read it and looked at him, nodding.

"Yep," Sir Larry said, flicking ash from his Kent III. "Same fleet registration account as the last one you gave me. The plot thickens as the curtains close on Act II. Hot on the trail now, milady?"

"Something like that." Monae was digging in her new Fendi beaded handbag with the snakeskin strap, which she had in rotation with the Paloma Picasso. By her normally frugal ways, the Fendi would have been a ridiculous splurge. But with the $500 in betting winnings from Devlin at her disposal, she'd fallen in love with the intricacy of the geometric beadwork, with *Ojos de Dios* ("God's eyes") patterns in pink, blue, green and white set against black.

"Please tell me this Archard Holdings is a shell company for the mob, and our beautiful sleuth is jamming a wrench in the gears of a vast criminal scheme."

Monae laughed. "As crazy as that sounds, you're not far off." She pulled out a $100 bill, the second half of the payment, and handed it to her CI, which was cop-speak for a confidential informant.

AT their new shared digs, Devlin didn't like the feeling of being followed. Or at least watched from a safe distance. In the wee hours at Monae's apartment, he would imagine the beige Plymouth parked across the street with a cigarette ember or two glowing in the black urban void. Sometimes the thought would take him to the window, where he would crack the blinds to see that at 2:30 a.m., no one was tracking him or his investigator. Devlin chalked up that good news to his former client and now go-to enforcer, Mike Jefferson.

Before Devlin met him, the former hockey goon and U.S. Marine had been a Phoenix cop for ten years, including being a member of the SWAT team and all-around badass. He looked very much like NFL running back Earl Campbell with his ebony skin, unruly beard and a neck thicker than most people's thighs. One night when he was off duty and headed home on his motorcycle, a driver clipped Jefferson and mangled his right leg. Jefferson found Devlin through a cop buddy who was in Devlin's group legal plan. Devlin rushed to the hospital to meet his new client, and as it turned out, Jefferson was a Buffalo native who, like his new lawyer, could recite the names of that season's starting offensive linemen for the Bills. Devlin's investigation immediately turned up two useful facts: the defendant blew a 3.2 on the breathalyzer; and he was also an off-duty cop. Devlin retraced the drunk cop's path on the night of the collision to five different bars near the college campus in Tempe. On behalf of Jefferson, who was 30, Devlin sued the bars under a dram shop statute. Jefferson lost his right leg below the knee; the perpetrator cop lost his job and pension, and got five years in jail. The various bars that had overserved the cop each settled for the insurance policy limits, a total that exceeded seven figures for Devlin's client. Because he had to wear a prosthetic, Jefferson was unable to work patrol ever again. But he did stay on the force as a public information officer, which he both hated (pushing paper vs. street prowl) and loved because at least he was still in the game.

In a legendary moment, Jefferson was off duty and waiting outside a store while his mom did some quick shopping. This was just days after he'd gotten out of the hospital, and he had not yet been fitted with his prosthetic. Unbelieving, Jefferson watched a shoplifter run out of the store, immediately followed by a uniformed Phoenix cop who took the thief to the ground. As the fight escalated, the shoplifter was getting the upper hand. Unable to walk, Jefferson slithered out of the car onto the hot pavement and bear-crawled his way to the fight, about twenty yards away. When he got to the scrap, Jefferson pushed himself up on his good knee and cold-cocked the shoplifter with a star-spangled left cross.

Once back in action, Jefferson took every opportunity to serve warrants and orders of protection in the grittier parts of Phoenix. On one call a defiant kid unleashed his deranged dog on Jefferson. The dog snapped its teeth onto Jefferson's prosthetic leg, recoiled in surprise and then lunged upward. To end the lethal threat Jefferson had no choice but to pull out his .357 and kill the dog in self-defense. The kid was so stunned by Robocop fending off his vicious dog that he immediately gave up and went prone on the ground.

With their Buffalo connection and a winning case together, Devlin and Jefferson were forever bonded in a unique way. Any time Devlin had an issue, problem or concern that might require certain skills—administered by a loyal friend built like a brick shithouse—he took Jefferson along. If they had been together on one of his hockey teams, Jefferson would have been Devlin's loyal enforcer, a title Jefferson relished and wore as a noble badge of honor. After Devlin learned that two thugs in a K-car had been tailing his girlfriend, he picked up the phone in his office, called Mike Jefferson and told him everything he knew.

"Think you can take care of that?" Devlin asked.

CHAPTER TWENTY-ONE

"Consider the situation resolved," Jefferson said, vaguely.

"I won't ask."

"You did your job," Jefferson said. "Now let me do mine."

AT least since the magical night with Monae nearly a year ago in Kingman, Devlin had solved his sleeping dilemma. After that crowning night of uninterrupted hours of sleep, Devlin had gone to his doctor for a prescription to calm his whirling mind. Insidious sleep interruption had not been an issue since.

Although Devlin's primary focus now was the formal complaint for the Ho-Chan Park wrongful death action, other cases continued. Two weeks before the planned trip to Los Angeles to meet Ho-Chan's mother, Devlin tied up the CandyMan case when he was able to wrench $50,000 from the other driver's insurance company. The cashier's check arrived from the insurance company the day before the L.A. trip. CandyMan and Sunshine came to Devlin & Associates together. CandyMan was in his trademark jeans, black T-shirt, leather vest and black boots. His limp from the crash was noticeably worse. Sunshine, too, was in her biker-mama gear, and she carried a large wrapped gift. After Devlin's one-third cut, that gave $33,000-plus for CandyMan to get his hip replacement surgery, with a chunk left over for his pain and suffering. Devlin gave them the check issued by Devlin & Associates. Immediately CandyMan's eyes welled up with tears. He couldn't manage any words, so he just reached out and shook Devlin's hand. Sunshine was teary, too, as she handed Devlin the gift.

When Devlin peeled off the paper he saw himself, painted in oils, standing before a jury. The anti-bra advocate Sunshine was also a very good artist. She had dug around at the library and found an old newspaper clipping about Devlin's trial against the nursing home operator in the seventies. Without an actual photograph, she had used her imagination and brought the Old Courthouse scene to life in a beautifully painted canvas. The meeting ended with an odd group hug among the biker holding his check, the free-spirited artist with the leather-face complexion, and the lawyer in a tailored gray suit and blue tie.

The next morning, June 6, 1985, Devlin and Monae took a yellow cab from Los Angeles International Airport to the Beverly Wilshire Hotel, at the intersection of Wilshire Boulevard and Rodeo Drive. Sloane Monae, who had been to Los Angeles for college volleyball games, was still thrilled because Devlin had reserved a suite at the plush property, which she need not know came at the princely sum of $675 per night. The hotel was only a twenty-minute cab ride to Ho-Chan Park's mother's apartment, just a straight shot east on Wilshire Boulevard through Koreatown. After checking in, Devlin and Monae spent a leisurely afternoon having lunch and then browsing the shops along Rodeo Drive. Devlin was mostly thinking about the meeting the next day. Back at the hotel, as Devlin was taking a shower, Monae undressed and let herself in to join him for a steam session. After, they went for an early dinner in West Hollywood and wound up at The Troubadour to see a band neither had ever heard of before: Guns N' Roses. The music and the club were too loud and raucous for Devlin and Monae alike, so they cut out before the band finished the set. In the cab ride on the way back to the Beverly Wilshire Hotel, Monae and Devlin had romance on their minds again. But by the time the cab cleared a late-night L.A. traffic snarl and they were back in their room, they collapsed onto the bed and fell into a deep sleep in each other's arms.

The next morning, the translator met Monae and Devlin in the hotel lobby. Sarah Sung was a 24-year-old Korean-American graduate teaching assistant at UCLA who knew her way around LA. Outside, morning fog shrouded the cityscape in a typical early chill. Sung drove them a short distance to the Original Farmers Market, a sprawling cluster of eateries, trendy shops and gourmet grocery stores. They climbed out of the two-door, micro-compact Honda Civic that had Devlin and Monae joking that they wished Sung had brought a more spacious K-car. They found a counter-service stand and ordered savory French crêpes and coffee, and as they ate Devlin laid out what they would need to discuss with Ho-Chan's mother. After breakfast Sung drove them east on Wilshire Boulevard, where they soon passed the art deco Wiltern Theatre. Then they were cutting through the dense Koreatown mix clustered with bars, Korean BBQ restaurants with tabletop grills, karaoke joints, hip speakeasies and clubs, traditional spas, bubble-tea cafes and specialty grocery stores. Sung turned south off Wilshire and found the apartment building between Koreatown and MacArthur Park. Again, Devlin and Monae had to wrench their lanky frames from the Japanese micro-car. Once they had, they were staring at a depressingly shabby apartment as the sun started to fracture the fog. The building was a sagging two-level affair that reminded Devlin immediately of Trevor Walsh's ramshackle apartment. Every American city had these same crossroad stops for the hard-luck demographic, a handful of them on the way up to something better but almost exclusively reserved for the have-nots. Despite the scant niceties, Monae noticed the fruited scent of night-blooming jasmine in the cool air. Palm trees and banana plants shaded what was left of the brown grass. The concrete sidewalk was heaved at ankle-twisting angles by the decades-long march of thick tree roots.

The trio climbed the stairs to the second level, where the burned-off fog had given way to the permanent poisonous drape that hung on the city. To the east, through the endless phalanx of telephone poles and dusky pollution, was the shrouded skyline of downtown L.A. Devlin found the correct door and knocked. It took a few minutes before the door cracked open, then wider, until Devlin and Monae saw Eun Jung Park, or "E.J." as everyone called her. It had been eighteen months since the fateful events of that Christmas Eve, and nine months since Goldie had introduced the thin file into Devlin's world, and now the lawyer was finally face-to-face with his client. She grasped a green oxygen tank on wheels that connected to a tube running up and then splitting into both her nostrils. She was diminutive, five feet tall on her tippy-toes and barely a hundred pounds. She smiled broadly.

Sarah Sung started speaking rapid-fire Korean. They went back and forth in Korean, and then there was a lot of smiling and nods back and forth among everyone. Eventually E.J. gestured the trio into her tiny apartment, which was officially a one-bedroom but felt like a walk-in closet. There was a disconcerting musty smell, an accumulation of three decades. It was dark, too, and cluttered with clothes, knickknacks, stacks of papers and a painted bookshelf crammed with sundry items—but no books—including a blender and a massive waffle iron with a frayed cord. Through the open back window over the kitchen sink, Devlin could see razor wire atop a gray block-wall fence, which surrounded some sort of automotive operation.

Every ten seconds or so the staccato tapping of air wrenches spinning lug nuts—*whir whir whir*—whined through the open window and bounced around the apartment. Devlin wondered how she hadn't been driven mad by the sound. For him, it was immediately irritating, like the intermittent chirp of a smoke alarm that needed a new battery. After more smiling and nodding, Devlin and Monae squeezed onto a dusty loveseat; E.J. and Sung sat on the only other two seats, which were two mismatched chairs at a small oval table three feet from the couch. E.J. had already prepared tea, and poured everyone a cup without asking. Devlin and Monae each took their cup, smiled and bowed their heads again.

"Tell her that I'm her lawyer, Connor J. Devlin with Devlin & Associates, and this is Sloane Monae, a private investigator who works for our firm. And that it's a pleasure to finally meet her."

With the teacups clinking softly, Sung started speaking Korean, and then spoke louder to top the volume of the *whir whir whir*. When Devlin figured she had said about the equivalent of what he'd just said, he expected her to stop. Except she just continued talking in Korean. And talking. And talking. She spoke for several minutes without stopping, not even for the air wrenches' *whir whir whir*. Then E.J. started talking, even faster, and then they were both talking over each other as the air wrenches continued, *whir whir whir*. Devlin looked at Monae and whispered: "I just told her to introduce us." Monae shrugged her shoulders and whispered back: "Lost in translation."

Finally, after several minutes, the two women stopped talking. The translator smiled and looked at Devlin. "She said it's nice to meet you."

Whir whir whir.

"That's it?" Devlin said.

Sung and E.J. both smiled and nodded. Devlin looked at Monae. "Looks like we're—" *whir whir whir*. Devlin stared through the open window in the kitchen and wanted to ask her to close it. But this was her space, her home, her life and her reality. Devlin's law practice was about the art of the human condition, and how to read and react to it. He wanted to understand each client's entire universe, not sweep in like some clichéd lawyer who started re-ordering everything to his liking. Instead, he would simply default to enduring any unpleasantries.

"Looks like we're in for a long day," he said, smiling at his new client. Then he quickly said to Sung, "Don't translate that."

Indeed, only Monae would get a brief break from that annoyingly loud cave over the next fourteen hours. In addition to the noise, by early afternoon it felt like it was 95 degrees inside. Everyone was sweating except E.J., who had apparently acclimated and was now fully inoculated to the smells, sounds and sweltering conditions. Devlin had to explain how he and Sloane Monae had pieced the evidence together to identify who had done such a horrible thing on a holiday night. This communication all had to be done back and forth through the translator and over the *whir whir whir*. There were also long delays every time anyone used Ho-Chan's name, because the mere mention of her son sent E.J. into a teary reverie for several minutes. Each time, all the other three could do was sit and wait for her sobbing to subside. Then she would dab her eyes with a tissue and eventually nod that she was ready to continue.

Whir whir whir.

Devlin then had to explain—through the translator and the cacophony of lug nuts being endlessly spun on and off—how a wrongful death case would work and

193

what E.J. could expect, which would be a jury verdict on her behalf, or a financial settlement if there were no trial, to compensate her for her loss and provide for her ongoing care. Devlin also desperately wanted to tell her what strategy he was recommending, whether they would go after the corporation or just the driver, whom they had identified as Delaney Dunne. But Devlin's mental back-and-forth had not yet provided any clarity on which strategy to pursue. Just when Devlin decided he would nail Becker, the likelihood of doing so just didn't seem plausible. Then when he was all in, at least mentally, to simply go after Dunne, an anger seethed in Devlin's belly about letting Becker slip away with no accountability for his part in the death of a human being. So instead, Devlin didn't mention case strategy and instead focused on a long list of care needs Devlin asked E.J. to detail.

To do so, Devlin spent the next hours asking about E.J.'s life, her connection to her son and how his death had affected her. She and her husband had emigrated from Korea to Los Angeles in 1925; their son was born the next year. She had been widowed almost thirty years now after her husband, who was also an accountant, succumbed to pancreatic cancer. She had moved to this cheaper apartment then, and had been barely subsisting ever since on her deceased husband's Social Security death benefit and much-needed financial gifts from her son. E.J. had suffered two heart attacks and a stroke, and now required 24/7 oxygen. She had no vehicle (she'd never had a driver's license or driven a car in her entire life) and used to walk to Koreatown to get outside and shop, but that was proving too taxing now. She didn't like leaving the apartment, because it was difficult hauling the oxygen bottle up and down the steps. Likewise, she no longer attempted to navigate the city bus system. At age 80, she was now a shut-in who felt imprisoned in her dark apartment with no other options to improve her surroundings.

The one bright spot and shining star in her life had been her beloved son Ho-Chan. In her eyes, he was the embodiment of the American Dream, the son of immigrants who had ascended to an important job with the U.S. government. E.J. did not really understand what her son had done in his job as a federal banking examiner, nor did she care. All she knew was that he had graduated with a college degree from an American university and had honored the family name by working for the United States of America.

Indeed, despite his meager government salaries through various posts, Ho-Chan had always managed over the years to send his mother money every month, which she used to buy food and essentials. This extra help was critical in bridging the gap between Social Security and what she needed to survive. To help his mother, Ho-Chan used to visit every couple months. To save money, he'd drive rather than take a flight. He'd leave Phoenix after work on Friday night, drive the five-and-a-half hours to Los Angeles and arrive at his mother's apartment by midnight, where he slept on the small couch. On Saturday she would be up by 5 a.m. and ready to start the day with her son, who was unable to sleep anyway due to her clanking around in the kitchen just a few feet away. They went out for breakfast, and then he would take her shopping in Koreatown to stock her kitchen until his next visit. Then they'd go to MacArthur Park for a walk and, later, out to dinner at Pink's Hot Dogs on La Brea Avenue. E.J. had been going there with her husband since it had opened in 1939, and she always ordered two hot dogs and took one home to eat for lunch the next day. On Sunday morning, E.J. cooked her son all his Korean breakfast favorites, starting with *gaeran tost-u* (egg toast), which was an egg sandwich with cabbage and a heavy dusting of brown sugar. She also cooked fried eggs and cut up the fruit they had bought at the market the day before. She toasted Japanese-style white bread from a Korean bakery and laid on a thick spread of local strawberry butter. E.J. asked about her son's work and whether he'd been dating. They reminisced about going to watch the Dodgers as a family, and the time Ho-Chan split open his tongue when he fell off his bike and hit the curb face-first. For E.J., the clock was always ticking down during these visits, to what she dreaded most.

Ho-Chan Park had to leave her apartment by noon Sunday so he could be back in Phoenix before 6 p.m. to get ready for the work week. Those teary Sunday departures had gotten increasingly more difficult over the years, as his mother's health declined and her loneliness and sadness expanded into an untenable state of despair. For the last several years, his intention had been to get them living in the same city, either moving his mother to Phoenix or getting a transfer so he could live and work in Los Angeles. But as the savings-and-loan investigation deepened and was centered in the Southwest, Ho-Chan was uniquely positioned in Phoenix and knew a transfer elsewhere was unlikely. At that point, just before his death, he had already scouted and secured a Phoenix apartment for his mother, with a deposit and signed lease agreement. He had planned to fly to Los Angeles on Christmas Day 1983, pack up his mother's belongings over the next couple days and then drive them both back to Phoenix in a rented U-Haul truck. He had taken the entire week off between Christmas and New Year's Day for that specific purpose, which was why he was working so late that Christmas Eve. That he had never arrived and didn't answer her calls had sent E.J. into a state of panic and anxiety that still had not fully abated almost two years later.

Since her son's death, E.J. had relied entirely on two different neighbors who would stop by to see if she needed anything at the store. She began to wonder, too, if her apartment was contributing to her declining health. Devlin had thought the same thing; he'd only been here half a day, and he was already feeling clammy, depressed and in need of a shower. At one point during her recitations in Korean, as he waited for the translation, Devlin was certain he felt something scurry across his ankle. A cockroach? Or perhaps it had just been a phantom sensation conjured by the general malaise of the apartment. Either way, it was unsettling. He couldn't imagine how horrible it was for her to essentially be trapped in here and tethered to an anchor, that clunky oxygen canister she had to drag through life.

By early evening, when the temperature inside had dropped to 85, Devlin realized the day would run even longer than they had planned. He gave Monae a $50 bill and asked her to find takeout food. Sarah Sung had to stay, otherwise all communication would stop, so she gave Monae her car keys. After Monae returned with a boxful of soft tortilla tacos with cilantro and room-temperature bottles of Coca-Cola, they continued the tediously slow Korean-English conversation. Sometime after 7 p.m. the *whir whir whir* mercifully stopped, and cooler air started to settle across the city. By the time they finished, darkness had long descended across Los Angeles. Now approaching 11 p.m., Devlin and Monae were both tired and sticky from dried sweat, as was the translator. E.J. was energized by it all and dreading the moment everyone would leave her alone and isolated again. As the trio stood to leave, E.J. got teary-eyed and said something to the student, who turned to Devlin and said, "There's one more thing she wants you to see."

Devlin smiled, nodded and bowed. They all followed the 80-year-old mother, and her oxygen bottle, from her cramped living room into an even more cramped bedroom where she flipped on a light that barely illuminated the dimness with a yellow hue. On one wall, opposite the twin bed where she slept, was a sprawling and impressive shrine to Ho-Chan Park. Hanging on the wall above a long dusty credenza were framed pictures of her son as a kid: holding a puppy with Mom and Dad at around age 7; riding a bike at around 10; a group shot with friends at a birthday party; high school graduation; a smiling H.C. at his college graduation from UCLA; and Ho-Chan in his government-standard white shirt and black tie working for the United States of America, standing in front of a slate-gray building. Also on the credenza were a cluster of youth sports trophies for soccer, baseball and track; high school and college report cards (all A's); a stack of kid drawings in marker and crayon; and the powder-blue folio that held his college diploma, a bachelor's of science in accounting.

E.J. lit each of the half-dozen votive candles on the credenza and then tried to say something in Korean to the young woman. But she could not get the words out through the tears, and she fell to the ground sobbing. Devlin helped her back up, and Monae moved to the other side to hold her as she cried. The day before, Devlin had embraced CandyMan and his artist bride; today it was the grieving Korean widow who'd lost her son. With her husband gone, too, she was all alone in the world, with only one advocate fighting for her cause: the Buffalo kid in the cherry-red Blazer.

Devlin was now standing a foot away from the photograph of the smiling Ho-Chan Park in his G-man business attire, a similar advocate for justice. E.J. picked up the photo of her son, said something in Korean and handed Devlin the framed image.

"She wants you to have this so you know why this case is important," Sung said.

"Tell her thank you, I accept and that I will keep this on my desk."

The student translated and E.J. nodded, bowed and smiled. Then E.J. paused and, in a light-bulb moment, held up her index finger, the universally recognized symbol for "one more thing." She started digging in the closet. She emerged with a white banker's box with a matching lid and handed it to Devlin. Hand-written on the top of the box was something in Korean, which Devlin assumed was a note to herself about the contents. E.J. spoke briefly in Korean.

"She says, 'This is very important,'" the student said. "It may help the case."

Devlin smiled, nodded and said, "Thank you. Thank you."

When he'd gotten the thin file from Goldie, Devlin only knew the victim as an "ASIAN MALE APPROXMITELY 50-YEARS-OLD" from a poorly written police report. Then the anonymous victim became a specific name and age, "Ho-Chan Park, a 57-year-old man," in Ford Rockwell's autopsy report. Now, as his mother slipped again into her endless dark space of grief, Ho-Chan Park was a living, breathing human being upon whom his mother had depended for her very sustenance and survival. In that moment, Devlin redoubled his intention to do everything in his power to help this woman through her loss: he was going to nail those bastards at Archard Holdings. Then, as he was hugging E.J., Devlin conjured a new rule, something he hadn't done in years, that honed his focus for the next play.

Rule #11: Misperception is, at times, more important than perception.

Chapter Twenty-Two

IN JULY 1985, DEVLIN WAS READY to enter the wolf's lair: Archard Holdings. Despite E. J. Park's health challenges, Devlin projected that she might live another ten years or more. He needed to get her moved out of that squalid apartment, set her up with daily health care and living assistance, and provide funds for another decade or longer. He knew he was playing a poker hand without any good cards, so he was ready to bluff with what he had—their employee Delaney Dunne, in a car registered to the corporation, and a wrongful death—and play it with all the confidence in the world.

Rule #11: Misperception is, at times, more important than perception.

Most importantly, he believed he would do right by his client. Added to her husband's Social Security death benefit, Devlin had to finesse enough compensation for her to live out her final days in improved surroundings with the assistance she needed. With that in mind, Devlin would go into the meeting with an inner ultimatum: either they settled on Devlin's number, or he was prepared to file the case and go to trial even with all the pressures and pitfalls that route would entail for both sides.

Just before 9 a.m. on a blazing, muggy morning in the desert, Devlin parked the Blazer and walked toward Archard Holdings. For good measure, on the way in he saw the orange Trans Am backed into one of the spaces near the door. Devlin stopped and admired the fruits of Monae's labor. The vehicle was immaculate and waxed to perfection, with the sun glinting off the chrome and gloss-neon orange. He studied the paint, as Monae had, to see if there was any mismatch between the front end, the hood and the rest of the vehicle. Even to someone who'd owned various high-end vehicles, the paint was flawless. He'd had one of these himself, a black Trans Am Super Duty with the trademark screaming chicken on the hood. Devlin still marveled that his super-sleuth girlfriend had found this vehicle and connected the dots, which was the only reason he was here today. Yes, she was unbelievable, in a multitude of ways.

Inside, the 20-something woman who greeted Devlin looked like she was styled more for a nightclub than work: voluminous blonde hairdo, black top with plunging neckline, tight miniskirt and spiky shoes. She led him to a plush conference room with a mammoth table at the center.

"They'll be right with you, Mr. Devlin. Please help yourself to coffee and pastries."

"Thank you."

Devlin took a seat near the middle; he wanted to see who chose the head of the table. There was a plate of thick cinnamon buns, slathered with white frosting, at the center of the table. The sweet aroma of the pastries commingled with the pungent scent of $200-a-pound Indonesian coffee brewing—depositor money was there for Becker to burn.

As he waited, Devlin studied an oversized triptych, a monochrome abstract, hanging directly in front of him. By 9:10 a.m. he had decided it was an ugly waste of decorating dollars, as four lawyers from Becker's general counsel came marching into the room. The lead lawyer at the head of the squad was a good-looking, square-jawed man in his early 40s who stood by his seat at one end of the table.

"So sorry to keep you waiting, Mr. Devlin," he said. "The whims of Mr. Becker know no clock." He stood with the palpable confidence of someone who had already won the case and was only here to report the bad news to the losing side.

"He's here?" Devlin said. "You should ask him to come join us."

The man just flashed a fat-chance smile and said, "Coffee?"

Devlin stood and extended his hand. "Connor Devlin."

"Odon March," he said, extending his hand.

"Is that your name, or a direct order?" Devlin said.

"Perhaps both. My grandfather told me our surname means 'wealthy defender,' which was prescient to my future profession."

"Or maybe you were supposed to play linebacker alongside Mike Singletary."

"Perhaps," March said.

The other three, two men and a woman, carried thick leather briefcases. Devlin wondered: since this was their first meeting, what could they possibly be carrying? The woman wore a dark pinstriped suit with a simple long skirt, a silver blouse and black heels. The men were impeccably dressed in well-cut suits. The introductions and handshakes went around.

"Natalie Grant," she said, smiling. "Junior associate."

"Connor Devlin," he said. "Pleasure."

"Steve Littleton, senior associate."

Devlin nodded.

"Greg Truax, junior associate."

"Four against one," Devlin said. "Hardly seems fair." Except really it was just March and Littleton who mattered; the two junior associates were just there to stack the deck.

"Oh, we are nothing if not fair," March said, pouring himself a coffee.

Then there was an awkward silence as the other associates poured and prepped their own cups. Once everyone was settled—March on one end, Devlin in the middle and the three other lawyers directly across from him—March spoke.

"Well, Mr. Devlin, would you like to proceed, since you called this meeting?"

"Yes, thank you," he said. "I'm going to tell you what we know, and I don't want to hear your version, or legal points of contention, or excuses. I'm just here to tell you what I've got. Then I'm going to give you one opportunity to resolve this amicably."

"Duly noted," March said. "I'm certain you'll enlighten us as to what this is all about."

"To start, we have your employee, Mr. Delaney Dunne, driving a vehicle registered to this corporation in the commission of an intimidation drive-by about one week before Christmas in December 1983. We then have a second incident, and a witness identifying the same vehicle, on December 24, 1983, the night on which Mr. Ho-Chan Park was struck down and died on Central Avenue in a hit-and-run sometime just before midnight. Not coincidentally, we know the victim was investigating Archard Holdings as a federal banking examiner at the time of his death. Not coincidentally, we know the first victim of one of this company's intimidation ploys, a Mr. Omar Sidi, is also a federal banking examiner investigating Archard Holdings. These facts lead me to believe that these two acts are connected and that, in both matters, the driver was not acting alone. I am representing the deceased's mother in the second, fatal incident, for which we are pursuing a civil action for wrongful death."

"Is that all?" March asked.

"No, it's not. What we don't know, but will find out, is what Mr. Dunne was doing in your company vehicle on Christmas Eve. My guess is that he was in the scope and course of his employment, even at that odd hour, because this was a planned and misguided scheme to scare off another federal banking examiner."

The two senior associates just stared impassively at Devlin. Taking their cues, the other two did the same. Devlin reached into his law case and produced a thick document that he set at the center of the table.

"This is the formal complaint, ready for filing. Yes, you can roll your eyes and pooh-pooh all this, but if we're unable to reach an agreement I will file this lawsuit with the court. Then we will subpoena all your documents and begin taking depositions from everyone who works here, from the lovely young woman who greeted me this morning to Mr. Dunne, and right up to and including Mr. Becker himself. Make no mistake: we will get to the truth."

March spun the formal complaint so it was oriented his way, squinted at it and then looked at Devlin and said, "And what is your number to avoid any unpleasantness?"

Without hesitation, Devlin said, "The demand is $5 million to settle the wrongful death action. I am willing to mediate it with a retired judge of my choosing, but at the end of the negotiation the $5 million is off the table, and we proceed to litigation. As I said, we will just keep going until we've exposed all of it." Devlin wanted to say more, about Becker ordering the hits, but such threats of criminal charges would be extortion.

"What are you implying?" Littleton asked.

"I'm not implying anything," Devlin said. "I'm being very direct. It's all right here." Devlin tapped the document he had been feverishly writing for the past month since meeting E.J. Park in Los Angeles. Seeing and feeling the depths of her health condition and squalor had been ample fuel for Devlin.

"Are you crazy?" March said calmly. "This is one of the most prestigious companies you'll ever encounter, with an impeccable reputation. These allegations are completely baseless and, quite frankly, preposterous. This is a folly and a blatant money-grab that will not work."

"Well, before you dismiss me out of hand you might want to consider the ramifications of doing so. Because I'm generous, I'm going to give you thirty days to consider the demand. That copy is yours. As I said, if you'd like to schedule a mediation we can do that, too. But after thirty days I will file the complaint with the court. Even thirty days is too long, because my client is elderly and infirm, so there is a real urgency to get this matter resolved, to improve her circumstances and health. But I want to be reasonable, too."

Another awkward silence ensued until Littleton said, "Is that all, Mr. Devlin? You came here to make these wild allegations, without any evidence, and demand $5 million? Or else?"

"As I said, we're not debating the case today."

Littleton was annoyed. "So, you have one of our employees driving around in a company car after work hours? So what? If he did anything improper he was clearly a rogue agent acting without our knowledge. There's no way any of this ever sticks."

Devlin stayed silent as he leaned into the time-worn comfort of one of his classics, courtesy of his former investigator Max Daniels, *Rule #3: Show your opponents death, and they'll accept sickness.* Devlin knew he had just showed them death, in the form of a damning fact sequence that ended with a man dying at the hand of one of their company employees. Even if these lawyers had already known about it, Devlin had informed them that someone outside their walls had put the puzzle together, too. Just as he'd suspected, the two junior associates sat with their mouths zipped, which is exactly what they had been instructed to do: watch and learn.

"I think we've heard enough," Littleton said. "Keep going, and we'll hit you with a suit for slander and notify the Arizona Bar Association of an unhinged lawyer in their ranks."

March stood, and the other three mimicked him like trained monkeys. Devlin stood, too. March extended his hand. "Thank you, Mr. Devlin. We will take everything you've said under close advisement, consider all our options and get back to you." Devlin knew this was the polite version of *Get the hell out of here, you ambulance-chasing halfwit.* Devlin was emboldened by his mission, which was to ameliorate E.J. Park's pain. So, as Devlin was shaking March's hand, he thought about E.J., alone and trapped in her cave-like apartment with the maddening *whir whir whir* and no other options in life. He pictured her collapsing in front of her son's memorial and recalled the story about the Korean breakfast she made her son to conclude each visit. Devlin could feel the desperation that had enveloped her. Ho-Chan Park was all she had left in this life, and this defendant was going to compensate her for that loss if Devlin had anything to say about it.

Except, as he had presumed, Devlin heard nothing from anyone at Archard Holdings until day twenty-nine of the clock he had started. Nadia Flores put the call through to Devlin, who was at his desk.

"We need another thirty days," Odon March said.

"Why?" Devlin asked.

"I'm not sure that's any of your business, but with our other commitments we have not had a chance to properly review your complaint with Mr. Becker."

"I told you before, my client is destitute," Devlin said. "Another thirty days is unacceptable. My client lives in a hovel. She needs oxygen 24/7, and she lost the only person she had left in this life, which was her son Mr. Park."

"I'm not sure what you want me to say."

"I just want you to understand the full gravity and urgency of this situation, that for another thirty days she will continue to suffer. For you this case is just another to-do on a long list; for her it's literally life and death."

"OK, well, all the more reason to give us a little more time to properly consider your demand."

Devlin sighed. He had already drawn his line in the sand, so why let them over-step? Because it was all part of the delicate art of negotiation, finding the sweet spot between hardball and flexibility as a means to the end: helping his client.

"I'll give you fifteen. But let me be clear: if the time passes without resolution, I will file the case."

"Understood. Thank you, Mr. Devlin."

Devlin hung up. He was fifty/fifty on whether they were just trying to burn up more time or seriously considering a settlement. Just as a hedge, he grabbed his yellow legal pad and began writing a notice of deposition for the first person on his list: Delaney Dunne.

THREE weeks later, Devlin wasn't surprised when he got the call. This time it was Steve Littleton.

"We need just a little more time."

"That's not going to happen," Devlin said.

"Look, we've been buried over here. Just give us a little more time. We want to do the right thing and work this out with you. Seriously."

"Well, seriously, the train has left the station."

"What does that mean?"

"I told your colleague Mr. March if you missed the last deadline I would file the formal complaint."

"Whatever," Littleton said. Then, just before he hung up, Littleton muttered, "Clown."

Just to see if they were bluffing, Devlin dragged his feet a bit on filing while he went to work preparing for depositions in the case. That way he wouldn't lose any time, while simultaneously clinging to the faint hope he might get another call to schedule the mediation, which was still the preferred and fastest route to help E.J. Park. Then, in December, in his last major official work act of 1985, Devlin drove to the Maricopa County Superior Court Complex.

After meeting E.J. Park at her apartment in Los Angeles, before the trio had reached the small Honda, the student translator Sarah Sung had told Devlin what Ho-Chan Park had written in Korean across the top of the banker's box: *If something happens to me, give this box to the police.* Sung also explained that E.J. told her that she had hidden the box so well at the back of the closet she'd completely forgotten about it until the big day when Devlin and his beautiful wife had come to her apartment.

"That's sweet," Monae said.

"Did you tell her we're not married?" Devlin asked.

"Didn't seem that important," Sarah Sung said.

Ever since that moment, the totality of the case had angered Devlin: corruption, financial crimes, the intimidation orders and the death of a wholly innocent man—a seething energy he had poured into carefully writing and revising the Ho-Chan Park wrongful death lawsuit, the document he'd dropped on the conference room table at Archard Holding, months ago. Today he'd asked Monae to come along, because she had been so instrumental in assembling the case.

They found the building and walked inside, Monae's heels clicking along the white linoleum floor, her Fendi handbag riding on her hip (minus the firearm, since she knew they'd be entering the court complex). Holding Monae's hand, Devlin stepped forward, set the thick document on the counter and pushed it across to the clerk, who officially stamped it "Received December 23, 1985," just one day before the statute of limitations expired.

Adalius Becker, and the corporation he helmed, were now officially in Devlin's crosshairs.

Chapter Twenty-Three

ON JANUARY 15, 1986, CONNOR J. DEVLIN'S FATHER died at Phoenix Municipal Hospital. As he had been doing for years, Devlin's father had come to Arizona for the winter months after the NFL season ended for the Buffalo Bills. Even while on vacation at the Arizona Biltmore, the senior Devlin wore a suit and tie every day, and was working almost to the moment he died.

Over the past few months, Devlin's dad had deteriorated as the tumor pressing on his vocal chords had made it difficult to speak. An ENT surgeon was confident he could perform a fairly routine, twenty-minute surgery that would alleviate the pressure and allow the senior Devlin to converse again. The younger Devlin was there post-op, and Dad seemed to be doing great. In fact, propped in bed at Phoenix Municipal Hospital—across the street from The Bunker—the senior Devlin was on the phone with an executive in the Buffalo Bills football organization. He finished his call and put the receiver on the phone by the bed. Devlin, his mom and his two sisters had been taking turns bedside, to make sure someone was there at all times.

"Look," he told his son. "I'm fine. I sent your mother and sisters away because I've got some more work to do. And I'm sure you do, too. No need for anyone to sit here. Go back to work, and I'll see you all tonight."

"All right, Dad." Devlin squeezed his dad's shoulder and smiled. This man was his steady bulwark against life, his mentor and confidante. While his father was not formally educated, he was intelligent, street-smart and always providing sage advice for whatever challenge, question or hurdle Devlin faced. He was brilliant with people, too, with a warm sense of humor that endeared him to many. That he was on the mend was fabulous, because Devlin couldn't bear the thought of losing him. He smiled at his dad again and left to go back to Devlin & Associates.

But as Devlin pulled up to the brick building, Nadia Flores was already outside in a panic, telling him someone from the hospital had called. Devlin jumped back into the Blazer and set his own personal land-speed record racing back to the hospital. When he got to the room, his father had already passed. Seeing his dad like that was an unfathomable shock, since he had just been talking to him.

His dad, old-school to the core, had refused to use a bedpan. After his son had left, he got up on his own to use the toilet. That simple exertion was just a little too much for his weakened body, and his heart gave out.

Back in the room, Devlin hugged his father and sobbed. That his dad was working until almost the moment he died, and had dispatched his son to go back to work, was exactly who he was. *Your work is to serve. Service is your work.* How was it that this omnipresent and powerful person was simply gone? That he hadn't even had a chance to tell his dad goodbye was a wrenching blow Devlin couldn't accept. This state of shock and sadness would linger for the next year and beyond.

The younger Devlin helped his mom with the arrangements to ship the body back to the only rightful resting place, Buffalo. Then Devlin, his sisters and their mother returned to their hometown for the memorial service, where Devlin gave the eulogy, a heartfelt and teary tribute to the old Irish bootlegger. The son joked that this father was a west-side Mick who had made good. His father had a special touch, had helped bring professional football to Buffalo in 1960 and, over the last twenty-six years, had become a local legend. The people seated at the memorial, at St. Joseph's Catholic Church on Main Street, were testament to the power and reach of the senior Devlin: members of the Buffalo Bills and Pittsburgh Steelers front-office brass; several former NFL coaches; Buffalo Mayor Jimmy Griffin and New York Governor Mario Cuomo; and a long list of former Buffalo Bills players. In the football universe, the capper to the season later that week was the swaggering 15-1 Chicago Bears crushing the New England Patriots 46-10 in Super Bowl XX. Normally a highlight of every year, the 1986 edition was tinged with sadness for

Devlin as he replayed memories of time with his dad. Devlin watched the big game alone, at his Scottsdale condo, because he wasn't in a particularly festive mood.

After watching the Super Bowl, Devlin got an idea to honor his father. He arranged to have the 1976 brown Cadillac Fleetwood Brougham shipped from Buffalo to Phoenix. Once it arrived, Devlin traded in the cherry-red Blazer and drove around town in his dad's Cadillac with a new car phone Devlin had mounted to the center console. The phone was an expensive technology toy that was supposed to revolutionize daily efficiency. Devlin wondered if he had had the phone earlier, whether he might have made it back to the hospital to say goodbye to his dad. But, in reality, the new technology never worked very well. The ringer was so loud that it shook the entire car each time it rang. Half of each conversation centered around "Guess where I am?" and "You're in your car?!" amazement.

IN April, Devlin got an angry call from Odon March asking him why he had filed the lawsuit when all they needed was a little more time. Time, Devlin told him, had run out. Devlin reminded March that the first deposition in the case, of Delaney Dunne, was already scheduled—which no doubt further angered March, because Devlin was about to officially breach the castle walls.

That same month, the judge granted relief and ordered that Bobby Swift be eligible for parole in thirty days. Prison administrators moved Swift from the hardcore Florence prison to Fort Grant, a minimum-security facility in southeast Arizona. Devlin started working on a plan to move Bobby Swift back to his mother's native Maine upon his release. In May, Devlin took the Cadillac to Fort Grant to spring Bobby Swift. Devlin had invited Monae along, but her agency was bringing in a reliable stream of investigation billings that demanded her attention. Her growing revenue had also allowed her to move the business out of her apartment and into her own rented office space near AAA Bail Bonds, where Devlin and One-Armed Lucky had once held court.

When Bobby Swift climbed in the Cadillac, he was a frail and ghastly white apparition. He barely said a word. He wore faded blue jeans, a black Iron Maiden concert T-shirt, black Converse Chuck Taylor high-tops and a white bandana around his head. His spirit was remarkably similar to that of Trevor Walsh: he had been broken completely by the prison experience. Gone was the swagger from the first time Devlin had met him. Swift also had really nice teeth, with a good smile that he only revealed after Devlin cracked a joke about his strict policy not to represent complete fuck-ups. Devlin's intuition told him this was not a career criminal, just a kid who had had one drug-induced bad night. Swift seemed anything but violent. On the drive back to Phoenix, Swift dug in his back jeans pocket and handed Devlin a crumpled white business envelope.

"What's this?"

"A thank-you. For what you done."

In total, Devlin had billed out just under $5,000 to write the Rule 32 petition that sprang Swift.

"That's all right, Bobby. We've been sending the invoices directly to Philadelphia Bank and Trust like you said. We're square."

"I know," he said. "But you walked my sorry ass from the River Styx to the light of day. I want to do this."

Devlin nodded. With the kid's $50,000 monthly oil royalty, the wealthy parolee could afford to say "thank you" however he saw fit. Devlin tucked the envelope in his jacket pocket and only looked at it later that night before bed. When he opened the envelope, Devlin just stared for a good five seconds: Swift had scrawled out a note authorizing a $100,000 check to be sent to Devlin & Associates. Devlin crossed himself as a sign of reverence for the largesse and immediately earmarked the funds for whatever expenses he would need to front on the Park case.

At the office the next day, Devlin had Nadia Flores credit Leander Farley's prisoner commissary account with $5,000. The jailhouse lawyer wouldn't ever see the light of day again, but he would never have to pay for cigarettes, chewing gum or the instant ramen noodles he coveted as an alternative to the cafeteria trough.

With Devlin still staying at Monae's place, he set Swift up at the Scottsdale condo for a few days as they worked out a plan for his new life. Devlin asked Swift to sleep on the couch rather than in Devlin's bed. There was doing right by his clients, and then there was "a little too close for comfort." Devlin didn't want the wiry felon between his sheets, and Swift readily abided by the request.

One of the conditions of Swift's parole was that Devlin would be an ongoing, guiding hand in his client's rehabilitation. Devlin wasn't taking any chances, so once they solidified the plan, he boarded a plane with Swift to hand-deliver the ex-con to his boyhood home in Portland, Maine, where his mother still lived. The $100,000 windfall from Swift's release was the beginning of a unique client association, unlike any he'd ever navigated. Devlin's role as lawyer quickly expanded to include various incarnations as surrogate father, big brother, friend, psychiatrist, priest, advisor and investment analyst for the parolee's $600,000-plus annual oil income. Devlin, who'd just turned 40 in 1985, began making monthly trips to Manhattan to consult with various brokers and investment bankers on Swift's behalf. In the shadowed city canyons of Wall Street, Devlin got an unofficial degree in investment finance and savvy sophistication.

And what Devlin learned in those conference rooms was that all the big money in 1986 was being played right in his own backyard. Federally backed and insured savings-and-loan institutions were returning huge profits to investors, with Arizona, California and Texas leading the charge. Thanks to Sloane Monae and Omar Sidi, Devlin knew exactly what was going on behind the curtain before the lid came off the scam. Stocks, too, had always made Devlin nervous, a money strategy moved more by emotion than actual empirical data and facts. Despite pressure from Swift himself, Devlin steered his client away from investing in any S&L or the stock market, and instead focused on a boring-yet-reliable plan to buy real estate, both raw land and commercial properties primed for development. It wasn't sexy, Devlin told Swift, but he liked tangible investments—land one could stand upon and proclaim as his own—that would build a fortune slowly while protecting Swift from the flash-fire vagaries and ruin of speculation. He told Swift what his old pal One-Armed Lucky had often said: "Big-Time, real estate be just like sex: get lots while you're young."

Meanwhile, Devlin had also just signed up the six hundredth cop in his group legal plan for law enforcement. The criminal felon Swift—who had been referred by yet another convicted criminal—was no less a client in Devlin's eyes than any he represented as a trial lawyer. The connecting thread was that the lawyer saw himself as a man for the people, people who had no other voice or leverage against corporate and government arrogance, greed and indifference. Swift wasn't bucking up against institutional powers, but he was certainly a human being who needed a guiding hand.

However, almost immediately, despite his roughly $50,000 in monthly oil royalties that afforded every possible opportunity in life, Bobby Swift proved a tough one to rehabilitate. He lived at home with his mother in a two-bedroom clapboard house built in the 1940s. Swift's paternal grandfather had specified that only blood relatives could be heirs to his oil fortune, so when Bobby's parents divorced acrimoniously and his dad remarried, his mom was left in the cold. Swift had offered to buy her a new house when he turned 18 and began receiving checks, but she told her son she was just fine with what she had.

Per the requirements of his parole, Swift had to attend twice-weekly individual therapy sessions and daily Alcoholics Anonymous meetings. Per court order, he also had to appear in person before his parole officer each month in Portland. Beyond that regularity, Swift quickly drifted back to the nightly bar scene and, although it was forbidden by the terms of his release, started drinking again. He frequently brought home women from the bars, against his mother's loud and consistent protestations. On nights he didn't find a pick-up at the bar, he'd search out a street prostitute. Swift had so much money that he was never without thousands in cash that he carried in a thick, rubber-banded roll of $100 bills. He'd find a prostitute—and even some young women who were not officially on the street but couldn't resist the offer of $500 in cash upfront to "hang out together" for an hour—and retreat to a darkened side street in his new silver-blue Buick Regal Grand National, with its 235-horsepower, turbocharged V6. The kid's lawyer, 2,700 miles away, was doing his best to right the already listing potential of Bobby Swift, but the ship was quickly taking on water.

ON a blazing June morning, Devlin waited in the air-conditioned comfort of the conference room at Devlin & Associates. He'd done his homework on the outside shop brought in by Archard Holdings: Forrest & Long, a national firm with offices in ten U.S. cities, including a hundred lawyers in a high-rise on Central Avenue just one-half mile from Devlin's building. Goldie had borrowed from Devlin's football heritage to dub the firm "Fourth & Long," as in the Dummy was going to need a miracle fourth-down Hail Mary to get Dunne to talk. To borrow another football metaphor, the defense had chewed up the clock. In a case he had filed in late December 1985, the action had stalled while the judge considered two different motions to dismiss, both of which she ultimately rejected. Still, the legal paper game by the defense had chewed up another six months without any progress toward resolution.

Nadia Flores buzzed, and over the squawk box said, "They're walking up. Looks like the client and a female attorney. I'll send them in."

Devlin stood and felt a surge of adrenaline: He was finally going to stand face-to-face with the driver of the Trans Am who, he believed, had hit Ho-Chan Park and left him dead on a rain-slicked city street. In a matter of seconds, the entire case flashed through Devlin's mind in a minute-by-minute timeline of events from Christmas Eve 1983, starting with Ho-Chan Park's sixteen-hour day at work, the exact time he left, the moment of impact and the Walgreens assistant manager seeing the orange Trans Am sliding toward the intersection with no headlights. Then Devlin's visit to Los Angeles to meet E.J. and seeing her frail condition, a life anchored to the oxygen bottle, and how deeply affected she had been by the death of her son. When Devlin saw Dunne's attorney, however, it knocked him back a bit, like an uppercut he never saw coming.

"Good morning, Mr. Devlin," Maria Ramirez said, shaking Devlin's hand and smiling. "I'm now with Forrest & Long, representing Archard Holdings and Mr. Delaney Dunne."

Ramirez looked even more confident than the first time they'd done battle in the Defective Manhole case. Her dark hair was now shorter and swept up above her ears in a stylish but no-nonsense cut. Her power suit of a silk blouse under a dark blazer and a slender skirt exuded class, and custom tailoring.

"When I heard it was you on the other side, I leapt at the chance to crush you again," she said with a slight, unreadable smile.

Devlin smiled back, with a raised eyebrow. "You leapt?"

"I'm kidding," she said, glancing at her client, who wasn't quite following the professional parrying. "Actually, I'm not kidding. Yes, I leapt."

"Just curious," Devlin said. "How did you—?"

"Go from defending the city against fraudulent claims to private practice?"

"Not exactly how I'd put it."

"Public service is a noble pursuit," she said, "but there's no nobility in poverty. Mr. Devlin, meet my client Mr. Delaney Dunne."

They shook hands and each nodded, but neither said anything. Devlin was already bothered by the conflict of interest he saw. "There's one thing before we begin," he said. "Ms. Ramirez, are you here today representing the corporation Archard Holdings *and* Mr. Dunne individually?"

"Yes. Is that a problem?"

"Well, clearly," Devlin said, "that's a conflict. You can't represent the interests of the corporation and Mr. Dunne simultaneously."

"Why don't you leave that to us to decide."

"How can we proceed if there's a conflict with Mr. Dunne's representation?"

"Look, I'm his attorney, and I don't believe there's a conflict, so let it go. If you feel so compelled, you can file a complaint with the state bar."

Devlin nodded at the stenographer, who had just taken her seat, and she nodded that she was ready to document every spoken word. Devlin spent the next two hours detailing the mundane: Dunne's upbringing and education (Devlin was surprised to learn Dunne had an undergraduate degree and had been accepted into law school but never attended), how Dunne had arrived in Arizona and met Adalius Becker just before leaving for law school, when he'd started working at Archard Holdings, and his job duties in excruciating year-by-year detail. After a short restroom break, once they were seated again Devlin dropped the hammer: "We need to talk about Christmas Eve and what happened that night."

Dunne was already shaking his head and looking to Ramirez, who said, "I've instructed my client not to answer any questions related to that night or any alleged incident."

Devlin had to try anyway. "Delaney, I know you want to do the right thing. That man was just doing his job. You can't ever make things right without going all the way. It's time to clear your spiritual slate."

"What are you, my priest?" Dunne said.

Devlin nodded. "Yeah, actually, in some ways I am."

"Again, as I said, I've instructed Mr. Dunne to take the Fifth on this line of questioning."

Devlin was reading Dunne's eyes, body language and fidgety gestures. Devlin sensed this was the moment: "We already know what happened that night. We know it was you driving the orange Trans Am registered to Archard Holdings. We have witnesses who gave us your license plate and put you in the vehicle. It's done, Delaney. Over. Now I just need to hear it from you."

"You're badgering the witness, Mr. Devlin. Will that be all, or was there another line of questioning you'd like to pursue?"

Devlin turned to her and said, "I just want to hear his side so we can clear this up. We believe Adalius Becker ordered intimidation plays on two different federal banking examiners. If Mr. Dunne was simply carrying out those orders as an employee of the corporation, and Mr. Park's death was a horrible accident, that will be helpful to Mr. Dunne, which you should acknowledge if you're representing his best interests. Otherwise, the other likelihood does not bode well for Mr. Dunne, as I'm sure you've explained—which is that Mr. Becker will deny any knowledge, and your corporate client will lay all this on your individual client."

Devlin could see Dunne was ready to crack: he *wanted* to talk. But there was no way she was going to let him say a word. Devlin could see him searching the inner terrain of a soul urging its host body to uncap the 55-gallon drum of toxic secrets.

Devlin charged ahead with, "Do you know what mitigating factors are?"

"Don't answer," she said.

"They're just facts that can help your case. We believe there are things you can tell us that might mitigate what happened that night. Becker ordered it, right? Both times?"

"Mr. Devlin! This deposition is now terminated." Then she turned to her client: "Do not say a word."

The only sound was the rattle and hum of the AC unit that was at the start of months of hard duty until the heat broke in October. Maria Ramirez stood and motioned to her client: *We're leaving now!*

Devlin took the opening: "Ho-Chan Park was 57 when he died that night."

"Mr. Devlin!" Ramirez said, scolding him. "Come on," she said to Dunne.

"We're off the record. I can say my piece as you walk out. He died alone on that cold, rainy street: no wife, no children and no relatives. His only family was his elderly mother, who lives in Los Angeles and relied on her son's financial support. Pretty much all he did was work around the clock trying to stop guys like your boss Becker, and it was all to help his mother."

Ramirez was shoving her client toward the door, but he was slow-walking it as he listened to Devlin.

"And for that, Ho-Chan Park earned a whopping fifteen grand a year. His parents came from Korea. His mother speaks no English and lives alone in a crappy apartment. You can help her, Delaney. She's been left with nothing and no one. She lost her only child. Do the right thing."

Dunne stared into the abyss, not saying a word. Had one been nearby, Ramirez would have used a riding crop to hasten her client's exit. They were out of the conference room and passing Nadia Flores seated at her desk, almost to the door.

Devlin followed them. "There's nothing we can do to bring Ho-Chan Park back, but you can still take responsibility. For his memory and legacy. For you. For his mother. There's good in you, or you wouldn't still be listening to me. You wouldn't have wanted to be a lawyer yourself without some sense of right and wrong. You wouldn't be here at all. Don't carry this for the rest of your life, Delaney. Not for someone like Becker. If you do, it's going to eat you alive. And I think you know that. All you have to do is come clean. That's the first step to turning your life around."

Devlin could sense the torment in Dunne, another lost soul like Bobby Swift.

"Good day, Mr. Devlin," Ramirez said as they reached the front door of Devlin & Associates. Then, when she and Dunne were standing in the outside light, Devlin sensed a fissure rippling through Dunne's inner stone facade. He stopped, turned and stared at his attorney, and then whispered something into her ear.

"Delaney," she said, literally pushing him along, "move."

CHAPTER TWENTY-THREE

Devlin watched until they were gone.

"That was intense," Nadia Flores said. "He wants to talk."

"He does," Devlin said.

"But he's not going to just hand you the rope to hang himself," she said.

Devlin nodded and said, "There's one part of this case that never made sense to me."

"What's that?"

"A day hasn't gone by since we connected the dots between that Trans Am and Archard Holdings that I haven't asked myself this question."

"Why use the company car?" she said, nodding.

Devlin gave her a look of surprise. She shrugged her shoulders and said, "I think it was calculated. A little leverage to protect himself."

"Exactly," Devlin said.

"He wanted to leave a clear trail back to Archard Holdings. In case things went south, just as they have."

"Otherwise they could just cut him loose at any time," Devlin offered.

She sighed and said, "I wouldn't hold your breath on ever hearing anything out of him."

The thought deflated Devlin, because his ongoing bluff hinged on the fear of the lawyers representing Archard Holdings, who had to believe Dunne might crack. Otherwise, if they could just keep him muzzled, they might never settle.

Chapter Twenty-Four

FOR HIS TRIP EAST TO SEE SWIFT IN LATE SUMMER 1986, Devlin had come up with a creative angle to get the backslider beyond drinking and one-night stands—to try to infuse him with some sense of culture, passion and purpose. Before broaching his unique idea with Swift and his parole officer, Devlin made numerous phone calls and worked his legal network and other contacts. Once he'd hammered out the details, he was ready to make his pitch to put Bobby Swift on a new career track. When pressed, and sober, Swift had expressed at least a passing interest in getting into the film business in some capacity. With his ability to potentially finance films, Devlin thought that was a good starting point. A movie about the pursuit of gangster Al Capone in the twenties was filming stateside. Devlin arranged permission for Bobby Swift to visit the set. The lawyer had also arranged for Bobby Swift to get an associate producer credit and very small back-end cut in exchange for investing $1 million into the production. Swift could visit the film set, meet the actors and experience something beyond the parochial life he'd known in small-town America and in prison.

Swift would actually get to work on the film, too, in September and October in a remote, natural setting Devlin thought would be perfect. A stately bridge across the Missouri River about fifty miles north of Helena, Montana, would serve as the location spanning the U.S. border with Canada where Prohibition-era whiskey runners would do battle with lawmen. Devlin thought proximity to the creative process, clean air and a full-scale film production might open something inside the ex-con, who was not overly giddy about the opportunity. For reasons Devlin couldn't unravel, Swift could have done almost anything with his inheritance, but instead operated with a glassy vacancy that rendered him completely devoid of any ambition. It was heart-wrenching and devastating to witness, but Devlin felt powerless, as though he was watching a puppy play next to a busy freeway, without any ability to intervene against the inevitable.

Devlin took a commercial flight to Maine to pick up Swift, and then accompanied him on another flight to once again hand-deliver the kid to his next destination in life: this time, Montana. As part of the crew of hundreds, Swift helped plant six hundred trees and hang olive-drab canvas and camouflage netting to hide the cabins and summer homes perched along the river. With at least cautious optimism that something might stick with Swift in this environment, Devlin returned to his Phoenix law practice during filming, which ran for most of October 1986. Despite the scene involving a shootout between Al Capone's gangsters and Prohibition agents, Swift seemed more interested in drinking with the crew at night and harassing the female extras. Swift couldn't even be bothered to meet the Hollywood luminaries who were gracious about taking time to talk to the crew, extras and locals.

Devlin pondered it all from his couch at the condo, with stacks of papers surrounding him and a yellow legal pad in his lap. It was October 25, with Game Six of the World Series on the TV. When the Red Sox scored two runs in the top of the tenth inning to take a 5-3 lead, Devlin turned down the volume, figuring heavily favored Boston was finally going to break the decades-long Curse of the Bambino. Just three more outs, and the Red Sox would be crowned champions for the first time since 1918. Devlin went back to work on his plan to breach the castle walls. Adalius Becker had to be raging mad and sweating that a trial lawyer had one of his own employees committing a crime in a company vehicle. Without knowing how much time had passed as he pondered the case, Devlin glanced up to see a ground ball roll between Bill Buckner's legs as Ray Knight of the Mets scored the winning run from second base.

"Game over," Devlin said aloud to the four walls of his living room. "Anything's possible."

"SIX months," Devlin said. "That's what I give the kid."

"That's a pretty quick assessment, right?" Monae said. "Maybe he just needs to blow off some steam after being in prison." They were on pillows in Monae's bed as the early-morning light seeped around the blinds.

"Some people are just wired wrong," Devlin said. "Time and money don't help the equation. I suspect he's drinking again, which is a violation of his parole. If he starts down the road of drugs, that will just accelerate the process."

"You think he'll end up dead?"

"That's my fear. Or back in prison. That's why I need you on this one."

"What'd you have in mind?"

"I need you to fly out to Maine and tail him for a couple days. I'm sure you'll be able to confirm what I already pretty much know."

"Which is what?"

Devlin paused and sighed. "My client's violating his parole. Any booze or drugs, and he's violating. I can't be party to a fraud if he's dodging his parole agent. And I can only ask or yell at him so many times about going to in-patient rehab. He just refuses."

Although she was nude, Monae went into work mode, grabbing her pad and writing notes. "Full name again?"

"Robert Earl Swift. Bobby Swift. He's staying at his mom's house in Portland, Maine. And off the record, I'm not looking for evidence to use in court or anything. This is just for my own peace of mind. I can't just let this kid slide off the deep end until he gets locked up or worse."

"So, I can go in and get you what you need."

"Yeah."

"You want photos?"

"Sure."

"Off the record," Monae said, "what about admissibility, Fourth Amendment?"

"Off the record," Devlin said, "I just want to know what's going on with the kid. He's breaking my heart. I've run out of ideas on how to help him."

Monae nodded. "Anything else?"

Devlin's frustration was boiling over. He hadn't made a trip back to Maine to see Swift since the movie-set disaster. When he did call the oil heir to talk about investments and check up on his overall condition, Swift was growing increasingly vague and disinterested in anything Devlin had to say. Of course, Swift was still paying the $15,000 monthly retainer to Devlin & Associates, but the lawyer was ready to pull the plug on taking any more of the kid's money. Once he had Monae's confirmation of illegality, Devlin hoped the threat of cutting off his representation would be the wake-up call.

"You OK?" she asked.

"It just saddens me to no end that this kid, with this second chance and all his money, is stuck. He blows his parole, it's going to be a cold reality when he goes back to prison. I just don't know what other smelling salts to wave under his nose to get him to wake the hell up and snap out of this deadbeat persona. It's really sad."

"No matter what you do for him, you know what the problem is, don't you?" she said.

"Drinking and drugs?"

"The money," she said. "Give any kid that much money, and I'll show you a kid who doesn't have a clue," she said. "No rhyme, no reason, no purpose. Nothing."

Devlin nodded.

"Well," she said. "Let me go do my thing. Maybe showing him some hard evidence will snap him back to reality. I'm pretty booked right now. Right after the first of the year, OK?"

"That's fine," Devlin said. "I just hope he makes it that long."

Chapter Twenty-Five

THREE MONTHS AFTER THE SHOWDOWN with Maria Ramirez and Delaney Dunne, Adalius Becker's hired legal guns had held true to form: Devlin hadn't heard anything in the wrongful death action on behalf of Ho-Chan Park. Over many years, Becker's in-house and outside counsel had done a masterful job of protecting the man at the top of the totem pole. And, from their perspective, dealing with this gadfly practitioner would be no different. But Devlin knew the non-response wasn't bad news, because his own version of Deep Throat had called for a second time. Because she was female, Devlin had come up with his own moniker, much more appropriate than the one from the Richard Nixon scandal: The Source.

"You've got them over a barrel," she had said. "That's why they're stonewalling."

"You're not going to tell me who you are?"

"They know if Delaney Dunne starts talking to save his own hide, then they're in big trouble, right up to Becker himself."

"Did Becker order the intimidation plays on the banking examiners?"

After a long pause she said, "Yes."

"Holy shit, you have to testify. You are the nail in Becker's coffin. If he directed

Dunne to scare them off, then he could be charged under the felony murder rule, too."

"I can't testify," she said.

"Obviously you work at Archard. Were you actually there when Becker told Dunne to intimidate Sidi and Park? Or are you getting this secondhand?"

"Get a pen and paper and take notes. I don't have much time. Tell me when you're ready."

Devlin grabbed a pen and his yellow legal pad. "Ready."

"Adalius Becker has schemes going on top of our schemes. He's siphoning money from Estate depositors to the parent company, Archard Holdings. He takes the cash inflow and uses it for all the lavish expenses. He's speculating like you wouldn't believe. He thought everything was good until these feds started snooping around, asking for financial statements and looking into his accounting practices. Except even his own accounting firm was asking the same questions, right? So Becker fired all his accountants and switched firms. Except he couldn't fire the feds. That's when he concocted this ridiculous scheme to scare them off. So, let me tell you: right now? Becker is freaking out. He can only keep the Ponzi scheme afloat with a constant and massive influx of new cash. But Archard Holdings is desperate for cash to cover all the real estate losses. Becker told all Estate's branch managers to push customers into 'high-yield' bond certificates, which are worthless junk bonds because Archard doesn't have any real assets to back them. I know Dunne wants out."

"He told you that?" Devlin asked.

"Yes. He told me it finally changed when Becker started stealing directly from everyday people, retirees trying to save. That's when the scam turned into something more heartless. More sinister. And now someone's dead."

"You have to testify, please," Devlin said.

"That's all for now. Just be patient. Give them a little more time."

"No, this has already dragged on for way too long. My client needs help now, not later."

"They're trying to buy Dunne, to keep him quiet and Becker in the clear. But that doesn't get rid of you, so they're going to need to pay you."

"Are you in these meetings when they're discussing this? How reliable is your information?"

"You want to know what Odon March calls you?"

"Of course."

"The no-good whiplash lawyer."

"Good. That means I'm under his skin."

"I have to go."

"Please consider testifying. Hello? Hello?" But she was already gone.

Then Devlin got a call from Odon March's personal assistant to set up a meeting that, because of Mr. March's busy schedule, would have to wait until the new year, 1987. The Source had been right: March wanted to get rid of Devlin. He shared the good news with his girlfriend and Omar Sidi over lunch. Monae and Devlin met periodically with Sidi, not for any pressing business purpose, but for the simple fact that they all worked on the same side of the law, albeit in different roles, and thoroughly enjoyed each other's company. Monae and Devlin had converted Sidi into a devoted aficionado of the house-special Tom Kha Gai soup and a stalwart regular at Ong Lek Thai Kitchen, which is where they always met.

Sidi, too, was cautiously optimistic that the U.S. government was tightening the noose and might soon seize Estate Savings & Loan for being insolvent. Sidi relayed that Becker was scrambling to keep his fraudulent empire afloat by asking for a lenient judgment from the Federal Home Loan Banking Board so he could transition into the safer home-mortgage arena. Devlin mentioned what he had learned from The Source—without disclosing *how* he knew—which squared with Sidi's own investigation. Indeed, Becker was out of money, a fact that meant Devlin was running out of time to get any settlement.

Sidi also told his friends that he had attended the Bank Board meeting that included two of the elected officials who were attempting to end the sprawling investigation. As the unraveling of the scam intensified, Becker filed a lawsuit against the FHLBB alleging members had leaked confidential information about Estate S&L. Sidi could only smile and offer, "I cannot say if that will be true or not. But Adalius Becker is criminal for one hundred percent."

Given Sidi's insider knowledge, the issue of collectability was now paramount in Devlin's strategy. Devlin had to get a mediation scheduled—like, yesterday—before the well ran dry and left E.J. Park destitute for the remainder of her days. He looked at Monae and admired that she had masterminded the investigation of the events of Christmas Eve 1983. She had not made a single misstep to be exploited by any of the defense lawyers. Not one, which had forever earned Devlin's high standard of professional respect. Personally, Devlin and Monae alike had been dancing around the issue of where things were headed with their relationship.

It was more than two years ago that they had consecrated their intimacy at the cut-rate motel under a neon glow. The intervening time had been mostly blissful. And, after two years, the spark and sheen of newness were gone. There were good days and bad days now, real-life normalcy when the masks and impossible best-behavior standards were no longer in use. What remained were two flawed human beings with their respective faults. Monae's smarts and independence could be off-putting when Devlin perceived her domineering manner as an attempt to push him around. And for Monae, Devlin's total devotion to his clients and cases via an iron-will work ethic often left little time for quality togetherness. Monae felt, at times, reduced to being an unpaid handmaid to Devlin's physical urges, when their sole time together was a quick union in bed. And because she knew he was immersed in his cases, it gave her an easy out to continue coasting without a heart-to-heart. The subtle tension held an unspoken truth for both: that it was time to go to the next step, whatever that meant, or move on. Amid that unspoken awareness, Devlin had moved back to his own condo, ostensibly to focus on the Park case. But, silently, they both also wondered what the move out of Monae's downtown apartment meant in the bigger picture of their developing relationship, if anything. The crack investigator was having difficulty solving her own interpersonal case. And, because it was her way, she mulled and endlessly analyzed "the next step" from every angle. She had pieced together one possible case theory about what might be holding her back, but she told herself it was ridiculous, à la Colonel Mustard in the library with the candlestick. *Really, you're going to risk losing him over that?* But if she had in fact correctly identified the dilemma, it was an obstacle that might never go away unless she let Connor Devlin go—a thought that filled her with dread. Around and around she went, trapped in the same mental loop.

THE lawyers were seated in the Archard Holdings conference room for the second time, on a rainy January day fading toward sunset. The matching beige chairs with shiny chrome legs might have looked good, but they were ridiculously uncomfortable. The late-afternoon desert light cast a dim ambience through the large window with a view north toward a craggy mountain. Insulated from the outside by the thick glass, Devlin could still smell the rainstorm now moving to the west. The same principals were gathered again: March and the other senior associate, Steve Littleton; and the two junior associates, neither of whom had ever spoken in Devlin's presence other than to greet him, Greg Truax and Natalie Grant. Except it was the latter Devlin was intently studying: Could she be The Source? And there was one new player.

"Mr. Devlin," Odon March said, "I'd like you to meet our senior partner who's here today from the Los Angeles office of Forrest & Long."

"Greg Garcia," he said, extending his hand.

"Connor Devlin, Devlin & Associates."

Devlin was familiar with the well-known defense lawyer by name and reputation, and had always been impressed (but never intimidated). Garcia had worked in Phoenix for a decade and quietly built a reputation as a brilliant and pragmatic practitioner. Polished, smooth and articulate, he was never ostentatious or flamboyant. He was polite, even affable, as he channeled his energy into tactical advantage. That he was here as a heavier buttress, from out of state, buoyed Devlin: they were scared that this case might have far-reaching implications. The Source had been right again.

"Just curious: where's Mr. Dunne's lawyer?" Devlin asked, noticing the absence of Maria Ramirez.

"We're taking care of Delaney now," Littleton said.

Devlin had nailed it: while Maria Ramirez seemed to have been wholly capable, Becker had ordered in the big guns.

"Shall we?" March said. Garcia sat at one end of the table and March at the other. Devlin ended up on the same side as before, with a view of the abysmal triptych and seated directly across from Natalie Grant.

"Let me first extend condolences on behalf of everyone here at Archard Holdings, and my firm as well, for the tragic loss of life in this case," Garcia said.

Devlin nodded.

"I can assure you Mr. Becker himself is beset with sadness about the horrible eventuality that occurred on Christmas Eve. And a good measure of our aim here today is to reach a mutual agreement to compensate your client for her loss."

Devlin nodded again.

"We've carefully reviewed your complaint, which is an excellent presentation of your case. Was there anything you'd like to say in the way of opening remarks?"

Devlin shook his head. "I think the formal complaint says it all."

"I would agree. With that, to start our discussion I'd like to briefly outline a few points. First, we stipulate that the vehicle in question is, in fact, registered to this corporation. Second, Mr. Dunne is a long-time employee of this corporation. And, third, he was driving the vehicle on the night of December 24, 1983, at or about the time of the incident. We do not dispute these facts."

Holy shit, Devlin thought. The defense itself had just corroborated what Devlin and Monae had no way of ever doing: putting Delaney Dunne behind the wheel. Devlin's bluff had worked. All the calculated gamesmanship, including giving the defense more rope with their delay tactics, might have just paid off. *Rule #11: Misperception is, at times, more important than perception.* Except Garcia was far too shrewd to make a clunky mistake, so Devlin immediately wondered if this was a planned hedge: put Dunne behind the wheel and cut him loose as needed to take the fall all on his own.

"However," Garcia continued, "while we can never know for certain exactly what Mr. Dunne, who has been a reliable employee with an impeccable employment history at Archard Holdings, was doing on Christmas Eve at such a late hour, we can assure you and your client that he was not in any way in the scope and course of his employment. We all work long, hard hours here, but not that hard and long. No one, including Mr. Becker himself, was working at midnight on Christmas Eve. I myself was trying to assemble a miniature kitchen for my daughter at that time, which made litigation look easy by comparison."

Devlin smiled. Garcia was polished as advertised, but he also brought rare qualities lost on many lawyers: humanity and a sense of humor. He had a daughter and was a dutiful dad, doing what all good dads did on Christmas Eve. In that way he was relatable—which was not to be mistaken for weakness in any way.

"Mr. Devlin, we want justice in this case just as much as you do. Our first step on that front was to place Mr. Dunne on leave, effective immediately, as we investigate your allegations. We are wholeheartedly taking up your cause, and will help with the investigation any way we can."

Devlin wasn't buying it. They were just putting Dunne on lockdown and paying him to keep his head down until the dust settled.

"Finally, Mr. Devlin, I just want to remind you that Estate Savings & Loan is a federally insured institution. We earn good returns for our depositors. And we are a good community partner, devoted to strong ideals and values. We are here today to do the right thing."

"Well, thank you, Mr. Garcia," Devlin said. "I don't have any kids of my own yet, but will remember what you said when it's time to assemble my first mini-kitchen." That drew a few stifled laughs. "Where does this leave us, then, with our demand for wrongful death?"

"Yes," March interjected. "Mr. Becker would like to offer a settlement to take care of the victim's mother, Mrs. Lee."

Devlin shook his head.

March looked annoyed. "Pardon me: is that not why we're here?"

"It's Mrs. Park," Garcia said, correcting his underling.

"I'm sorry. I meant..."

Devlin did not step in to relieve him of his embarrassing gaffe, but Littleton did: "Mrs. Park. He knows her name. We have another pending legal matter involving a Mrs. Lee."

Devlin doubted that very much. And he wished he could just clear everyone out and deal one-on-one with Greg Garcia, a true gentleman lawyer, who now took back the reins.

"We are prepared to offer your client $100,000," Garcia said. "Pending your approval, we could prepare the paperwork, get everything finalized and have a cashier's check payable to your firm within seven days."

Devlin was not impressed that they had just offered to pay six figures. But they were feeling the heat. And he also thought, *Not even close,* which conjured another new one. *Rule #12: The other side always has more money to give.* Devlin was duty-bound to present the offer to E.J., via the translator Sarah Sung, along with his recommendation that she turn it down. In the meantime, he planned to start scheduling more depositions the moment he left this building. But he nodded as though he were considering the unacceptable offer. Mostly, he was staring intently at the young Natalie Grant and wondering again if she was the one dropping the bread crumbs.

Garcia knew they were in trouble and was trying to buy the case cheap, which wasn't going to happen. *Rule #3: Show your opponents death, and they'll accept sickness.* The degree of sickness they were willing to accept remained to be seen.

THE next month, Monae confirmed Devlin's worst fears about Bobby Swift, with photographs to prove it all. He was drinking again, cavorting with prostitutes and, sadly, dealing and doing drugs. Powder cocaine primarily, which Swift preferred as a status symbol over crack cocaine because the high lasted longer and, he bragged, it was way more expensive. Swift had money to burn, and burn it he did. He started by snorting cocaine, and by the time Monae was tailing him he was injecting. Swift's mother had finally had enough and kicked her son out of the small family home. Although he had enough money to buy any property in town and beyond, Swift was living in a dank basement apartment that smelled like wet dirt and cat urine. Putting aside any Fourth Amendment concerns since this was strictly intelligence collection,

Monae had smelled the place herself by taking a peek when she knew Swift was out drinking for the night. She easily jimmied the flimsy doorknob lock and found, as documented in her report to Devlin: "... a sizeable stockpile of cocaine packaged for sales, two scales powdered white, a box of small baggies, $85,213 in cash in a black garbage bag, two 9-mm pistols, three used condoms and seven used syringes scattered on the unfinished cement floor."

Upon reading her report, Devlin asked her to destroy all the photographs and any other documentation of her trip. Devlin had tried a dozen times to convince Bobby Swift to enter treatment. Devlin had used every tactic from tender-and-gentle sympathies to tough-love ultimatums heavily laden with F-bombs. He had even made two more trips to Maine to try to sway Bobby Swift in person. None of it had pierced Swift's bubble of torpor.

Devlin called Bobby Swift's apartment at 5 p.m., which according to Monae's intel was about an hour after he woke up each day and a few hours before he would venture out again to drink, sell drugs and conjure the next party with plentiful cocaine supplied by Swift. The kid answered on the tenth ring and still sounded dead asleep. Devlin was careful with his wording.

"Bobby, it's Connor Devlin."

Silence.

"Your lawyer. Calling from Phoenix, Arizona."

"Hey..." Devlin couldn't tell if it was a flicker of recognition or feigned awareness. "What's up?"

"What's up is that you're violating your parole with drugs and alcohol. You're also a convicted felon and prohibited possessor, Bobby; you can't have firearms."

"How you know all that?"

"I just know." Devlin could barely contain his sadness that manifested as anger and sweeping heartbreak.

"So, what's that mean?" Swift asked.

"Well, as an officer of the court I would be duty-bound to report any alleged parole violations to the authorities."

Silence.

"Bobby?"

"Not if you're not my lawyer, right?"

"I don't think that's the best solution, Bobby."

"Yeah, but if you're not my lawyer then no reason to rat me out."

"Bobby, don't do this. You'll regret it."

"Thanks for everything you done, but I'm good now," Swift said. "You're fired."

"Bobby?"

The line went dead. Devlin's greatest fear had come to fruition. Despite everything he had done and tried, in the end he had failed Bobby Swift. Now it would only be a matter of time.

Chapter Twenty-Six

A MONTH AFTER THE LOWBALL OFFER, Devlin heard from The Source again on a chilly February afternoon.

"You need to depose Adalius Becker next."

"Fat chance, right? He'll just take the Fifth."

On the deposition front, Devlin had been methodically working his way down the list he'd made. He'd already deposed the two cops who were first on scene on Christmas Eve; Ford Rockwell; Ho-Chan Park's supervisor; the Walgreens assistant manager; and, from Archard Holdings, a handful of the lower-level employees and the fleet manager. Unfortunately, none of the dozens of hours of testimony had turned up much that was useful. Most notably, Devlin lived with the sword of Damocles dangling overhead. Devlin knew from Sidi that Archard Holdings was in serious financial trouble as the federal investigation inched forward. If Devlin somehow proved the wrongful death was part of a larger conspiracy, and the company went bankrupt, they would never see a nickel. Or, if Dunne's actions on Christmas Eve were deemed intentional, then the insurance company would be off the hook for the vehicle policy, individual or corporate, since insurance did not extend to intentional acts.

"Doesn't matter," she said. "Becker is worried Dunne might talk, because he thinks he's weak. You've got them in a box: now you need to keep squeezing."

"Will Becker ever agree to a deposition?"

"Doubtful. But he's also arrogant and may be thinking he can put you in your place. Either way, the threat of the deposition is your leverage to get them to settle."

"At some point you need to tell me who you are. Is this Natalie Grant?" Devlin thought he detected a slight pause, as though he'd nailed it. But he couldn't be sure.

"Who I am doesn't matter. Garcia wants them to pay up, to end this, so they can deal with all the other heat coming their way."

"You seem to be in the loop on everything." But, again, all Devlin heard next was a dial tone.

Within a week The Source again proved correct, as Devlin had officially scheduled a deposition with the evil overlord himself: Adalius Becker. That he had been able to schedule it at all was somewhat shocking. Garcia had managed to push it out until June, which Devlin was willing to concede for a shot at Becker. Of course, that was Garcia's bigger play, to run the clock as long as possible within the legal bounds, because Devlin's client was now 82. At that advanced age, anything was possible. If Garcia could hold the line until E.J. Park died, the only living statutory beneficiary to any claim was gone, and Devlin's case would die, too. Devlin wanted to call the ever-affable Garcia and tell him exactly what he thought of his heartless ploy to deny his client some comfort. And then he recalled another of his dad's sage maxims.

Never pass up an opportunity to keep your mouth shut.

"Right again, Dad," he said aloud.

IN June 1987, the outgoing head of the Federal Home Loan Bank Board deferred judgment on Adalius Becker. And the incoming chief was more sympathetic to the real estate mogul's supposed plight. In an unprecedented move, the board led by the new director agreed to a memorandum forgiving Estate S&L and granting a clean slate for any violations up to that point. During lunch at Ong Lek Thai Kitchen, Sidi was incredulous at the move and resolved to redouble his efforts to bring down Becker: "For one hundred percent you will see him in orange jumpsuit."

Meanwhile, on the other side of the world, well out of Devlin's purview, the leader of Hungary was ousted from power within the ruling Communist party, along with others. Although Devlin never saw the headline, something was afoot in the geopolitics of Europe.

As he continued his fraud, Becker neared completion of a pair of opulent resort properties in California and Texas, which had already cost more than $700 million combined. Those projects, Garcia told Devlin, unfortunately required Mr. Becker to be out of state until late summer, which meant the deposition would have to wait. Devlin countered that he would agree to that as long as they concurrently scheduled a mediation. Garcia agreed and said he would get back to Devlin with possible dates and times. Devlin continued with his other depositions in the case, too, to keep the ball moving if they had to go to trial.

Concurrently, true to Mike Jefferson's word, neither Devlin nor Monae had seen the shit-box again. Devlin suspected this was the sensible influence of Garcia, who would immediately shut down any such ongoing mafia-goon idiocy. At lunch one day, Jefferson had made a vague reference to how he'd resolved the matter by saying it was impossible for anyone to eat corn on the cob "with no fucking teeth."

"*The Blues Brothers...?*" Jefferson had said, as follow-up.

Devlin didn't get the film reference.

"'Tucker McElroy, lead singer, driver of the Winnebago'? Come on, man."

Devlin just smiled, shook his head and let it go. He loved Mike Jefferson like the brother he never had, and knew it was better not to ask. As Sidi told his two new friends, "For one hundred percent we have neutralize the shit-box."

Chapter Twenty-Seven

LATER THAT SUMMER, DEVLIN SAT staring at the oversize triptych, the monochrome abstract, once again in the conference room at Archard Holdings. Before coming to this meeting, Devlin had called Goldie, driven over in the Cadillac and entered the dark stench of The Bunker.

"Where are you on the conspiracy, Dummy?" Goldie asked, rolling the lit cigar between his fingers and peering at Devlin through the brown cloud.

"They put Dunne on the record as the perpetrator in the hit-and-run. But there's no way we'll get Adalius Becker as the one ordering the hit."

"Agreed. That would be this lowlife's word against the head of a corporation. Mediation is your only shot to do right by your client. And to do that you're going to have to let the big fish swim away. Even a half-assed hack like you can see that."

Devlin had finally conceded that, but hearing Goldie confirm it was painful, because Becker should go to prison for what he'd done. Devlin was also angered that The Source was not willing to come forward, because he felt she had a duty to do so. Then again, he understood: she'd be exposed and discredited, her testimony easily discarded as hearsay. The Source was a legal apparition, useful to Devlin but officially nonexistent. As Devlin and Monae had discussed, they'd solved the case, knew Becker was guilty... and had no direct evidence.

"You have an obligation to your client," Goldie said. "It's a miracle you took it this far. Beyond a miracle, really. Reel in your catch and leave the whale for the feds. Sounds like they're about to pull Becker onto the ship and gut him anyway. Your only duty now is settling your case and taking care of Ho-Chan's mom."

Devlin shook his head. "That scumbag's direct order resulted in the murder of your friend."

Goldie blew out and nodded through the cloud. "The law is an imperfect arbiter of justice. Don't step on dollars trying to pick up dimes. Go settle. Becker will get his due, like Al Capone—a murderer getting nailed for cooking the books. I'm still dumbfounded you took it this far. C'mon, Dummy, I gave you an unsolvable case."

"Still—"

"Get the hell out of here with that sorry-ass look, and go finish what you started." Devlin stood and turned to leave. "And one more thing, Dummy."

"What's that?"

"Remember who they are when you go into this mediation. You get me?"

"I get you," Devlin said, nodding and smiling: "Fuck a shifty witch."

IT was now a week after that meeting with Goldie, as Devlin sat waiting for the legal team representing Archard Holdings.

"That beard looks stupid," Devlin said to David Nash, who sat next to him at the conference room table with his wispy white beard minus any mustache.

"This from a flunky who represents shit-bird felons, drunk strippers and horn-dog doctors who can't keep it zipped," Nash said.

"At least I don't look like an idiot."

"Debatable."

Greg Garcia, in a gray suit with a crisp white shirt and blue tie, walked into the room followed by the same four lawyers: senior associates Odon March and Steve Littleton, and the two juniors, Greg Truax and Natalie Grant. Devlin had the same thought as before: she had to be The Source, right? Devlin led the introductions and then kicked off the mediation.

"If it's amenable to everyone, we'll let Judge Nash make some opening remarks," Devlin said. With nods all around, Devlin looked to his old friend. "Judge?" Devlin had heard Nash's prelude so many times he could have recited it himself.

"There are no facts, only interpretations," the mediator began. "That's Nietzsche, and in the arena of law he is precisely accurate. Each side here today has a different version of the same story. Both sides must concurrently consider the calculus of settling today versus going forward to a trial. There are risks and benefits to both that you must each carefully consider. Let's start with today: there is a potential price to each of you in reaching resolution today. For the plaintiff, there is the possibility of accepting an offer that is far less than a jury might award. For the defense, there is the possibility of paying an amount far more than a jury might award. The benefits to settling today are similar for both sides. The conclusion of the case brings clarity and resolution, and avoids the time and financial costs of preparing for a trial."

He paused, looked at the six lawyers, and then continued. "Of course, not reaching a settlement today and going forward means extending the timeline of this case for another six months, a year, or longer. Along with that, going forward means assuming the costs—mental, emotional, physical and monetary—to properly prepare the case for trial. Proceeding to trial also introduces the wild-card variable we all know as the jury. Most jurors have an innate instinct that usually comes to the fore during opening statements. The entirety of the trial, all your carefully prepared evidence, is seen through a simple filter: does this square with the original gut feeling inside each jury member?" This next bit was Devlin's favorite part: "No matter how airtight, there isn't any case that can't be lost in open court. Nor is there any case, no matter how long a long shot, that can't be won. And then, even after a verdict, there is the appeals process that might further drag out final resolution for more years. This is the cost-benefit analysis each of you must carefully consider today."

With that, the judge was like a fight referee dispatching the opponents to their separate corners. Devlin would stay put in the same conference room while the five other lawyers retreated to March's sprawling corner office with Nash. Forty minutes later, Judge Nash walked into the conference room with a solemn look. He was shaking his head.

"Lowball?" Devlin said.

"No," Nash said. "On the contrary: two-point-five. March said he can messenger the check before week's end."

"Two-point-five?" Devlin said.

Nash nodded.

"Holy shit: we jumped from a hundred grand straight to two-point-five."

"Right?"

"How do we play it?" Devlin asked the seasoned negotiator.

"Tell me: just what the hell do you have on these people?"

"What do you mean?"

"Devlin, come on, you've got the wrongful death of an unmarried guy, no kids, with an 80-year-old mother as sole beneficiary?"

"Eighty-two."

"OK, whatever; you see my point: a case that hinges on this real estate guy in a company car doing fuck-all on Christmas Eve at midnight? They could just call him a wild-card employee who went off the rails, and disavow any knowledge of his after-work activities."

"They're still afraid Dunne might start talking and connect the dots back to Becker."

"How do you know that?"

The Source, of course. "I just know."

"OK, Uri Geller, then that's your leverage if they really want to get rid of you. I wouldn't push this anymore. You've already won: take this offer and run."

"Rule #12: The other side always has more money to give."

"What? I have no idea what you're talking about, nor do I care."

"We need to counter," Devlin said confidently. "The demand is still $5 million."

Nash whistled through his teeth. "You sure?"

Devlin nodded.

"OK, let's start small to see if there's wiggle room. I'll tell them if they're at three, then you're at four-point-seven-five. But I don't see how you have any leverage here, because no way you want to risk going to trial."

Devlin nodded. "Do it, old man."

"Respect your elders."

"Then please, you dinosaur fossil, get the hell out of my sight."

Almost two hours later the judge was back, nodding his head.

"I like that Greg Garcia guy. He's good people. Those other two senior yokels: not so much."

"What'd he say?"

"If you're at three, they're at two-point-seven-five," the judge said.

Devlin pondered. "The head of this corporation is directly responsible for the death of a human being. If money is the only recourse, then they're going to have to open the checkbook."

The judge nodded. "As much as I hate to say it, I think you might be right."

"Go for it. Go big. Tell them again the demand is five."

"Wait, just like that, back to five? That's not exactly negotiating."

"I told them at the beginning I wasn't going to negotiate. Five million."

"No, you can't go back to five," he said, standing. "I'll tell them you're firm at four-point-seven-five." The judge was gone about thirty minutes and came back smiling, with a thumbs-up.

"They went for it?" Devlin asked, standing.

"No, they're breaking for lunch and gave me this," he said, waving a paper menu. "He said we can order whatever we want!"

Devlin could only shake his head. They ordered sandwiches and potato chips, ate and waited another hour before Garcia summoned Judge Nash via his secretary. Nash finally returned to Devlin in the conference room just after 4 p.m.

"Tell me," Devlin said.

"Four flat," the judge said.

"Fuck you: he said that?"

Nash was nodding. "Four million dollars. The offer is good for seventy-two hours, to allow you time to consult your client, and contingent on ending the negotiation now. No more back-and-forth."

"What do you think?"

"I think I'll take you to the floor if you don't accept… what are you doing? I know that look."

"I sure as hell wish I could put Adalius Becker on the stand and get him to cop to ordering the hit. A jury would clean his clock. Eight figures for sure."

"Maybe on *Perry Mason*, but that's not going to happen in the real world. Take the settlement."

Devlin pondered and then, almost imperceptibly, nodded. "Contingent on my client's approval."

Judge Nash stood. "Wise choice, son."

The case that had started as an impossibly thin file, with a deceased man on a holiday night and no defendant, was ending here with a $4 million victory as Devlin stared at the hideous triptych. But he still wasn't across the finish line, because there remained a looming issue: collectability. Would this company be solvent long enough to pay out millions to a plaintiff's attorney?

"And…" Devlin said.

"Yes?" the judge said, just before he reached the door.

CHAPTER TWENTY-SEVEN

"Tell them Becker can go fuck himself."

The retired judge and the lawyer smiled at each other, and then both chuckled. Then the judge said, "I'll paraphrase."

IT was another sixteen months, in January 1989, before Omar Sidi's team had the distinct pleasure of ordering Becker to stop transferring cash from Estate S&L to Archard Holdings. By cutting off the cash, the probability of Becker's demise increased exponentially. Regardless, he tried to perpetuate the fraud by arranging a new round of junk-bond deals. In one month alone, through the failed eleventh-hour attempt, the flailing Becker managed to lose another $12 million.

In April 1989, talks between the pro-democracy Solidarity movement and Communist authorities in Poland led to a landmark deal on partially free elections. Then, that same month, Archard Holdings went bankrupt. On the day, Sidi himself helped seize Estate S&L as a small army of federal agents rushed into the building. Devlin had beat the clock: by the time of the raid, the $4 million paid out to Devlin & Associates in late August 1987 was just another ledger line in volumes of red ink.

After the feds swept in, Sidi and his team discovered the full depths to which Becker had operated his fraudulent empire with a wanton disregard for the regulators, whom he openly disparaged as government minions trying to enforce rules that did not apply to his fiefdom. The work once undertaken by Ho-Chan Park and carried on by his best friend Sidi fully unmasked a confusingly connected web of some fifty subsidiaries in real estate, banking and insurance businesses, including overseas operations Becker had managed to hide from regulators. Sidi told Monae over lunch that the federal government was on the hook for more than $4 billion to cover Estate S&L's losses after seizing the institution. In the aftermath, Becker's fraud left more than 38,000 customers holding worthless bonds, a total loss topping $400 million for the people unwittingly caught up in the scam. Many of the victims were retirees who lost their entire life savings. Along with the financial devastation, many suffered attendant emotional despair. Some committed suicide. The shockwave of damage caused by Adalius Becker would reverberate well into the 1990s and beyond.

Then, on June 4, 1989, after weeks of mounting protests, the Communist Chinese government military and pro-democracy demonstrators clashed in Beijing's Tiananmen Square. Early on a sultry June morning, Devlin read the story in *USA Today* on an airplane, during the one-hour flight to Los Angeles. That week he had signed two new clients, including his first aviation case, a Grand Canyon tour-helicopter crash, which would be a wrongful death action against the tour operator for pilot error. Devlin had battled several other high-profile firms to get the case. To do so he'd started exploring the possibility of using animation for the first time to show his case to the defense and, if it went to trial, the jurors. The other case was a referral from one of the officers in Devlin's group legal plan, which had surpassed a thousand paying members. Devlin had decided to stop adding any new members, since he was now getting all the cases he could handle. The new referral was a food-poisoning case against a Mexican buffet restaurant chain, which had almost killed his 54-year-old female client.

Once on the ground in Los Angeles, thirty minutes after hailing a yellow cab, Devlin was standing in front of E.J. Park's new residence just before noon. On his first solo trip here after the case concluded, Devlin had traveled to Los Angeles to personally deliver the settlement check to E.J. He'd driven E.J. to a local bank to help her set up an account with the trust department. Devlin brought in two other key professionals who worked in Los Angeles, including an estate lawyer and an independent financial advisor. This assembled team had guided E.J. in managing such a large sum. The advisors also eventually helped find E.J. a new apartment and move her belongings. Devlin had returned to Phoenix after more than a week, leaving only once he felt she was on solid footing. A busy caseload had intervened since, but now Devlin was returning as promised to see her new apartment and how she was faring.

She had settled on Carondelet Street, east of her old place and south of Wilshire Boulevard. The historic building had been converted into luxury apartments called MacArthur Regency, a residence that was as close as one could live to the greenery of the large urban oasis she loved. Gone was the mishmash of gang graffiti, homeless tent cities and razor wire from her previous neighborhood. As Devlin approached the building he walked past well-tended flower beds packed with hibiscus with wide blooms, petunias and violets. Thick evergreen vines of star jasmine with white blooms infused the air with a strong, sweet scent as Devlin stepped into the spacious lobby where a uniformed guard sat at a desk. Devlin took the elevator to the tenth floor and found E.J.'s apartment.

She pulled open the door, oxygen bottle at her side, and began smiling and nodding immediately. Devlin smiled and nodded, too, gave her a hug and stepped inside. Each of the restored apartments retained the original 1925 light fixtures, hardware, plaster and ornamental ironwork that evoked E.J.'s early years in Los Angeles with her husband and son. Beautifully installed dark hardwood floors replaced the musty carpet at her previous place. By comparison, the eight hundred-square-foot one-bedroom looked positively cavernous. Gone was most of the clutter and debris. Devlin had asked the firm he hired to help E.J. buy whatever new furniture she wanted. Replacing the old couch and wobbly kitchen table with its mismatched chairs was a coordinated living room set, a glass coffee table and a small circular table with two matching chairs. E.J. had brought along the old painted bookshelf, which she had re-crammed with assorted items. Devlin smiled when he saw the blender and waffle iron with the frayed cord jammed in the shelf. A calm silence had replaced the annoying staccato of air wrenches.

Most striking of all, and the single quality that had to be improving every facet of her outlook and demeanor, was the quality of natural light flooding the space—the raw material of mood and health. To the east, E.J. had two large sets of windows with spectacular views of MacArthur Park and its towering palm trees and large lake. Every day, E.J. rode the elevator down to the lobby and was able to wheel her oxygen bottle the short distance to the park, where she loved sitting and just watching the day go by. Simply being able to go outside and immerse herself in the greenery had completely changed her life and outlook. Devlin took her hands, smiled and bowed.

"I am so happy for you," he said, speaking slowly and loudly as if that would help her better comprehend. He was not sure if E.J. fully understood what he had done when he took a twenty-percent cut of the settlement rather than the customary one-third. That's what he had decided as he stared at Becker's ugly triptych the day of the mediation, that Devlin would take less to ensure Ho-Chan Park's mother received as much as possible. In doing that, she would never have anxiety about her ability to pay her bills and medical costs. She had already told her lawyer, too, that after her passing she planned to donate whatever money remained to three designated organizations. The first two had propelled her family's collective securing of the American Dream: a nonprofit organization that advocated for immigrant rights, and her son's alma mater of UCLA. Finally, one-third of her estate would go to a nature conservancy fund for upgrading and maintaining city parks throughout Los Angeles.

E.J. smiled widely. Devlin figured she had to understand at least some English after living in L.A. for decades. But the UCLA student Sarah Sung had said on the first trip that E.J. had remained astonishingly insulated from learning the second language. Devlin could have easily arranged to have the translator accompany him again, but he had decided that his presence, smile and energy would suffice in communicating everything to E.J. She took Devlin's hand and led him back to her bedroom, where the shrine to her son had been meticulously recreated exactly as Devlin remembered it. Except here it was much cleaner and not coated with dust. Devlin wanted to tell her that leaving so many candles burning was a distinct fire hazard, but then decided she had lit them just prior to his arrival. He had brought back the framed photo of her son, too; he nodded his thanks and then indicated that it belonged with all her others. E.J. took the frame and set it on the credenza.

She knelt before the shrine and, following his Catholic dictates, Devlin knelt beside her as they held hands. She had folded a blanket that cushioned the hardness of the wooden floor for these prayerful moments. Kneeling with her conjured the unfortunate mental image of Tom Scarsdale in his orange polyester suit jacket. E.J. did not cry, but rather closed her eyes and moved her lips without saying anything aloud. Devlin did the same. He gave thanks for being able to provide a grieving mother this new comfort. He asked that her son be blessed and protected, and she, too, for all the remaining days of her life. Then, somehow, Goldie popped into this sacred mental space like a sixty-five pound bulldog, snorting, farting, drooling, knocking things over and—if such a thing was possible—smoking a fat cigar.

Fuck a shifty witch.

Devlin recalled that night at home as he read through "the file" Goldie had given him, a total of three sparse pages, and he thanked the stone-age mentor for believing in the kid. The Dummy had prevailed. Recalling the meager start to the case conjured Sloane Monae and her incredible sleuth work, and the odd emptiness Devlin now felt when he compared the first L.A. visit to this solo trip.

She was definitely ensconced in his heart, and he was excited to call her as soon as he got back to Phoenix later that night.

Epilogue

IN SEPTEMBER 1989, THE FEDERAL GOVERNMENT HIT Adalius Becker with a $1.4 billion fraud and racketeering action. Although not detailed in the newspapers by name, Delaney Dunne's inside cooperation had been instrumental in building the case. Devlin had been right: at some point Dunne had finally cracked to absolve himself of the darkness he carried.

Due to the sprawling nature of the fraud case, Maricopa County prosecutors deferred to federal authorities and never pursued state charges. Concurrently, because Dunne had agreed to cooperate in the federal investigation, the Maricopa County prosecutors allowed him to plead in the hit-and-run to the lesser charge of negligent homicide, rather than manslaughter. This was a serious break. Rather than intentional, the death of Ho-Chan Park would officially be deemed "accidental" under the plea deal, because Dunne had never intended to kill him. The Christmas Eve intimidation ploy was supposed to be nothing more than a scary drive-by in the night. At Dunne's sentencing, he faced a wide punishment range of anywhere from two to ten years, and ended up getting seven. There was, however, no evidence other than Dunne's testimony to charge Becker criminally for his part in Ho-Chan Park's death. As Goldie had said, the whale was being gutted in other ways.

EPILOGUE

Devlin had a tremendous measure of pride in the fact that it had been his gumshoe girlfriend who had tracked down Delaney Dunne, who had then flipped to help prosecute the greatest fraud perpetuated in the twentieth century. It was a rare daily double for Devlin, a case with both criminal and civil charges, and was exactly the type of corporate greed, deception and malice he had signed up to expose: *when you turn on the light, the cockroaches scatter.* Also not detailed in any official newspaper account was the secret treasure trove of documents in the banker's box E.J. gave Devlin—including Ho-Chan Park's personal diary—which was the final dagger in putting together the case against Becker. Park had collected and notated much of the damning evidence, it appeared, with the help of an insider at Archard Holdings. At some point, Park became so concerned about his evidence being stolen that he packed it all into a single banker's box and hid it away at his mother's apartment in Los Angeles. Devlin figured his secret ally The Source was the one who had helped Park put together his case, but Devlin hadn't heard from her again. He was still putting his money on it being Natalie Grant, a lawyer with a conscience inside the castle walls, but he just didn't have any way of knowing. The next month, the U.S. government subpoenaed Becker to testify before the House Banking Committee. Becker, however, invoked his Fifth Amendment protections by keeping his mouth figuratively duct-taped as the FBI seized his latest resort projects. Ultimately, Becker's empire of dirt completely crumbled.

With the case behind him, Devlin had more time to follow the increasingly curious news coming out of Eastern Europe. In September, Hungarian officials opened the border with Austria to allow the departure of more than thirty thousand East German refugees, the first such exodus since Devlin was a junior in high school. The next month anti-government protestors overshadowed the celebrations of the fortieth anniversary of East Germany. Ronald Reagan's Soviet counterpart Mikhail Gorbachev said "Life punishes those who delay."

In November, Sidi told Devlin the cost of the overall S&L crisis had passed $500 billion. The national media coverage often focused on Phoenix's own Adalius Becker as a figurehead who best encapsulated the excess, greed and hubris in the feeding frenzy of a sprawling, government-propelled fraud. Becker continued to blame government regulators for the failure of Estate Savings & Loan, and sued for control over the bank even as his legal fees topped $1.5 million per month.

"BOBBY Swift is dead," Devlin said, shaking his head as he sat with Monae at Ong Lek Thai Kitchen. They were having a late lunch, so the restaurant was mostly empty and quiet, except for "Girl You Know It's True" from Milli Vanilli. No one was watching CNN on the muted television mounted in a corner of the bar.

"I'm so sorry," she said. "I know you did everything you could."

They were, as always, sharing the Tom Kha Gai soup and one plate of Chicken Pad Thai, and each had iced tea.

"He was just a kid," Devlin said. "Early this morning, I guess. His mom called me. She found him in his old room. I guess he broke the window at her house, climbed in at some point during the night and then OD'd on heroin. In the end, we all just want to go home."

Although he knew Bobby Swift made the choice to stay on his dead-end road to nowhere, it didn't diminish the sadness pulsing in Devlin. And the more he followed the despair, the faster he fanned the flames. Maybe he should have hand-carried the misguided heir to a detox center and shackled him there. Maybe he should have moved Swift to Arizona instead, where Devlin could keep him on a shorter chain. Although Bobby Swift clearly had some aberrant disposition toward self-immolation, his lawyer would forever shoulder the blame for Swift's demise and ponder the lingering question: was there something else Devlin could have done to save Swift's life?

"Stop it," Monae said.

"Stop what? You solved an unsolvable murder. Our pal Omar helped unravel the biggest fraud of the century. I couldn't keep my client alive. Those are the facts."

"Except, you *won* the case. Ho-Chan's mother has a new peace and comfort, thanks to you. Dunne is in prison. And Becker will soon be joining him. Winner, winner, winner. I'm not coming to your little pity party."

Devlin managed a rueful smile. "You're right."

It had been five and a half years since she first spied the rogue lawyer at the prison in his well-cut suit—tall, uniquely handsome and bespectacled, just the way she liked.

"You know," she said, "with all due respect, I'd rather talk about us than Bobby Swift. We've been avoiding this for a long time."

"OK. But I'm not exactly sure what we're avoiding."

Monae knew the essence of what she wanted to say, because Lord knows she'd thought about it for more hours, days and weeks (OK, *years*) than she wanted to admit. But she was also afraid that when she finally blurted it out—what was holding her back—it was going to sound really stupid. Or selfish. Or just ridiculous. So it was still easier to keep avoiding.

"Did I tell you I found a larger office space for my agency? Moving on up."

"Congratulations."

"Thanks. This builds my new brand: the Monae Group."

"I like it. Shouldn't you have 'investigations' in there?"

"I thought about it, but that's a little too specific for me. This sounds more professional in a vague sort of way."

"You are the consummate professional. And a sexy one, I might add."

He reached across and touched her hand, and they both felt the glow. Then she pulled her hand from the table and reached for her iced tea. "We're getting off track: where were we?"

"You said we're avoiding something."

"Oh, right."

"Are we talking about getting married?" Devlin said. "I mean, if anything, I know I've been mostly married to my work. That's just what I do. But I do want more... someday."

"Me, too," she said, thinking, *What day will that be for me?* And then, as long as they were on the subject: "What about kids?"

"Sure," he said. "Absolutely."

"You're 44. The clock's ticking."

"Are you asking me to marry you?" Devlin said with a devilish glint in his eye.

"That's not the way this works. I'm a modern woman and all, but still a traditional girl. So the right guy will know *he* has to ask *me*."

Milli Vanilli had ended, and KISS—unmasked!—was singing the title chorus to "Lick It Up." They both started laughing, a little relieved for the distraction.

"Oh my God," she said. "Remember this?"

"Our first date. You already wanted to kiss me."

"It wasn't a date," she said. "We were working."

"You still wanted to kiss me."

"Maybe," she said.

"Instead I made you wait."

"Oh, please," she said. "You just didn't have the *cojones* to make the move."

"Yeah, you had to wait until the next trip for those."

"Stop."

Except he was right: that night on their second trip had been magical, unplanned and perfect, even as it went against all her carefully structured order, reasoning and rules. That's what her Devlin did to her; he allowed her to topple the cross-referenced and color-coded matrices she built, and just *go with it*. With whatever came next. She liked how he had opened up those parts of herself, her base instincts—including an untapped, feral sexuality and a greedy selfishness that had also spurred her to new heights in her career. She loved being comfortable revealing herself both physically and emotionally with him; it was something she'd never felt with any other man… especially the physically naked part.

Yes, as implausible as it seemed even to her, Devlin was her first and only lover. This was the revelation she'd never been able to share with him: that she had been a 29-year-old virgin when they landed in bed at the Good Night Motel. Her silence was not because of anything he would do or say in response. She knew it wouldn't matter to him, but it mattered to *her*. She was proud of her selectiveness, but she also felt a nearly subconscious, gnawing sense of her life choices narrowing. She was reasonably confident Devlin was the best she would find, but… still. She had no comparison points, sexually or even in long-term relationships. So there was a nagging anxiety about closing all other doors after only being with one man. It was a classic Sloane Monae battle, between a searching heart and a regimented brain.

"Well," she said, "just to put it out there, there's something specific I wanted to talk to you about."

"Of course," he said. "Anything."

Why did he have to be so understanding? Then the fear returned, and she talked around the edges again. "Well, it's just that after five and a half years we sort of need to be thinking about what's next. I'm 34. I didn't used to buy it, but the biological clock is real." Then, with a barely perceptible catch in her voice: "But there's something else."

Devlin was not trying to be insensitive, but he was stunned into silence. He pointed at the TV and said, "Look."

There were images of people atop the Berlin Wall, which had separated communist East Berlin from democratic West Berlin for nearly thirty years. The people were dancing, drinking from champagne bottles and hoisting pickaxes. For Monae, ten years Devlin's junior, the wall had been less of a formidable symbol of oppression and Cold War politics. She had been five when it went up, while Devlin was learning about it in high school history class.

"Yeah," she said distractedly, "the end of an era." Now she was off track again. The longer she waited, the more uncertain she was about what she wanted to say.

And how. And even why. She looked at him and decided that she was going to find the courage to at least talk about it, to tell him her doubts and how they might work through them, together. Or not—because that was the risk of intimacy: taking a plunge into the shadows. She was finally ready to make that leap, so here goes…

"Connor J. Devlin. The one and only."

Monae and Devlin both looked up to see an elderly man with a head full of wispy white hair. Devlin did not immediately recognize him.

"Yes, sir," Devlin said, shaking the old man's outstretched hand.

"You don't remember me."

"I'm sorry," Devlin said. "You got me there."

"It's been a long time," he said. "But I never forgot you."

Monae sighed. Of course: another star-struck fan on the long list of male and female admirers, all stepping forward to congratulate the great trial lawyer.

"My memory fails me, too, son," the man said. "I can't remember the exact year. But you came through my courtroom. I know it was you for the plaintiff, because you won big against all odds."

"What was the case?"

"You successfully sued the hell out of a nursing home."

Then it hit Devlin square: here it was, the third ghost from the seventies Devlin had long ago predicted. First there was One-Armed Lucky, then Trevor Walsh. And now this gentleman caller: Judge Elmore Stearns, who had already been old that fateful day they first met almost twenty years ago. *Jesus, he must be 110.*

"Judge, I never told you this, but did you know you actually presided over my first case ever?"

"The nursing home case was your first?"

"No, sir, years before that, in 1970. A drunk lawyer called me to a bar and then sent me to court without any preparation on a case that was some low-level criminal offense I can't even remember."

"Nor can I, son."

"But I sure as hell never forgot you and how you wiped the floor with me that day. Then when I saw you on the bench for the nursing home case, I thought I was done before we started. You were none too pleased with me throughout that trial, if you recall."

"I do. And I was always harder on those I respected. As much as you might have thought I was exacting some personal vendetta on you, I did not believe your evidence justified that trial. But you proved me wrong, sir. And in the process, you impressed the hell out of me."

This was truly a monumental turn: the old magistrate was now addressing the original Dummy as "sir." Devlin thought back to being that 25-year-old lawyer who had received a brutal beat-down in his first case, the day Devlin had been summoned to the toilet stall by the inebriated attorney who dispatched him to court, for his first case ever, on a wing and a prayer.

"Well, your honor, thank you."

There was an awkward silence as the old retired judge stood there, looking somehow troubled. Monae remained poised. She hadn't totally lost her courage, but it was slowly slipping the longer she waited. And really, her virginity didn't even matter: who the hell cared anyway? If anything, what man wouldn't want to be the first? *Get a clue, Monae.* She re-oriented her intention and told herself she could do this. She would share everything—most importantly, even her fears and doubts—with the man she loved.

That is, if this other guy would ever leave. Devlin, too, was wondering why the judge was still standing there.

"Well, again, it was great to see you, Judge."

More silence. Then the judge blurted out, "I have a case for you."

Oh, good Lord, Monae thought.

Devlin could see her obvious frustration. "Judge, could you leave me your number, and we could make an appointment to discuss it at my office?"

"Retired."

"Excuse me?"

"Retired judge. Many moons ago, son. I just turned ninety. Still kicking."

Devlin smiled.

"Do you have a pen?" the old man asked.

"I do," Monae said, reaching in her new Dooney & Bourke purse, a flap-and-tab shoulder-strap bag in black pebbled leather with the signature raised figure of a duck on the back. She was careful to conceal the pistol as she dug for the pen. Devlin took the pen from Monae and smoothed the damp cocktail napkin that had been under his iced tea.

"Did you see what's happening?" the old man said, pointing at the dismantling of Communism, in the waning weeks of a decade, playing out on television.

"I did," Devlin said.

"Stunning turn," the judge said. Devlin's extended hand still held the pen and napkin, which the judge ignored. "That's why I need your help."

What a tenacious old man, Devlin thought. "OK, Judge. I'm happy to take a look. We could even meet tomorrow, say in the afternoon. Three work for you?"

"How about going *mano a mano* with a great legal mind, although he's a real son of a bitch. Sorry, ma'am."

She smiled. "You should hear *him*."

"What do you mean, Judge?" Devlin asked.

"Lawyer v. lawyer," he said. He took the napkin and pen.

Devlin decided the old man must be off his meds. He stood and extended his hand to end the impromptu meeting. The judge shook the lawyer's hand and then pulled him in close. "Your client would be my granddaughter, because that bastard lawyer killed her husband in broad daylight."

Acknowledgments

SPECIAL THANKS TO THE FINE TACTICIANS on the literary front: Jim Moore, for our camaraderie, friendship and your ever-reliable editing hand; Pat Lichen, for your similar editorial prowess and scene refinements; Sarah Cook Design for the cover and interior layout; and Debbie Francis and Faith Van Buskirk, for everything else.

Like many creative endeavors, this book took much longer to bring to fruition than I ever would have imagined—an entire decade. As they will, life challenges intervened on numerous fronts to stall the work. In the end, it was the man who lived these events (who chooses to remain anonymous) who rekindled the flame and allowed our collaboration to blaze back to life. I'd like to thank you, as always, for your advocacy, your dedication to a common vision, your keen insights on narrative and our ongoing friendship. I am forever grateful to you for our opportunity to create, laugh and build something meaningful together.

LANDON J. NAPOLEON is the award-winning author of numerous fiction and nonfiction books. His critically acclaimed *Devlin Series* of novels are all based on the actual career arc of a street-smart trial attorney starting in 1970. The series charts the savvy fighter's career rise decade by decade.

His debut novel *ZigZag* received starred reviews, was a Barnes & Noble "Discover Great New Writers" finalist, and was adapted for a feature film starring Oliver Platt, John Leguizamo and Wesley Snipes. His nonfiction biography *Burning Shield: The Jason Schechterle Story* documents the inspiring true story of a rare human being with an undeniable will to live. The book debuted in the Amazon TOP 100 for biographies and memoirs and was an "Arizona Republic Recommends" selection.

He is a graduate of Arizona State University (bachelor of arts in journalism) and the University of Glasgow in Scotland (master of philosophy in creative writing). He lives in Arizona.

www.landonjnapoleon.com

Made in the USA
Middletown, DE
20 September 2021